FALLEN
MASTERS

·JOHN EDWARD·

FALLEN
MASTERS

A Tom Doherty Associates Book
New York

This is a work of fiction. All of the characters, organizations, and events portrayed in this novel are either products of the author's imagination or are used fictitiously.

FALLEN MASTERS

A Tor Book
Published by Tom Doherty Associates, LLC
175 Fifth Avenue
New York, NY 10010

www.tor-forge.com

Tor® is a registered trademark of Tom Doherty Associates, LLC.

ISBN 978-0-7653-3271-4 (hardcover)
ISBN 978-1-4668-0072-4 (e-book)

First Edition: September 2012

Printed in the United States of America

0 9 8 7 6 5 4 3 2 1

Jill Fritzo
The world is a brighter place because you are in it.

Acknowledgments

More than a decade and a half ago I was approached to write a book about my life and the psychic experiences of clients—it was called *One Last Time*. Unbeknownst to me at that time, I would go on to write seven more books on the subject of spirituality—both fiction and nonfiction. Hold the psychic jokes please!

Over the years I discovered that, while many people are wide open to the potential of going "above and beyond," there are also many who are deeply rooted in their belief systems yet are curious and inquisitive of the infinite possibilities of the "Other Side." Through fiction, I learned that I could convey a message of spirituality, kindness, and love that allowed the reader (whatever their religion) to contemplate, without giving up or abandoning their faith. I love taking people on these journeys of potential.

People often ask, "Where do you get your ideas from?" and quite honestly I can only say that I believe most of it is channeled creatively in some way. I've been blessed with guides—both here and on the "Other Side"—and I want to take this opportunity to thank a few of my earthly guides for stewarding this new work of fiction: Claire Eddy, for not being "Lost" on the subject; Greg Tobin, for your guiding light and literary tailoring; Corinda Carfora, for always being one of my original Publishing Angels and just "here and there"; and Tom Doherty, for the opportunity to bring a message of love and humanity to the world by igniting people's imagination. To my family: my love and appreciation. And to the *Fallen Masters* in all of our lives . . . here's our story.

FALLEN
MASTERS

PROLOGUE

· *Twenty-eight years ago* ·

Ten-year-old Charlene St. John glanced at the clock. It was almost 6 P.M. and her father should have been home by now. Her father, Ian St. John, was a Scottish immigrant who had fallen in love with the African-American woman who worked at the laundry where he took his clothes each week. Ian and Louise had married and moved into a small house in Denbigh, a suburb of Newport News, Virginia.

Ian worked for the Northrop Grumman Shipbuilding Company in Newport News.

With only a rudimentary education, he was not one of the white-collar engineers or technicians. He was, he liked to say, one of the men who held the ships together.

"If men like me dinna screw in the bolts and tighten the nuts, the ship would come apart and sink to the bottom of the sea," he insisted.

Ian took pride in his work, and the walls in the living room of his house on Loraine Drive were lined with photographs of the USS *Ronald Reagan,* and the USS *George H. W. Bush*. These were nuclear carriers of the Nimitz class, both of which he had worked on for years.

"Mama," Charlene pleaded, her hands over her heart, "is something wrong? Did Daddy call and say he was going to be late?"

"No, darlin'," Louise said. "But you know what your daddy says about traffic on Warwick Boulevard. In the morning going toward the shipyard, it's like pushing down on a coiled spring. And in the evening coming back home, it's like pushing on that same spring from the other direction. I'm sure he's just tied up in traffic or something. Probably a wreck somewhere, and that brings traffic to a complete halt."

"Oh!" the girl said. She put her hands to the sides of her head. "Oh, Mama! There *was* a wreck, and Daddy was in it. Daddy is dead!"

"Charlene, what are you talking about?"

Charlene began crying inconsolably.

"Hush now, dear," Louise said. "You want your eyes looking all red when your daddy comes home?"

"He's not coming home, Mama. Never again," Charlene said.

"Now, Charlene, stop it. You're making me nervous."

The doorbell rang.

"See, there's your daddy now." Though, even as Louise said the words, she had a sinking feeling. Why would Ian ring his own doorbell?

When Louise opened the door, she saw two uniformed police officers standing on the front porch, a black male and a white female. The police car was parked out on the street, right in front of her house.

"Mrs. St. John?" the male police officer said.

"No," Louise said quietly—so quietly that she could barely be heard. She held her hand out in front of her, as if holding the police officers off, and stepped back into the house, away from the door. "No, no, no, dear God in Heaven, no!"

"May we come in for a moment?" the policewoman asked gently.

"No, no, no, no—," Louise said, burying her face in her hands and shaking her head.

Charlene, who was no longer crying, came to the front door. "You may come in," she said.

"And who are you?" the policewoman asked, smiling at the little girl.

"My name is Charlene, and my daddy is dead, isn't he? He was killed in a car wreck on Warwick Avenue." As she said this, she clasped her hands over her heart again.

The two police officers looked at each other in shock.

"Has someone already called?" the policewoman wondered. "Nobody is supposed to call before we get here."

"Nobody called," Charlene said. "But Daddy *is* dead, isn't he?"

"Yes, sweetheart, I'm sorry to have to tell you, that is true," the policewoman answered.

"Mrs. St. John, is there someone we could call? A relative? A close friend, perhaps?" the police officer asked.

Louise was still sobbing and totally unresponsive.

"Mama has a good friend named Norma Keeler," Charlene said.

"Do you know her telephone number?" the policeman asked.

Charlene led the policeman over to the telephone, then pointed to a number that was written on a pad on the wall.

"Thank you," the policeman said as he picked up the phone and dialed the number.

"Mama," Charlene said. She stood next to her mother and wrapped her arms around her. "Mama, it will be all right."

"Oh, Charlene, how did you know?" Louise asked, putting an arm around her daughter. "How did you know?"

They could hear the low-key voice of the policeman on the phone.

"What do you mean, how did she know?" the policewoman asked.

"She knew," Louise said. "Even before you got here, she knew."

"But how?" the policewoman asked.

Charlene stood there like a little statue or a sentry on watch, gazing up at her mother; then turning to the lady cop she quietly said, "I felt it, here," and put her hands over her heart for the third time. Charlene's mother began to keen softly, and the look on the young girl's face as she comforted her mother brought tears to the policewoman's eyes.

Part
·ONE·

CHAPTER
1

Dave Hampton had the looks of a star. With a full head of dark hair always perfectly coiffed, blue eyes, and well-chiseled features, he could have been the lead in a dramatic television show. He was, in fact, a television star, but not in a drama series. He had his own news, commentary, and talk show airing at six o'clock eastern time, Monday through Friday. From Maine to California, millions of Americans adjusted their schedules so they could watch the show live, and those who couldn't watch it live recorded it.

Hampton specialized in controversy and conspiracy theories. There were few who were ambivalent about him—the public either loved him or hated him. "Innovative, brave, probing," his supporters said. "A wacko, conspiracy nut-job," his detractors said.

Today his guests had discussed such subjects as whether or not the United States was purposely not drilling for domestic oil in order to exhaust all the oil reserves of the rest of the world, to whether or not Errol Flynn was actually a Nazi spy.

The guests were gone now and the show was on a commercial break before the final segment, which Hampton called "Critical Update."

"Back in one minute thirty seconds, Dave," the director said, his voice audible in Dave's ear plug.

"I don't see my CU queued on the teleprompter," Dave said.

"Sure it is," the director said. "Untapped Oil Reserves."

"That's not the one I want. I changed it, remember? I want Sinister Shadow."

"You mean you were serious about that?"

"If you don't put it on the teleprompter, I'm going to try and wing it, and that will make it worse."

"All right, all right," the studio floor manager said. "Just a minute."

Dave stared into the three teleprompters, which were just below the camera lenses. "I'm waiting."

"Coming up—now," the director said.

The story on the teleprompter changed, and Dave acknowledged, "Thanks."

"We're going to hear about this one, Dave. This is the kookiest of them all."

"I wish you were right," the studio floor manager said.

"Come on, you mean you actually believe this?"

"I'm afraid I do," she said.

"Ten seconds, stand by."

Dave nodded and looked at the camera. When the red light came on, he began to speak.

"Have you ever had one of those feelings that nag at you? You know what I'm talking about, a smell that is familiar but you just can't place it, a voice, face, or event that is just on the other side of memory, or a tune that haunts you from your past?

"I'm having just such a sensation now. There is something up, something going on—and though I don't know what it is, I know that it is *mon-u-ment-al*! It is of earth-shaking proportions, and when I say earth shaking, I'm not just engaging in hyperbole.

"Whatever this is—and for lack of a better word, I am going to call it a sinister shadow—it is hanging over our heads now like the fabled Sword of Damocles. Is this merely another one of Crazy Dave's conspiracy theories?

"No, I'm not saying that there is a Nazi settlement on the moon, or there are aliens among us in high-ranking positions. I'm not saying that the Illuminati control all the governments of the world.

"I can't be weaving a conspiracy out of this, because I don't have enough of a grasp on this to formulate a hypothesis, or even to ask a question.

"Let me keep this very simple: Responsible and believable people, speaking off the record and with the assurance of anonymity, have told me of a disturbing paradigm, great and troubling movements that are taking place in religious, scientific, and political circles. I don't know what it is— but I do know that it is making strange bedfellows, bringing about cooperation between the most disparate sectors of all human society. And while this cooperation would normally be considered a good thing, I am told these meetings are not the result of some universal brotherhood of man. This coming together is not anything born of altruism but rather a desperate seeking of the deliverance of humankind from this—sinister shadow.

"I feel as if all humanity is in a car, driving toward the edge of a cliff, headed toward one final catastrophic car accident. And the biggest problem is that while some of us can see the accident coming at us in slow motion, we can't figure out how to put on the brakes. I don't have the answers, but I can promise you that I am going to do my level best to find the truth and bring it to you. The one thing that I know in my heart is true is that something of epic proportions is coming toward us, and we soon might be faced with making some pretty important choices.

"Choices, ladies and gentlemen. Choices that might change the world."

Hampton, in his signature sign-off, held his hand up, palm facing the camera. "From New York, this is Dave Hampton. Good night, America."

As soon as he had delivered the sign-off, the telephones in the cable network studio began to ring off the hook, and within the hour, emails and tweets flooded into Dave's own phone and swamped his website. Dave looked at the response and was both relieved and afraid. He had taken a gamble tonight and knew that the network would be breathing down his neck for what it would probably consider a bold stunt just for ratings.

But people were interested in—no, deeply concerned about—his report and felt they had to reach out to him to express their emotional responses to the news. He just wished he knew what he was going to tell them, for if his sources were correct, the truth was far worse than anything they could imagine.

CHAPTER 2

· Vatican City ·

Giovanni Giuseppe Battista, known to the world as Pope Genaro I, strode purposefully along the corridor of the Apostolic Palace in the Vatican with two of his most senior and trusted cardinals. The Holy Father, as spiritual leader of the world's 1.4 billion Roman Catholics, felt the burden weighing heavily on his shoulders this day.

He was a tall man, rail thin at age seventy-two, who wore thick wire-rimmed glasses that gave him an intellectual look, which belied his deeply held commitment to charity for all people and his natural personal humility. In the deep pocket of his white cassock, the familiar "uniform" of his religious office, he fingered a simple wooden set of rosary beads and prayed silently, almost unconsciously.

As Genaro walked to what might be most important meeting of his life, he found himself thinking about the nature of time. With a heavy heart, Genaro was struck by a sense of ending rather than beginning—on the line of human history that stretched back some tens or hundreds of thousands of years, depending on where one pegged the creation of the first man. And to his sorrow, he silently prayed for the billions of souls who currently resided on the planet Earth, whose ultimate salvation was his greatest care, for he feared that in this most crucial hour he might fail them as their shepherd.

He and Cardinals Luigi Morricone and Zachary Yamba were the last to walk into the meeting of representatives from the world's greatest religions, representing a huge percentage of the entire world's population. The pope sat in a high-backed chair (with his cardinals at designated spots behind the pontiff) at a huge conference table that had been set up on the floor before the altar in one of the most familiar worship spaces on the planet: the Sistine Chapel. Countless prayers had been offered to heaven in this sacred space but never had it been the site of such a meeting that crossed over such ancient and complicated divides—chasms even— between and among the faiths of the world. Never had there been an event that would warrant a gathering like this. Until now.

The major religious traditions were represented by nine persons, one person each for this ad hoc council, called the Council of Faith. "Cataclysmic change is descending upon the earth," the Holy See had stated in its invitation to the various religious leaderships. "We invite you to gather to discuss the opportunities for great change." Rather a mysterious summons, yet the response had been unanimous. All those bodies who had been invited had dispatched an ambassador to Rome, for each had held a piece to the enigmatic puzzle that faced them. The duty to save their followers trumped any conflict in ideology.

The Dalai Llama, exiled spiritual leader of Tibetan Buddhists and one of the most recognized faces in the world, had flown in from London for this "summit of summits," as some in the press had dubbed it. "Enlightenment not shared is not enlightenment at all," he had said upon his departure from Heathrow amid extraordinarily high security.

A Hindu holy man of Mumbai, India, had provided this insight: "This is but another turn in the eternal cycle of death and reincarnation. In our belief, Shiva the destroyer and Vishnu the preserver are forces of dark energies and light and are the fabric of our universe."

Representatives of Judaism and Islam, two faiths that had sprung from the same patriarchal figure, Abraham, came to sit side by side for this conference of world religions, as had Orthodox and Protestant Christians. The Tao, the ancient "way" to faith and salvation, was represented as well, as were Sikhs, who believed in a continual cycle of reincarnation until all beings merged with One God.

Genaro welcomed them to his home and the members of the extraordinary body listened to his words, spoken in Italian and English, with translations provided by linguists brought along for that purpose. Only the Dalai Lama sat imperturbably alone, a solitary saffron-robed figure among a collection of clerics vested in the differing styles of their religions.

"Our human situation is being affected, or perhaps I should say *afflicted*, in a way not seen since some of our most ancient scriptures were written down by distant ancestors. Both science and religion are reporting strange phenomena in this age, unlike any in memory. These forces, which may be called 'evil' are manifesting themselves in the lives of many billions here on

Earth. Why? Well, that is for us as theologians to attempt to answer. But even before that, it is our responsibility to *act* to save our fellow human beings from a dark terror unlike any other known to mankind.

"There have been natural phenomena of late that, in themselves, are not threatening to the entire world, but taken together indicate the possibility of malevolent forces at work: earthquakes, floods, potential pandemics of disease, even mental instability that manifests itself in man-made catastrophes such as war and genocide. There have always been events that have created misfortune and disaster for man, but the level of instability has struck us as something new. Something which may endanger all of humanity."

Pope Genaro looked around the table that gleamed and reflected the room on its brilliant surface.

"But we do not represent all the faiths of this world. We cannot be universal, by our very nature. Therefore, how can we speak for any who are not represented here? There must be millions of them . . . ," stated the imam, a world-renowned Muslim scholar from Alexandria, Egypt. He spoke the words aloud, but each of the men at the table—and all were men—held the same thought in his mind.

"Of course, we can only do our best, both in the name of those of our own faiths and for all the people of the world. That is what we are called to do," the chief rabbi of Jerusalem responded.

The Sikh leader, a tall man in a somber gray suit with a starched white turban, smiled sadly and said, "All gods are subject to mankind's ways, whether they care to be or not. That is, when we choose the path of evil over the path of good and betray the soul for base purposes, not only do we ourselves suffer, but so does the force for all good in the universe."

"Let us be faithful, then, to our beliefs and in one another," the pope said. "And let us convoke this urgent meeting with prayer. I ask that each leader present offer a prayer of his choosing, in the words of his faith, to move our minds and stir our hearts with purpose in this hour. For we each have been given signs, regardless of our beliefs, and these signs point to a coming event that threatens the future of man. We may not be able to avoid this fate, but we must strive to help all of mankind face this crisis."

Outside Rome, in the Italian countryside, farmers awoke that day to discover that a large meteorite had fallen to earth and scorched their land. Livestock lay dead throughout a several-square-kilometer area, and crops, mostly barley and corn, were ruined. Their lives were ruined, as well, with the loss of half a year's income and the need to replenish the dead livestock that would have provided milk and meat for hundreds of families in the region.

The event made the local newspapers and television news but got little mention beyond that.

CHAPTER
3

Marcus Jackson was a very popular President of the United States. As an African American who had faced cultural and political obstacles all his life with quiet determination and a solid core of honorable ethics, he worked tirelessly toward his goals, and those traits helped him to achieve the nation's highest office. Married to a Vietnamese woman who was a naturalized citizen, this power couple was a poster for tolerance and social cohesion. It didn't hurt that their fifteen-year-old son was a charming and intelligent young man who seemed to be cut from the same cloth as his father. While his parents worked hard at shielding their son from the world and its evils, his sunny personality had shone through and he succeeded in winning the hearts of the most recalcitrant. Not since the Kennedys had a presidential family been so embraced by all Americans.

POTUS, as he was called now (because he had spent twenty years in the military and felt most comfortable with this nickname), stared at a large flat-paneled television screen displaying the huge devastation caused by a massive earthquake in Turkey. Deep in his heart he knew that this would be yet another crisis for his office to deal with. Although he was given the immediate reports of the quake from his State Department personnel, he wanted to see how the media were covering the cataclysmic event.

"The unusual thing about the earthquake is the area that it has affected," the announcer was saying. The scope of the earthquake was unprecedented. It had covered almost 200,000 square miles, or roughly two-thirds the total area of Turkey. Equally alarming was the strength of the earthquake, which at 9.5 on the Richter scale, matched the Chilean earthquake in May of 1960, one of the most severe in history.

"We, of course, have no way of determining yet the extent of casualties from

the earthquake, but estimates run as high as two million," the announcer said in somber tones.

"Obviously, we are unable to get to some of the more remote parts of Turkey, but here are pictures for Istanbul."

The screen was filled with images of the city, now reduced to piles of rubble, dazed-looking survivors walking around as if lost.

"Here is the famous Blue Mosque, built by Sultan Ahmed in the seventeenth century. As you can see, the cascading domes have all collapsed, as have the six minarets."

It was during this initial report that the breaking news came that Charlene St. John, the internationally known song diva, was going to give a concert from Mexico City, with the total proceeds "one hundred percent," the announcer stressed, "to be given to Turkey relief. We are told that not even the normal expenses of producing such a show will be deducted from the gross proceeds."

"Charley, find out if that is true," POTUS said to his appointments secretary. Charley was Charley Crawford, the captain that POTUS had pulled from a burning Humvee at Saba al Bor, Iraq, nine years earlier, and was POTUS's most trusted aide.

"Yes, sir," Charley replied, limping out of the room on his prosthetic leg.

Jackson stared at the footage of the devastation that rocked Turkey and knew that the American response would have to be swift and massive. After watching several hours of nonstop news reporting from the devastated nation of Turkey, Jackson was brought out of the hypnotism that was the news cycle by Win Jackson, the President's lovely wife, who reminded POTUS that she had purchased a pay-per-view for a current Charlene St. John concert as she was one of St. John's many devoted fans.

"As horrible as it is, the devastation in Turkey will still be there after the concert," Win said. "You spend so much of your time worrying about the problems of the whole world, it seems. Could we not have a little beauty in our lives?"

"Of course we can," POTUS said, smiling gently and switching channels.

Charlene St. John was dazzling in a sequined, body-hugging dress that caught the spots and winked back in thousands of tiny flashes of light. She began the concert with *Ave Maria*, then *Panis Angelicus*. After that she covered some songs, then sang a few of her own. Every song was met with a thunderous ovation.

Then the lights changed and she stood alone in a single blue spot, surrounded by darkness. The darkness was filled by a few bars of music.

"Oh," Win said, leaning forward expectantly. "Listen, this is her signature song. Isn't it beautiful?"

> *Do you see the light*
> *Of all creation: the day, the night?*
> *A universe of peace and love*
> *Of goodness that comes down from above*
> *Take his hand*
> *And you will understand*
> *That we are one*
> *We are one*
> *We are one*

After the concert was over, POTUS called his aide into the office. "Charley, would you try to get Miss St. John on the telephone for me?" POTUS said.

After a number of minutes, Charley handed POTUS the receiver. "I have her for you, Mr. President," he said.

"Thank you," POTUS said. "Charlene?"

"Hello?" Charlene replied in a tentative voice.

"Charlene," the president said. "I hope you don't mind my using your first name, but tonight, you put yourself on a first-name basis with the entire world. I would like to invite you to the White House. I want to personally thank you for all you have done. I don't know if you fully understand this, Charlene, but your singing has awakened angels all over the world. Your one voice has made a difference. Will you come?"

"I—I would be honored, Mr. President," Charlene replied. She felt frozen, and all her natural shyness bubbled up inside, rendering her close to speechless at this moment.

"The honor is mine. My family would love to meet you, too. My wife, Win, is always commenting how much she loves your songs. And my son, Marcus Jr., has a little crush on you, I think. He's fifteen and at that awkward age, you know."

"Oh, I know all about awkward, Mr. President."

POTUS laughed. "See, that's why I want you to visit us. You're down to earth for such a big celebrity."

"Well, I can now say the same of you, sir."

POTUS hung up the phone and thought how such beauty could coexist with such sadness in the world. And how one voice singing in the darkness had a way of lighting the way. He hoped that this thought would sustain him as he dealt with the crisis in Turkey.

CHAPTER
4

Dr. Jason Chang, a trim, middle-aged Asian-American, had been a space shuttle astronaut in the late 1990s and early 2000s, having logged more than sixty days in space. He had gained fame during one spacewalk when, as he and a fellow NASA astronaut had been repairing the shuttle's exterior, a freak accident occurred. A piece of space junk severed the other man's all-important EVA line and he had risked his own life to save his colleague.

No longer an astronaut, Chang was now one of the premier astrophysicists, not only in NASA but in the entire world. He was the "go to guy" for any anomaly, from errant asteroids to black holes, from star nurseries to black matter.

Dr. Chang put double cream and double sugar in his coffee as he looked at galaxy cluster Abell 2744, nicknamed Pandora's Cluster. The presentation pieced together the cluster's complex and violent history using telescopes in space and on the ground, including the Hubble Space Telescope, the European Southern Observatory's Very Large Telescope, the Japanese Subaru telescope, and NASA's Chandra X-ray Observatory. The slides were time sequenced with one second representing twenty-four hours.

"Whoa," Chang said. He moved the presentation back by two months, then reviewed it again, this time taking as long as thirty seconds with each frame. After that, he did a quick calculation.

"Craig," he said. "What is the redshift of Pandora's Cluster?"

Dr. Craig Walcott laughed. "What are you doing, Jason? Testing me? It is z equal to 0.308."

"Uh-uh," Chang said. "Take a look at this."

Craig looked at the figures, then at the screen, then at the figures again. "Wait a minute," he said, "0.512? This can't be right."

"Run them yourself."

"No, I wouldn't question you. I mean you are the—" Dr. Walcott stopped in midsentence and reran the figures. "Damn," he said. "I don't understand this. Did we make a mistake with the first calculations?"

Chang moved to another computer, tapped in a few keys, then brought up the initial photos of Pandora's Cluster. He ran the figures on that. "Z equals 0.308," he said.

"Abell 2744 has not almost doubled its distance from us in twenty years. That's impossible," Craig said.

"What time is it in Moscow?"

Craig looked up at the array of clocks on the wall. "Sixteen thirty," he said. "You're going to call Dr. Kolnikov?"

"Yes. I have a theory about this, but I want to run it by him first."

Chang initiated the call, then after a moment said, "Dmitri?"

"Jason, my friend, it is good to hear from you. How is young John? Are you still raising him to be a cosmonaut?"

"Astronaut," Dr. Chang said. "We raise astronauts in America."

"Ah, indeed."

"Dmitri, I want you to do me a favor. I want you to take a look at Abell 2744 and give me the redshift."

"Z equals 0.308."

"Is that your calculation from the latest photos?"

"Why do you ask?"

"Please, just take a look at the latest photos and do a new calculation. I'll wait."

"Very well," Kolnikov said.

While he waited, Chang took a swallow of his coffee, then made a face. "It's grown cold," he said.

"I'll get you another cup," Craig offered.

"You know how I like it?"

"Yes, you like a little coffee with your cream and sugar."

As Chang held the phone, Walcott poured a new cup of coffee for him from a pot on a side table, doctored it appropriately, then brought it back. Chang took a swallow before Kolnikov's voice came back on the phone.

"This is not possible," Kolnikov said.

"What did you come up with?"

"Z equal to 0.512. But how can this be?"

"Examine the slides very carefully," Chang said. "I think there are only two possible solutions. Dark energy is increasing at the rate of expansion beyond anything we have experienced so far, or there is a gathering cloud of dark matter that has suddenly entered our galaxy."

"This will require more study," Kolnikov said. "We will work together on this."

"Thank you, my friend," Chang said as he hung up.

"Jason," Dr. Craig Walcott asked with concern in his voice. "If what we have here is an expanding cloud of dark matter, and if it would move into our galaxy, our universe, or impact with Earth, that could be—"

"A terminal event," Chang said.

CHAPTER
5

Patricia Rose Greenidge fell into her favorite easy chair in her modest living room with the heaviness of the entire world's cares pulling her down with the force of iron weights. Known as "Mother Earth" or Mama Greenidge, or simply as "Mama G," the elderly native of Grenada closed her eyes and tried to block out the visions that had disturbed her of late—more than ever before.

The nighttime sky above had revealed strange new patterns that she could see with her naked eyes, breaking from the expected movements upon which she and others based their charts—and had done so for thousands of years. It seemed as if she could actually see the planetary bodies moving of their own volition. Never had she experienced such phenomena, and she was at a loss as to how to interpret such signs.

"As above, so below," she had often said regarding her knowledge of astrology and the insights that the stars and planets offered to human beings. If only they would observe, watch, and listen to the messages that, she believed, God was sending them in the movements of heavenly bodies. In her latest visions she saw a dark cloud coming to obscure the light of the sun, and knew full well that it was no eclipse. What else could it be? What were the heavens holding for Earth's future?

She knew what it meant—even though she tried, pleaded, bargained with God for it to be some misinterpretation on her part. And if this meant what she thought it meant, should she share this? Was she blessed or cursed with this knowledge?

Mama G was not some quaint old black woman in a bamboo, palm frond, and flattened beer can shack, talking about ancestors' island juju, reading chicken bones, and casting spells for the native islanders. She was much more sophisticated than that, and had developed a following of millions of souls the world over who listened to her nightly radio and Internet broadcasts and read her blogs and books. She was a media phenomenon whose audience had grown exponentially over the past fifteen years, since near the turn of the millennium, when her astrological readings and teachings had captured the attention of more and more people around the globe.

Although she was not educated beyond high school level, Mama G had studied the ancient wisdom and esoteric teachings of the stars on her own, and no one understood or taught astrology the way she did, with her island intuition and unique insights into traditional ways of matching the power and position of the stars with human life.

As an astrologer with psychic powers, she wrestled with the conflicts that sometimes arose between her access to knowledge of the metaphysical nature of the world and her deep faith in a loving God who had created the universe, of which she knew in her heart she was but a minute part.

Patricia Rose Greenidge did not believe in predestination, the belief that all events throughout eternity have been preordained by divine decree, including each individual's ultimate destiny. No, she could not go there. She thought, instead, how sad it was for those who believed that their own lives were plotted out in their entirety—either by an astrological chart or a divine plan that could not be altered.

If that were the case, how could one learn anything from life? Why would you try to improve yourself, help others, or strive to do better? The answer is, you wouldn't. In the predestination scenario, you would simply accept that your lot in life was set in stone based on God's unchanging will—period. End of story.

Instead, Mama G believed—and preached constantly—that human beings decide what it is their souls need to learn and experience before they incarnate on the Earth plane. She saw her role—that is, how she employed her God-given gifts—as that of a guide for others on their earthly journeys, which often put her in direct conflict with some of her more conservative family members and neighbors. The world embraced her, but her own island sometimes judged her harshly, and even ostracized her.

But Mama G persevered, knowing deep in her heart, in the very core of her being, she had a purpose, and that purpose revealed itself each day as she sought to help others.

She could not, and would not, attempt to force her own vision on any individual who sought her guidance. She understood that her purpose was to help people unlock their own free will and inner resources to cope with life and to find their own way to the Source. She often urged her listeners to, "Live passionately in the days that have been given to you. Be of help to others in your life as an instrument of the Universe. Do good at every opportunity—and do nothing rather than something that would harm another person."

But what good were such noble intentions in the face of the momentous catastrophe that Mama G foresaw as a coming storm on the horizon of time?

Mama G had studied where the Earth had been and where it was going. Now, as the Earth and its people entered into the new Age of Aquarius, a twenty-six-thousand-year cycle was coming—some would say colliding—to an end. The Earth neared an alignment with the stars in relation to the sun, which would rise on the winter solstice at the very center of the galaxy in a short time. In metaphysical and astrological terms, the people faced the end of days, and Patricia Rose Greenidge could not see beyond that point to a future for mankind.

She was aware, too, of the end of the Mayan calendar that charted the very same epochal cycles she was appreciating with profound questioning, now, of what she must do.

O Lord, she prayed in silence, *show us the way to understand the true knowledge of our existence in whatever time is left to us.*

Mama G knew that the world was facing a chance for change. But if the people did not grasp it and make the necessary changes, the chance would be lost forever. She knew, too, that she was being deliberately blocked by some unknown force: Her abilities, once so free-flowing, were being limited or harnessed in some way.

It was as if the gathering clouds of darkness sought to muddy her thoughts, muffle her words, and stall her actions by shifting the energies around and within her in ways contrary to what she had known for her entire life. Something was different this time, and she wasn't certain exactly how or why. *And I don't know what I can do about these dark energies,* she thought grimly.

What if they are more powerful than we poor human beings can handle?

· Belfast ·

The body was that of a young woman. She was completely nude when she was found and the police were called. The coroner had arrived with a police escort, and as he examined the body, he spoke into a small hand-held recorder.

"I am Dr. Colin O'Reily, medical examiner duly constituted and commissioned to disturb the corpse in the course of my examination. The body is that of a Caucasian female, young—late teens to early twenties. The right side of the face is distorted because of an irregular deforming wound that involves the lateral aspect of the orbit, brow, and the right maxilla. A large amount of dried blood is present on the skin. There is a deep incision over the inner lateral aspect of the left breast that is approximately twelve centimeters in greatest dimension and very deep. I am probing inside the wound and . . . it is as I expected. The heart has been removed."

Despite the fact that the crime scene lay in the midst of a busy city, with life and traffic humming along all around the field where the police now stood, an eerie veil of silence had descended upon those present. The examiner paused to take a breath.

O'Reily was a veteran of some thirty years in his profession, but this— dear Lord, this was the worst he had ever encountered.

"Continuing, there are what appear to be scars on the inner aspect of her left thigh I . . . it appears to be letters. I can make out V-I-V . . . Viva. *Viva Domingo*. I am taking samples of debris from the inner aspect of the thighs as well as samples of pubic hair.

"Turning her over, I see . . . I'll be damned. Erin, would you be looking at that now?"

Erin Donnell, who was one of the homicide officers on the scene, looked as directed. She was much younger than the coroner and not much older than the dead woman.

"Dear God in Heaven, what is that?" Inspector Donnell asked.

"It looks to me like some sort of glyph. Though what it might be stymies me."

Meticulously carved on the corpse's back, apparently when she had still been alive, was an elaborate design, now somewhat smudged and dirt-caked. Whatever the symbol was, it was clear, however, that the young woman had suffered unimaginably before her death.

The police covered the victim and began the laborious process of removing the body for an autopsy. But the one thing that stuck in all their minds was that the animal responsible for this could not be what they would conceive of as having any kind of human emotion. All those present silently uttered a desperate prayer, asking an unseen Power for forgiveness of their own shortcomings and peace for this girl who had met such a grisly fate in this desolate place.

CHAPTER
7

· Long Island ·

B eyond the rolling lawn that extended some one hundred yards from the patio and pool of her palatial estate, Charlene St. John could see the morning light touch the gentle waters of the Long Island Sound.

Each day that she awoke here—and lately she had been touring less and staying home more—she rose with a prayer of gratitude for this beautiful gift, this place that provided refuge, peace, and comfort. She loved it here. Yet there was a sadness in her heart that had never been salved and, she feared, never would be.

Charlene St. John McAvoy's working-class family slipped into poverty after her father was killed. But her mother had always worked hard to provide for them, and the bond between Charlene and Louise grew strong over the years as they tried to survive on her mother's meager earnings. The strange premonition of her father's death weighed on Charlene's mind, but no other such event had occurred and after a few years she came to the conclusion that it was only the incredible connection to her father that had allowed her to have such knowledge.

Her childhood had been one of hard work and discipline and Charlene's only solace during those long years was her love for music, and for singing. By the time she was fifteen, her mother had recognized that her talent was unique, and at her urging, Charlene entered, and won, the nationally telecast show, *Talent Search America.* By the time she was eighteen, she had climbed up the music charts to international fame, and she was able to give her mother everything that she had ever been deprived of—security from want, and a lifestyle of comfort and joy. And when Charlene finally decided to embark on her own life as an adult she was able to purchase a fine home that her mother could call her own.

She had been blessed with an incredible instrument, a voice that could touch hearts across all boundaries. Now thirty-eight, she had sold well over 100 million albums and regularly packed the largest arenas in the world whenever she went out on tour. Even in a music industry beset by revolutions in technology and distribution, she stood head and shoulders above other performers, one of the brightest stars in the entertainment galaxy.

The public knew her—or thought it did—as the superstar who had been in love, very publicly, with a very different sort of superstar. They also knew that she had lost the love of her life, tragically. They could not know that Charlene felt in her heart that she would never experience true love again in this lifetime. . . .

· Three years earlier ·

It was halftime of the Super Bowl game between the New York Jets and the St. Louis Rams. There were eighty-five thousand people in the stands, and the Jets—who were the underdogs—were leading 17 to 14. The excitement was electric as the football experts, former players and coaches themselves, began to discuss the first half.

"Clearly, the Jets have been able to run against this vaunted Rams defense, and that has been the key so far," one of the analysts was saying.

"But they're going to have to open up their passing, don't you think, Tony?"

"I think we will just have to wait and see what the Jets come up with in the second half," said Tony as he saw the director motioning for them to wrap up the chatter. The halftime show was about to start. The commentators shut off their mics and started to vent once again about how halftime shows were a complete waste of valuable airtime, and that no one actually watched them.

The next shot on the JumboTron showed a small woman walking to the center of an immense stage. There were no dancers, no manic band playing, just one singer with a microphone and a lone spotlight. She seemed like a single candle shimmering in the darkness. And then she began to sing.

I've a life to live
Open up my heart and give
To someone, somewhere

I know that we will be together
Heart touching heart forever
Someone, somewhere

The crowd at the stadium, normally restless during halftime, grew quiet and attentive. Those who had left their seats for halftime refreshments paused where they were and looked down at midfield where Charlene, without elaborate stage setting and with no flashing play of laser lights, stood alone—one small woman, holding the souls of over 100 million people with her voice.

Sports fans all over the country refilled food bowls and complained loudly that the only thing these shows were good for was to get a much-needed bathroom break. But they suddenly stopped when they heard Charlene's voice. Phone calls were interrupted, curses broke off, yelling quieted. There was something about Charlene's voice, a unique, haunting quality that crossed all music genres to resonate in the hearts of those who heard it.

When Ryan McAvoy was nineteen years old, he developed a microchip no larger than a dime that could manage and store 1 million gigabytes of information. Now he was a billionaire many times over and considered by the popular magazines that followed such things to be the world's most eligible bachelor.

McAvoy was at that fateful Super Bowl game; in fact, he had bought ten thousand tickets, which were distributed to military, police officers, firefighters, and EMS personnel. When he came down from his skybox seat to walk through the section that was occupied by the beneficiaries of his largesse, everyone assumed he was coming to say hello. And that is exactly what he did, until he reached the barrier between the stands and the football field. Once there, he reached under the railing where he had previously taped a long-stemmed blue rose. Then, before anyone could stop him, he vaulted over the railing and walked calmly out onto the field.

At first the security guards were too shocked to react. They all recognized him, and no one thought that he would be a stalker, or would mean any harm to anyone. But they had a job to do, and several of the guards started after him cautiously. There were several frantic voice exchanges between the security forces and the stadium officials, who feared that this was part of Charlene's performance and were terrified of a lawsuit. By the time the decision was made to intercept this incredibly famous individual, Ryan had managed to mount the stage, and when they reached him, he was already on one knee in front of Charlene.

"Excuse me, Mr. McAvoy," one of the security guards said. "We don't mean to be rude, but just what are you doing out here?"

Ryan looked up at Charlene, and there was something in the expression on his face that reached her. Although she had been frightened when he started toward her, now she felt no fear whatsoever. She felt, as she wrote in a song later, a "magic moment."

"Please," Charlene said to the security guards. "Don't take him away. Let him speak."

The guards looked at one another as if trying to decide what to do. The senior guard present shrugged his shoulders and stepped back, giving Ryan his moment, still wondering if this was some sort of elaborate piece of performance art.

Ryan extended his arms to either side, then sang two lines from her signature song, "Someone, Somewhere":

I know that we will be together
Heart touching heart forever

"Charlene, my beautiful Charlene, you don't know me yet, but I am the man you are going to marry. I love you."

Ryan had managed to obtain from the show's producer a lavalier microphone, set to the same frequency as the microphone Charlene was using, so his proposal was heard all over the stadium, and all over the world.

For a moment, the massive crowd was stunned. Was this part of the show? No, it couldn't be—and yet, somehow, it seemed so right. They waited to see how Charlene would react to this oh-so-public pronouncement of love. Then, when Ryan stood up and handed her the rose, she took it and held her hand out for him to kiss.

The crowd cheered and applauded.

Ryan turned and left the field amid the cheers of the crowd coming from both Jets and Rams fans. He winked and placed his hand to his heart. It reminded her of the same gesture she had made when her dad passed. Eerie and touching.

The scene of Ryan's proposal was shown on every news and sports show, not only in America, but also around the world. It had gone on YouTube, and by evening already had well over half a million hits.

"The Jets won, forty-four to twenty-seven," one of the beautiful blond cable newscasters said that evening, "but the second half was almost anti-climactic given the event that occurred during the halftime. One can only wonder, what was Ryan McAvoy thinking? And what is Charlene think-ing now?"

When Charlene examined the blue rose more closely that evening, she found a slip of blue paper that matched the rose petals so perfectly, she al-most didn't notice it. When she removed the paper and opened it, she found written in gold ink:

> IF YOU WANT TO TALK TO ME, MY CELL NUMBER IS
> 310-555-0178.

Charlene laughed, wadded the paper up, and threw it away.

That night, she awakened at about two in the morning, and she lay in bed for several minutes, unable to go back to sleep.

What had awakened her?

Why couldn't she go back to sleep?

She relived the halftime incident when Ryan McAvoy came out onto the field. She had not recognized him, and didn't know who it was until someone told her. She had heard of Ryan McAvoy, of course. Who hadn't heard of him? He was one of the ten wealthiest men in the world. What could possibly have been going through Ryan McAvoy's mind to make him do something like that?

Was he serious? Who did things like that? And just what kind of re-action did he possible hope to get from her by doing such an outrageous thing?

She fluffed her pillow, turned over, fluffed her pillow again, and turned over again. She looked at the digital clock, and the red glowing numbers said *2:16*.

2:39 . . .

3:10 . . .

3:27 . . .

With a sigh, she sat up and turned on the light. What had she done with that piece of paper that she found in the rose?

She had thrown it in the trash can.

Charlene got out of bed and walked into the kitchen area of the suite where she was staying. The coffee grounds had been emptied into the trash can and she had to go through them until she found the paper. It was wet, and coffee-stained, and most of the words were smeared so that she couldn't read them.

She couldn't make out the first few digits, though she was pretty sure that it had been a Los Angeles area code. Taking the paper back into the bedroom, she picked up her cell phone and looked at it.

"Charlene," she said aloud, "if you do this, you are as crazy as a loon." She giggled. "But no crazier than he was for coming out onto the football field in the first place."

She glanced again at the alarm clock as she dialed his number. The time was 3:43 A.M.

She heard the called phone ring. It rang four times and she was about to punch the call off when she heard someone pick up.

"Charlene," Ryan said, "what took you so long?"

Not since the last royal marriage in London had there been a more fairy-tale wedding. This American prince had won the heart of his princess, and they were married in the Cathedral of Saint John the Divine in New York. Charlene was not Episcopalian, but Ryan was, and he thought that marrying someone whose last name was St. John at the Cathedral of Saint John the Divine was appropriate.

The cathedral was filled to overflowing, but there were no cameras allowed in the church. There were plenty of cameras outside, though, and the police had blocked off traffic on Amsterdam Avenue.

They were married for less than two years, "The Couple" that every magazine and television show pointed out as an example of a marriage of famous people that could not only survive, but thrive in the public eye. The world was waiting for a child to complete the storybook couple's charmed life, when they learned that Ryan had been diagnosed with a quick-acting, and inoperable brain tumor.

Charlene canceled all her concerts and tours. She spent every minute with the man who had become her whole life. There were rumors of special treatments, all in a vain attempt to forestall the inevitable.

Not since the public mourning after the death of Princess Diana had the grief been so widespread. More than one newscaster choked up when news of Ryan's death was announced. And the young widow, Charlene St. John McAvoy, achieved legendary status in the hearts and minds of people around the world. To the tabloids, her day-to-day life was busy, filled with activities, and she devoted a good chunk of her time to charities created in Ryan's name. But the reality of Ryan's death threatened to engulf her.

She had lost her center, and while her closest friends, mother, and family tried to help, she couldn't see a way to any kind of future that didn't have Ryan in it. Her mother offered to come and stay with Charlene for as much time as she needed her, but Charlene refused, saying that her mother had suffered too much as a widow herself and she wouldn't want her to go through that again, even if it was to comfort her daughter. And so Charlene created a cocoon around herself, a cheerful façade that she presented to the outside world, but when she finally came home, she retreated to the sanctum of her bedroom and cried herself to sleep most every night. She was alone with her grief in the huge house that she and Ryan swore would be their nest, a place they would grow old in, a happy home that would ring with the glorious sound of many children.

CHAPTER
8

· Washington, D.C. ·

President Marcus Jackson had left his desk and was sitting on one of the two facing wheat-colored sofas separated by a cherrywood table. A huge presidential seal was the centerpiece of the oval carpet. Ollie Mc-Kenzie, the President's science adviser and Dr. Jason Chang were sitting on the sofa across from him. He finished reading the report the two men had given him.

"I tried to put it in as plain a language as I could, Mr. President," Chang said. "I wanted you to be able to get through all the scientific jargon so you would understand it."

"Oh, I understand it, all right," POTUS said. "What you are saying here is that there is a possibility that this mysterious dark force, whatever it is, is going to intersect with Earth within a matter of days? Weeks?"

"We think less than a month. We can't be certain."

"Why can't you be certain? Isn't it a matter of speed and distance? I am reminded of the old mathematical problem: 'How long does it take a train doing fifty miles an hour to go from point A to point B if they are one hundred fifty miles apart?'"

"It isn't that simple. This dark matter is not moving in any clearly defined direction or velocity," Chang said.

POTUS put the folder down then held his hands together in an almost prayerlike manner. "Are you aware, Dr. Chang, that there is a gathering of the world's religious leaders to discuss this?"

"I'm sorry, we have tried to be very careful about letting any of this information out, in order to prevent any kind of world panic."

"Do you remember when you first contacted me about this?"

"Yes, Mr. President."

"How long before that initial contact had you been aware of this"—he made a motion toward the manila folder—"dark matter?"

"Only a couple of days."

"Would it surprise you to know that the religious leaders have been dealing with this thing for at least six months?"

"How could they? I've checked all our tracking—this had not even manifested itself six months ago."

"And yet, more than one religious figure—and from more than one religion, I might add—were aware of this as far back as six months ago."

"I don't know how to respond to that, Mr. President."

"Nor do I," POTUS said. "All right, I'll ask you again: What do you need? What can the government do?"

"I'm afraid, Mr. President, that I just have the problem. I don't have a solution."

"If you have a solution, or even a request that might help you find a solution, call me."

"Yes, Mr. President."

"In the meantime, I will do what my religious adviser has suggested that I do. I will pray."

"That can't hurt," Chang said.

As Chang left the Oval Office, President Jackson reflected on the previous conversation. He was faced with a situation that no president, king, or emperor before him had ever faced. He was being told by scientists and religious leaders alike that there was a possibility that all humankind could be destroyed by some mysterious black cloud from outer space.

"Just my luck," POTUS stated quietly in an attempt at dark humor. "I get elected president and the world comes to an end."

He thought: *This is where Superman or Doctor Who would descend and save the planet—as well they should!* But what human power could save the Earth from such a destructive force? It would take every ounce of spiritual strength he—and every man and woman—possessed to find a solution. If one were to be found at all.

God help us, every one, he prayed silently and intensely.

CHAPTER
9

The director of the National Aeronautics and Space Administration had convened a meeting of the International Scientific Council in Houston, bringing together the leading scientists and those in positions of power from every continent on earth to focus on the emergence of scientific evidence of a strange dark energy that threatened the planet. After opening the meeting he turned it over to Dr. Jason Chang, who had first noticed the phenomenon.

"I wish first to thank you all for coming to this conference and second to commend you on the preparatory work that you did in record time to present important data here to the international community. We have more than ninety nations and every continent represented. In short, we have evidence of a force that is a form of dark matter, with no known origin, which is expanding within the universe.

"We are here to discuss just what is the physical and scientific nature of this dark matter. And if we determine that this force is dangerous, what can we do to prevent this new force from damaging or destroying us?"

As he consulted his notes on the laptop screen, he tried to hold in his emotions and remain the cool, competent professional in a leadership position during a potential crisis. Could he steer these scientists, bureaucrats, and politicians toward a constructive, unified conclusion and even toward the correct action for the sake of their planet?

Never had Chang felt so vulnerable, not even in his astronaut days when he had been disconnected from his own EVA line, the umbilical cord that connected him to the space shuttle, and to life. Then there had been only one choice, only one right action—to try to save the life of another human being. Here, in the face of this amalgam of scientific reality and moral imperative, he simply did not know the answer—or the answers—and he would have to trust the minds of many others even as he tried to guide them to the right choices that might affect every person on earth.

In this task, he reported directly to the President of the United States. The two had spoken the week before the opening of the international conference. Chang had briefed President Jackson on the agenda and the expected attendees.

"Can we get a handle on this phenomenon, Dr. Chang?"

"We are going to try, Mr. President. The Russians, Japanese, and Australians are particularly cooperative and open to sharing their own research with the rest of us. We have opened all our satellite data to scientists around the world. It's the only way we will be able to ask others for their research results. Either we all cooperate or we all go down together."

"What, exactly, do you mean by 'all go down'?"

"A terminal event, Mr. President."

"Terminal event?"

"The end of all life on this planet."

"It's that serious?"

"We believe it might very well be the case, Mr. President."

"What can my administration do to help you in your work? What resources do you need to stem this tide?"

"Well, at the moment, it is a matter of data-gathering and analysis. For that we need global involvement—without delay. You can encourage the Chinese and the Europeans to be more cooperative. I don't think they realize what is at stake here."

"I'll contact the leaders today—personally. Meanwhile, good luck with your meeting. You have a lot on your shoulders."

Jason Chang realized that what the President had said was true. But that didn't help very much. Now, as he gazed out at the faces of so many scientific colleagues and competitors, he tried to put aside the burden of what he knew and focus on the simple yet urgent duty of communicating his knowledge with those who had answered his invitation.

This moment was very much like the liftoff of the space shuttle—at which time he had to put out of mind all the information he had crammed into it for years. Instead of thinking, he became pure action and reaction. He recalled the fearsome thrill of the shuttle's thrust into flight even as he stood before his global peers—then he put all emotion out of his mind.

"For this task," he continued, "all of us as men and women of science must put aside purely national and parochial interests for the good—I should say, for the survival—of the planet.

"What we at NASA have been calling dark matter has appeared from nowhere—or, more correctly, from a point near galaxy cluster Abell 2744. We may never know its source, but we do know it is constantly expanding and moving dangerously close to Earth. Concurrently, there is evidence of substantial increase in solar activity. There is no way, yet, of calculating when the planet will physically encounter this dark matter. We estimate, however, that it may occur within weeks—not months, and certainly not years. How many days or weeks? This is infinitely faster than climate change, a 'greenhouse effect' on fast forward."

Chang saw the assembled scientists shift in their seats and whisper to one another. He knew what they were thinking, because he had thought the same things himself when the bizarre phenomenon had first been revealed to him. . . . Now, what would they do with their thoughts? Could they come up with an idea to conquer this seemingly insurmountable threat?

There were far more questions than answers in his mind at this point.

"My friends, let's take a look at the data available to us and decide how we can help one another find a solution for our world."

CHAPTER
10

POTUS and his staff discussed whether he should keep his appointment to speak at the National VFW conference in San Antonio, or stay in Washington to deal with the earthquake in Turkey.

"Mr. President, your core constituency is made up of veterans and their families," Charley said. "The way I see it, you don't have any choice. You have to go to San Antonio."

"But wouldn't it seem rather uncaring if I did that?" POTUS asked. "I mean here the poor people of Turkey are suffering unspeakable privations, while I enjoy the pomp and ceremony of a speech that is like preaching to the choir."

"On the other hand, the country needs to see that business is still being conducted. I think it is important that you do go."

When POTUS called in the Speaker of the House and the Senate Majority Leader, both of whom were members of the opposing party, and they agreed with his staff that he should go, he made up his mind to do so.

Inside the boardroom of Air Force One, POTUS sat in an overstuffed leather chair at one end of the long oak table, conducting a meeting with people from his inner circle. Charley Crawford sat just to his left, tapping into a laptop, and Freddy Harris, chief of the President's Secret Service detail, was standing in front of the door that led into the boardroom. Win sat on a chair near her husband and as she watched him she was overwhelmed with pride and love at his calm and assured manner.

Here she was flying on Air Force One, arguably the most elegant and powerful mode of transportation in the world, and she contrasted that with her experience as a child on the overcrowded, leaking boat in which she and thirty-three others had escaped Vietnam. A short while ago the chef of Air Force One had served a meal of bacon-wrapped filet mignon, asparagus spears, and rice. It was rice instead of baked potato as a concession to Win. They ate from gold-trimmed Air Force One china, and drank from crystal embossed with the presidential seal, and Win was humbled by the unique gifts that life had given her.

The pilot's voice came over the speaker. "Mr. President, ladies and gentlemen, we've been given priority clearance, and we'll be landing at SAT in about fifteen minutes."

"Wow, we've been given priority clearance. Can you imagine that?" Crawford asked, and the others laughed.

The presidential limo was parked on the tarmac right beside the plane, and after POTUS, his wife, and his son came off the airstair, they got immediately into the car that was to take them to the Gonzalez Center, where the VFW convention was meeting. They were led and trailed by police cars, and flanked on either side by police motorcycles. Just before they turned off South Alamo onto East Market, POTUS saw someone holding a sign. The sign read:

PRESIDENT—AN AGENT
FOR THE DARK FORCES
OF THE UNIVERSE

"That's a strange sign," POTUS said, pointing through the window.

"What sign? I don't see any sign," Win said.

"It's right there, right on the curb, not ten feet away. And you don't see it? It's right—" POTUS paused in midsentence. "It's gone. Where did it go?"

Win smiled. "Darling, don't let anyone else know you are seeing things. Otherwise, I fear they might start questioning your sanity."

A moment later the car turned off East Market onto Convention Way. There were several people being held behind a rope line by police officers. Here, too, were three signs.

WE LOVE YOU, MR. PRESIDENT
THANK YOU FOR COMING TO SAN ANTONIO
WELCOME, MR. PRESIDENT!

"Do you see those signs?" POTUS asked.

"Yes."

"Why do you see them? Because these are 'good' signs?"

"No, I see the signs because they are there."

"Uh-huh," POTUS said.

"Mr. President, there is a side entrance where we can take Mrs. Jackson and Marcus Jr., so they'll be only about a hundred feet from their box," Freddy said. "Tim and Mick will meet them there." Tim and Mick were two other members of the Secret Service detail.

"Good. Can you take me there as well?" POTUS joked.

"I'm afraid not, sir. As you can see, there is an honor guard waiting for you," Freddy said. "You and I will be getting out here."

POTUS looked through the window and saw an honor guard of twelve; six on either side. The honor guard of ten men and two women was made up of veterans wearing the uniforms that represented "their" war, including every war from World War II (an old veteran, standing tall and proud in his ribbon-bedecked olive drab Ike jacket) to Afghanistan.

A Korean War vet in his "pinks and greens" uniform, with the silver leaves of a lieutenant colonel on his epaulets, called out as POTUS approached. "Present arms!" His voice was still strong and commanding.

As one, the honor guard brought their highly polished M1 rifles to the present arms position, holding them trigger guard facing out, with the stacking swivel even with their eyes. As a soldier himself, POTUS was impressed with the precision of this mismatched group of veterans. He saluted as he started through the corridor.

Then time turned once more on its eternal wheel. . . .

CHAPTER
11

A re you sure he's a doctor? Or is he an actor sent here to portray a doctor?" one of the new nurses asked Rae Loona, the head nurse at St. Agnes Hospital. She was talking about Dr. Tyler Michaels. "He's a dreamboat!"

It was funny that Dr. Michaels would be compared to television doctors, because his future was charted for him when, as a boy, he became entranced with the TV show *M*A*S*H*, which in its day was even more popular than *Grey's Anatomy*. Others watched the show for the black humor, or the political satire, or even because of its military theme.

But young Tyler had been intrigued with the life-and-death decisions Hawkeye, Trapper, B.J., and Colonel Potter, his old-time TV heroes, had to make every episode. He knew that someday he was going to have to make those same decisions—not in the army, he had no intention of joining the army or any other branch of military service. He would be making those life-and-death decisions in a civilian hospital.

Tyler had attended Vanderbilt University for undergrad and medical school. "You are as good a student as I have ever encountered," Dr. George Gibson, one of his professors told him, shortly before he graduated. "But you are too full of yourself."

"I don't consider confidence as being tantamount to conceit," Tyler said. "And don't you think that a doctor, especially a surgeon, who is about to cut into a person, should have confidence in what he is doing?"

"Find some way to tone it down, Mr. Michaels," Dr. Gibson said. "Confidence in the operating room is one thing. Conceit in life is something altogether different."

Tyler was forty-four years old, but a healthful diet, a workout regimen, and—he would be the first to admit—being born with good genes caused many of the nurses, as well as some of his patients to have, as one young woman put it during a break, "thoughts that were not pure."

The other nurses had laughed because she said aloud what many of them kept to themselves.

Dr. Tyler Michaels drove a mint-condition 1967 Corvette. It was black, and the scooped side panels were red. The vanity plate read CUT. He had thought of having it say HEALER, but that was already taken.

One could perhaps forgive Tyler for having a God complex. He seemed to have it all: He was living his dream, acknowledged without question as the best surgeon in St. Agnes Hospital, many said the best in all of Atlanta. And the ones making such claims were other doctors and nurses, people who could validate their claims.

Tyler did not use the word *surgery* when he spoke to his patients. Instead he preferred to term his procedures "positive invasive techniques."

Some might even consider it ironic that *Tyler* had a "God complex" because he was an atheist. Both his parents were atheists: his mother, who was a lawyer working for an appellate judge, and his father, who was a physicist. They taught Tyler to set unsubstantiated belief aside, to adopt what they called the "scientific approach" to existence.

"No creaky, old bearded man sitting on a throne in the clouds gave me anything," Tyler liked to say. "Everything I have ever earned is by the sweat of my brow and the power of my intellect."

"What makes you think that those of us who believe in God picture him as some bearded old man sitting on a throne in the clouds?" Karen asked.

Karen, Tyler's wife of seven years, who was eight months pregnant with their first child, had an unwavering faith, and she desperately wanted Tyler to find a faith—any faith. It didn't have to be Mormon like hers; she just wanted to know that her child would be raised by two parents of faith.

Karen Michaels felt that Tyler's parents had done him an injustice by raising him as a nonbeliever. She made him promise that he wouldn't stop her from giving their child both: a love of science and a love of God.

"I won't stop you from trying to indoctrinate him in your faith," Tyler said. "But when I think he is old enough to understand, I intend to inculcate him in the beauty of science. And he will learn, quickly, that science and God are incompatible concepts."

"Not according to Emanuel Swedenborg," Karen said, surprising Tyler. She was always tuned into forward thinking and the latest in New Age and metaphysical thinking. It drove him nuts, of course.

"Who is he? Some TV evangelist?" Tyler bowed his head, closed his eyes, and extended his arm, palm out. Then, assuming the singsong voice of an evangelist preacher, he said, "Send me one hundred dollars-uh, and I will send you a genuine prayer cloth-uh, that has a picture of Jesus Christ with eyes that glow in the dark-uh!"

"Stop it," Karen said. "That's sacrilegious. Even though I know you're kidding—aren't you?" She went on, seriously: "Emanuel Swedenborg was a cool seventeenth-century scientist and inventor, and one of the most important persons in Swedish history. Geez, I can't believe you don't know this. His early life was devoted to science—and he made a ton of discoveries—but as he got older, he focused on the spiritual aspects of life, where he experienced dreams and visions."

"Dreams and visions? Get real. He might have been a scientist early in his life, but if you ask me, he turned into a kook—or a drug addict," Tyler scoffed.

"Just promise me that you won't try to poison our son's mind against religion, that you will let him grow old enough to make up his own mind," Karen said.

Tyler wanted to tell her that she would be doing exactly what she was asking him not to do, but he knew how important her faith was to her, so he gave in to her entreaty.

Tyler was a true workaholic who spent more time at the hospital than he did at home. Karen loved him very much, and learned to accept his commitment to work by focusing on the coming baby, and also by writing and illustrating what she hoped would be the first of many children's books. She was an experienced editor herself, having edited both adult and children's books, and now she was going to move over to the other side of the desk in hopes of being an author. She had also attended three or four writers' conferences where she took classes on writing and, more importantly, was able to convene with many writers who were successfully published, as well as editorial colleagues in the business.

She was writing her first book for their unborn son, Jeremy Tyler Michaels, and planned to have it finished and ready for submission on the very day she and Tyler brought their baby home together.

Karen had a rare talent for planning—and for following through with her plans.

"We will bring him home together, won't we?" she asked Tyler. "Even if you are on call, you will take enough time off to bring our baby home."

It was Christmas Eve, and Tyler and Karen were curled up on the leather couch in front of the fireplace, listening to a CD of the Mormon Tabernacle Choir singing *"Lux Aurumque."* Tyler might be an atheist, but he did have an appreciation of beautiful music.

"We will bring him home together," Tyler promised.

Karen smiled at him. "You are making that promise on Christmas Eve," she said. "And any promise made on Christmas Eve can't be broken."

"You mean like a 'spitting in the palm of your hand' promise can't be broken?" Tyler teased.

"If that's what it takes," Karen said.

Tyler made the motion of spitting his hand; then he rubbed it on her protruding belly. "Here," he said. "I'm making the promise to both of you."

Karen laughed, then lifted his hand from her stomach and kissed it. "It isn't just bringing him home, you know," she said.

"What do you mean?"

"Tyler, I so much want you to be a part of the baby's life. Please, try to be more present after he is born—if not for me—then for him."

"I'm well ahead of you, my love," Tyler said.

"What do you mean?"

"The baby is due the first week of January. I have already told the hospital that I intend to take a four-day holiday over the New Year's weekend. No pager, no patients, no calls, no surgeries."

Karen's face lit up. "Oh, Tyler, do you promise?" she asked.

"I promise."

With the baby scheduled to be born in the first week of January, Karen was well aware that the New Year would bring all sorts of life changes. It was, she knew, going to be a new transition for both her and Tyler. How would Tyler handle it? Would he realize that he had new responsibilities, and that the child's very future would be shaped by Tyler's actions? She could only hope and pray that Tyler would rise to the occasion and become as incredible a father as he was a surgeon.

CHAPTER
12

Being on staff rather than a visiting physician had one perk that Tyler especially appreciated: He had a marked parking spot, and though he was senior enough to have taken one of the spots nearest the physician's entrance to the hospital, he chose one over in the corner instead. On one side was the brick wall of the hospital building, and on the other side was the utility building that housed the air-conditioning unit. That way there was very little opportunity for someone to misjudge their parking place and damage his car. Also, it kept his car out of sight. The Corvette was worth, conservatively, sixty thousand dollars. It would be quite a tempting target for an automobile thief.

Tyler parked in his spot, then completing his parking ritual, fitted it with the canvas car cover that he kept in the trunk. With the car covered, and out of harm's way, he entered the hospital by the physicians' entrance. Tom Claiborne was working on a circuit-breaker panel.

"Ready to sell that Vette, yet, Doc?" Claiborne asked.

"Not yet," Tyler said.

"I'll give you an arm and leg for it," Claiborne said. "In fact, if you wait for a moment, I'll give you the leg right now."

That was Claiborne's sense of humor. He had lost his left leg below the knee in an industrial accident but had so mastered the use of his prosthetic limb that Tyler knew him for two months before he realized he had an artificial leg.

"Now tell me, Tom, just what would I do with an extra leg?"

"Well, seein' as how your chief of surgery is always ridin' you, you could stick a boot up his ass and still have two legs left," Claiborne said.

Tyler laughed. There were some who worried that Tom Claiborne's dark sense of humor might harbor some deep-seated psychological problem, but

Tyler had visited with Claiborne more than anyone else in the hospital, and he believed that it was just the guy's way of coping with it.

When he stopped by the nurses's station on the recovery floor, he saw the chief of nurses making an entry in the computer, tapping the keys with two fingers as fast as the average person could type using the QWERTY method.

Rae Loona was a fifty-eight-year-old African-American woman with a cartoon-print six-inch headband and an Afro that, according to her, had not gone out of style and never would.

"When are you going to learn to type?" he asked.

"When you learn to rap," Rae shot back without looking away from the monitor.

Tyler picked up the file folders that were lying in the "rounds" basket. "How was Mr. Underhill's night?" he asked.

"The night nurse said he was quiet," Rae said. Finishing whatever she had been typing, she sent it to the printer then stood up and came over to the counter. "How is Karen?"

"She's tired of being pregnant," Tyler said. "I told her to stop being such a baby."

"What did she say to that?"

"She told me she would stop being such a baby when I carried one in my belly for nine months."

Rae laughed out loud and slapped her hand down on the countertop. She pointed at Tyler. "She got your little pink ass with that one."

"How do you know my ass is pink?"

"You're a white boy, aren't you? You think in my thirty-five years of being a nurse, I haven't seen ten thousand pink asses?"

"I've often wondered why you're still here."

"That's 'cause my Johnny hasn't returned my calls. If my Johnny Travolta would have me, I'd be out of here so fast—well, I can't even tell you how fast, 'cause there's no words to describe it. *That's* why I'm still here."

Before Tyler made his rounds, he stepped into the physicians' lounge for a cup of coffee. There were three interns there, drinking coffee and laughing. They grew quiet and stood as Tyler came in.

"Gentlemen," he said. "How is it going?"

"Fine, Dr. Michaels," one of the interns replied.

"You're Dr. Poole?"

"Yes, sir."

Tyler poured himself a cup of coffee. "Tell me, in writing a medical report, what does the SOAP method mean?"

"That's an acronym, Doctor," Poole replied. It mean 'subjective, objective, assessment, and plan.'"

"Very good. And to what does the subjective refer? Dr. Blake?"

"The subjective part of the report tells what the patient says about his symptoms in his own words," Dr. Blake said.

"And the objective?"

Dr. Urban, the remaining intern, replied. "The objective part of the report details what the doctor sees and hears when he observes the patient."

"He?" Tyler said.

"Yes, sir," Urban replied, not sure why Tyler questioned him.

"How many interns are here at St. Agnes right now?"

"There are nine of us," Urban replied.

"Uh-huh. All men?"

"No, three are . . ." Urban paused in midsentence. "Oh. I meant what he *or* she observes."

"Good for you," Tyler said. He finished his coffee, then picked up the stack of files again. "Well, gentlemen, are you ready to make the rounds?" he asked.

"Yes, sir," Dr. Urban replied.

At her nurse's station, Rae Loona watched the three eager young interns trailing along in Tyler's wake. She knew, as they knew, and every intern past or present who had interned with Dr. Michaels in the last ten years, that they could learn more in one hour with him than they could learn in an entire semester of medical school.

CHAPTER
13

When the phone rang, Karen Michaels checked the caller ID before she answered. It read DR. J. D. KIRBY.

"Hi, Daddy," she said brightly. "Or is this Mom?"

"It's me, sweetheart," Edna Kirby said. "How are you doing?"

"Still pregnant," Karen said. "Just like I was when you called yesterday."

"And the day before and the day before that," Edna said. "I'm just thinking that maybe your father and I should cancel the cruise."

"What? No! Why in the world would you want to cancel the cruise?"

"So we can be here for you when the time comes," Edna said.

"Don't be silly, Mom. Tyler will be here. There's nothing you or Daddy can do when the baby is being born. I will need you *after* the baby is born. You said you would come for the first week and I'm holding you to it."

"Oh, there is no way you can keep us away," Edna said. "You think we don't want to be there to see, and to play with our grandson? And then give him back to you when he needs his diaper changed?" she added with a little laugh.

The cruise was a vacation and fellowship retreat sponsored by the church her parents attended in Nashville. Her father was chief of residents at Nashville General Hospital. Dr. Henry Emory had been on staff there, and when Emory left Nashville to come to St. Agnes as chief of surgery, Dr. J. D. Kirby had recommended that he try to recruit Dr. Tyler Michaels. He had also played a hand in getting his daughter together with the young surgeon, whom he thought showed more promise than any other surgeon he had met in the previous ten years.

"Did you have a good Christmas?" Karen asked.

"Oh, we had a good enough Christmas, I guess—except you weren't there," Edna answered. "We had a beautiful church service, then a potluck dinner. Everyone dressed up for it. But I wish we were together. I miss you and want to see you with the baby on the way."

"It was a nice Christmas for us," Karen said, but with hesitation.

"Nice?" Karen's mother's voice had a questioning lilt to it. "What do you mean, nice? Did something happen?"

"No, Mom, really. It was fine. Tyler gave me the most beautiful diamond pendant you ever saw. It's just that—" She stopped in midsentence.

"Don't just leave me hanging, sweetheart. It's just that, what?"

"Well, Tyler is so sweet, like I said, he gave me the most beautiful diamond pendant." She laughed. "And he bought Jeremy a football. Not a little one, mind you, a full-sized, real football. It's as big as Jeremy will be when he is first born. But to Tyler, Christmas is just—things."

"It's about tradition and family, built on a foundation of faith and values."

"I agree. You know that. Oh, Mom, I wish for anything, something—I would settle for him being a little more spiritual. I don't care about him being religious. I mean, I can't really complain too much. After all, he has never tried to change me, he accepts—no, more than accepts, I think he even respects that I am a person of faith. But he—"

"Sweetheart, you hold on to your faith," Edna said. "There's no need for you to preach. Tyler will come around. This, I know in my heart."

"I hope so, Mom."

"Are you going to celebrate New Year's Eve?" Edna asked.

"Yes. They are having a reception at the ballroom in the W Hotel. Tyler said we could stay home and pop a big bowl of popcorn, then watch New Year's come in on TV, but I'm the one who pushed him to go." She laughed. "Next New Year's Eve we'll have to hire a babysitter!"

"Well, have a good time, dear. But don't get too tired."

"I won't. And you and Daddy have a good time with the cruise."

Karen had silently hoped they would change their minds and stay, so she wouldn't feel alone, after all, on this special night. Despite Tyler's attempts to be there for her, she felt abandoned—by everyone—and somewhat depressed, but she decided she would keep it to herself, to hang on and think about the positive outcome that lay ahead . . . after all, her baby had not abandoned her. He would be with her forever. She could count on that.

·Grenada·

Patricia Rose Greenidge, Mama G, sat in her chair and rocked back and forth slowly as she watched a log burn in her patio fire pit. It wasn't a high, lapping blaze, but a long, low blaze that was blue closest to the log, then orange and yellow before dissolving into little curls of smoke. The outside evening air was unseasonably cool.

She drank a cup of tea and tried to deal with the visions that were dancing through her head.

She saw a big building, surrounded by towering Corinthian columns, and inside that building, an assembly of some sort. It was not the national parliament of Grenada, nor the Congress of the United States, nor was it the General Assembly of the United Nations.

She didn't know if she was asleep, dreaming this, or fantasizing in some semiconscious state. Okay—she wasn't asleep, she knew that. Her eyes were open and she was fully aware of the burning log in the fire pit.

There seemed to be some debate taking place.

"We need someone with a foot in both worlds," someone said.

"There are those whom we can talk to," another said. "One of them is here, with us now." All Councillors turned to look at her with paternal hope for the future.

"Yes, I am aware that Patricia Rose Greenidge is here. I summoned her."

"You summoned me here?" She stood in a state of awe, with more than a little annoyance stirred into the mix. She wore a colorful housedress, not having gussied up for this occasion, because she had been summoned without warning. Then, as she looked around and became more accustomed to being there—wherever "there" was—a sense of shock and unreality over-whelmed her.

"You are aware of us? You see us?"

"Yes."

"Do you know where you are?"

"I am on the patio of my house. At least I thought I was."

"Yes, but you are also with the Council of Elders."

"Who are you, child? And where are you?"

"I am the Governor. I preside over the Council of Elders on what you may call the Other Side." The voice did not speak aloud but simply en-tered her consciousness with authority, overwhelming in its power.

"Oh dear Lordy Lord, now I think I've flipped for sure." She was in awe, but she was herself, after all. "I am willing to believe I am not where I thought I was, but do I have to fear where I am?"

"No, you are right where you need to be."

"Why am I here?"

"It is our hope that you can help us," the Governor said. "All of human-kind is under assault by the Evil Ones. You face a grave danger as never before in history."

"The Evil Ones? Danger? You'll have to speak plain to this simple lady."

"Yes, they are the Forces of Darkness. And they are more powerful than you can possibly know."

"But aren't you the Forces of Light? The Good?"

"Yes."

"Lord knows, I've had signs of being called to meet you."

"Yes."

"What would you have me do? I'm one person. Good Lord and butter, I know that I am but a simple woman, but I have faith and know that if we pray hard enough, the forces of good will always win out over evil. You tell-ing me that I have been wrong my whole life?" She tilted her head with natural curiosity, almost like a child.

"We want you to—"

Pop! In Mama G's patio fire pit, a trapped gas bubble in the log deto-nated loudly, sending up sparks and a small flare.

Mama G looked about her, now visibly shaken, having a weird, al-most metallic taste in her mouth that she could not explain—a kind of interdimensional bad breath that made her terribly uncomfortable. A dark and sinewy figure moved quickly into the tropical bougainvillea and the darkness, carried away by the scent of the frangipani trees. She shuddered at knowing that she had just experienced both light and darkness in battle.

She saw nothing else except those things that were so familiar to her: an old black-and-white picture of her parents in an oval frame, a vase that had belonged to her grandmother, a curved glass secretary and bookshelf, her cat curled asleep on the back of the rattan sofa.

"What would you have me do?" she asked again.

The place she had just visited, the Council of Elders, the Governor, all were gone.

Had they ever been here?

Or, more to the point, had she actually been there?

She was already interpreting visions, premonitions, troubling feelings that had been plaguing her. But what good were such aphorisms and noble intentions in the face of the catastrophe that Mama G foresaw as a storm on the horizon of time?

Her faith was shaken, and the power of prayer—a thing that she had always relied on—seemed suddenly like a very small candle with which to fight the darkness.

·London·

Asima moved across the street as swiftly as she could. The chaos in Piccadilly Circus on this warm day was overwhelming, with cabs, buses, and tourists bustling about everywhere. Car radios and street speakers were amplifying the latest hit by Charlene St. John, the American pop star. A vibe of compassion could be felt even amid the urban clangor.

This was not the environment Asima had envisioned for raising her children. She had instead dreamed of a bucolic setting, either here in England or in her native Grenada. But she had followed her husband, Muti, here, and she did not regret that. It was part of the package.

She hurried herself and her little ones over the crosswalk and made it safely to the other side of the buzzing street.

Education was important to Asima. Having been raised in the Muslim tradition, she had also grown up in the New World with all its opportunities of that tradition as well. She had graduated at the top of her class, and it was then that her dream of raising her family there, or someplace similar, had first occurred.

She had been inspired to write about island life, about her own life. She was confident that one day she would take her life story and share it to inspire people all over the world. She would help to educate them about the true beliefs and traditions of Islam in a world distorted and diluted with terroristic ideologies and discolored by violence.

Though she held a Ph.D. in political science and world philosophies, at one point Asima put her life—and her dreams—on hold. She had gotten married. She had rewritten her first book at least three times, but still she felt it was not ready to put out for publication. Since that time she had written two more books, but was still working on the ending chapters of the third book. She and Muti had several children, the oldest a son named Shakir, age fourteen.

Most people would never see Asima in the role of erudite professional, writer, teacher, or activist. Not because she wore traditional clothing or lived within a culture that was sometimes antithetical to women's progress, but because of her beauty. Even as she walked with her children along a bustling urban street, many people, men and women, stopped to stare at her. She carried herself with a melodious, radiant energy, and her dark eyes, eyebrows, and eyelashes were so pronounced that she never needed to wear makeup. Her cheekbones were sculpted in a way that was the envy of any model. Her figure was no different than it had been at nineteen when she had first met and fallen love with Muti Faradoon.

He was her hero, her heart, her true soul mate.

Even though Muti was far more traditional in his beliefs than she, she had long ago decided that she would sacrifice her personal and professional desires to be with him. Beneath the cultural stamp, he was still somehow different. He understood who she was. Their courtship had been quick, and their love strong from the very first moment they met. Muti possessed a childlike innocence and humorous demeanor that had been challenged only once: when two of his brothers were killed in a suicide bombing on the border of Syria and Iran ten years ago. To this day, Muti never discussed the bombing. He always just said that they, Rami and Hamir, were victims of "a senseless plan."

Of late, however, Muti seemed different. Asima recognized the change in him, and she tried desperately to get him to talk to her, to let her in on what was troubling him. However, he would not share his private thoughts anymore, at least not with her. This lack of conversation was only getting worse, and to Asima, who prided herself on her ability to communicate with anyone, the silence was deafening.

"We used to speak to each other only with our eyes, and our souls danced together," she told him. She had bittersweet memories of blissful, romantic, spiritual lovemaking, but now when they were together in bed it seemed purely mechanical on his part. She could not reach him. He was fast becoming an island—but an arid desert island, not a place where she wanted to live. Not like her beloved island nation. This was more like Atlantis, sinking slowly into the abyss . . . a place she could not go.

The loss was compounded by evidence that Muti was dragging their firstborn son, Shakir, under with him.

The shadows of Muti's dead brothers, Rami and Hamir, seemed always present in their lives, and in their home. He now spoke of them incessantly to Shakir—and to Asima, when he spoke to her at all. His elder brother, Omar, who had been in London even longer than Muti and had welcomed the family into his home for several months before they found their own place, was an overbearing presence at their flat. He was a successful restaurateur and Muti worked fifty or sixty hours a week for him in one of three locations. They were on the verge of opening a fourth place.

Shakir idolized his father. The sun rose and set on anything and everything Muti said. Shakir listened for hours as Muti spoke to him about their ancestry, the family's history in Iran over many generations, and the losses the family had suffered. He painted a picture of the world as a dark place that required a man to adopt a warrior mentality in order to fight his way through to victory against a host of enemies, seen and unseen.

Asima wanted only what was best for her three children, and for Shakir, she only hoped that one day he would find success in America. She did not see the United States as the land of the infidel or the sleeping giant waiting to pounce on the rest of the world. No, she saw the whole world in the same way: Each country was like a child behaving badly, one that needed a parental figure to step up and lay down the rules and regulations so that one child would not be able to bully any other child for too long a period of time.

It was clear to most people, and to Asima as well, that the United States' reputation was not so pristine as it had once appeared, but it was a place and a culture that held such great promise nonetheless. She held on to high hopes for her family, and Shakir was her golden child. He was destined for great things, this son of hers and Muti's; of this she was certain. He wanted to be an architect.

But as Muti became increasingly callous and empty, Shakir seemed to be maturing much faster than he ought to—and acting older than he was. Certainly he was behaving in ways Asima did not favor. One day she heard him weeping in his room after Muti had been picked up by his brother Omar for work.

When she walked into Shakir's room, he had his iPod blaring in his ears, and he was wiping tears away from his eyes. On his bed were charts and diagrams drawn on beige typing paper and a photo layout of the newest restaurant that Muti and Omar were opening in Piccadilly. She was baffled at what this was all about and deeply disturbed.

Asima felt in that moment that Shakir was feeling the pressure of being Muti's son and Omar's nephew—that their dreams for him were much different from his own or Asima's. Muti had told Shakir that he was to take his place in the family business. That would mean his desire to be an architect would have to be put aside for now. His urge to design and build would take a backseat to Muti's will for him. . . .

Asima was walking with her little ones to the new restaurant location off Piccadilly Circus to meet Muti and Shakir there for an early dinner. It was a routine gathering, but she felt a strange foreboding this time that was different and disturbing to her soul.

In the cluttered office at the back of the new restaurant, Muti and Omar were huddled, speaking in hushed tones. Because construction workers were making sufficient racket out front, they did not have to whisper, but they were used to talking like this, and they were paranoid about being overheard—by anyone.

"The sign is close at hand," Omar said. He held up a copy of a local Farsi-language newspaper, then a copy of an English-language tabloid with blaring headlines: 11TH NEW ZODIAC BODY UNEARTHED IN BELFAST. The men pored over the news story, especially the diagram of the field in which the bodies had been buried in shallow graves.

Muti said, "So, when do you think the final revelation will come? It has to be very soon. We are ready." He looked eagerly at Omar.

The eldest son in the family, Omar had been calling the shots for his younger brothers for years. It was he who had assigned the bombing to Rami and Hamir. It was he who had arranged for Muti and his family to relocate to London, and he who had found a place for Muti in his thriving Persian restaurant business. He was a puppet master who, in turn, took his instructions from a dark, ethereal force that had no name—that is, no name that he shared with Muti.

"The world will be watching Belfast, just as we are. Then the world will witness attacks on each continent as our strategic action is unleashed." He smiled and sat back, drumming his fingers on the office desk. "We hold no enmity for Christians, Jews, or any religion, nor any Muslim sect here or anywhere. We are called to act against a weak mankind who are blind to the will of the Almighty. They have been soiled for centuries by false beliefs and false prophets. Now will come the time of the cleansing."

"Brother, I have long wanted to avenge our younger brothers, and we have both worked for long years to assimilate ourselves here in London, indeed in the very heart of the city. I must say I am impatient and on edge, waiting for the final signal."

"Yes, Muti, you have been most faithful to our cause, even though you cannot fully understand the scope of this war—or its ultimate outcome. But I can tell you that the forces of righteousness—which some call the Dark Side—plan to control the energy of the human spirit. This has been revealed to me. I speak this as the truth. You have put your trust in me and placed your life and the lives of your family in my hands. I could not ask any more of a friend or a brother than that. We are truly one now, and we will be one in the glorious new world."

The younger man looked down at the papers strewn over the desk in the restaurant office: bills and letters, advertisements, newspapers, sample menus, maps of the city. His eyes focused on one piece of paper, a drawing his son Shakir had made of the new place's main dining room. He said, "We must tell Shakir what part he will play in the plan. It has been two years since we agreed that he is the chosen one who will carry out this act of vengeance in our name."

"It is a great honor for him and for our family," Omar said, nodding gravely. He looked at Muti, trying to detect any sign of doubt or wavering in his commitment to the act. He saw none. "Your wife will be here soon. Let us be seen taking care of our business when she comes."

That night, as she lay in bed alone, Asima suddenly remembered an incident from her university days in Grenada. A brief encounter in the market with an older woman, a native of the island, who had told her something about herself that, over the years, she had nearly forgotten. Now it seemed prophetic and deeply disturbing.

"Girl," the woman had said, reaching out to touch Asima with both hands on her cheeks, "my name is Patricia Rose Greenidge, but most folks just call me Mama G. I am what they call a seer. Oh sure, it goes by other names like psychic, soothsayer, oracle . . . but me, I'm just a God-fearing woman with a gift of knowing. I only claim to be what I am." The woman smiled, exposing large white teeth and a warm fire in her dark eyes. "You are beautiful, both in your body and your soul. One day you will make a great sacrifice—the greatest sacrifice that could ever be asked of a woman and—" She paused significantly. "—a mother. You will help many in a way that you cannot know. Yet you will know it at the time. You will be a hero and the mother of heroes."

Asima thought about that encounter from her past and wondered why of all times this would come to her now and knew that as much as she tried sleep would not come easily that night.

· Melbourne, Australia ·

Dawson Rask was in a garden of beautifully sculptured shrubbery in Hampton Court Maze. He had started out with other visitors and a guide, but somehow he had become separated, and as he tried to find his way back to them, he just got deeper and deeper into the maze. Then he tried to find his way out, and he could swear that the path that was open but a moment before was now closed.

"This is dumb," he said. "How can I be lost in a three-hundred-year-old garden in the middle of the day with hundreds of people within the sound of my voice?"

As he stood there, the shrubbery began closing in on him, actually moving toward him so that the place where he was standing became more and more confined.

"Ah!" he shouted.

His shout woke him up, and he lay there breathing heavily, thankful that he was not actually lost, though he was wondering, just for a moment or two, where he was.

He was in Melbourne, Australia, and it was, according to the digital clock on the bedside table, 3 A.M. Okay, it was 3 A.M. here, but back home in New York, it was 5 P.M. That meant that it was also P.M. by Dawson's body clock.

Dawson sat up and swung his legs over the side of the bed. Reaching over to the bedside lamp, he turned it on. The light illuminated the hardcover book that lay on the table. Both the title of the book and the author's name were in gold embossed letters. It was a beautiful book, and it was selling very well both in the United States and in foreign sales. The book was just released in Australia, and Dawson had made the long—very, very long—flight from New York to promote the book.

He reached down to touch it, feeling a bit of creative pride; then he walked into the bathroom. After turning on the light, he looked at himself in the mirror. Unshaven, he saw gray among the stubble, as well as a few gray hairs waving from the top of his head, like excited fans at a red-carpet premiere. All of this paled in comparison to the "baggage" directly under his eyes. He had passed the forty-year milestone last month.

"Dawson, don't get old," he said aloud. Then he chuckled, because he was repeating something his ninety-year-old grandmother had told him when she would sometimes complain about the aches and pains of aging. She had been dead for eight years now, but she had been such a vivid part of his life that he still remembered her fondly, especially her sense of humor.

His body clock might tell him it was 5 P.M., but he clearly had morning mouth, so he brushed his teeth, then turned sideways to look at his body. Now, *that* he was still happy with. He had been blessed with good genes and a muscular build that enabled him to maintain the body of a Greek statue. It was still clearly defined but required a daily workout regimen in order to be sustained.

Realizing that sleep was not going to be an option, he decided to get a jump-start on the day of media and press interviews. *The Moses Mosaic* was his third novel, following hard on the heels of two previous international bestsellers.

"A writer?" Miss Hall had said. Miss Hall was his freshman high school English teacher. "Dawson, I don't mean this as a put-down, but you have dyslexia. The first time you turned in a paper, I thought your name was Noswad."

It wasn't just the dyslexia Dawson had to overcome. It was also that he was following in the wake left by his brother, Boyd, who was two years older. Boyd's transgressions were infamous, and he had left all the teachers embittered and predetermined not to let another Rask run amok in their classroom.

But Dawson, despite, or perhaps because of, the legacy left by his brother, excelled in high school, not only in academics, where he overcame his dyslexia, but in athletics, becoming a conference champion cross-country runner. A writer for *Profile Magazine*, while doing a piece on Dawson, wrote:

It is fitting that the bestselling author, Dawson Alexander Rask, ran cross country in high school and college. Cross country is a grueling sport that pits the runner against himself as much as against the other participants. It requires strength of body, as well as strength of character. Dawson Rask's character, Matt Matthews, exhibits those very traits, and one must wonder, as one always does, if Matthews isn't Rask.

Dawson had been born and raised in Decatur, Illinois. His grandfather had served in the Korean War, his father as an army draftee in the early 1960s. When he came back he began teaching at Milliken University in Decatur, becoming a full professor a few years later. Dawson's father didn't talk much about his military service, which included a two-year tour in Vietnam in 1965 and '66—and when he did talk about it, it was always some innocuous story or a humorous event. He never talked about any combat experience, and Dawson would not have known that he won a Silver Star if he had not accidentally found the medal and the citation.

Because of his father's position, Dawson could have gone to school at Milliken very cheaply, but he chose to attend Washington University in St. Louis, instead. Washington U. was a fine school with a great academic reputation, and he was able to put together several academic scholarships, including one scholarship from a beer company, simply because he was the son and grandson of veterans. He also chose Washington University because, while it wasn't in his hometown—and he did want to get out on his own—it wasn't so far from Decatur that he couldn't make it back home on long weekends.

His brother flunked out of Milliken, as well as Southern Illinois University at Edwardsville. He wasn't dumb; in fact, Dawson knew that his brother was quite intelligent. But it never was a matter of intelligence with Boyd. It was Boyd's psyche. He was a congenital troublemaker who was caught drinking when underage, and using pot when he was older.

As he had in high school, Dawson ran track and cross country at Washington University in St. Louis. One good thing about running in high school and college is that the athlete could continue with that sport for many years by participating in fun runs and marathons. And it was the running that helped him keep the trim body that he still enjoyed. Dawson earned a degree in English, and his father thought that he was going to become a teacher; in fact he urged him to do so. But Dawson moved to New York where he found a job as an associate editor at Penword House.

He did well and moved up to editor, then senior editor. That was when he met Mary Beth Williams. Mary Beth had no desire to ever be published.

That was important to someone who was an acquisitions editor, someone who could fulfill the dreams of struggling writers all over the country. He used to attend writers' conferences, and had to exercise restraint and common sense in order to resist the flirtations of women who made it clear that they would do almost anything to have their book published. That she didn't give a fig for what he could do for her was one of the first things that endeared Mary Beth to him—just one of many—and he fell hopelessly in love. They were soon married, and their life together was about as perfect as anyone could ever hope for. But all that changed one bright September morning.

Mary Beth was a financial wizard, a bond trader with Cantor Fitzgerald. She worked on the 101st floor of the North Tower of the World Trade Center. Dawson had often replayed his last telephone conversations with her on that terrible September 11, 2001. She had just been promoted, which allowed her to have a desk next to one of the windows, and she wanted to celebrate by having lunch with him at Windows on the World.

"Remember," she said early that morning. "You must be wearing a jacket and tie."

"Windows on the World is pretty expensive," Dawson replied. "Couldn't we just celebrate at a burger joint somewhere?"

"You don't worry about how expensive it is. I'm paying for it. This is my celebration, remember."

Dawson got to the office early and was starting on at least ten submissions he had to look at, all ten from respected agents, which meant he had to do more than just scan them. He was about thirty pages into *Remembered Faces, Forgotten Names* when his cell phone rang. Seeing that it was Mary Beth, he picked up.

"I know, I know, jacket and tie. I won't forget," he said.

"Dawson," Mary Beth responded, "I'm not calling to talk about that. I've been trying to reach you for fifteen minutes, but the phone lines have been jammed. The World Trade Center has just been hit by a plane."

"What? Where did it hit?" He looked at his watch. It was just past 9 A.M.

"I don't know. Below us somewhere."

"A small private plane?"

"I don't think so. The explosion was too loud, and there's smoke everywhere."

Dawson could hear a lot of confusion in the background, shouts of anger and fear.

"The sprinklers haven't come on! Why haven't the sprinklers come on?"

"Where is the fire extinguisher?"

"Someone used it to break out the window."

"Mary Beth, I hear a lot of commotion in the background. Is it really that bad?"

"It's pretty bad," Mary Beth said, strangely calm. "Someone just came back in and said that all the stairwells are blocked, we can't go down."

"Dawson, my God! Come out here and see what is on the TV!" Sam Bryant said. Sam was the publisher of Penword House. "I turned on the TV and CNN is reporting that an airliner just flew into the South Tower of the World Trade Center."

"North Tower," Dawson said. "I'm talking to Mary Beth now. She's in the North Tower."

"Both of them got hit," Bryant said. "And they are now just saying that this is no accident!"

"This is bad, Dawson," Mary Beth said. Now he could hear the fear in her voice. "This is very bad."

"I'm sure that help is on the way," Dawson said. But even as he said that, he could see on the TV screen smoke billowing out from the point of impact and obscuring the entire top of the building. He thought of telling Mary Beth of the second strike but didn't want to frighten her more.

He started to say something, but his telephone connection with Mary Beth suddenly went dead. He stood before the television in the office, less than two miles from the World Trade Center in Midtown Manhattan. In fact, if he were to go to the top floor in his building and look out the south-facing windows, he could see with his own eyes the ugly sight of the white and black smoke rising into the azure late-summer sky.

He looked at his watch. It was now forty-five minutes past nine o'clock. He held his portable phone in his hand, hoping, praying that it would ring again. He could not imagine what Mary Beth was going through in those moments. The television news broadcasts repeatedly showed the images of the two jetliners crashing into the buildings.

He tried again and again to reach Mary Beth, to no avail.

Suddenly, at almost precisely ten A.M. his coworkers, who had filed into the room and were gathered around the television, gasped as one. Dawson willed himself to look at the screen and listen to the news anchor: "The South Tower is collapsing. It's going down! Oh, my God. . . ."

There were sobs all around him, both men and women weeping.

He punched the button to dial Mary Beth's number yet again. There was a busy signal. He cleared the line so he could receive a call—her call, he prayed. He slipped into a nearby office that wasn't his, but it was empty and a few steps away from the chaos in the other room.

Dawson Rask was not a religious man. For his entire life, he had been self-sufficient, pulling himself up the ladder in his chosen profession by wit, skill, and hard work. Knowing he wasn't always the smartest or smoothest person in the room, he had vowed that no one would ever out-work him. That's why he put in fifteen- or twenty-hour days sometimes. Mary Beth had called him on it, and lately he had pulled back a bit, especially since they were both something of workaholics. Well, hadn't Mary Beth just been promoted? He had almost completely forgotten about that in the fog of the past hour . . .

Thousands of days and life's ups and downs had passed since the last time he had prayed. He couldn't even remember when that had been or why. Now, he was grasping at anything—anything—that might save the woman he loved and their yet-unlived life together.

He closed his eyes tightly and held his breath, uttering a prayer in silence.

His phone buzzed, and he picked up immediately. "Hello. Hello. Mary Beth?"

"Yes, darling." Her voice was muffled, and he could hear her covering a cough.

"What's happening now?"

"It's . . . getting hard . . . to breathe," Mary Beth said. Her voice was different, distant and somewhat dreamlike. But who was dreaming? This was a real-life nightmare that neither could comprehend.

"Lie down, Mary Beth. Listen to me, put your nose to the floor. There should be an inch or two of air there." He sympathetically crouched down to mimic what he was telling her to do, even though she could not see him. He desperately tried to think of what he could do. He sat on the floor, scared and helpless.

"Dawson, I think I'm not going to make it out of here. Tell me you'll be okay."

His mind had been a jumble, chaos and irrational anger mingled with pity and bitterness. He felt the tears streaming down his face. He couldn't help looking at his watch again. Why was he so obsessed with the time? What was it? About twenty-five minutes after ten o'clock. He could barely see the watchface anyway because his eyes were misted and his vision fogged.

"Daw, honey, listen to me. I love you."

"Our house, our kids," Dawson blurted, running through his mind what his plans were, what their world was going to be . . . "I love you. I love you," he said in reply, wanting to keep her on the line—to keep her alive and present in his life—but he knew that his last words to her weren't heard. "Hold on, Mary Beth! Hold on—"

He heard someone scream and rushed back into the office with the television. On the TV screen, he watched the North Tower collapsing at about 10:28. Dropping the phone, he sank into the nearest chair and wailed. It had all happened in a little less than two hours, though it had alternatively seemed like endless days or mere seconds. He looked down at the phone lying on the floor, an ugly, dead object. He hated it. The last he had heard from Mary Beth was on that damned thing that lay there like a corpse. The worst thing he could have imagined had come true in his life—and for tens or hundreds of thousands of others.

A few of the men came over to him and, awkwardly, silently, rested a hand on his shoulder for a moment. Several of the women, themselves crying, came over to hug him. Dawson had never felt such bitter pain in all his life. . . .

That was more than a decade ago, yet he had relived it each day since—thousands of times, over and over again. It was a wound that had not healed, and he doubted it ever would.

CHAPTER
18

S everal big HDTV screens were scattered around the ballroom of the W Hotel so that no matter where anyone was, they had a good view. As the New Year broke around the world, each screen carried the countdown. Some time zones were seen in replays of the event. One that particularly caught Karen's attention was the replay of Australia's fantastic fireworks display over the Sydney Opera House and Harbor Bridge.

Except for a weeklong vacation in Canada and a quick weekend in Mexico, Karen had never been out of the country. She was looking forward to the day that Tyler and their baby could travel with her and see the world like her parents were doing this year.

Tyler made very good money and they wanted for nothing. It gave her a sense of confidence that they would be able to bring their son up in affluence, providing him with every advantage. But even as she wrapped her mind around that sense of security, she realized that they were paying for it in other ways. Sometimes she wondered what their life would be like if Tyler were not a doctor, if he could belong to her—and their son—and not to the hospital.

It wasn't as if the medical profession were new to her. Her father was a doctor, and she could remember times when some crisis at the hospital would take him away from the family at inopportune times. She had starred in the senior play when she was in high school, but her father didn't see it, because he had been called away by a medical emergency.

But those incidents, though frequent, never seemed to keep him away as often as Tyler was away. Maybe now that he had proved himself to be the best, he would ease up a bit, start backing off so many surgeries, and spend more time at home.

Even as she was thinking that, she knew she was kidding herself. The hospital would always be the other woman. She had to accept that. While she was coming to terms with her fairy tale's reality ending, the count-down to the New Year was happening—both on the TV monitors, and with the revelers in the room.

"Ten . . . nine . . . eight . . . seven . . . six . . ."

Tyler put his arm around her shoulders and got ready to bestow her with a New Year's kiss.

"Five . . . four . . . three . . ."

Buzz, buzz, buzz!

It was Tyler's pager. The pager he had promised would be turned off!

"Two . . . one! Happy New Year!"

All the couples in the room celebrated the moment with a kiss. But Tyler had taken out his pager to look at the ID to see what code was plugged in.

"It's . . . ," he started to say, but when he looked back toward Karen, she was all the way across the ballroom. He saw her wiping her eyes as she turned the corner to leave.

"Karen!" he called, but she didn't look back. Tyler hurried across the ballroom, picking his way among the kissing couples and the popping bal-loons. "Karen!" he called again.

He caught up with her in the hallway. She did not come back to him at his call, but she at least stopped, and was standing there waiting for him as he approached.

"Karen, what are you doing? Why did you run out like that?"

Everyone in the ballroom shouted, "Happy New Year!" They could hear horns blowing and people laughing. There could not have been a greater contrast between the celebration going on not more than sixty feet behind them and the two people standing all alone in the shadows of the empty hallway.

In the ballroom now, people began singing.

Should old acquaintance be forgot,
and never brought to mind?
Should old acquaintance be forgot,
and old lang syne?

"You shouldn't even have to ask why I left," Karen said.

"I promised you I would be here with you for New Year's, and I was," Tyler said.

"You were here physically, but you weren't here," Karen said. "Not really. The moment that pager went off, you jerked it out of your pocket."

"Well, that's what a pager is for," Tyler said, trying to soften his response with a smile.

"You said you would leave your pager turned off. I know, I know, I'm not being fair," Karen said. "But I'm hormonal and cranky, and I'm just not in the mood for a dose of doctor disappointment."

"What about a dose of Doctor Make-You-Feel-Real-Good?" Tyler asked, turning on the charm.

For auld lang syne, my dear,
for auld lang syne,
we'll take a cup of kindness yet,
for auld lang syne.

"It won't work," Karen said. "Tyler, you told me, you *promised* me, that you were *not* going to be on call tonight. You said that tonight was the first day of the rest of our lives. This was supposed to represent our future. *This* is how you see our future? Well, I'm here now to tell you that this is *not* how I see my future."

"You don't understand," Tyler said.

"What is it I don't understand? I've been around doctors for my entire life. My father is a doctor, and I am married to a doctor. Is there some secret known only to doctors and not to their children or spouses that I don't know?"

"It's Dr. Emory," Tyler said.

"What?"

And surely you'll buy your pint cup!
And surely I'll buy mine!
We'll take a cup of kindness yet,
for auld lang syne.

"If I told you, you would just mark it down as another example of my— what did you call it? Unbridled self-assurance, I think you said."

"No, I think I called it conceited."

"Yes, well, I was just trying to make it sound better," Tyler said. "Anyway, I think he is jealous of me."

"Why should he be jealous? He is a fine doctor with an outstanding record," Karen said.

"I won't argue with that. But be that as it may, he has put me on a type of academic probation for what he has labeled a few bad judgment calls over the last few months."

"What sort of bad judgment calls?"

"Nothing specific, other than the way he says I present myself to the patients, and the hospital staff. It seems that Emory sees me as an egotistical hot shot in a lab coat and he wants to make an example out of me. Poor, innocent me. Can you imagine that?" Tyler made a face, still trying to use his boyish charm on Karen, but she did not seem affected in the least.

"How long has this been going on?" Karen asked.

"How long? I don't know. The better part of a year, I suppose."

"A year? This has been going on for a year and you are just now getting around to telling me about it?"

"Suppose I had told you, what would you have done? Called him, and asked him to please not be so hard on your husband? Karen, do you think I want that?"

"I could at least get his side of it," she said.

"Why in heaven's name would you want his side?" Tyler asked. "I'm your husband, for crying out loud. Isn't my side of it enough?"

"It might have been, if you had told me before now," Karen said.

Tyler sighed in frustration. "This discussion isn't getting us anywhere except to make matters worse," he said. He leaned down and kissed her on the cheek. "Look, the page was an emergency. There was a bad accident out on 285. Multiple collisions, multiple traumas, and the hospital is understaffed. I've got to go. You can see that, can't you?"

"I suppose so," she said. She looked at him, hoping that he would say something gallant, like: *You know what? How about I drive you home first, just to stretch this moment out a little longer.*

But that's not what he said. Instead, he kissed her on the forehead and said, "You take the car home, I'll grab a cab out front. When I get to the hospital, I'll call you if it looks like it's going to be an all-nighter."

Karen nodded without responding. The one thing her mom always told her was that "great expectations lead to greater disappointments," and that was certainly the case now.

For auld lang syne, my dear,
for auld lang syne,
we'll take a cup of kindness yet,
for auld lang syne.

"You do understand, don't you, Karen?" Tyler asked. "Please tell me you understand."

"I've been married to you for seven years," Karen replied. "I understand."

Tyler looked at Karen as if trying to decide whether that was an expression of understanding or continued frustration. He had no choice but to consider it as an expression of understanding, and again, he kissed her on the forehead. "Do you have your keys, or do you want mine?"

"I have my keys," she said, fishing them from her purse.

"You are an angel."

We two have run about the slopes,
and picked the daisies fine;
But we've wandered many a weary foot,
since auld lang syne.

Karen watched Tyler move quickly toward the lobby with an enthusiasm for healing and a passion for the adrenaline rush. Could she deny him this? Was there anything more pathetic than the wife who has been jilted by a husband for his mistress? Even if that mistress is his work?

Karen started down the hallway past an abstract piece of artwork that was hanging in the corridor. She could still hear the music behind her, though the words and melody became more and more indistinct as she walked away.

For auld lang syne, my dear,
for auld lang syne,
we'll take a cup of kindness yet,
for auld lang syne.

She walked through the dark parking lot until she found the Volvo S80 that they had bought two years ago. She had picked the car out because he was so entranced with his 1967 Corvette that he really didn't care what sort of "family" car they owned.

She clicked the opener and saw the parking lights flash and the interior light come on. Out here she could hear fireworks, and looking down toward Turner Field she saw them bursting through the air in a myriad of colors and shapes.

After opening the door, she slipped in behind the wheel, feeling somewhat embarrassed that she would have to push the seat back farther than Tyler had it. Nothing to be embarrassed about, she told herself. "I'm pregnant and he isn't."

She rubbed her slightly aching tummy and said aloud, "Happy New Year, Jeremy. Let's go eat ice cream. How about a pint of Rocky Road and Phish Food?"

S now was not rare in Atlanta anymore, what with climate shifts in recent years, but it was infrequent enough that, unlike northern cities,
Atlanta had no snowplows or salt reserves to deal with it. That, coupled
with the fact that the citizens of Atlanta were still not used to such driving conditions, made the roads extra hazardous.

There had been no snow when Tyler and Karen had left home earlier
tonight, and now he was having second thoughts about sending Karen on
home alone. He thought about calling her on the cell, but knew that making her answer her phone while she was driving in this weather would
make things even worse. Tyler made a mental note to call her after he got
to the hospital, just to make certain she got home all right.

"Driver, could you hurry it up a bit more?" Tyler said.

"Maybe you ain't heard, mister, but there was a big pile up out on 285.
This ain't the kind of weather to be hurryin' in."

"You're right, I'm sorry. But please, drive as fast as you think it is safe.
The reason I'm going to the hospital is because of that wreck. I'm a doctor."

"Okay, Doc, I'll do what I can," the driver replied.

The driver did go faster, and Tyler could feel the car slipping from
time to time as the wheels lost traction. It made him worry all the more
about Karen.

When the driver reached St. Agnes, he started to turn into the front
entrance, but Tyler called up to him.

"Go to the emergency room entrance around to the side," he said.

"You got it," the cabdriver replied.

Inside the hospital it looked like a plane had crashed. There were patients everywhere. The more serious cases were lying on gurneys in the

halls; the less serious ones were sitting in the waiting areas. Some were weeping; some were shouting for attention. There was a frenetic activity of nurses triaging patients and instructions being called back and forth. The noise and chaotic activity would discombobulate most people, but it served to give Tyler a clarity that many would love to develop.

Tyler's ability to think and act rationally during chaos was a gift, though he didn't see it that way. And just as some military geniuses could react brilliantly to challenging situations in combat, Tyler could react to medical crises. He was blessed with the ability to prioritize, to listen, and to plan, which made him a perfect doctor for emergency room medicine.

Because of that, Dr. Emory wanted Tyler to take the position of head ER doctor, but Tyler loved to cut. He needed to be a surgeon; it was how he defined himself, and when he declined to take the position Emory offered him, the troubled relationship between the two men escalated.

Though he was not the chief resident, his commanding attitude and energy caused other doctors to come him with questions about their own patients. And now he was exercising the authority that came so naturally to him, barking off orders, demanding tests, and deciding where the patients should be. Having come straight from the party, Tyler was still wearing his tux, his hair was perfectly styled, and he looked like a glossy magazine advertisement for "the good life."

Though wearing a tux added to the illusion of emergency, his energy and his sense of control of the situation enabled him to calm the troubled seas with no more than a word and a touch. He dived into the thick of things, and every concern in the world took a backseat to the event at hand.

For Karen, it had been a harrowing drive home. One of the cars coming toward her started sliding on the snow; then it turned broadside and she was sure it was going to slide into her. Instead, it slid all the way across the road until it was finally stopped by hitting the curb. Twice she thought she was going to slip into a skid, but she remembered her father's instructions to always "turn your wheels into a skid," and that worked for her both times.

She was sweating by the time she got home, partly because she had the defroster going at full blast and it was blowing hot air into her face, but partly because the drive itself had been so taxing. Then, to make matters worse, when she turned into the driveway, the remote would not open the garage door.

"Ohh! I don't need this!" she shouted as she pushed the button several times with the same negative results. Now, instead of being able to exit the car in the protected confines of the garage, she was going to have to go through the snow.

With a sigh of frustration, she opened the car door, stepped out into ankle-deep snow, and because, as a very pregnant woman, she was wearing flats, felt the frigid snow on her feet immediately. She had felt guilty about paying so much for the shoes, which were beautiful on the ballroom floor but beyond useless in six inches of snow.

Karen started toward the front door; then disaster struck, and she fell.

Though she tried to turn her body, she was unable to do so, and she fell facedown with her pregnant-protruding stomach taking the brunt of it. She had never experienced such pain. It went all through her, from her stomach down her legs and around her back. She managed to get up onto her hands and knees, but a wave of nausea overtook her, and she threw up.

Finally, shakily, she was able to regain her feet and she managed to make her way unsteadily to the front door. It wasn't until she reached the door that she realized she had dropped the keys in the snow when she fell, and she had to go back out, in the dark, and search through the cold snowdrifts for them. It took her at least two minutes until she found them; then once again, she had to work her way back to the front door.

She was shivering with cold and her hands were shaking so badly that she was barely able to get the key in the lock.

Stepping into the foyer, she turned on the light. Then she walked over to sit on the sofa. Her head was spinning, and she was still in pain. Pain. Pain! She didn't realize until that moment that she was having labor pains and they were severe.

"No, no, no!" she cried. "Oh dear God, no . . . Tyler, I need you now!" In her mind, she cursed Tyler for not being with her, for abandoning her. She didn't want to feel such anger at him, but it welled up inside regardless.

She had thought that he might have called her to check on her, but he hadn't. She couldn't call him; she knew there was an emergency at the hospital, so there was no telling where he might be right now. If he was just cutting into someone, the last thing he would need is for his cell phone to ring.

Another pain hit her, this time so severe that it doubled her over. She picked up the phone and dialed 911.

"Nine one one," the operator answered.

"My name is Karen Michaels. I need an ambulance right away," Karen said, her voice strained.

"What is the nature of the emergency, Karen?" the 911 operator said, her voice pleasant, caring, and calm.

"I'm in labor. . . . I've fallen, and I'm in labor! Please, send an ambulance to 2117 Peach Blossom Terrace. Tell them I want to go to St. Agnes Hospital. My husband is a doctor there and he is on duty now."

"An ambulance is on the way, Karen," the 911 operator said. "I want you to stay on the phone with me until they get there."

"All right," Karen said.

"Karen? Karen? Karen, are you still there? Answer me, please."

Karen blinked her eyes a couple of times and realized she had passed out momentarily. "How long was I out?" she asked.

"Oh, thank God you are still there," the operator said. "About a minute, no longer."

"I'll try and stay with you," Karen said.

"How long are you pregnant, Karen?"

"Eight . . . almost nine months now."

"That's long enough, don't you think? Do you know if the baby is a boy or a girl?" the operator asked, trying to keep Karen engaged.

Karen carried on a conversation with the operator, though it was difficult to do so, until she heard the ambulance out front. She dropped the phone then, and stopped fighting to stay conscious.

She came to once in the ambulance on the way to the hospital, and was aware of an oxygen mask over her nose and mouth.

"Hang in there, Mrs. Michaels," the EMS technician said. "We're almost there."

She could hear the siren and for one disconnected moment wondered what unfortunate person was being rushed to the hospital.

CHAPTER
20

"To various and sundry of you out there, I bring greetings," Dave Hampton said, holding his hand up, palm out. His worldwide cable news broadcast reached millions each day on TV and via the Internet. Over the past few years, especially, his audience had grown exponentially as he delved into the "news behind the news" from his own unique perspective. Of late, he had been delivering a particularly powerful message that some of his critics called a "doomsday" message, dismissing him as a scaremonger. But his audience only got bigger the worse the news got.

"You don't want to miss the show today. Call your relatives and friends, call anyone that you care about, and tell them that they must watch this show today.

"Why?

"Because today I am going to lay out for you, as clearly as I can, the danger—no, 'danger' is not a strong enough word—the perils facing us. And folks, when I say facing us, I mean every man, woman, and child who is of good heart.

"I now know, though I am not at liberty to reveal my sources, that the President has hosted meetings with people of religion and science to deal with this crisis that faces us.

"Religion and science together?" Dave smiled at the camera. "Isn't that a little like matter and antimatter?

"A preacher and scientist went into a bar. The bar disappeared in a puff of smoke."

"Okay, that was a weak joke, I'll admit. It might even have been a sick joke.

"But you do get my point, I hope. Normally the Big Bad Wolf is the budget or lobbyists or right-wing or left-wing conspiracies. I've been a whistle-blower on many topics, but none has scared me half as much as this black cloud. If something is out there, some deep, dark, sinister shadow, a force of evil that is threatening us, it is threatening scientist and preacher alike, is it not? And is it not in the nature of man to form alliances for survival?

"This, I can tell you from a scientific viewpoint. A few weeks ago, a scientist at NASA, while studying pictures of space, noticed an anomaly. The redshift of Abel 2744 moved from z equals 0.308, to z equals 0.512."

Dave chuckled. "Z equals zero what? Dave, what on Earth are you talking about?

"Well, that's just it. I'm talking about nothing of this Earth. I'm talking about a cluster of stars, officially Abel 2744 but referred to as Pandora's Cluster. And from that cluster a mysterious cloud of dark matter is coming toward Earth. If you don't understand dark matter, then you can just refer to it as I have been. That's why I think of it as a dark or sinister shadow, without real substance but very real nonetheless.

"Interesting, don't you think, that this evil would be coming from Pandora's box? Or, in this case, Pandora's Cluster. And it is evil, my friends. It is more than just a scientific observation; it is a manifestation of evil.

"On another but related note, in recent days all eyes have been focused on the heavens, and I have reported to you from this desk on the strange goings-on that even our top scientists have had trouble following.

"It seems that billionaire Roger C. Bracken's attempt to send an unmanned spacecraft to the moon blew up shortly after launch this morning in rural Oregon.

"Was this attempt by man to answer some of our most troubling questions thwarted by forces we do not—and perhaps cannot—understand?

"Pandora's Cluster, anyone? You make the call."

The broadcaster held his hand up, palm out. "From New York, this is Dave Hampton. Good night, America and the world."

Off camera, the news broadcaster slumped in his chair. For the entire program he had kept it together as he reported on the dire events he saw unfolding on the planet and beyond. Now he felt the weight of the danger the world was facing and the choices—good, bad, and indifferent—that mankind had made in the past. And the choices that would have to be made in the very near future.

CHAPTER
21

· *Melbourne, Australia* ·

After Mary Beth was killed, Dawson quit his job. He could no longer face going to work in the same place where he had shared that final thirty minutes with Mary Beth. For a while he did consultations with writers, and he took jobs writing for hire, doing several Westerns under a house name.

Then he wrote *The Cain Collage*. In this book he introduced the character of Matt Matthews, an Indiana Jones type. On the day the planes hit the World Trade Center towers, Dawson saw the curtain pulled back to reveal evil, the dark forces of the world, and "good versus evil" was the theme of his book. *The Cain Collage* became a runaway bestseller, and he followed it with *The Mizraim Montage*, using the same character and the same good-versus-evil theme.

Dawson looked at the book again. His name was above the title, and above that, in shining blue foil, was a legend: NEW YORK TIMES BEST-SELLING AUTHOR. He had to admit, that had a good sound to it.

And now he was on a promotional tour, not the 5 A.M. local TV show in places like Mobile, St. Louis, and Dallas, but ten thousand miles from home.

He could hear the same repetitive questions coming at him, but this time with an Aussie accent:

"What was the motivation behind the series?"

"How many books do you see yourself writing for the character in this series?"

"Are you excited for it to be a movie?"

The funny part about doing these interviews was that the interviewer had hardly ever read the book. The producers of the show would glance at the press release notes, then formulate questions for the host to ask, squeezing them into a two-minute segment.

Sometimes that canned procedure would have ludicrous results.

"I got the idea from an exhibit I saw in the American Museum of Natural History in New York," Dawson would say.

"So, where did you get the idea for this story?" the interviewer would ask, not having listened to what Dawson had just said.

Non-writers probably thought that such things as book signings and publicity tours were the glamorous side of the business. Authors knew that such events were arduous and disagreeable, but it was the nature of the business and absolutely necessary to do these interviews to allow people to know the book is out. Having sold over 1 million copies of each of the previous books internationally gave Dawson Rask the luxury of not having to worry about supporting himself. This also allowed him to dedicate his time to the ancient texts, symbolism, and mystical mysteries that his readers so appreciated.

Dawson considered himself a student of the ancient wisdom. He loved to interview the philosophic minds of today's generation, at least those that he felt would be the ones most remembered. From astrologers to atheists, metaphysicians to quantum physicists, there was not a concept or discipline that he didn't like to imagine.

He particularly loved the research that inspired him to create the character of Matt Matthews, who blogged his findings on his websites and created a buzz in the Internet world. Matt was a reflection of Dawson—not who he was, but who he would like to be.

And like his character, Dawson was what others would call "a cool dude." He was personal friends with "Oprah people," from athletes, to show-business personalities, to the ultra-wealthy, to sitting and former Presidents. His tweets had 8 million followers and counting, and he could start a frenzy with a single released thought.

Dawson was once fined by the City of New York for asking his fans to drop off cans of soup for a local shelter at a City Hall town meeting that was attempting to shut the shelter down. There were fifteen hundred cans dropped off within the hour—forty-five hundred in less than two hours.

The event put a strain on the New York City Police Department, blocking pedestrian and car traffic for over three hours. He had hoped, by his suggestion, to generate local awareness of the situation, but it became national, appearing on every broadcast and cable network news show that day. Dawson knew his popularity, and respected it. His goal was to use his popularity, and his gift for writing, to educate as well as to entertain.

In contrast, Dawson's brother, Boyd, had overcome the less-than-stellar reputation he had realized in high school. President of a refuse collection company, he had become very successful in part because of his willingness, indeed his eagerness, to do business with the mafia.

"My brother dumps his garbage on the public, and I haul it off," Boyd liked to say, criticizing his brother's elitist way of making a living.

Dawson knew that Boyd was very jealous of him. Dawson had risen above his brother's shadow and sibling competition to sibling victory. And he believed, sincerely, that it had become almost a Cain and Abel rivalry, a theme of good versus evil.

Some literary critics had actually pointed that out as a continuing theme in his novels. A *New York Times* reviewer wrote:

> Though elements of the picaresque color the major players of this author's books, there seems to be in each of them a theme of sibling rivalry, sometimes satirical and overplayed, sometimes as subtle as the base note of a quality perfume. And, as the notes in a perfume produce the final, blended scent, so too, do the "notes" of Rask's novels combine in such a way as to produce a satisfying read.

The reviews, as well as the sales of all three of his books had been outstanding, and his agent wanted him to release the rights to his first two books to make them Hollywood blockbusters.

Dawson said he would agree, as long as he maintained creative control over the storyline. He simply didn't need the money to sell out his vision.

He told his agent: "If I had a son and a daughter, named Mike and Emily, I wouldn't allow a complete stranger to pay me a million dollars for each so he could call them Mark and Carrie!"

It was too early to use any of the hotel's valet services, so Dawson ironed his own pants and shirt, got dressed, then looked at the clock. The glowing red digital clock said that it was 6:30 A.M. He picked up the phone.

"Good morning, Mr. Rask," the man at the front desk said.

Dawson smiled. He almost expected the man to say, "Throw a shrimp on the barbie."

"Yes, is my driver here yet?"

"He is indeed, sir, sitting in the lobby as we speak."

"Good, tell him I'll be right down."

Dawson had not yet met his driver, as arrangements had been made by his publisher and publicist. But when he stepped from the elevator, there was little doubt that the tall man wearing a blue blazer, tan slacks, and what Dawson would describe as a Greek fisherman's hat was his driver. His suspicion was corroborated when the tall man stepped toward him.

"Would you be Mr. Rask, by chance?"

"Not by chance," Dawson replied. "I worked hard to get here."

The driver laughed politely. "Your car is out front, sir."

The black stretch Mercedes was parked under the porte cochere on the other side of the drive in the area reserved for VIPs. The driver held the door open for him, which always made Dawson feel a little self-conscious. The steering wheel was on the right, and even though he knew they drove on the left side of the road here in Australia, it was still a little jarring.

On the way to his first interview, on a national radio show, he experienced an anxious feeling. Why? he wondered. He was certainly well seasoned by now—he had done hundreds of these things over the last three years.

A few seconds later, he felt clammy and nauseous—not carsick nauseous, just nauseous—and he actually thought for a moment that he might need to vomit. As he rolled the window down to get a breath of fresh air, he saw a large statue of a lion. But it wasn't an ordinary statue, because this one seemed to be moving.

That's not possible, he thought.

"We are here, Mr. Rask," the driver said. "I will be waiting for you in the car park, reading your novel. If you need anything, call me on my mobile. Here's my card . . . Jack Ransom."

Dawson happened to look down on the passenger's side of the front seat and saw a newspaper. He didn't notice the headlines, nor did he read any specific article, but for some strange reason, disconnected words from different parts of the page seemed to leap out at him.

Joy . . . Cancer . . . Belfast . . . Mere . . . Christianity . . . November.

The words seemed to float above the paper, and he felt a wave of dizziness come over him. He closed his eyes, and bracing himself with one hand against the top of the car, he reached up with his other to press his hand against his forehead.

"Perry Landers," the driver said.

"What?" Dawson asked.

"I asked if you are all right," the driver said.

Dawson blinked a few times and stared at the driver. He could have sworn that he heard the driver say "Perry Landers."

"Mr. Rask?" the driver asked, his words a bit more anxious this time.

"Oh, uh, yes," Dawson said. "I'm fine. I'm just trying to get used to the difference in time between here and home."

The driver smiled. "I know what you mean," he said. "I visited my first cousin in the U.S. a couple of years ago. He lives in Nashville. You're sure you are all right?"

"Yes, I'm fine, thank you."

Despite his reassuring answer, Dawson knew that he wasn't all right. Something was wrong and he knew it. It was as if had received bad news without actually receiving it. The air felt heavy, and there was a knot in the pit of his stomach.

"Perry Landers," the driver said again.

"What?" This time Dawson barked the word.

"I said have a good interview, sir."

"Dawson?" his Australia-based publicist called out to him. "You're on in five minutes. Please come inside now."

CHAPTER
22

· Vatican City ·

The papal apartments wrap around the Courtyard of Sixtus V on two sides of the top floor of the Apostolic Palace in Vatican City. Since the seventeenth century, the papal apartments have been the official residence of the Holy Father. The apartments include the pope's bedroom, an office for the papal secretary, the pope's own private study, the dining room and kitchen, and a smallish but comfortable living room with the latest TV equipment.

There is housing for the nuns who run the papal household, as well as a roof garden that Pope Benedict XVI used to enjoy especially. Nearly everyone in the world is familiar with the image of him blessing visitors and tourists in the piazza from his study near his bedroom. The pope lived and worked within these confines as his predecessors had for hundreds of years before him.

Pope Genaro had invited Cardinals Luigi Morricone and Zachary Yamba, his two closest confidants, into his study so they could discuss the problem facing not only Catholicism, Christianity, and all the other religions of the world, but all of mankind. As a cardinal, Genaro Giovanni Battista, now Genaro I, had been particularly close friends with both Cardinals Morricone and Yamba. He had known Morricone since both were parish priests.

"May I express a concern, Holy Father?" Cardinal Morricone asked.

"Of course, Luigi."

"The concern I have is that we may be sounding the drum to a danger that does not really exist. As you know, from the time Our Lord walked upon the earth, there have been rumors of the end of the world. And when the rumors prove to be false, the person who started the rumor loses face."

"Do you think I am concerned that I might lose face?"

"It isn't just you who will lose face, Giovanni. We cannot allow such a thing to happen to the Vicar of Christ."

"But I feel it here, Luigi," Genaro said, putting his hand over his heart. "I know that it is a message from God. And I am not the only one who has felt it. You heard the words of Rabbi Yahman and Imam Abdul-Majid. They, too, have received a message from God. Even the Dalai Lama is aware of the dark forces that are arrayed before us."

"But, Holy Father, what can we do besides warn the people?" Cardinal Yamba asked.

"We can unite the people," Genaro said. "There are almost seven billion people in the world. Surely there is enough truth, light, and goodness among those souls that we can mobilize against the Evil One. We are on the eve of a new year. Tomorrow I will give the blessing, and I will call for the power of daring and assurance in God and in man to follow the way of peace, to be a light of goodness and brotherhood. It is something that all must do: individuals and nations, religions and science."

"Do you think the evil we face is Satan's doing?" Yamba asked.

"Do you think it is not?" the pope answered.

"I am sure it is."

"The Evil One has tried before to use his power against mankind, and always before, God has been able to defeat him. But in the last one hundred years, Lucifer has gained so much ground in the hearts of man that the most evil who have ever lived, and the most evil who are among us now, could tip the balance of power between good and evil. And I am sure you remember the adage from Edmund Burke, 'All it takes for evil to triumph is for good men to do nothing.'

"It is vital that we do all that we can to combat it."

"What will do, Your Holiness?" Morricone asked.

"We must pray, Luigi. We must pray as we have never prayed before. We must pray that God uses us as his instrument in this epic battle, that we can mobilize the good who have come before us, and those who are with us now, to combat the legions of hell."

"Yes," Morricone said. He sank to his knees in prayer. "We must pray."

The pope closed his eyes tightly, his face ashen as he poured out his soul in prayer with the men who stood closest to him in this hour of dark destiny.

I lizea Ibanga arrived at John F. Kennedy International Airport exhausted. It had been a thirty-six-hour trip from her home in Kenya to the United States. She had been invited to testify before the United Nations' Commission for Refugees. In a blur of movement, UN officials and security people whisked her off the plane and into a private helicopter that flew over Queens, over the East River, and deposited her in a condominium just a few blocks from the headquarters of the international organization.

She was numbed by the trip and so took a bath—the first real hot bath she had taken in months—before the session with the commission. She would be in New York for two days, then back home, back to the chaos and fear that had been her life for . . . how many years? Well, for *all* her life.

Ilizea was a refugee from the interminable conflicts in Rwanda: tribe on tribe, faction against faction, that had torn the nation apart and cost hundreds of thousands, if not millions of lives over the past two decades. She was orphaned, jobless, physically scarred, alone in the world. Yet as she luxuriated in the bath, drawing soap over her tired body, she closed her eyes and breathed in the scented steam and remembered what had brought her here.

The children. *Save the children.* That thought and that thought alone had occupied her mind and soul for the past ten years.

Starting with her little brother. When the militia had come to her village to execute a night raid, Ilizea, sixteen at the time, and her brother Mfon, then eight, hid in the shed behind her family's house—under a pile of kindling wood and a few tools that her father possessed. This was the drill her parents had made both of them perform many times, until they were sick of it and made jokes about it.

But when the time came, it saved their lives. Their parents did not survive. The militia cut them and sixty others in the village to pieces and took all the girl children over the age of twelve with them. All that were left when the troops drove away were about thirty kids, mostly boys, mostly naked or in rags, and Ilizea and her brother. Ilizea was the oldest, and they looked to her for leadership. They looked to her to save them. What now? What would they do? Where would they go?

"Come with me," she said simply. She counted them, had them gather whatever food they could find and water in portable containers. Whatever they could carry they carried on their backs and in their hands. "Come with me," she said, and they followed her.

They walked out of their village and headed east. For more than a month she led them through the hills and forest lands, avoiding population centers wherever she could. She brought them into western Kenya. Every single child survived under her care. They were weak and hungry, incredibly dirty, but each had a smile on his or her face when they arrived at a safe place—an orphanage where they would be kept until permanent arrangements could be made.

Ilizea worked for the next four years at the orphanage and made trips back to her home to bring out more refugee children and even some adults. Miraculously, she worked unmolested for all that time and could account for hundreds of lives saved.

She wanted to ask the United Nations for support in her work. She couldn't be certain they would do anything at all, but speaking to the commission would be good publicity for the cause.

Ilizea Ibanga dried herself off and dressed in a new suit that a supporter had provided for her. She ran a brush through her hair. A knock at the door signaled the time had come for her to go to the UN.

Whatever happened, she had done what she could, what one person could, to save some lives, to *save the children*. . . .

CHAPTER
23

Dave Hampton gazed into the camera as he read a breaking news bulletin:

"On the heels of the strange hurricane activity reported in the Atlantic Ocean that now threatens the entire East Coast of the United States come reports just moments ago of seismic activity in Asia—in fact, throughout the vast Pacific Rim region of the world. Just moving on our newswire are these reports of earthquakes in Japan, Vietnam, Indonesia, Malaysia, New Zealand, and Australia, with tremors felt as far away as Hawaii, Vancouver, Seattle, and Los Angeles.

"Measurements of these quakes vary from a minimum of 7.1 on the Richter scale to the 9.1 quake in Japan, which just last year was devastated throughout its southern islands by a similar phenomenon. Viewers, something is unfolding on a cosmic scale that we can only begin to guess at.

"Earliest estimates of the death toll already top two hundred thousand. And let us not forget the recent events in Turkey, a country that has seen a huge chunk of its population decimated by yet another natural disaster. Coincidence, ladies and gentlemen? Sadly, I think not."

Dave Hampton was sitting in his high-backed, overstuffed leather chair sipping a root beer as he listened to Gaye Mullins, the assistant to the president of the American News Channel network.

"You are beginning to make some people nervous," Gaye said. "Your conspiracy theories have been great theater up until now, and the more you were reviled against, the better your ratings. But this theory that you've been pushing lately, musing about this . . ."

"Sinister shadow?"

"Yes." Gaye brushed back a fall of blond hair. "Dave, what are you doing with this—this doom and gloom thing? Where are you going with it?"

"I wish I knew," Dave replied. "I could be flippant and say that I'm going wherever it takes me, but I have no idea where that may be."

"Do you know there is a movement under way to boycott businesses that advertise on your show?"

"How could I not know that? I've probably gotten ten thousand emails on that subject."

"You can see then, can't you, why we at ANC would be a little concerned?"

"Have my ratings dropped?"

"No," Gaye said. "Quite the opposite. They have increased by almost twenty percent since you started on this."

"Then why is ANC concerned?"

Again, Gaye brushed her hair back, mostly a nervous gesture.

"Because the negative publicity about your show is increasing exponentially, and by extension, that publicity is reaching the entire network."

"You know what they say, Gaye. All publicity is good publicity."

"Dave, let me ask you something. And this is a personal question, from me to you. I'm not representing the network on this."

"All right, ask."

"Do you believe what you are saying? Do you believe the world is about to come to an end?"

"I don't believe I have said that, Gaye."

"No, but you are certainly implying it."

"No such implication is intended. I am merely reporting on something that nobody else seems to be covering. Something is going on, Gaye. I don't know what it is, but it is wide, deep, and it is reaching out across all humanity, regardless of nationality, religion, or race. And it is very frightening."

"You are frightened?" Gaye asked.

"I'm terrified."

"I, uh, please, Dave. Tone it down just a bit."

"I'll do this," Dave promised. "I won't speak of it again until I have something more to talk about. Something more concrete."

"Thanks," Gaye said. "I think."

Gaye left the room, and Dave, having finished the rest of his root beer, crushed the can and launched it in a basketball shot toward the waste can on the far side of the room. It dropped in.

"Three points in any auditorium," Dave said under his breath.

CHAPTER
24

M r. Hampton, we just got a call from a woman in Grenada who wants to speak to you. She has been calling and Skyping all day, and she won't stop until she gets you. She's on your Skype now. She says she has some important information for you," Julie said. Julie was a smart twenty-one-year-old intern who believed, sincerely, that her internship here would be a gateway to a television career of her own.

"I'm not sure working for me is going to get you anywhere," Dave had told her back when she signed on. "As you will discover after you've been here awhile, I'm considered somewhat of a kook."

"A kook with more viewers in your time slot than all the other cable networks combined," Julie had replied.

"That's true."

"What's the woman's name?" Dave asked.

"What's her name?" Julie asked into the phone. She nodded, then looked back at Dave. "She won't give a name."

"So I'm supposed to talk to any kook who comes in asking for me? Tell Jerry to send her away. That's what we hired him for, isn't it?"

"He can't talk to her," Julie said. "What? Tell him what? Are you crazy? I can't tell him that."

"Tell me what?" Dave asked. "Now you've got me curious."

"It's embarrassing."

"Now you've really got me curious."

"She says when you were fourteen, you had a—uh—" Julie blushed and stopped in midsentence.

"I had a what?"

"You lost your virginity to your mother's friend."

He turned redder than a radish, blushing as he was put firmly in his place. "My God! How could anyone know that?"

Julie laughed and quickly covered her mouth with her hand. "You mean you did? Your mother's friend? She's old!"

"She wasn't always old, kid," Dave said. "Tell Jerry to connect her."

"Are you serious?"

Dave reached out for the phone.

"Jerry? Yes, this Dave Hampton. I'll have Julie brief her over Skype. What does she look like?" Dave laughed. "Lena Horne? You old fart, how is Julie supposed to know what—? Never mind. I'll tell her."

Five minutes later Julie reported back to her boss that the older, regal-looking light-skinned woman was very much for real. Dave said, "Thank you, Julie," and he switched on his desktop.

"I can stay here if you need me for anything."

"Thank you, Julie," Dave repeated, and he took Julie by the arm, then escorted her out of his office.

"Good evening," Dave said, half looking at his computer screen and multitasking by reading some papers on his desk and punching in a text message on his handheld mobile phone. "I didn't get your name."

"My name is Patricia Rose Greenidge, but everybody calls me Mama G." Her voice was soft, melodic, and had a strong Caribbean accent.

"Mama G? *You* are Mama G? I've heard of you, your radio broadcasts, your webcasts."

"I'm flattered."

"Why didn't you just tell Jerry your name?"

"My name doesn't always open doors."

Dave chuckled. "I must confess, Mama, you came up with one hell of a way of opening this door. How did you know that? How could you possibly have known it? I was so embarrassed, I never told a soul. Not my best friend, and certainly not my mother."

"My guides told me. They tell me all sorts of stuff when necessary. And that was necessary for me to know to get through to you. They also revealed to me that dark forces are descending upon us. And you know this, too."

"You—you know something about this?"

"I know that you have been chosen," Mama G said.

"Chosen by who?"

"By the good guys."

"Mama, you aren't making a lot of sense."

Mama Greenidge smiled. The image of her face filled his entire screen.

After all, she did not yet know completely what her mission was, but she felt she was doing exactly the right thing in reaching out to Dave Hampton. She felt it with all the passion she possessed, even though she couldn't prove any of it—yet.

"Yes, I am, Dave, and you know that I am making a lot of sense because you know exactly what I'm talking about."

"All right, maybe I do have an idea. But if the—let's call them the Forces of Light—chose me, what exactly have they chosen me for? What do they want me to do?"

"They want you to rally the people."

"All right, I'll do that. I suppose in a way, I am doing that now. But to what end?"

"As I understand it—"

Dave held up his hand to stop her. "Wait, before we go any further. You say as you understand it. Why do you understand it? Where are you getting your information?"

"From the same source you are," Mama G said. "The only difference between us is that I've had a lifetime of living with that world! Or should I say, the *real* world, as well as *our* world. And so I am better able to interpret it."

"All right," Dave said. "I interrupted you, I'm sorry. As you understand it, to what end am I to rally the people?"

"There is a war brewing, Mr. Hampton. A war of celestial forces and with consequences far beyond the sum total of all the wars ever fought by man."

"Who will be fighting this war?"

"Good versus evil."

Dave laughed out loud. "Good versus evil? Excuse me for laughing, but isn't that the cliché of all clichés?"

"Hardly a cliché. Think about bullying, lying, all kinds of crime that are committed every day. Think about a good kid in school trying to do the right thing or a policeman risking his life to keep somebody safe. Good versus evil isn't a cliché, it is a fact," Mama G said. "It will require the combined good of every soul that has ever lived, as well as every soul that is alive today. The forces of evil will be recruiting from the same pool of souls, living and dead. We must unite if we are going to defeat them."

The smile left Dave's face and now he stared at Mama G with an expression of fear and worry.

"I believe you," he said. "I don't know why I believe you, I just know that I do. I will do everything in my power to make this happen. But I'm going to need help."

"You will have help," Mama G said.

"From you?"

"From me, from the Council of Elders, from the combined good of every created soul, living and dead. Each person has the choice to use their free will to choose the positive life force, which we know as love, or the negative or evil in their everyday lives. This is where it matters most—one choice at a time. And we have help, if we are willing to look and listen. Great minds from our past have glimpsed reality and will coach and guide us and the others who are being contacted even as we speak. The Council is using all the means at its disposal. All for the good."

Dave had tuned her out for a moment as she spoke. He wrote out some numbers in bold marker on a sheet of paper and held it up to the Skype cam. "This is my cell number, my home number, and my private number here at the studio. How may I find you, stay in contact with you?"

Mama G nodded. "I'm easy to reach," she said. "I am here to help. So are you. More light will come in through two windows than through just one."

Dave felt a moment of warmth. He didn't know exactly what was being asked of him. But he felt relieved from being anxious and expectant, if even for a brief flash of time. "And, for God's sake, don't tell anyone else about my little—uh—experience with my mother's friend."

· Long Island ·

It had been exactly nineteen months, two weeks, and three days since the death of her beloved husband, Ryan, and Charlene's grief had not gone away. She was someone who lived her life with words, powerful words that, set to music, could soothe the troubled soul. Hers and her fans', so they told her. But there were words she never wanted to hear again, words that were also powerful, but evil in their construct, words like *cancer, metastasize,* and *malignant.* Even such words as *chemotherapy* and *radium treatment,* words that were supposed to cure cancer, were painful because the treatments did not work.

"Inoperable means terminal," Ryan said once during the extreme nausea of his chemotherapy. "So why am I having to put up with this?"

The telephone rang. It was probably her mother, or her manager, or one of her friends trying to cheer her up.

They didn't understand. She didn't want to be cheered up. She wanted to wallow in her grief; she found a perverse comfort in it.

She heard Sue answer the phone.

Good for Sue. Sue Bailey was her personal assistant, and was adept at running interference with the many newspaper reporters, magazine feature writers, television talk show producers, and would-be authors who thought that Charlene "owed her story to the public." This was at least the fourth time the phone had rung already this morning, and it was still early. She was thankful to Sue Bailey, who was utterly proficient and professional in dealing with each call.

Charlene saw Mr. Fitzpatrick run across the lawn, then dart up a tree. Mr. Fitzpatrick was what she had named the resident gray-tailed squirrel. At least she thought it was the same creature. . . . The squirrel went inside a hole in the tree, disappearing, then reappearing a moment later with a nut in his mouth. Sitting on the limb of the tree, the squirrel looked around to make certain that he was safe; then he held the nut between his two front paws and began gnawing on it, totally content with his environment and life.

"I know it sounds crazy," Charlene said to herself. "But, at this moment if I could, I would trade lives with you, Mr. Fitzpatrick. You have a warm nest to live in, a limb that gives you a beautiful view, and a supply of food. You have no one to grieve over. Do you even know what grief is?"

"Charlene, the cook wants to know if you want breakfast," Sue said, coming into the sunroom then. Sue was a healthy-sized Southern lady, not fat but strong looking. She was more than Charlene's personal assistant; she was her traveling companion while on tour, and more than once she had, by sheer presence and strength, opened up a path for her through grasping fans and aggressive paparazzi.

A few moments earlier, Charlene had moved from the white leather sofa to the window box seat, and she was sitting there now with her legs drawn up, her arms wrapped around them, and her head resting on her knees.

"Maybe some toast and a cup of tea," Charlene said.

"Charlene, you have been living on nothing but toast and tea for how long now? How about a good breakfast this morning? I know you like cheddar cheese and mushroom omelets. I'll tell him to fix that for you."

"Really, I don't think I could hold it down," Charlene said.

"You don't have any say in the matter," Sue said. "If necessary, I'll hold you down and have Lucien spoon-feed you."

Charlene chuckled. "All right," she said. "Tell Lucien to fix me an omelet. I'll try to eat it."

"Thank you," Sue said. She turned away, then looked back toward Charlene. "Don't think I couldn't hold you down, missy. And I wouldn't need Mule to help me."

Mule was James "Mule" Bailey, Sue's son, and an all-pro defensive lineman for the New Orleans Saints.

Sue ate at the table with Charlene. Lucien Garneau, the cook, had gone all out with the omelet, perfectly prepared and perfectly presented. Lucien had been the head chef at La Provence Restaurant, a small, exclusive, and very pricey restaurant in the East Forties in Manhattan. Ryan and Charlene had eaten there shortly after they were married, and Ryan was so taken with the food that he hired Lucien away at three times his restaurant salary. He was an unnecessary extravagance now: since Ryan had died, Charlene rarely invited guests over, and her own eating was sporadic at best. Often she would have a peanut butter and jelly sandwich and a glass of milk. But when Lucien prepared even that for her, he did so with panache, trimming off the crust, cutting it into fourths, and spearing each quarter with an orange twist. She kept him on, not only because she felt an obligation to him, but also because having him here reminded her of Ryan.

After breakfast Charlene returned to the sunroom, then walked over to the window to look for Mr. Fitzpatrick, the squirrel. When she didn't see him, she felt a sense of loss.

"Are you all right, Mr. Fitzpatrick?" she asked. "Please tell me that you didn't wander off and get caught by a dog. You do know to stay out of the street, don't you? Do you have anyone to worry after you?"

·London·

Asima had been so proud of Muti and Omar for assimilating them-selves into the culture of London. By building three Persian restaurants and planning to open a fourth, they had become very successful. They were living the true Western dream.

But lately little things did not seem right to her. Conversations stopped in midsentence, whispered telephone calls, expressions of hate and disdain for the West that the brothers made no effort to hide. She did not want to admit it. It couldn't possibly be true, could it? Could she have been taken in by Muti and Omar?

The location for the newest restaurant in Piccadilly Circus, the Times Square of London, opposite the theaters and Ripley's Believe It or Not! museum attracted thousands of people every day. Had they chosen this location for the traffic it would bring to their restaurants? Or was there a more sinister purpose?

Muti seemed different and Asima recognized the change in him. She tried desperately to get him to speak, to let her in on what was troubling him. He would not share his private thoughts; at least not with her. This lack of discussion and conversation was deepening, and to Asima, a communication specialist, the silence was deafening.

Muti was speaking; he just wasn't speaking to Asima. He and Omar, though, were plotting their future actions, following a plan laid out for them by a person they referred to simply, as "the One."

The One had appeared to them one night when they were discussing the wrongs that had been done to them by the West, and to their family and friends, grieving over brothers whom they would never see again in this lifetime. He had sat at a corner table in their restaurant, hunched over a single steaming cup of coffee that never seemed to diminish, though they watched him drink it, and never cooled, though it had sat for over an hour without being refreshed.

The One was dressed in black, with a black hooded jacket. He remained in the restaurant after everyone else had left. Muti and Omar approached him.

"We are closing, sir," Omar said.

"I will leave after we have spoken," the One said.

"But if we leave the door unlocked and the blinds up, those who pass will think we are still open, but we have closed the kitchen and can feed no more."

"Your door is locked and your blinds are down. No one will come in," the One said.

"No, I haven't yet . . . ," Muti started to say, but when he looked toward the front of the restaurant he saw that the blinds were down, and the CLOSED sign had been turned in the door.

"Omar, did you—?"

"No," Omar said.

"You two have been chosen," the One said. "This is a call to action."

"Who has called?"

"You have been called," he said without answering the question.

"What have we been called to do?"

"It is a call to action against all mankind, not just Christians, or any specific Muslim sect, or any religion—but all mankind. It is a cleansing of those not on our path of righteousness."

"A cleansing," Omar said. "A much-needed cleansing. I have been saying this all along."

"Yes. A necessary cleansing. You will need a martyr. A young martyr. I believe you have such a person in Shakir. Can there be a more noble beginning for a boy of faith?"

"Surely you mean an ending," Muti said. "For if Shakir martyrs himself for the cause, for his uncles, will it not mean his death?"

"It will be his rebirth in the other world, a world where he will be received with honor, and glorified, and empowered beyond anything imaginable on earth."

"What would you have him do?" Omar asked.

"Omar, this is one of my children," Muti said, wondering how this being would know anything of his family, much less have the authority to announce that his firstborn son was to be a martyr to some nameless cause.

"And you are my younger brother," Omar reminded him. "You will do as I say. And I say that Shakir will be martyred." Muti stared at his brother in dismay, and then turned and looked into the eyes of the One. And recognized the passion—and something else—that he had been seeing in his brother's eyes for some time. Tears came to his own eyes as he realized that he had already embarked on a path that he could not abandon.

"Do you read the papers?" the One asked.

"Yes."

"Have you read of the murders in Belfast?"

"I have read of them."

"The sign for you will be the twelfth and final murder to take place in Belfast. The heart of each of the victims has been removed. When the twelfth murder takes place, the last heart will be procured and the circle will be complete. The hearts have been buried and the placement of the bodies from an aerial perspective will to point to a date in the future . . . when the planetary lineup is completed. Then, my followers, when the last body is found with its inscription of a glyph, it will be the call to action not just for you, but for an organized cadre around the world, a thunderous movement that will shake the world. Fear and panic will rule. And that will lock the code to our cleansing. When that happens, you and many others around the world will launch coordinated attacks against mankind. We will see justice, and humanity will finally be set on the right path."

"What is the code?" Omar asked.

"You will know."

"How will we know?"

"You will know," the One repeated.

"If we must do this, let me martyr myself," Muti said, feeling locked into this future but praying that he could at least save his beloved son. "I will not sacrifice my son and his future when he does not yet believe. I do believe. Let me take his place."

"No, Muti," insisted Omar. "Shakir's very innocence is what makes him the proper messenger. We will instruct him to the honor being bestowed upon him."

"But—"

"No more . . . The decision is made." Omar looked toward the front of the restaurants and saw that all the blinds were up, the OPEN sign was pointing toward the street, and the One was gone. He was in charge of the operation, and he needed to regain control over his brother and family. "We'd better get this place shut down."

"But I thought it was."

"Can you not see now, Muti, that the One was sent to us to give us this message? Can we deny this charge?"

"I don't know."

"Shakir is the chosen one. He has been blessed by Allah."

Or cursed, Muti thought, but he didn't say the words. He thought of Asima at this moment, since it was her son they were talking about—as well as his.

CHAPTER
27

Conditions at the hospital were still erratic, and even Tyler was beginning to feel the pressure. Why wasn't Henry Emory here? There was no excuse for him not being here now.

"Where is Dr. Emory?" Tyler shouted to Rae Loona, the head RN on duty.

"He is unreachable, Dr. Michaels. We paged him four times!" she yelled back.

"Well, page him again, damn it! And if he doesn't answer the page, call him at home!"

"You think I didn't think of that?" Rae replied, and when Tyler turned he saw her staring at him with such an intensity that suggested she would resort to physical violence if he ever spoke to her like that again.

Tyler looked back at her with a sad puppy dog look and a devilish wink, and Rae, no longer able to maintain the evil stare, began laughing.

"Mikey, you are one crazy doofus, did you know that? But don't be disrespecting me when I haven't had my caffeine. Did you know I gave up caffeine, Mikey?"

Tyler hated when she called him that, but it was also oddly endearing, so he just went with it. "I take it that's because the love of your life doesn't use caffeine?" He couldn't resist.

"Of course. My John Travolta doesn't allow such poison to pass his lips. That's why I love him. Or, I should say, that's one of ten thousand reasons I love him!" Rae handed Tyler his white coat. "Take off that penguin jacket," she said. "You're scarin' my patients."

"*Your* patients?" Tyler asked as he took off his tuxedo jacket and handed it to her. He put on the doctor's white coat.

"My patients," Rae said, handing back the jacket. "And don't you forget it." She turned to the doctor and added, "Mikey, we are going places. And I mean go-ing pla-ces!"

He had no clue what she was talking about, but he was used to that—and he didn't question her.

Nobody in the history of St. Agnes Hospital had ever messed with Rae Loona. Some even nicknamed her *Rae*ving *Loona*tic. Although she had been at St. Agnes for only thirty-five years, legend had it that she had been there for a century. And certainly her presence was so dominating that it seemed as if she had been there that long. Onetime director of nursing for the entire hospital, she had stepped down after several years to devote herself to clinical work on the floor. She loved her patients. She was passionate, determined, and dedicated—with a vengeance.

Rae had lost her only child to cancer and her husband to heart disease. Since that time the patients had become her family, and she rejoiced with them when they recovered, wept for them when they did not.

She was an RN—a registered nurse, with a button that proudly proclaimed: "RN MEANS REAL NURSE." As far as she was concerned, LPN meant, "let's play nurse," not licensed practicing nurse. None of the other alphabet nurses were allowed to work with or around her. And if any LPN gave her any of their crap, she would highlight the word "practicing."

Rae was famous for single-handedly getting the hospital through a nursing crisis a few years earlier.

Already experiencing a nursing shortage, the condition was exacerbated when a strike occurred. She called a meeting of the nurses who worked with her. The meeting was unauthorized, but nobody on the hospital staff would dare to call her on it.

"Listen to me," she told the nurses. "If you walk out of this hospital for any reason other than death—and when I say death, I mean your own, and even then you better be three days dead before you leave—especially if you leave because of some dispute over salary, I will personally make sure that any salary increase we get won't do you any good because you won't be working here anymore."

"How are you going to do that, Nurse Loona?" one of the other nurses asked. "You don't have the authority to fire us."

"Oh, I have no intention of firing you," Rae said. "If I fire you, you can draw unemployment. No ma'am, you will leave here of your own accord."

"What makes you think we would do that?"

Rae smiled at the nurse, but it wasn't a friendly smile, it was the smile of a lioness contemplating her meal.

"Trust me, child," she said in a voice that was a mixture of steel and velvet. "When Rae says you will be leaving of your own accord? You will leave of your own accord. There'll be no *Welcome Back, Kotter* here for you! Wasn't my Johnny so haaaaandsome as a Sweathog?" It was a rare day when she didn't talk about the love of her life, John Travolta—to whoever would listen.

And there was no misunderstanding what Rae meant. She would make life in the hospital hell on earth for them.

That nurse, and all the other nurses learned that negotiating and salary disputes were a distant second to the quality of patient care. And as Rae described it later, "Once they were lost, but now they are found; were blind but now they see."

For a period of six days, there were only ten nurses looking after three floors of patients. Rae made sure that administration knew who the dedicated ten were, and every one of them wound up getting a five-thousand-dollar bonus. Rae negotiated that for them, not for herself. Each of the nurses got it, but she declined. Not one of those ten RNs ever forgot that level of dedication, and each one of them has made sure that Rae, who had no family of her own, was never alone on a holiday. This holiday she was with her family, in the ER, doing what she did best: running St. Agnes.

Everyone who knew Rae, or even knew about her, knew that they needed to stay on her good side. (Younger nurses had to be convinced that Rae actually had a good side.) The stories about her were priceless and relentless. The doctors for a fifty-mile radius knew the story of her pushing a patient in a bed out the front door of the hospital when the insurance company said they would no longer pay for treatment. There was Rae, pushing a patient down Peachtree Avenue saying that she was headed to Southside General.

What people didn't know was that Rae had called the local TV stations, and CNN, and all had camera crews waiting outside to cover the story of how St. Agnes would turn its back on a twelve-year-old boy whose single mother couldn't afford treatment. Miraculously, the good-natured board of trustees decided to take his case pro bono.

A reporter for the *Atlanta Journal-Constitution* wrote a story about her, calling her the "crazy middle-aged black nurse from St. Agnes." WSB TV-2 interviewed her about that story and she remarked that the writer was incorrect, she wasn't black.

"I beg your pardon?" the interviewer asked, the expression on his face showing his obvious confusion over her answer.

"I'm more of a Hershey's milk chocolate," she said with a straight face. What she didn't say out loud was that she was convinced that her Johnny Boy—John Travolta—drank gallons of chocolate milk every day. She had nothing upon which to base such an assumption other than her super-active fantasy life. And she didn't care who knew it!

Everyone on the hospital staff who watched the interview got a big laugh out of it, and they felt a sense of pride about working with her. And ever since that time, Rae had found dozens of Hershey chocolate bars, mysteriously and anonymously left at her nurse's station. She kept a supply in a *Grease* mug on her desk. Generally, she gave them out to the children, to each child patient when she could, and to children of patients' families.

"I will try Dr. Emory again," Rae said. She held up her finger and wagged it at him. "But not because you told me to. It's because I was goin' to try him again anyway." She picked up the receiver and began punching in numbers.

That reminded Tyler that he had intended to call Karen, so he reached for one of the other phones and started to call home, when he recognized a patient that was lying on one of the gurneys.

It was an old high school classmate, Buddy Amendola. Buddy had been the starting quarterback on the high school team, then was recruited by the University of Georgia but didn't have what it took to make the team there. Dropping out of college, he had come back to Atlanta and was now a police officer. Tyler had run across him a few times since then, mostly when he was bringing in either a shooting or traffic victim. Now he was a victim himself, his uniform soaked by his own blood, urine, and snow.

Without completing his call, Tyler hung up the phone then hurried over to his old friend. Buddy was trying to speak, but was inaudible.

"What happened to him?" Tyler asked one of the interns.

"He was attending the nine-car pileup out on 285 when a vehicle hit him head-on. He didn't even see it coming. I think he has cerebral edema. His blood pressure is dropping, he has been in and out of consciousness, he has thrown up, his eyes are blinking and rolling and his heart rate is dropping."

Tyler shone a penlight in Amendola's eyes.

"Good call," he said to the intern, who beamed under Tyler's compliment. "Get him up to the OR."

"Dr. Michaels, we can't take him to the OR," Nurse Loona said.

Calmly and with calculated precision in his voice, Tyler turned to face Rae. "What do you mean we can't take him to the OR, Nurse Loona?"

There was a different atmosphere to the hospital tonight. There were no rabbits for her to pull out of a hat, this was a grave and grim circumstance. The hospital was at capacity, the holiday weekend was anything but a holiday, and having the hospital inundated with twenty-four people with various degrees of injury up to and including critical, was overwhelming even to Rae. "Sir," Rae said pointedly, "there is nobody to operate on him. We can't locate any of our on-call staff. In case you haven't noticed it, the weather is a bitch and the hospital's communication system is not operational during this whiteout. I know that to Yankees, a little old six-inch snowfall is nothing, but to us folks here in Atlanta, Mikey, it's a blizzard. And Rae doesn't have a good feeling about how this is all going down."

Sir? Rae had called him sir? Tyler detected concern in Rae's voice, and the fact that she referred to him as sir slightly unnerved him. Tyler knew people said he had ice water in his veins because he never got flustered, no matter the crisis. What people didn't know, was that Tyler fed on Rae's steadfast strength, and to know that tonight, even Rae was showing some of the pressure, he had to take a few deep breaths in order to steady himself.

"Okay, here is what we are going to do," Tyler said. "I want you to call over to EMS and see if they can reroute any other patients that are noncritical to Southside General and Atlanta Mercy."

"All right," Rae agreed without complaint or other feedback. That was another good thing about Rae, Tyler thought. For all the acid in her tongue, she knew when she could talk back and when she ought to follow orders without comment.

At that moment, three more EMS crews arrived, bringing in the remainder of the crash victims. One of the vehicles involved had been a church bus with four adults and eight teenagers on board. Two of the adults had been killed outright, and the other two were critical. The two adults killed had been the parents of two of the teenagers.

"Triage! Triage!" one of the EMS men was yelling.

Tyler took a quick look at the injuries and determined that Buddy needed him the most, and first. As he began prepping for surgery on Buddy, he told one of the nurses to hang a couple of bags of antibiotics on the two young teens whose parents perished in the accident.

"What else do we have?" Tyler asked.

"A senior with a double hip fracture, and a drunken college kid with a broken arm, leg, and nose. They think the kid may have been the cause of the whole thing."

"We have a woman in labor here!" a nurse shouted.

"What do we do?" another nurse asked.

"The kid is going to be born with or without a doctor," Tyler said. "That's been happening since the beginning of time. If it is a girl, tell the parents to name her Agnes after the hospital. Page orthopedics for the other two, and get a psychiatrist to consult with the college lush. I'll be in surgery."

Prepped, wearing scrubs and latex rubber gloves that allowed him to feel the touch, Tyler let the OR nurse put his surgical mask on; then he walked into the operating room where Buddy, clothes cut from him, lay under a sheet.

"Buddy, I remember when three big linemen tried to turn you into a post-hole digger," Tyler said quietly. "If you survived that, you can survive this. And I promise you, I'm as good at this as you ever were at throwing a football."

Tyler held his hand out. "Scalpel," he said.

CHAPTER
28

Things were still hectic in the emergency room. Susanne, one of the ER nurses, had called orthopedics on Dr. Michael's authority, and now she was trying to calm the senior with the hip break. Mr. Reynolds was clearly suffering from dementia and had no idea where he was or what was happening to him, and he was starting to become volatile. Sue hated to use restraints on the older patients, but they tended to rip the IVs out of their arms.

"Dillon, you are going to have to help me here. Get him restrained."

"Yes, ma'am," the young nurses' assistant replied. Dillon was conscientious and did his work well. He was also quite strong, and it was that—having a strong arm the nurses could call upon when need be—that made Dillon more valuable than some of the other nurses' assistants.

Leaving Mr. Reynolds in Dillon's hands, Sue turned her attention to the patient in bed four. This was the pregnant woman, and her water had just broken.

As Sue got closer, she spoke to the woman, keeping her voice upbeat so as to keep the woman calm. "Okay, now, let's have a look-see here," she said. She picked up the EMS chart, then gasped. The name on the chart read KAREN ANN MICHAELS.

"Oh, my God," she said. She looked into Karen's face and saw her eyes closed, but whether she was holding them closed or she was unconscious, Sue didn't know.

"Rae!" Sue called. "Rae, you better get over here quick!"

"What is it?" Rae asked. She had heard the fear and shock in Sue's voice, so she responded quickly without any acerbic comment. When Rae walked into the triage room and saw the patient, she didn't have to check the EMS chart. She knew instantly who it was, and her stomach dropped. Her maternal instinct kicked in.

"Well, now," Rae said, speaking as calmly and soothingly as she could. "It looks like Jeremy may be coming a few days early. I guess he just got tired of waiting."

Karen's eyes opened, fluttered, then closed again.

"Karen, honey," Rae said. "Listen to my voice. Stay with me, dear, okay?"

Karen's eyes opened again, and Rae saw a flicker of recognition in them. "Rae, I was—it happened so quickly—I don't know . . . Where's Tyler?" she asked. "Where's my husband. Please, can someone get Dr. Michaels?"

Rae looked at the nurses' assistant standing there in a state of shock. It was clear that he had never seen this much death, blood, and trauma. And now there was a woman in labor.

"Go page Dr. Michaels and tell him that his wife is in labor down here—*stat*! He will want to know." She even pushed the paralyzed kid. She didn't like the way Karen looked, but she dared not say anything for fear of frightening Karen any more than she already was.

"But Dr. Michaels is—," Dillon started to say.

Rae cut him off in midsentence. "Listen to me, and don't give me any backtalk," she said. "You go get Dr. Michaels, and tell him that *his wife needs him*!"

When Karen looked away, Rae shook her head with a twisted look and squinted eye, as if telling Dillon that she understood Dr. Michaels was in surgery. What she wanted him to do was walk away and at least look like he was getting him. The reality was that this baby was coming— with or without Tyler Michaels.

CHAPTER
29

D r. Emory and his wife had been celebrating New Year's at home with no more than half a dozen other professional couples, none of whom were doctors. They had not been watching television, so Emory knew nothing about the accident. He did not have his pager or his cell phone on, and though he didn't realize it, the phone downstairs was unplugged.

As a result, nobody heard the phone ringing in his home office, or the one upstairs in the bedroom.

It was not until two o'clock when he and Millie, having told their guests good-bye, went up to go to bed that he saw the blinking red light on the phone. When he picked it up, he found four messages, all saying the same thing: There had been a major accident, and the hospital was swamped with injuries.

H enry Emory was an ex–U.S. Army surgeon who, during the Vietnam War, was stationed at the Third Field Hospital in Saigon. He was there during the TET Offensive of 1968, and could remember when wounded soldiers were brought in by the hundreds. Not since then had he walked into a hospital with such an aura of intensity as he encountered now.

He had a sense of command authority about him that intimidated many of the younger people on the staff. Behind his back, they referred to him as Darth Emory, and he found out about it. The scary part was that he liked the title.

He assessed every corner of "his" hospital as if conducting a military inspection, and he did not like what he was seeing tonight. Chaos seemed to be the order of the day, and in his position he had to worry not only about patient care, but about the hospital's liability risk as well. The hospital already had four lawsuits pending, and one was just settled out of court.

When young, idealistic high school and college students came to talk to him about becoming a doctor, anticipating his encouragement, they were often surprised to discover that he tried to dissuade them from entering the medical profession. In his opinion, you go to school for years, rack up a lifetime of student loans and personal debt, work for years for free, and unless you go into some high risk specialty, it takes too many years to realistically pay off one's debts and actually make something of a living. One or two malpractice claims and the overpriced insurance could shut you down. "Drive a truck, sell insurance, open a restaurant," he would tell wannabe doctors.

This was a virtual war zone, but as he moved from patient to patient, reading and assessing charts and lab results, he was surprised to discover that there was some order in the chaos. And it was not his. When he looked through the glass doors and saw Rae holding the hand of one of the patients in such a compassionate way, at first glance it didn't surprise him. This was Rae, after all. Then he took a second look and saw that she was with Karen. He pushed through the door and immediately started to assess what was happening.

He looked at Rae as if to ask where Dr. Michaels was, but she pretended not to understand the look, because she was hesitant to tell him. She could tell Emory was burning with anger.

Tyler was on medical probation, and as such, was denied privileges in the OR, whether supervised or not. In light of the tragic accident, Rae hoped there would be leniency, but Tyler was such a badass and hot shot—a younger reflection of Dr. Emory himself—that their relationship could only go one of two ways. Either Emory would treat him like a son and take him under his tutelage or it could get much worse for Tyler Michaels. The expression on Emory's face told her all she needed to know. It was going to get worse.

Rae had Karen in the stirrups and prepped for delivery, and the contractions were coming fast. The portable ultrasound was being done by the tech, and that's when they saw that the baby was in a breech position. The fetal heart monitor wasn't detecting the baby's pulse.

Dr. Emory shook his head and looked at Rae. Despite his reputation as a hard-ass, Rae knew about his relationship with Karen's family, and that Dr. Emory had known Karen from the moment she was born. And she knew that he was genuinely concerned about her.

"Rae, call up to the OR and get it ready for a C-section," he ordered.

"Yes, Doctor," Rae said.

"Where the hell is Dr. Michaels?" Emory asked again. "Why isn't he here with her?"

"Dr. Michaels is in surgery, Dr. Emory," the tech said. He was unaware of the restriction on Tyler, unaware that he had just betrayed a confidence.

"What?" Dr. Emory exploded.

"What is it?" Karen asked in a weak voice. "What is wrong?"

"Nothing, sweetheart, don't you worry about it. Uncle Hank is here," Emory said, patting her hand tenderly.

"The surgery," Emory said to Rae. "Was it life threatening?"

"I—" Rae wanted desperately to say that it was, but she couldn't. "I don't know," she said. "I know that Dr. Michaels was concerned about him. It was an old friend of his, a police officer who was hurt while he was working the accident."

As furious as Dr. Emory was about Tyler choosing to perform a surgery that was not life threatening, that was paling in his personal frustration that Karen's family was in the Caribbean on a cruise and probably unreachable due to the weather and communications. She shouldn't be dealing with this alone.

For her part, Karen was trying to do her breathing, she was trying not to push, but she was also having a hard time feeling connected to her body. As strange as it seemed, she was starting to lose interest in everything that was going on.

That wasn't right, was it? Labor should feel more intense, more painful, not disconnected.

Her perspective shifted to being above her body looking down at those working on her.

"What are you doing down there?" she said. "I'm up here." She giggled. She found it hilarious to be suspended just below the ceiling, watching as they were working so feverishly on that woman on the bed.

The woman on the bed did look like her. She couldn't deny that. But that wasn't her. It couldn't be. She was up here.

Suddenly she was back in her body with her heart racing and adrenaline pumping.

"*Ty-ler!*"

Did she actually shout the word? Or did she just think it? She would have to . . .

Karen's world went black.

As Tyler was finished with the initial cuts on his friend, eliminating the swelling in his brain and stopping the bleeding, it became clear that this was not so bad a situation as he first had thought. Maybe there was a part of him that wanted to be the hero to this man who had been the hero quarterback, throwing the winning touchdown pass in the state finals. He wanted to save his friend, the friend to everyone. Tommy had always been the good guy. Everyone loved Tommy; that's why they called him Buddy. He was the world's buddy. Tyler had just saved everyone's hero, and that made him a—

"Dr. Michaels?" the OR tech's voice buzzed through the intercom.

"Yes?"

"Dr. Sanford is prepping to come in and finish."

"Good," Tyler called back. He was only too pleased to have one of the "old-timers" see the quality of his work.

Dr. Sanford came in to assess the situation. "Looks like you have everything under control here," Sanford said. "There's an emergency C-section next door in OR-2. You want to stay here, or help with the C-section?"

"If I want to see a naked woman, I'll look at a skin magazine or go to a strip club," Tyler replied.

There were two female nurses in the OR, and the roll of their eyes showed that they considered that remark to be offensive. Realizing that he had committed a faux pas, he cleared his throat and looked sheepishly at them. "I beg your pardon, ladies, I had no right to mouth off like that. Dr. Sanford, if you don't mind, I'll finish, but I would appreciate your assistance."

"Of course," Dr. Sanford said.

Tyler didn't need Sanford's assistance, but he knew that he would be gold in Dr. Henry Emory's eyes after Sanford told him what an amazing job he had just done.

Karen took her last breath after severe cardiac arrest on the operating room table. It was not detected that she had ruptured her aorta in the fall. The trauma had not only affected the baby, but had also caused severe internal bleeding. Nothing could be done now. Had she been treated an hour earlier, had Tyler been with her when the fall happened, both mother and child would have had a chance.

Tyler was still in OR-1, totally oblivious of the fact that Karen and his child were twenty feet, and a lifetime, away from him. His world was changing forever.

Even as Dr. Emory was losing her, he was weeping openly and unashamedly over his surgical mask. She was gone, and his only hope now was to save the child. But when Jeremy was delivered, it was clear that he had passed first.

After Tyler finished with Buddy, he saw that there was still activity on OR-2, so he decided to step in and see if they needed him. He was still wearing his surgical mask, so the grin of achievement was obscured, but not the twinkle in his eyes.

He saw Rae first, standing by the operating table with tears sliding from her eyes. He knew that Rae was a very compassionate nurse, but she was also the consummate professional. Then, when he saw who was on the table, his insides turned to hot molten lead and his head began spinning. Then his world exploded as he heard the words he would never forget.

"Call it," Dr. Emory said in a choked voice.

"Time of death of the mother, 2:23 A.M." It was not Rae who called the time, but one of the other nurses.

Rae was crying harder now, and Tyler could see her body shaking as well as hear the sobbing.

Again, with a choked voice, Dr. Emory said, "Call it."

"Time of death for the child, 2:24 A.M."

"No! No! No!" Tyler screamed, and he dropped to his knees, weeping loudly, banging his hands against his face. Rae came to him quickly, knelt beside him, and wrapped her arms around him, comforting him as she would a child, though her tears were as bitter as his.

Dillon, the nursing assistant from the ER, burst in. "Dr. Emory, we have a problem in the ER. The two teens that Dr. Michaels triaged earlier, the ones whose parents died in the crash—they just coded, sir. Both of them. Apparently they were allergic to the antibiotic."

·Atlanta·

O h, she looks so lovely, Dr. Michaels," Hiram Welch said. "You will
be quite pleased, I think, when you see her." Welch was the funeral
director.

"I don't want to see her," Tyler said.

"What? But of course you will want to see her, to tell her the final
good-bye."

"I don't want to see her! I want the casket closed! Do you understand that?"
Tyler shouted the words so loudly that some people came from other
parts of the funeral home to see what was going on.

"Well, yes, of course—if it is your wish, the coffin will be closed. I assume you mean for the child as well."

Tyler glared at him with such anger that Welch cleared his throat nervously. "Both of the coffins will be closed," he said.

On the day of visitation Tyler stood up front alongside the two closed
Eternal Cloud caskets, described by Welch as "stainless steel, blue-mist,
brushed caskets, allowing the natural steel finish to show through, providing a dignified and peaceful presentation." One of the coffins was full
sized, the other very small. They were pushed very close together, as if
Karen were holding her child.

Tyler saw his mother and father come into the back of the visitation
room. He had talked to them on the phone, but this was the first time he
was seeing them since Karen had died.

Dr. Paul T. Michaels, always quick to point out that he was a Ph.D.
and not a medical doctor, and his wife, Margaret Elaine, both lived in
Atlanta, so they didn't have far to come. They were both atheists, but not
the run-of-the-mill, quiet, "you believe what you want and I'll believe

what I want" kind of atheist. They were what Tyler liked to call, "in your face, practicing, proselytizing" atheists.

In fact, Tyler's father had recently written an article for *Atheism Today* magazine, beginning with the words: *"Our existence is human centered, not God centered, nature oriented, not deity oriented."*

"You know, Tyler," Paul said to his son as he came up to speak to him. "Both your mother and I have buried our parents, and others that we cared about, and we take comfort in the knowledge that death, like birth, is the natural order of events. There is no need for the false comfort of a 'hereafter.' We say a respectful good-bye, then we get back to our lives."

Tyler nodded but said nothing.

"So I need to ask you. Do you have this all under control?"

"Sure, Dad. It's been two days," Tyler said. "How could I not have it under control? Let's go golfing next week," Tyler had replied in as sarcastic a tone as he could, and was glad to see, by the sharp intake of breath and narrowing of his eyes, that his father caught the sarcasm.

"Yes, well, we are here if you need us," Paul replied.

There were six folding chairs under a canopy alongside the green-carpeted open graves at the cemetery. Tyler sat in the first chair, his parents sat next to him, then came Karen's parents, and finally Dr. Emory. During the graveside service in the cemetery, Paul and Margaret Michaels sat there with detached expressions as prayers were said, and when the "sure and certain hope of resurrection" was promised they looked on their fellow mourners patronizingly. Unlike many of the other women, his mother did not weep. She and his father wore what they imagined were appropriate expressions of sadness.

Karen's parents were always there for her in life, and they were there for her and for him in death. They had taken that cruise excited to come back and be grandparents, only to learn that they were coming back to bury their daughter and her child.

They had been very solicitous of Tyler, looking at him with sadness and pity. He didn't want that. He wanted their anger. He wanted them to blame him for the death of their daughter and grandson. He wanted them to look at him in the same way that Dr. Emory did, with disdain and disgust. He wanted them to hate him as much as he hated himself. They did not. They looked at him with love and pity because he had nothing now, no family and no faith. Tyler was isolated and alone.

When the graveside services were over, everyone but Tyler started to leave. He stood there alongside the open graves with tears streaming down his face as he stared down at the two, as yet, unclosed graves. He heard people talking quietly as they walked away. He didn't hear well enough to understand all the conversations, but he clearly heard someone say, "If he had been there with her, she would still be alive."

Car doors slammed, engines started, and the cars began to leave the cemetery, but still, Tyler stood by the open grave.

Karen's mom walked up to him. "Are you okay?" she asked.

He shook his head as tears continued to slide down his cheeks. "No, I'm not okay," he said quietly.

"It's time to leave now, hon. They have to close the graves. It's time to let them rest in peace."

Tyler looked at her, then in a moment of pure selfish need, lashed out at her. "I could have saved her, you know. If I had been there for her, this would not have happened. But I wasn't there, because I chose to abandon her and play the hero—I was being the hotshot, performing surgery—as it turned out, not even emergency surgery! Do you understand that? *She is dead because of me! Jeremy is dead because of me!*"

Karen's mother looked shocked for a moment, then processing what he was really saying, realized that he *wanted* to punish himself.

"Tyler, there are forces greater than you and a scalpel at work here. There is a master plan, and I don't begin to try to understand it. Sure I question it, but I don't doubt its existence. God has a purpose for you, one that is far greater than you ever have known. Please don't let Karen and Jeremy's passing be for nothing."

As she got to the last part of it, Tyler could see the anger and pain whirling in her eyes and voice. She hugged him and walked away. Karen's dad nodded, and they turned together to walk toward their car.

When they got into their car, Tyler saw that the only people remaining were Welch, the funeral director, and the two men who would be closing the grave. They were standing off to one side, where they had remained discreetly out of the way of the mourners.

No, they weren't the only ones remaining. Back in the shadowed corner of the canopy, he saw one more person. Rae Loona. She nodded at him, and he nodded back.

Seeing Rae there, that awful moment came back to him. He replayed Karen's death scene in his mind. And as he looked at the two open graves, one adult and one child, a pattern began to develop in his mind.

Tyler had first met Karen on February 23. That was 2/23. Karen's death was called at 2:23 A.M.

As he looked down at Karen's casket, there was a plaque that read BELOVED WIFE, MOTHER, AND DAUGHTER.

There was also a small number plate on the casket, and the number was *223*.

He thought of that for a moment, considering the coincidence; then he looked back at Rae. "You're still here," he said.

"I thought you might need some company," she replied.

"Thank you for staying." He walked away from the grave, and seeing him leave, the funeral personnel started toward the grave to take down the canopy and take up the chairs and green carpet.

"What are you going to do now?" Rae asked, hugging him.

"Nothing. Go home, I guess."

"I'll bet you didn't eat lunch," Rae said. "Do you want to go have lunch?"

"I'm not really hungry. What time is it, anyway?"

Rae looked at her watch. "Two twenty-three," she said.

"What?"

Rae realized then that that was the exact time that Karen's death had been called, so when she repeated the time, she said the words quietly, almost reverently. "Two twenty-three," she said.

Tyler nodded. "Thanks for the invite," he said. "But I think I'll just go home and crash. I need some time alone."

"I understand," Rae said. She hugged him again. "Mikey, when you go before the hospital board this week, just know that whatever happens, I will always be your friend, and that you are the best doctor I've ever known."

He really was, she realized, a friend. He made her think. He made her appreciate what she had and what love meant. Almost as much as her devotion to John Travolta . . .

When she had lost her own son and husband, she had found comfort in Travolta's films, classics such as *Grease* and *Saturday Night Fever,* which she watched over and over again, literally dozens of times each. She also loved laughing at *Look Who's Talking* and was amazed at *Phenomenon* and *Michael.* Her Johnny moved her and motivated her as few people—real or on film—ever did. She had liked him a lot before he lost his son, but now she felt a kindred connection—and great admiration—as a parent who had lost a child as well.

Tyler had almost forgotten his summons before the hospital board. He knew that it was not going to turn out well.

"Thanks again," he said.

When he walked back to his car, he happened to notice the license plate number of the hearse across the drive. It was *223*.

When Tyler got home, he just crashed on the couch. He rolled over and saw a tote bag on the side of the couch with a classic Winnie-the-Pooh logo on it. In it, wrapped in blue tissue paper, was a card from Karen and Jeremy. It read, *Dear Daddy, thanks for being the best husband and Dad in the world.*

Tyler felt each syllable like a kick in the stomach. It was as if someone had reached in and grabbed his heart and was squeezing it. He howled in pain, a primal pain of loss beyond measure. When he pulled himself together and grabbed a glance of his appearance he looked haggard and pale. He had not only skipped lunch, he hadn't eaten in a couple of days, and still didn't feel like eating.

Reaching into the Winnie-the-Pooh bag, he found a self-published advance copy of Karen's book that was titled:

223 Blue Butterflies Say I Love You
by Karen Ann Michaels

Emotionally depleted, his scientific mind and internal coincidence meters reeling, Tyler was now officially freaked out.

· *Vatican City, New Year's Day* ·

The *Te Deum* was sung as thanks for the year just ended. Genaro I stepped out onto the loggia from the Apostolic Palace and looked at the tens of thousands of people gathered in Saint Peter's Square. Just before the pope delivered his message, he bowed his head.

"Not my words, but yours, O Lord."

Looking back up, he began to speak to the crowd.

"We give thanks for God's grace and love. At this, the beginning of the New Year, we pray for God's mercy, that He guide us through the precarious times we face.

"In the coming days, we will face perils such as those never before faced by mankind. These difficult times will require solidarity among all God's children, of all races and nationalities, and of all who recognize His dominion over us, in whatever religion they have chosen to reach Him.

"The Earth is at a tipping point. In the last century, men and women have turned their back on the Church, they have embraced the secular over the spiritual, and they have fallen short of God's goodness and glory.

"Because of that, Satan has chosen this time, and the generations now present on this planet, to push out God and establish his kingdom on Earth. We will be besieged by a dark cloud, a cloud of evil. This evil cloud will incorporate all the authority of Satan, plus the combined power of all the evil that has ever resided in the soul of man, from the beginning of time until the iniquity that inhabits the souls of those living today. Each of us will be faced with a choice—to give in to this temptation of the easy path and journey toward the negative and the ways of chaos and destruction, or to choose to fight for all that is good and pure in the cosmos.

"We must unite in this struggle as never before—every man, woman, and child—link the righteousness of our souls with the goodness of all those who have gone before us, and who now, even though they dwell in Heaven, will join with us in the holy fight of good against evil.

"Each of us must ask ourselves not what we can get from God, but—am I open to receiving God's love?

"What may I do to help bring peace to this world? What good acts may I take today, as one soul, one of God's children among many—in my own home to bring the light of goodness, in our neighborhoods, and our nations on Earth? How can we act out of love today?

"The gift to us is free will and free choice. Along with that gift comes the *responsibility* to avoid evil, to make the *right* choices each day.

"And now, as we leave behind the days and hours of the year just passed, we give thanks to God for His just and merciful judgment and elevate our thanks to Him and His love for us."

·*Dallas, New Year's Day*·

Ten thousand people had come to the Preston Forrest Baptist Church for this special New Year's Day service. The Reverend Glen Dale Damron was in the pastor's study talking with his two assistant pastors, the youth minister, and the senior of his deacons.

"I've received a message from God," Damron said. "And I am going to share that message with our people today. I tell you this so that when I start my sermon, you don't all look at me like I'm crazy."

The clergymen in the study looked at one another in confusion. It was left to the Reverend E. D. Owen, the more senior assistant pastor, to ask the question. "Brother Glen Dale, what is the message?" he asked.

"I'd rather not say here," Damron said. "I intend to speak the words from the pulpit, exactly as God gives me those words to speak. But I will say, this will be different from any sermon I have ever given, or for that matter, any sermon you have ever heard."

"I wish you wouldn't do it," said Jim Penny, president of the Board of Deacons.

"Why would you say such a thing, Brother Jim?" Owen asked.

"When you say this is going to be different from anything we have ever heard, it makes me nervous. There are already those who call us Bible-thumpers, fundamentalists, and religious kooks."

"Are you ashamed to be regarded a Bible-thumper, Jim?" one of the other assistant pastors asked.

"No I am not, brother, and you know it," Penny replied. "It's just I don't think we should depart from the message of our Lord and Savior, Jesus Christ."

"Brother Jim, if you don't want to hear this sermon, then you are free to leave the auditorium," the Reverend Glen Dale Damron said. "But I do wish you would stay, because in this fight that God is asking us to undertake, it will require the soul of every righteous person. And I consider you to be not only a friend and an asset to this church, but also a righteous person."

"And this—this message you will be delivering today—you say it came from God?"

"It will come from God," Damron said. "The message I received was to step up to the podium and begin to preach. God will give me the words to say."

"Whew," Pastor Owen said. "I'll give you this, Glen Dale, you certainly have a lot more courage than I have. You are going to be speaking to ten thousand people in the auditorium, and as many as a million through our television ministry, and you have no idea what you are going to say."

"I have no idea at all," Damron said. "Could I ask you all to join me in prayer now?"

The five men stood in a circle with their heads bowed.

"Heavenly Father, I ask you to bless these, your servants, as we set out to do Your work today," Damron said.

"And, Heavenly Father, give Brother Damron tongue to speak Your words," Owen added. "In Jesus' name, we pray. Amen."

As Damron took his position, the congregation was singing:

> What a fellowship, what a joy divine,
> Leaning on the everlasting arms;
> What a blessedness, what a peace is mine,
> Leaning on the everlasting arms.

When the song ended, Damron stepped up to the podium, gripped both sides, and bowed his head.

"May the words of my mouth and the meditations of all our hearts be acceptable in your sight, O God, our strength, and our Redeemer."

Damron looked out over the congregation, the largest Baptist church in Dallas, and one of the largest Baptist churches in America. He saw the eager faces looking up at him, and the three cameras that would be sending his message out through the Christ Alive Network, by satellite all over America and around the world.

Dear God, he thought. *Bring forth the words.*

"We give thanks for God's Grace and love. At this, the beginning of the New Year, we pray for God's mercy, that He guide us through the precarious times we face.

"In the coming days, we will face perils such as those never before faced by mankind. These difficult times will require solidarity among all God's children, of all races and nationalities, and of all who recognize His dominion over us, in whatever religion they have chosen to reach Him.

"The earth is at a tipping point. In the last century, men and women have turned their back on the Church, they have embraced the secular over the spiritual, and they have fallen short of God's goodness and glory.

"Because of that, Satan has chosen this time, and the generations now present on this planet, to push out God and establish his kingdom on earth. We will be besieged by a dark cloud, a cloud of evil.

"This evil cloud will incorporate all the authority of Satan, plus the combined power of all the evil that has ever resided in the soul of man, from the beginning of time, until that iniquity which inhabits the souls of those living today. Each of us will be faced with a choice—to give in to this temptation of the easy path and journey toward the negative and the ways of chaos and destruction, or to choose to fight for all that is good and pure in the cosmos.

"We must unite as never before; every man, woman, and child, link the righteousness of our souls with the goodness of all those who have gone before us, and who now, even though they dwell in Heaven, will join with us in the holy fight of good against evil. . . .

"Each of us must ask ourselves, not what we can get from God, but—am I open to receiving God's love?

"What may I do to help bring peace to this world? What good acts may I take today, as one soul, one of God's children among many—in my own home to bring the light of goodness, in our neighborhoods, and our nations on Earth? How can we act out of love today?

"The gift to us is free will and free choice. Along with that gift comes the *responsibility* to avoid evil, to make the *right* choices each day.

"And now, as we leave days and hours of the year just passed, we give thanks to God for His just and merciful judgment and elevate our thanks to Him and His love for us."

·*Edison, Maryland*·

Jack Fender took doughnuts to the office that morning. He had worked at the real estate office as an agent for nearly ten years. Not the most successful agent, however. In fact, the sales manager, Joanie Sampson, was thinking of firing him if he didn't close on a sale before the end of the quarter. He had become a drag on the budget, the low producer for the past sixteen months straight—and on and off for the two years prior to that.

"That's so sweet of you!" the receptionist exclaimed when Jack walked in at nine thirty. She immediately got up from her desk to follow him into the lunchroom, where he placed the box of treats on the counter by the coffeemaker. The little room was filled with the aroma of freshly baked doughnuts and freshly brewed coffee.

Each of them took a doughnut and a cup of coffee back to the reception desk. He sat and chatted with her for a while.

"Gotta get a sale, you know," Jack said, his mouth flecked with sugar, then took a sip of his coffee. He put the coffee cup down on the desk and reached into his jacket pocket.

The two commiserated about the weather. It had been rainy the past few days. Today looked better: sunshine in the forecast. He asked whether Joanie was in yet.

"Yes, she was in when I got here," the receptionist said. "She's such a go-getter. Always first in and last out in the evening." She was smiling when Jack pulled out an automatic pistol and shot her in the chest. As she lay bleeding on the floor, he shot her in the head, execution style.

Then he walked down the narrow corridor past his own small office where he had spent less and less time since the new year. He walked into Joanie Sampson's office without knocking.

"What—?" the sales manager blurted, but her words were cut short as Jack shot her twice. She slumped over, instantly dead, as he turned and left. There was no one else in the company at work yet. The other agents were out meeting with clients or hadn't yet started their day.

Jack got into his car, a five-year-old SUV, and drove home. It took about six minutes. His wife was in the kitchen. Their two youngsters, Jacob and Brittany, were at school, in second and fourth grade, respectively, just a few blocks way.

Honey, is that you?" Jill Fender called out. She closed the dishwasher and turned it on, then wiped her hands on a dishtowel and sighed. She wondered what he was doing home at this hour. He needed to be out there selling homes and finding new clients. They were underwater with their mortgage and two months behind in payments—so it could be disastrous to fall behind another month. He needed a paycheck. *They* needed a paycheck.

Jill walked out of the kitchen, down the hallway toward the front door. Yes, he was home, all right. He stood just inside the door.

Jack and Jill Fender. Ever since they first started dating in high school, they had been subjected to the inevitable jokes: "Jack and Jill went up the hill. . . ." They had enjoyed it for a long time, through the early years of their marriage and even beyond the time their two kids were born. Then—it seemed like overnight—he had stopped laughing about those "Jack and Jill" jokes. He had stopped laughing about anything.

"What's up?" she asked as she approached. She saw him standing there, his arms at his side. Then she noticed the gun in his hand. "What the heck is that, Jack?"

"I've gotta close a sale. Sell a house, you know."

"I know, honey. You're fine. Do you need something?" She was thinking that he had left some paperwork in his study downstairs in the basement. But the gun . . . why was he holding a gun? Her thoughts were incoherent, scattered.

"No," he said. He held up the pistol and shot his wife twice. Then he went outside, closing the front door behind him. He sat in the front seat of the car, on the passenger side, as if waiting for someone to drive him somewhere.

I've done what you wanted me to do. Now can you let me sell a house?

No one answered his unspoken question. Half an hour later the police found him there in his vehicle, shot dead by his own hand. There was no note left behind.

CHAPTER
33

·New York City·

"F rom New York, a bold fusion of entertainment, edification, and enlightenment for all America, it's the *Dave Hampton Show*. And now,
here's Dave!"

The off-camera voice was loud and enthusiastic, reminding some of
the courtside announcer introducing players at a basketball game.

When the camera moved to a closer two shot on the set, it found Dave
sitting in one chair and his guest in another. It continued on in until it
had a one shot of Dave.

He held up his hand, palm out. "To various and sundry out there, I
bring greetings," he said.

The studio audience applauded.

"My guest today is Dr. Craig Walcott. Dr. Walcott is an astrophysicist
with NASA and a Senior Fellow from Yale University. Dr. Walcott, I
want to thank you for coming on my show today."

"It is good of you to give me this opportunity," Dr. Walcott responded. If central casting had been asked to supply a geek for a show,
they could have done no better than Walcott. He was short, thin, nearly
bald, and wore dark horn-rim glasses. All that was missing was a pocket
protector for his pen.

"Have you ever seen any of my shows?" Dave asked.

"I have."

"Yes, and in fact, did not one of your people get in touch with me
about the dark energies, and ask if I would have you as a guest?"

"That is true."

"Is it also true that there is now some scientific evidence for this phenomenon?"

Dr. Walcott screwed up his face as if trying to come up with just the right answer. "You are giving it a more ominous tone than I think may be required at this point. I prefer to call it—in fact, science calls it—*dark matter*."

"And, what is dark matter?"

"The scientific definition is that it is a hypothesized form of matter particle that does not reflect or emit electromagnetic radiation. We can determine the existence of dark matter only because of its gravitational effects on visible matter, such as stars and galaxies. Approximately four percent of the gravitational effects observed are from visible matter. That leaves ninety-six percent presumed to result from dark matter."

"So then, dark matter does exist," Dave asked.

"You are asking me to state an absolute, and I can't do that," Dr. Walcott said.

"But you have just given us a definition of it."

"Yes, but I specifically said that it is a hypothesis."

"Is there currently a scientific hypothesis, subscribed to by scientists from all over the world, that a large cloud of dark matter is moving toward the Earth?"

"Yes, that is true."

"And isn't there also a hypothesis that this cloud of dark matter is moving more quickly than previously thought?"

Dr. Walcott didn't answer right away, but it was obvious by the expression on his face that Dave's question had hit a nerve. "We don't know, but that may be the case," he finally answered.

"Dr. Walcott, I realize that your world is scientific, and I know, too, that you, as all scientists do, deal more in probabilities and hypotheses than in, as you stated a moment ago, absolutes.

"Would it surprise you to learn that, in addition to the scientific study of this sinister shadow, there is also a conclave of religious leaders from every major religion in the world to discuss this very subject?"

"I don't know why they would," Dr. Walcott said. "Until we examine this phenomenon further, we don't know all its implications."

"You mean the implications of good and evil?"

"Good and evil?"

"Could it be that this thing we are facing, what you call dark matter, could in fact be a manifestation of age-old evil? One that goes beyond our mortal plane, one that involves the very structure of the soul?"

"There is no scientific proof that there is even such a thing as a soul," Dr. Walcott replied.

"Didn't you just tell us, Doctor, that there is no scientific proof, no absolute as it were, of the existence of dark matter? And yet, you are dealing with it."

"Well, yes, but—"

"Hold that thought, Dr. Walcott," Dave said. He smiled into camera two. "We'll be right back."

"And we're down for three minutes," the floor director said.

"Mr. Hampton, that's not a fair comparison," Walcott said while they were in break.

"You say it isn't a fair comparison, but did Dr. Jason Chang not tell the President that we could be dealing with a terminal event?"

Walcott gasped. "How did you know that? That has been classified as top secret."

"How long did you think you could actually keep something like that a secret? Something that would affect every living being on the face of the Earth?"

"You must not broadcast that," Walcott said. "To do so would cause a world panic. There would be the potential for pandemonium, all based on speculation. We don't know that this is true."

"On the other hand, if it is true, and if the religious disciplines of the world are correct, that this is the physical manifestation of a battle between the forces of good and evil, then would it not be incumbent upon me to rally those forces of good?"

"We're back in ten," the floor director said.

"Please don't ask me that question," Dr. Walcott said.

"I won't mention Dr. Chang's call to the President, but some of my questions and comments might make you uncomfortable."

The red light came on.

"We're back, and my guest is Dr. Craig Walcott, an astrophysicist with NASA. Dr. Walcott, do you believe in good and evil?"

"I'm—I'm not sure what you are talking about."

"It's a simple enough concept," Dave said. "Mother Teresa would be an example of good, Adolf Hitler would be an example of evil. Would you agree with that?"

"Yes, of course."

"And do you believe, metaphysically, that the forces of good and evil are always in conflict?"

Dr. Walcott pulled at the collar of his shirt. "Metaphysically, I suppose I would say that I agree."

"And, continuing in the same metaphysical mode, are not the forces of evil sometimes referred to as dark forces?"

"Mr. Hampton, I'm not sure where you are going with this. I think before I answer any more of your questions, I would need to examine your hypotheses."

"All right, Dr. Walcott, here it is. Is it not possible, as the religious representatives of some six billion souls now believe, that what you and the other scientists are calling dark matter could be the dark forces of evil? And if that is so, would we not do well to prepare to do battle with that force?"

"And how would you do that?"

"By mobilizing the good within and among us," Dave said.

·*Hong Kong*·

Francis Chun Yin was half-British and half-Chinese (the product of a colonial-era marriage) and all entrepreneur. By age twenty-three he had established himself as the top bond trader in his company, and within a few years he took his newfound wealth and invested it in a technology firm that wanted him as CEO.

He stood out among his peers in school and in his profession, not only because he was much taller than average, but also because he had a zest and love of life that seemed unique. Girls were always attracted to him, and he was an unfailing gentleman, but he hadn't ever married. As he approached his thirty-fifth birthday, he began to question himself and to look inside, asking, *What is my purpose? Why have I been able to accumulate so much in so little time? Where am I going?*

Two months earlier, Francis Chun Yin journeyed into the mainland. He called it a pilgrimage, though it was really a tour of manufacturing plants that he controlled and various financial headquarters that he had worked with over the past decade. It would change his life in ways he could never have predicted.

In Guangdong Province, toward the end of a grueling month of tours, meetings, conferences, and decision making, he came to Shenzhen, a city of 12 million, for the last week of his visit. His company's largest manufacturing center—more than a factory, a kind of city within a city—was located there, amid the teeming, busy population that fueled a booming economy for the nation, even as the world's major Western economies were floundering and teetering on the edge of collapse.

Bleary eyed, the tall Eurasian entrepreneur, dressed in jeans and a polo shirt, asked to be shown the inside of the plant. After some initial resistance, he received the official guided tour. He asked for more. He wanted to see more. He wanted to see it all.

Perhaps he shouldn't have been shocked. There had been news reports, especially in the United States, about the conditions at the mammoth factories in China that employed hundreds of thousands of workers each. He learned about worker burnout and suicides. People came up to him as he walked the factory floor to tell him their stories. He gave them his email address and phone number so they could register complaints. That was when he learned that workers were denied access to electronic communications, period: No cell phones. No email. No contact with the outside world. It was illegal.

In his hotel room after four nonstop days of touring and personally speaking to hundreds of managers and workers, he made a decision.

Francis returned to Hong Kong and immediately issued a set of decrees of workers' rights and privileges—and expectations—that would free them from the virtual slavery he had witnessed in Shenzhen. Every person would be given a smartphone—the same kind manufactured in the very plant he had visited. He called the provincial governor to inform him of what he was doing and announce that he was prepared to face the consequences of his actions. By then, he hoped, it would be too late for the government to do anything about it. He spent every waking and working hour from that point on determined to give *his* workers some real hope for their own lives and those of their families. It may not have made any financial sense, but Francis knew that this was the right decision and one that needed to be made now.

·Long Island·

Charlene might have eaten lunch—she couldn't remember. She had listened to music most of the afternoon, classical, and now she was looking at a book of art. What held her attention for the moment was *The Night Café*, a painting by Van Gogh.

The picture was dominated by the pool table that sat in the middle of the café, on a wide-plank floor. There were also, around the edge of the café, and the picture, a few scattered tables with condiments. A waiter in white was standing next to the pool table, while a man and woman, seeking as much privacy as they could, sat at the back corner table. There was a sleeping man at another table, while two more men were engaged in conversation at a third.

Charlene got the impression that the conversation was low, malicious, and conspiratorial. That impression was aided by Van Gogh's own comments about the painting.

> In my picture of the "Night Café" I have tried to express the idea that the café is a place where one can ruin oneself, go mad or commit a crime. So I have tried to express, as it were, the powers of darkness in a low public house, by soft Louis XV green and malachite, contrasting with yellow-green and harsh blue-greens, and all this in an atmosphere like a devil's furnace, of pale sulfur.

Ryan had been particularly intrigued with this painting, and tried to buy it from the Yale University's Art Gallery, but they wouldn't sell it.

"Charlene, go upstairs, take a shower, and get dressed. We are going out tonight!"

The words were spoken by Pamela Johnson, who had just burst unannounced into the room.

Pamela, who had a Ph.D. in theology, was a frequent television guest any time the conversation had to do with such things as religion in our society, theological concepts, religious history, or even the occult. Thin and striking, she was an African-American woman who reminded many of a young Diana Ross, with dark eyes and amazing cheekbones.

Dr. Johnson was the first of six children her mother had borne, only two of whom, Pam and her brother Julius, had the same father. Pam's mother and father were married, and though they struggled to survive—Pam's mother was a maid for the Rail Haven Motel, and her father worked at the Scott County Milling Company in Sikeston, Missouri—they had a small house in a modest neighborhood and life was hard but good. When Pam was nine, her father was killed when he fell from the top of one of the grain elevators while trying to change a vent cover.

She shared that early experience of loss with her friend Charlene.

After that, Pam's life changed drastically. Unable to keep the modest home in a middle-class, integrated neighborhood, Pam's mother was forced to move to Sunset, a neighborhood so bad that the police never came into the area. Pam witnessed murders, saw drugs sold and used on the street. She was beaten up three times by her mother's boyfriends, all of whom became fathers of Pam's younger half siblings.

Very early in life, Pam developed a love for reading, and found that she could lose herself in a good book, whether it was a novel or book of philosophy or history. She was a straight-A student at school, given special attention by several of her teachers who saw her potential and realized the reality of her life.

When Pam said she wanted to go to college, her mother, who had been trying to talk her into dropping out of high school, laughed at her.

"You ain't never goin' to 'mount to nothin', 'cause there ain't no one in our family that ever has," Doris Johnson declared. "And as for goin' to college you can just get that idea out of your head right now. You may as well say you want to go to the moon. It ain't possible."

"Mama, we have gone to the moon."

"Yeah? Well, you ain't goin' to college."

Doris Johnson was wrong. Some of Pam's teachers got together and secured enough scholarship funding for Pam that she was able to attend Washington University in St. Louis. Graduating with a straight 4.0 average, Pam continued her education until she earned a doctorate. Now a tenured professor of theology at Drew University in New Jersey, she was a much sought-after speaker and consultant.

It was Sue who had introduced Pam to Charlene, and they had been fast friends ever since. Through all Pam's trials and tribulations, she had hung on to her faith—and now, when asked, she would say that the Ph.D. in her name stood for "Power to heal disasters." That was her remedy for everything—that, and her unwavering faith in God.

"Hi, Pam," Charlene said. "Look, I really don't feel like going anywhere. But if you want to visit for a while, that would be all right."

"Maybe for you, but it's not all right for me," Pam said. "What do you think? That I want to sit around you while you're in the blue funk? Girl, I'm not going to let you bring me down. I told you, we're going out."

"Going out, where?"

"Columbia University is holding a lecture for alternative thought and belief tonight, and there are going to be speakers on all sorts of subjects, from faith to quantum physics. There is even going to be a psychiatrist there who will be speaking on reincarnation and past-life regression therapy."

"Oh, I don't think so . . . ," Charlene said. "Really, Pam, I thank you for thinking of me, but I'm not in the mood."

"Sue!" Pam called.

Sue came into the sunroom, though, as there was no sun now, the room was illuminated by a couple of table lamps.

"Sue, get this woman's clothes ready. She's going out tonight."

A broad smile spread across Sue's face. "Oh, Charlene, good for you."

"I'm not going anywhere," the world-famous singer protested.

"It's going to do you a world of good," Sue said. "What do you think? The blue Celine, or the red Van Noten?"

"I *really* don't want to go," Charlene said.

Pam held the telephone in her hand, and she dialed Dellafiore's Restaurant. "Yes, I'm calling for Stardust Enterprises," she said when the phone was answered. "I'd like the private back room, please, for four people. Yes, that is correct, Stardust Enterprises. Just a moment." Pam covered phone. "What's the code number?" she asked.

Sue started to answer but Pam held up her hand, indicating that she wanted Charlene to answer.

"Zero two eight seven," Charlene said.

Pam smiled, then repeated the number into the phone. By forcing Charlene to answer, it meant Charlene had agreed to go. "Seven o'clock," she said.

While closing the phone, she made a shooing motion to Charlene. "Hurry and get ready," she said.

"I'll wear the black—," Charlene started to say, but Pam interrupted her.

"No black," Pam said. "You'll wear the red Van Noten."

"The blue Celine," Charlene compromised.

Forty-five minutes later, Charlene and Pam were sitting in the backseat of a Cadillac Escalade. The back windows were so darkly tinted that nobody could look in. Raymond Evans, who, in his younger years had driven race cars for Ryan, was driving.

"I don't know why I let you talk me into this," Charlene complained. "Really, I am going to be such a wet blanket."

"No, you aren't," Pam said. "I'm not going to let you be. If you are too much trouble, why, I'll just reach over and pinch your nose."

Charlene laughed. "You would, too, wouldn't you?"

"In a rabbit-running minute, I would," Pam said.

"Rabbit-running minute? Is that one of your academic expressions?"

"Nope. It comes right out of swamp-east Missouri," Pam said.

Charlene laughed again. "You're going to make me feel better no matter what, aren't you?"

"That is my intention," Pam said.

When the giant SUV pulled up in front of the restaurant, a dozen paparazzi were on hand. Cameras began flashing as Joseph, the owner of the restaurant, greeted Charlene and escorted her inside. Despite the melancholia that had enveloped Charlene for so long, she was able to muster a smile and wave to the paparazzi and those who just happened to be passing by and recognized her.

The patrons of Dellafiore's Restaurant were used to famous people coming through the doors, from show business folks to sports figures to high-profile politicians. They considered it gauche to gawk, but Charlene St. John was different. In the time since her husband had died, Charlene had become nearly a complete recluse. She had kept up with the business by releasing two albums in the last two years, both of which went platinum, and the pay-per-view concert and a few other performances and personal appearances. But two years had passed since her last major tour.

Because of that retreat from the public eye, even Dellafiore's most jaded diners looked up from their meal to see Joseph escorting Charlene and her friend to the back of the restaurant.

As she passed by one of the tables, the diner there, a well-known television actor, smiled and spoke to her.

"Hello, Charlene. How are you doing?"

Charlene smiled back at him. "Hello, Michael," she said. "I'm doing well, thank you."

Once they stepped into the private dining room and the door was shut behind them, the restaurant owner escorted them to a private elevator. The elevator led to a basement hallway and exited two blocks down and behind the location of the restaurant, near the delivery entrance where Charlene's driver, Raymond, was waiting. Charlene hugged Joseph, who had clearly done this for a few "special" patrons before, and she and Pamela proceeded to what was to be a life-changing event.

Raymond drove expertly through the city traffic until he reached the campus of Columbia University. Pam led Charlene to Pupin Hall, then into the lecture auditorium itself. The lights had been dimmed inside, with the only illumination being small floor lights to enable passage up the aisles. Because it was dark, and because so many of the attendees were interested in the upcoming program, no one noticed her, and Charlene and Pam were able to take their seats without bother.

The seats were padded and comfortable, and as Charlene sat there she thought of the enticing food aromas she had experienced at Dellafiore's. Tables were extremely difficult to get there, but she had used the restaurant as a ruse to enable her to come here unobserved. Now her several days of eating nothing but peanut butter and jelly sandwiches caused her stomach to revolt. She had been that close to real food, but had simply walked by it without so much as an appetizer. She should at least have taken some cheese.

The barely audible conversations from the audience and the soft whisper of the air-conditioning made Charlene sleepy, but before she drifted off, Pam glared at her as if she were a child misbehaving at Mass. The thought made them both laugh.

The audience grew quiet as the lights onstage shifted to a hue of blues and purples. For a moment Charlene had the feeling that she was about to take the stage, for she had performed in this exact lighting many times before. An applause that could only be described as polite greeted the man who walked out onto the stage. This was the speaker, Dr. Emile Zuckerman, according to the program.

Dr. Zuckerman appeared to be in his late forties, or possibly early fifties. He was wearing a jacket and button shirt, but no tie. His salt-and-pepper hair was cut short. He was of average height and weight with a pale complexion and eyes so blue that Charlene could tell the color from her seat. Dr. Zuckerman looked out over the audience for a long moment, without speaking. He held the silence for so long that some in the audience began to wonder if the esteemed lecturer had suddenly and unexpectedly developed a case of stage fright.

Then, his first four words hit Charlene like an unexpected blow to the solar plexus: "The dead can speak."

What does he mean, the dead can speak? Charlene thought. If the dead could speak, did he think for one minute that Ryan wouldn't have spoken to her by now? Their love was as strong as the cinematic love between Patrick Swayze and Demi Moore in the movie *Ghost*. Perhaps even stronger, because Ryan wouldn't have to go through Whoopi Goldberg, he would speak to her directly.

If he could. Which he can't, because regardless of what Dr. Zuckerman just said, the dead cannot speak.

Charlene was so incensed by the idea that she started to stand up to shout out loud that he was lying, and she was proof that he was lying. "This guy is crazy. I'm not going to stay for this nonsense," Charlene whispered, furious.

Before she could stand, though, Pam reached out to hold her in her seat. "Don't you say anything, don't you even wriggle around in your seat if you don't want me to open a can of whup-ass on your bony frame," Pam hissed.

At first, Charlene's eyes opened wide at the unexpected reaction from Pam; then the absurdity of Pam opening a can of "whup-ass" on her caused her to smile broadly, and she smothered a laugh, shared by Pam. After that, she turned her attention back to the fool onstage who had just told her that "the dead can speak."

"Let us start with the fact that ninety-one percent of Americans believe in the survival of the soul," Dr. Zuckerman said. "That gives us a basis upon which to explore the possibility of the living communicating with the dead.

"Descartes said, 'I think, therefore I am.' The 'thinking' he asserted was beyond the physical, thus, a manifestation of the soul."

As Charlene listened, the inner turmoil she had been feeling released its hold on her, and she began to relax, to let his words resonate in her—and this was a sudden flash of realization—in her *soul*.

Pam was listening like everyone else in the auditorium, but she was also keeping a close eye on her friend. She had heard Dr. Zuckerman speak before, and she had read many of his books and papers. When she learned that he would be lecturing at Columbia University, she was determined to see to it that Charlene attended the lecture. She was sure it would be good for her friend, and now she felt rewarded for her determination. As she watched Charlene gradually lose herself not only in the words, but also in the deep, spiritual meaning of Zuckerman's lecture, she could see the moment that the pilot light, extinguished by the wind of Ryan's death, was reignited.

"And now," Dr. Zuckerman said. "I want all of you to conduct a little experiment, a journey into the recesses of our own soul. We will do that by means of a meditation exercise."

The lights grew much dimmer, so that the audience was now in total blackness, the only light being a small purple halo that hovered around the speaker. His words were quiet, repetitive, entrancing, and Charlene felt a light-headedness—a tingling that moved from her toes up to her head. She escaped her body and seemed to drift in the darkness above, fixated upon and circling around the purple halo that surrounded the soft, almost melodic, entrancing words from the speaker—words that lost coherency but somehow imparted a meaning much greater than the sum of their parts.

Charlene thought that when you meditated you were supposed to feel serene and quiet. Instead, something else was taking over, her pulse was racing, and she could actually hear her heart beating in her ears—and then everything went black.

CHAPTER
36

What had happened to the speaker, to Pam, to the auditorium? How did she get here, and more important, where was *here*?

The shrubbery was crisp and clear, sculpted like the most beautiful castle grounds of Europe that were maintained by ten generations of gardeners. And she had never seen flowers like this, the colors so bold and sharp, the fragrance intoxicating, not only appealing to her olfactory senses but also somehow—and she didn't know how this was possible—emitting musical notes in perfect harmony.

Beyond the garden, she could see sunshine dancing like jewels on the water. Waves came rolling from the sea, crashed upon the shore, then left rainbows in the sand as they retreated. Never in her life had she been anywhere more beautiful or more beguiling than this place. As foreign as it was to her, as improbable, there was nonetheless a comfort to it, a welcoming warmth that was beyond all understanding.

Yes, this was her place, more home than any home she had ever before experienced. All the trappings of her life; her wealth, her fame, her success, were but unneeded, indeed, unwanted encumbrances. She would gladly shed them and stay here, forever.

Then, in the distance on the beach, in the bright light of sun between sand and sea, she sensed more than saw a man standing there, waiting for her. Suddenly she was ten years old again, and that long unrequited wait in her small house in Denbigh was over. The man in front of her was her father!

Charlene ran toward her father with the wind at her back—but no, she wasn't running, she was gliding, for there was nothing physical in her movement except for the closing of the distance between her and her father. But when she reached him it was physical because she could feel his arms around her, and she could feel his breath upon her neck as he spoke to her in the Scottish accent she had not heard since she was that ten-year-old girl.

"*Och*, and when did mi' wee *bairn* become such a beautiful lady?" he asked.

As he pulled her away from him to look at the woman she had become, she felt tears rolling down her face.

"Oh, Daddy, Daddy," she said. "Do you know how much Mom and I have missed you all these years? You were not only my father, you were my hero. When I read books about knights on prancing white horses, you were my knight—my Scottish knight with claymore and shield." Even as she spoke to him, she asked herself, *Is this a dream?*

"I know how ye loved me, lass," Ian replied. "I can hear it now in your singing, a voice that all Heaven can hear." Ian laughed. "*Och*, and many 'tis the time I've told the chorus of angels here that the sweet voice they envy is that of mi' own daughter."

"Daddy, this is the best dream I have ever had. I'm so glad that I fell asleep during that boring lecture."

Ian smiled at Charlene and put his finger under her chin. "Ye are not dreamin', lass. For 'tis all real. You are here, and 'tis your own father who is talking to you. You have a gift, my girl, from God's Forces of Light. The world needs you. That's why you were put on the Earth in the first place."

Charlene knew, now and forever. He had passed over in the car accident. Yet he was speaking to her in this moment, and where he was—and where she was—did not matter. "I *know* that it's my imagination," she said. "But I don't care. I have never been so happy in my life. I want to hang on to this delusion as long as I can."

The smile left Ian's face, and his expression became one that Charlene could well remember from her childhood when he was telling her something and wanted to make certain she was understanding him. He would say, "Listen to me, lass. I promise you, you are here and I am here, and never has anything been more real than this moment."

"This can't be real, Daddy," Charlene said through her tears, wiping them away. "If this were real, don't you think Ryan would be here? I know, I know. You don't know Ryan, he came after you, long after you. But he was my husband, my love, my reason for living."

Ian smiled again. "Lass, sure an' you would nae be for thinking now, that I dinna know mi' own son-in-law? I know Ryan, and he is here."

"This can't be happening," Charlene said through tears. Then, "Is this Heaven?"

"This is where you are supposed to be," her daddy said reassuringly.

"If Ryan is here, where is he?" she asked.

"Honey . . . I am here." The voice, truly Ryan's voice, came from behind her and she spun toward it.

Ryan was on one knee on the ground, extending a long-stem blue rose, just as he had on that magic moment at the halftime show of the Super Bowl game, now so long ago.

I know that we will be together, heart touching heart forever," he sang to her, not in the funny, off-key voice he had used when first he met her, but in the voice of an angel, as if Nat King Cole, Elvis Presley, and Luciano Pavarotti had all gotten together and lent him their voices to make one beautiful voice.

Ryan stood then, and Charlene allowed the spirit of him to wash over her as if she were the shoreline and he was the water. With every breath she took, more of her physical being, or at least her perceived physical being, was being eroded away to be replaced by the essence of pure and unadulterated love.

As he stepped closer, she was mesmerized by how handsome he looked. She knew somehow that he was in spirit form, but it was his physical form that she was seeing now, and if possible, he was even more handsome than she had remembered. All those months of his sickness had been washed away and he radiated his essence.

Charlene reached out toward him; then she quickly pulled her hand back. What if she tried to touch him only to find out that he wasn't real? She couldn't stand that, for if she felt nothing, she would awaken to discover that this was nothing but a dream after all. No, she didn't want that; she would not be able to stand that. To lose him again would be even worse than when she lost him the first time.

She would not touch him—she would enjoy him while she could.

However, Ryan was not to be denied, and he reached out to her, pulling her to him with a kiss that was more intense than any kiss they had ever shared before. When he kissed her, she felt a surge of energy permeate her being, an energy beyond anything she had ever experienced, more wonderful than anything she could even comprehend, and she knew, at that moment, that Ryan was real, as her father had been real, and that this place, wherever it was, was real as well.

"You are here?" she said when, finally, the kiss ended.

"No," he said. "*You* are here."

"I don't understand."

"You will understand, in time."

"Ryan, is this Heaven? I mean, the beautiful shrubbery, the lovely flowers, the wonderful sea and shore. Is this Heaven?"

"Heaven is what you want it to be," Ryan said.

Suddenly Charlene gasped and put her hand to her mouth. "Ryan! Have I—?" She paused, not certain she could complete the sentence. "Have I died?"

"No, darling, you haven't died. Nobody really dies here. I am the one who died—for lack of a better word—remember? You are still very much alive. And as you can see, hear, and feel, so are *we*. Just vibrating at a higher frequency—like a note that humans cannot hear, but dogs can." He laughed with a heavenly mirth.

"Then, I don't understand. If I am alive, what am I doing here, in Heaven, with you?"

"You are here for a reason," Ryan said. "It was not mere coincidence that Pam brought you to the lecture. Nothing is mere coincidence."

"Then why am I here? What is the reason?"

"God needs a favor," Ryan said.

Charlene laughed.

"Why do you laugh?"

"God needs a favor? From me? Ryan, on the surface of it, can't you see how silly that sounds? God is—well, God. If God needs something, why doesn't He just do it? What possible favor could I do for God?" Her voice dripped with sarcasm, with a foundation of anger for having to help this Supreme Being who took the loves of her life away from her.

"The world is in chaos. You can make a difference, honey. You can be a game-changer. . . . Will you help?"

Suddenly what had been humorous turned to anger, the intensity of her anger erupting like a volcano. She was inconsolable and all the grief she held on to for months came pouring out.

"The Universe or God or whatever the hell you want to call this needs my help? Where was he when I was crying myself to sleep at night when my father died? Where was he when I was wishing my heart would just stop beating so I didn't have to feel the pain in my chest when you died? Tell me . . . *where was God at that moment?*"

Charlene did not expect an answer to her question, nor did she receive one, then.

As Charlene stood there on the shore, her back to Ryan, she saw a huge wave coming toward her from the sea. The wave, glistening in the sun, was the most beautiful shade of turquoise she had ever seen, growing higher and higher as it approached. The wave curled at the top, but wasn't spilling over. Instead, it shed spindrift, like sparkling diamonds, from a peak that was at least ten feet high.

Charlene continued to watch as the wave rushed toward her, mesmerized by its beauty, somehow unafraid even though she knew it was going to hit her. It spilled over right on top of her, but even though a wave that large should have knocked her over, it didn't. The breaking wave did not leave her drenched either. Instead, if left her inspired and enlightened.

If asked to put into words what she felt, she would not be able to, yet she knew God in that moment. She knew unconditional love and it rivaled any feeling that she ever felt before. It was as if the wave had been a living water to quench the deepest thirst—of faith, love, and understanding.

She looked back at Ryan and saw him smiling at her.

"You felt it, didn't you?" he asked. "You felt God's love."

"Yes," Charlene said, her voice sounding so small and insignificant in this place. "Do you feel this?"

"This is my existence now," Ryan said. "Consider the gulf between the poorest beggar on earth, holding out his hand in the hope that someone will give him a crust of bread, a pauper with no place to lay his head, and the life I lived on Earth, with so much money that I could have anything man is capable of producing. The difference between what I was then and what I am now, is many times greater than that gulf between the beggar and billionaire."

"Ryan, what is this all about?" Charlene asked. "You said God wants a favor. What kind of favor?"

"I will try to explain it to you," Ryan said. "But I will be able to open the window only a tiny crack. You will have to open the door to understanding yourself.

"There are positive and negative forces in the Universe, and the veil between those forces is weakening as the Dark Forces are gaining strength. We are all a blank slate when we come into our physical form, and our ability to make choices—our free will, as it were—is being lobbied by these positive and negative political forces."

"Ryan, you are saying things like positive and negative forces, but what you are talking about is simply good and evil, isn't it?" Charlene asked.

"Yes."

"I don't understand. Oh, I understand good and evil, all right. But I don't understand what role I can play."

"There is a war brewing, a war of apocalyptic proportions, and souls are at stake. Believe me, Charlene. You can make a difference."

What Ryan was saying was overwhelming, and Charlene was trying desperately to understand him, and to ascertain her role in this war he was talking about. He was still talking to her, but the words were fading in and out, and she was straining to hear.

Then, like a television screen during a storm, the beautiful scene around her began to drop out. Ryan was fading out of view and Charlene knew she was being pulled away from the loves of her life. She reached out toward him, not just to touch him, but also to grab hold of him, to anchor herself in this place, but her fingers grasped only thin air. She was being pulled by a riptide of reality back to her seat in the theater.

There was a huge whooshing sound followed by a bang, and that was when someone called an ambulance.

CHAPTER
38

Dr. Tyler Michaels sat at one end of the long conference table in the boardroom of St. Agnes Hospital. Jay Abernathy, the hospital administrator and chairman of the board; Dan Meyer, the hospital attorney; Dr. Emory and Dr. Peter Presnell from the St. Agnes medical staff; and Dr. Mel Gunther and Dr. Maxwell Urban from the Georgia Composite Medical Board were all sitting around the other end of the table.

That left Tyler somewhat isolated. At least he was sitting, and not standing before them like a schoolboy summoned to the principal's office.

Abernathy sat with his hands folded on the table before him, and he began to speak in a cold, emotionless voice. "Dr. Michaels, after careful consideration, this board has found you in abuse of the standards of this hospital, to wit: You performed a surgery in violation of a temporary probation denying you OR privileges. In addition, the surgery you performed was not emergency surgery, and in so doing, you absented yourself from triage during a massive influx of emergency patients. Worse, you ordered antibiotics to be administered without a direct diagnosis, exacerbating their medical condition into what could have resulted in death had it not been for immediate remedial action by Drs. Emory and Presnell."

Worse than the cold, impersonal enumeration of the charges against him was the expression on Dr. Emory's face. It was a cross between self-righteousness and smug victory.

"Have you anything to say in your defense?" Abernathy asked.

"There is no defense against the truth," Tyler said. "And everything you said is true."

There was a subtle change in Dr. Emory's expression. Clearly he had expected Tyler either to deny the charges or plead with the board for leniency. He was visibly disappointed that Tyler had done neither.

"Very well, Dr. Michaels. It is the recommendation of the board of directors of St. Agnes, and concurred by the Georgia Composite Medical Board that you are to be put on professional suspension for two years. Your license is not being revoked, but you will not be allowed to use it for the next twenty-four months. In addition, you will be required to undergo a psychological evaluation before being reinstated officially."

"If I may, Mr. Abernathy?" Dr. Emory said.

"Go ahead."

"Tyler," Emory said, "as far your surgical skills are concerned, you are the best I have ever seen. You have a God-given talent that is rarely equaled. But it takes more than touch and dexterity to be a good surgeon; you must also have the right mental and psychological mind-set. And that, you clearly do not have. Despite what you think of me, I took no joy in bringing you up before this board, and I take no pleasure in seeing these sanctions applied to you. My hope and fervent prayer is that you take these two years to reevaluate your priorities, and that you return to medicine a complete surgeon."

"Thank you," Tyler said, not knowing what else he could say.

CHAPTER
39

Under other circumstances, the two-year probation the Georgia Composite Medical Board had just hit Tyler Michaels with would have been devastating. But now, in a perverse way, he was glad for it. He needed to be punished for having let Karen and his baby die. Tyler had once read about the members of strict religious orders, who in the Middle Ages practiced self-flagellation using a cattail whip that was flung over the shoulders repeatedly during private prayer. In his current state, the concept of self-flagellation did not seem all that absurd.

During the weeks and months that followed Karen's funeral and his expulsion from the medical community, Rae Loona became the only constant in Tyler's life. Amid the grief and despair, she was a bridge, a connection to Karen and the baby.

Rae had been with Karen in her last moments. She was there for her when he was not, and now Rae was there for him. So when Rae rang his doorbell, he was very happy to see her.

"Mikey! Damn, you look like shit."

"Thank you, thank for saying so. I appreciate looking like I feel. Because I feel like shit."

"It's been weeks. Do you plan on starting your psych program or are you going to let the bullies in the boardroom dictate your future? You know I implied that you needed to do that surgery, yet you and everybody else didn't want to hear it when I testified. That is bullshit. You wanna throw a pity party?"

"Funny, I was just thinking about flagellation, and here you come, like Mighty Mouse, to save the day. Let me take off my shirt so you can get to my back."

Rae laughed. "Honey, don't think I'm too old to enjoy seeing a good-looking man without his shirt. Say, my true sweetheart, Mr. John Travolta." Tyler rolled his eyes at that. "But that's not why I'm here. Now, go take a shower, shave, oh, and make sure you put on some clean underwear. You are so nasty lookin', ain't no tellin' when you last changed drawers. Mikey, haven't I told you: We are going places!"

Tyler smirked and was about to say he wasn't going anywhere, when Rae added, "Or I will strip you down myself and see what the Good Lord never intended for me to see. Now, do what I told you, and let's go!"

Half an hour later, showered, shaved, and in clean clothes—it actually felt good to be showered and in clean clothes—Tyler was ready to go to wherever it was Rae had planned. He picked up his car keys from the hall tree.

"Huh-uh, honey, we ain't goin' nowhere in your old white man Volvo," she said.

"I haven't driven the Corvette in two months," Tyler replied. "I don't even know if the battery is up."

"Honey, we are goin' in my RX-8." Rae drove a blue Mazda RX-8 sports car with a bumper sticker that read I DON'T DRIVE ANY FASTER THAN MY ANGELS CAN FLY. Her license plate said IHOTMAMA. She was a little heavier than she liked to be, which she attributed to menostop, not menopause. She also had a daily ritual of double-stuffed Oreo cookies, "No more than I can hold in one stack between my thumb and forefinger" and iced milk for breakfast.

"Get in, Mikey," she said, clicking the remote to unlock its doors. "We are going places. We have a date with destiny."

"Destiny," "fate," "luck," were words that, in Tyler's mind were synonymous with angels, Santa, and God. He shook his head and smiled, but he didn't want to be disrespectful to a woman who was only slightly younger than his mother, and much more of a friend than any he'd ever had.

"Where are we going?"

"Places, Mikey. We are definitely going places." She laughed as she started the car.

An hour and forty-five minutes later, they were at Hartsfield Airport, boarding a flight for New York. Two and a half hours after that, they were summoning a taxi at LaGuardia. After getting hotel rooms at the

Algonquin, they took a taxi to Pupin Hall at Columbia University, where they were to listen to a lecture by Dr. Emile Zuckerman.

Rae got tickets in the second row, stage left. Tyler had no idea what to expect from this night, but he was feeling glad that she'd dragged him out. It was actually the first time he'd "felt" anything in months.

According to the program Tyler was reading, Dr. Zuckerman had studied cellular psychology and wrote about his findings in multiple journals and a few books. One of the books Tyler had even heard of: *The Universe as Organism and Source of Energy*. Karen had read the book, and had tried to talk Tyler into reading it, though he kept putting it off. Maybe he would have to read it now, especially after attending the man's lecture.

Dr. Zuckerman began by speaking about the soul and the survival of consciousness. He talked about experiments with mediums and measurable data and findings and how he put his reputation on the line to show that, as he put it, there "just might be something else."

Rae looked at him and handed him an envelope. As he started to open it, she took it back and said, "Not yet. I'll tell you when to open it."

Tyler listened to Zuckerman speak and was perplexed. Here was someone who seemed to be a respected scientist who was willing to take the path of science to examine the validity of the soul. At that moment, Tyler heard someone behind him, as if the person had leaned forward to whisper in his ear.

"Dr. Zuckerman is not the first person to walk this path. Science and faith are two branches of the same plant, both needing water and sunlight to survive."

Tyler twisted around to see who was speaking so loudly in his ear in what he thought was a bad Swedish accent. His jumpy movement startled Rae, and the two of them started to giggle. That's when he noticed two women seated nearby. Rae and Tyler looked at each other in disbelief. The famous singer, Charlene St. John, had taken a seat directly in front of them.

Tyler listened to the speech, fascinated by the points Zuckerman was making. He was a man who believed strongly, almost devoutly, in the primacy of science, and yet this man was attacking Tyler's doubt—enough to make him begin to question his own belief, or rather his own skepticism. . . .

Suddenly in front of him, Charlene St. John's head rolled back, and she fell from her seat. Instinct and training took over, and Tyler and Rae went to her aid.

"Whoa, mister. Hey. You ought not to touch her, if you don't know what you are doing," one of the other members of the audience said.

"He's a doctor, and I'm a nurse," Rae said authoritatively.

"Cardiac arrest," Tyler said. He and Rae positioned Charlene in the aisle, flat on her back, then he banged his fist on her chest, then leaned down to listen, then banged his fist again until her heart resumed beating.

Rae had already dialed 911, and she and Tyler stayed with Charlene until the ambulance arrived. Had they not been there at that moment, one of the greatest singers in the world would have died.

Tyler and Rae had saved her life.

CHAPTER
40

A few hours had passed since Charlene's attack. Pam was hoping that it was simply exhaustion and dehydration. Paul Maxwell, Charlene's business manager for the past twenty years, was in the ER with Pam. The expression on his face was beyond worried. It was sick.

And why not? Pam thought. After all, Charlene was his golden goose. Just his percentage of what Charlene was earning had made Paul a millionaire many times over.

No, that was mean of her. Pam knew that Charlene was much more than a meal ticket for Paul. She knew that Paul could not love her any more had she been his own sister.

"Tell me again what happened?" Paul asked.

"I've told you."

"Tell me again, I'm trying to wrap my mind around this. She was hypnotized? I've read about things like this, mass hypnotism at these cult events. What were you attending, a séance?"

"It was not a séance, and she was not hypnotized," Pam insisted. "I told you, Emile Zuckerman is one of the most respected men in his field."

"Yeah, well, if you've got a kooky field, then it doesn't take a whole lot to be one of the most respected kooks, does it?"

"He is hardly a kook. He has consulted with presidents of the United States."

"Really? With the last bunch of presidents we've had, that doesn't say a whole lot for him, does it?"

"Paul, I know you are upset and worried. I'm upset and worried as well," Pam said. "But I resent your implication that because I took her to the lecture, I am somehow responsible for this."

Paul ran his hand through his hair and looked earnestly at Pam. "Forgive me, Pamela," he said. "I know you would do nothing to hurt her. God knows, you have almost single-handedly brought her through these last two years since Ryan died. You're right, I am not myself, but I have no right to take it out on you."

"Don't worry about it," Pam said. "We are all in this together."

Charlene made a sound then, and Pam stepped to the door and called out to the attending physician.

"Dr. Vaill! Dr. Vaill, come quickly, please!" Pam said. "I think she is waking up."

Dr. Elyse Vaill, wearing horn-rimmed glasses and a white coat, was a mature woman with a dignifying gray at the temples who exuded calm professionalism. Pam had made the comment when she first saw her that she looked like a doctor out of central casting; she could have played one on a soap opera.

Charlene was fully conscious now and she looked around, a little surprised to find herself in a bed, in a hospital emergency room.

"What am I doing here?" she asked. "What happened?"

"You've had a mild myocardial infarction," Dr. Elyse Vaill said.

"A mild myocardial infarction? What is that?"

"In layman's terms, a small heart attack."

"A heart attack? But isn't that something that only old people have? I'm in the prime of life," Charlene said.

"Not necessarily. But unfortunately, while we have procedures and medicines to deal with a heart attack, that isn't the real problem." The doctor cleared her throat and looked not only at Charlene, but at Pam and Paul as well.

"In doing the tests to discover what might have led to the attack, we have discovered a tumor behind your heart. It is constricting the blood supply to your head and your lungs."

"A tumor? You mean, as in cancer?" Pam asked.

Vaill nodded. "I'm afraid so," she said.

Pam grabbed Charlene's hand and began squeezing it as her eyes welled with tears.

"How bad is it?" Paul asked.

"It's not good," Vaill said. "It appears to have been there for some time, and has already grown quite large. More than likely this is what has been contributing to the lethargy that your friend here says that you have been having."

"Is it growing?" Charlene asked.

"From the results of the test, it is quite possible that this tumor will continue to grow and, I fear, quite rapidly."

"You haven't said the word yet," Charlene said.

"What word?" Dr. Vaill asked.

"Don't play games with me, Doctor, please," Charlene said. "I'm not afraid of the word, I heard it used with Ryan. The word is 'terminal.' What I have is terminal, right? How long do I have to live?"

Dr. Elyse Vaill did not, at first, give a verbal response. Then she said, "Other than an increasing tiredness and weakness, you probably won't experience much pain. And what pain you might experience, we will be able to control. For how long, that I cannot say for certain."

"Thank you, Doctor, for being up front with everything," Charlene said.

"I wish I could give you better news," she said. "I'll—uh—go now and let the three of you talk. If you need anything, please let me know."

A long silence descended over the room after Dr. Vaill left.

"We'll have to tell Sue," Charlene said. "She's at home."

"No, she is here," Pam said. "She is calling your mother."

"Does she know?"

Charlene shook her head. "I don't think so. None of us knew until a moment ago. I called her when you were in the ambulance."

Even as they were talking about her, Sue came into the room. "I called your mother," she said. "She's taking the first flight out of Miami that she can get."

"Thank you, Sue," Charlene said.

Sue saw the tears sliding down Pam's cheeks and a drawn expression on Paul's face. "What is it?" Sue asked. "What do you know that I don't know?"

"She . . . ," Pam started, but she choked up and couldn't finish the sentence. She waved her hands and shook her head. "She . . . ," she started again.

"It's terminal, Sue," Charlene said.

Sue had been through the diagnosis and quick demise of Ryan.

"Oh, no," she said. "No, please God, no."

"Are there news people here?" Paul asked.

"Yes. There were too many people at the auditorium when Charlene passed out," Sue said. "Also, the EMS people tweeted the news to the local gossip rags that she was being brought in to the hospital."

"What do they know?"

"Nothing, so far," Sue said. "I told them that Charlene had been feeling low about Ryan, and hadn't been eating, and that was what caused her to pass out."

"I don't know how long that story will hold up," Paul said. "I mean, now that she has been diagnosed. And there were witnesses at the lecture who watched Tyler get her heart started again—and the EMTs who helped."

"Dr. Vaill won't tell anyone anything," Pam said. "We were talking earlier; she knows the importance of Charlene's privacy and doctor–patient confidentiality. She's bound by privacy laws, as are all hospital staff. If they value their careers, they won't say anything. There's really nothing we can do about the EMTs and audience except hope none of them run to the media."

"Of course, when we cancel the show in Mexico City, there will be more questions asked," Paul said.

"We aren't going to cancel the show in Mexico City," Charlene said.

"What? Of course we are. You can't do a show now. Not in your condition," Paul said.

"Oh, but I can, and I will," Charlene said. "I have been grieving for almost two years. I did the pay-per-view event only because I didn't have to tour and it gave me something to do. Likewise with the albums. It was only the devastation of millions in Turkey that finally roused me to do a public concert at all. You heard Dr. Vaill, and really, when have I not been tired after a show?"

"That was because you work so hard preparing for your shows. And the shows themselves are a drain," Paul said. "And that's when you were healthy."

"But I wasn't healthy," Charlene said. She put her hand over her heart. "I've had this time bomb ticking inside me now for a long time. Maybe that is what was making me so tired then. And if I was able to do the shows then, I can do this one now."

"Charlene, I don't know," Pam said.

"I *do* know," Charlene insisted. "Pam, Paul, I want to do it. I have to do it, don't you understand? This will probably be my last show, and I want it filmed and preserved. It will be my farewell. Think of Michael Jackson, and how he died before he was able to do his farewell show.

Don't you think he would have wanted to do that show? I certainly do. I know that I don't want to go out like this."

"You are sure?" Paul asked.

"I am sure."

"All right," Paul said. "Pam, Sue, let's go talk to Dr. Vaill and see what we will have to do, medically, to get ready for the show."

Pam was pleasantly surprised that Paul wasn't pushing her friend to do the show. "Charlene probably could use the rest anyway," she replied.

Charlene watched them leave her room; then she turned on her side, being careful not to disconnect the lines that led to the monitor, and looked through the window. She was in New York Presbyterian Hospital and as she looked out onto Broadway, she was surprised to see that it was daylight.

She looked over to the table beside her bed and saw Dr. Tyler Michaels's card. He had scrawled his cell phone number on the back. She dialed it on her own handheld and held it to her ear with some difficulty. When a woman's voice answered, she was surprised, but then the person identified herself.

"This is Rae Loona. Hello, Ms. St. John. Tyler is right here. He was just temporarily separated from his phone!" Rae's positive energy shone through even on a mobile telephone call. Charlene could hear Tyler snatching the receiver from Rae with mock exasperation, saying, "Why are *you* answering my phone?" and heard Rae laughing in the background replying, "It's what I do, Mikey."

Tyler Michaels said, "Hello."

"You know, Dr. Michaels, I won't be able to stop thanking you every minute for a while. I hope you'll forgive me in advance."

"I am glad I was there to help," Tyler said. "Really, it's my job, Ms. St. John."

"I appreciate that. And I want to invite you and Nurse Loona to the Academy Awards ceremony in March—as my guests."

"No, really—we couldn't—"

"If you ask Rae, I sincerely doubt she would say no."

"Well, I suppose . . ."

"I'm reserving the two tickets for you, and you better show up. That's all I'm going to say about it."

"I'll tell Rae. Do you want to stay on the phone to hear her scream?"

"I better not. I might have a relapse. Thank you so much, Dr. Michaels."

Charlene smiled—a big, genuine smile—for the first time in at least several days.

After hanging up, she decided to tweet her fans, who by this time had probably heard she was in the hospital:

> Feeling great after a bit of a scare. Doc gives me clean bill of health.
> On to Mexico City!

But all she could think about was what had happened—not what happened to get her here, but what happened while she was—what? Unconscious? In a coma? In a trance?

She had seen her father and Ryan, had talked to them, had felt her father's embrace and her husband's kiss. That long, wonderfully intense kiss. Had she made all that up? Was it just a hallucination?

It had to be. The reality was, she was here, in a hospital, diagnosed with a terminal illness, and all that she had experienced was nothing more than a dream.

The reality that what she had experienced—or thought she had experienced—was just a dream, hurt more than the news that she had an inoperable malignant tumor. With all that she had been through, how could she have allowed herself, even in a dream state, to be so vulnerable?

"Because I'm a fool, that's why," she said aloud.

There was an audible click; then a nurse's voice came over the intercom. "Did you want something, Mrs. McAvoy?"

"What? Uh, no, nothing," Charlene said.

What was this? Were they listening in? Was there a TV camera in the room as well as a hidden microphone? The idea probably wasn't that farfetched. After all, they had a machine connected to her that could tell some nurse at some distant location what her heart rate was, what her blood pressure was, and how rapidly she was breathing, or even if she was breathing at all. For all she knew, they could tell what she was thinking.

Charlene felt anger, not at the idea that she was being monitored, but because what she had experienced—or thought she had experienced—never really happened at all. The more she thought about it, the more intense her anger became.

She heard the sound of shattering glass and, startled by it, turned to see what had caused it. An elderly white-haired woman with a pushcart of books and magazines from the ladies' auxiliary was standing in her room.

Charlene glanced down at the floor to see what had fallen, but there was nothing there. Had the hospital volunteer picked it up that quickly?

"What can I do to make you more comfortable?" the woman asked, her voice as old and strained as she looked.

"Nothing, thank you," Charlene replied.

"Oh, but I've so many things here," she said. "Magazines? Newspapers? I've quite an assortment, as you can see."

"No thank you," Charlene said again.

"Life Savers?"

"Look—" Charlene read the woman's name tag. "—Betty Jean. I—I appreciate everything you are doing, but I don't want a thing. You've been so kind. I hope you can understand that."

"Of course I can, dear," Betty Jean replied, the smile never leaving her face. "I'll just let you rest, then."

"Thank you," Charlene replied.

The hospital volunteer pushed her cart to the door, then came back to the bed.

Lord, what does she want now?

Betty Jean took Charlene's hand in hers and, putting something in it, smiled again. For some reason, at that moment, she looked ageless rather than aged. Charlene could almost imagine an aura of light around her.

"Charlene," she said. The voice was not old or creaky, but resonant and soothing. "Ryan and your father want you to know that it was all real. And you are going to be one for so many."

"What?" Opening her hand, Charlene saw a roll of Life Saver mints. When she looked back up, the old woman and her pushcart of magazines and newspapers were gone.

"Wait, come back!" Charlene called.

The woman did not reappear.

"Pam! Pam, are you out there?"

Something in Charlene's voice must have frightened Pamela, for she came running in immediately.

"Stop that hospital volunteer," Charlene said. "Tell her to come back in. I need to talk to her."

Pam looked confused. "What hospital volunteer?"

"What do you mean, what hospital volunteer? I'm talking about the old lady who was just in here," Charlene said. "She just this second left the room—you had to have seen her. Tell her to come back, I want to talk to her."

"Honey, there was nobody in your room," Pam said. "I've been right outside the door ever since we left you to yourself. No one has come in."

"But you have to have seen her!" Charlene said desperately. "She was just here!"

Pam shook her head. "You must have dozed off and dreamed it," she said. "I swear to you, no one entered or left this room. Let alone an old hospital volunteer."

Charlene opened her hand and showed Pam the roll of Life Savers. "Then, would you please tell me where this candy came from?"

Pam shook her head. "I don't have the slightest idea."

On the plane back to Atlanta the next day, Tyler sat quietly looking through the window, listening to the soft whisper of air slipping by the airplane at well over five hundred miles per hour.

"Dr. Zuckerman is not the first person to walk this path. Science and faith are two branches of the same plant, both needing water and sunlight to survive."

"What?"

Rae looked at him.

"Did you say something?" Tyler asked.

"No. You looked like you needed some time to think," Rae said. "I didn't say anything."

Tyler nodded and looked through the window again. It couldn't have been Rae, anyway. Whoever it was had spoken in a Swedish accent.

That's funny. Last night at the lecture, someone behind him had said the same thing, and in the same Swedish accent. What was going on, here?

"When you get home, read the Bible. You will gain a deep spiritual meaning and insight, even from the smallest and most trivial incidents. You will encounter psychic experiences in your life that cannot be explained simply by science. Do you think it was mere coincidence that you were sitting behind Charlene St. John last night? God has a purpose for you, one that is far greater than you ever have known."

Again the words, which he now realized had to be in his mind, were spoken with a Swedish accent.

But the voice in his head had raised legitimate questions. He began thinking about what had happened last night, how they had just happened to be sitting behind possibly the best-known singer on the planet. Was it a mere coincidence that he had been sitting behind Charlene St. John? And why were the voices in his head suddenly speaking in Swedish accents when he didn't even know any Swedes? The one thing that Tyler knew for a fact was that they had saved Ms. St. John's life. Which was what doctors did, not that Tyler felt very much like a healer at the moment.

"You were great last night, the way you handled that emergency," Rae said.

"Was I?" Tyler replied. "The funny thing is, Rae, I don't even know if I will ever be allowed to practice medicine again."

"Don't worry about it. God has a purpose for you, one that is far greater than you ever have known."

Tyler felt as if ice-cold water had splashed down his back and spine. The voice in his head had just used those exact same words. And those were also the very same words Karen's mom had said to him at the cemetery.

Rae pulled an envelope from her purse. "Remember when I showed this to you last night?"

"Yes, I remember. You said you would tell me when it was time to open it."

"Now is that time," Rae said, handing the envelope to him.

Tyler opened the sealed flap. Inside the envelope were business cards for all the houses of worship in the area, from synagogues to mosques, and all the Christian denominations: Catholic, Baptist, Methodist, Episcopalian, and Mormon, among others.

Rae watched Tyler as he perused this very eclectic collection of religious institutions. She waited for a full minute before she spoke again, this time in a raised voice. *"Pick one, damnit!"* she said.

"How am I supposed to know which one to pick?"

"Pick one and speak a language. Any language. Or you can do what I do. I go to them all. I treat God like food."

"You treat God like food? What do you mean?"

"Like food," Rae repeated. "I can't just eat Italian all the time. Sometimes I have to have some Chinese, or maybe I need a little Mexican. Some variety."

Tyler felt tears start to well up in his eyes. In order to break the seriousness and to suppress his emotion, he looked at one of the cards and raised an eyebrow and asked with severe doubt, "I don't see anything for the Church of Scientology here? What about it? Do you sometimes have to have a little Church of Scientology?"

Rae smiled back to him and quipped, without missing a beat, "Tell me, have you ever seen John Travolta dance? Honey, that white boy has rhythm—more than rhythm. He can park his slippers under my bed any-time! *Whoo hoo*, Mikey—*whoo hoo!*"

Tyler laughed quietly and felt a burden leave him. He was breathing again. Correction, Tyler's *soul* was breathing.

He wished he could change this moment—rewind the clock to the point when Karen and Jeremy might have been healed. Then they would be with him now and he with them. . . .

CHAPTER
42

American News Channel had made arrangements with its sister broadcast company, Euro News, for Dave Hampton to do his show from its Ireland studios. He could have taped his show for rebroadcast, but he preferred to do it live. Dave was back for a second time, despite his producer's exasperation last time and the network's discomfort with the cost. But it was Dave's show, and until he really screwed things up, he would get his way in most things. He had managed to get the coroner and the police detective who were working the cases.

"How many have there been so far?" Dave asked.

"Eleven," the policeman, Eric Vaughan, said.

"And I'm told that there are striking similarities in each of the bodies you have found."

"Aye. The first few were young, attractive women. All were naked."

"But then the next few victims were men?"

"Aye. And not young either."

"But you, Dr. O'Reily, in your examinations, despite the gender switches and other factors, you found that there were still similarities."

"Yes," the coroner replied. "All had the words 'Viva Domingo' carved on their inner thighs."

"Viva Domingo? As in, *Viva Zapata!*?"

"Perhaps, though I don't know of anyone named Domingo."

"Were there other similarities?"

"All had their hearts surgically removed, and all had an archaic or mystical symbol carved on their backs."

"I believe you have pictures of this?"

"I do."

"I want to caution our audience, these pictures are rather graphic," Dave said. "But we have cropped them so that you see only the symbols. And what I call your attention to is the absolute intricacy of these carvings. It is as if whatever demented soul did this thought that he had all the time in the world."

The pictures were flashed on the screen, one after the other. The glyphs and figures looked almost as if they were tattooed on the skin by a very skilled tattoo artist.

"Are there any cases in recent history like these?" Dave asked.

"No," the policeman said in a distinctive Irish brogue. "This is—there's no other way to say it—evil incarnate."

"Evil incarnate," Dave said. "Yes, that is precisely what it is."

Dave looked at the pictures for a moment, then looked back toward the camera.

"Many of you may remember there was a serial killer who operated in Northern California in the late 1960s and early 1970s. To this day, the killer's identity remains unknown. The killer himself coined the name Zodiac in a series of letters he sent to the press, all of which contain cryptograms. His victims were four men and three women between the ages of sixteen and twenty-nine.

"The cryptology was broken in only one of his letters, and in it, he said that when he dies to be reborn in the afterlife, that those he killed will be his slaves.

"Are we dealing with a copycat killer here? Or is this the same killer who terrorized California so many years ago?

"Or—" Dave paused in midsentence, then lifted his hand to his head and made a circle. "—here is where people are going to say that old Dave is crazy, but is this something much more than a copycat, or even the original Zodiac killer? Is this a physical manifestation of the sinister shadow I have been speaking about?

"Folks, I'm telling you, don't dismiss this concept of good versus evil, of the power of darkness doing battle with the power of light. I feel very deeply—and I cannot tell you where this feeling is coming from—that we are soon, all of us, going to be engaged in some cataclysmic battle for survival. And not just survival of our human existence, but the survival of our very souls."

Dave held his hand up, palm out.

"From Belfast, this is Dave Hampton. Good night, America."

·Grenada·

Mama G watched from far away in her island home, smiled, and nodded with appreciation for Dave Hampton doing his job, what needed to be done. She hoped the distraction of these murders would not keep him from his larger task.

The other TV channels and newspapers were finally taking the story seriously and listening to Dave's perspective, quoting him and sending their own reporters out to cover the breaking news.

She went to her computer to write a new blog to tell the world how she felt. All things in time. As above, so below . . .

·Danton, Missouri·

The pressed had dubbed him the "Church Burner." Carl Turner delighted in the name. He goaded his friend, Brent Begley, into more action with the promise of more headlines. Carl called their nighttime forays into arson their "playdates."

They met up on Sunday morning at church but said nothing to each other at that time. Their families had belonged to the First Baptist congregation for generations, and they had attended Sunday school together for ten years. Throughout the two-hour service of preaching and prayer, they sat attentively. In the afternoon they ate Sunday supper with their families. Then, at midnight, they met in the First Baptist parking lot and set out on their mission of destruction.

They easily broke the front door lock of the Missionary Community Church in Charlestown and moved swiftly, expertly in the pitch dark. They had reconnoitered the church a few weeks previously, attending a Sunday worship service, coming in a few minutes after it started and leaving early, before it ended—leaving no impression of themselves behind among the congregants.

Now they were all business, lifting benches and chairs to create a pyre around the pulpit. Then they gathered all the hymnals they could find, and collection baskets and paper and picture frames, and piled them, too, and doused the material with a gallon of gasoline.

"Come on," Turner urged. "Move it." The only words he had spoken since entering the sanctuary. He tore three paper matches from a convenience store matchbook, struck them, and tossed them into the pyre. He then ignited the remaining matches and dropped them in a puddle of gasoline.

Whoosh! Smoke and fire blew in every direction. The two young arsonists fled, jumped into the still-running car, and sped off to their next destination—another church about one hour away. It would be their tenth immolation in just six weeks. And they had more work to do—much more.

From the Charlestown, Missouri *Telegraph-Reporter*

Two Locals Arrested in Church Arsons;
Suspected "Church Burner" to Be Charged

DANTON—Two men were charged Friday morning with setting fire to a church in eastern Missouri. Local and federal authorities said the men may face charges in nine other church fires that have taken place over the past several weeks.

The men, Carl Robert Turner, 20, of Danton, Mo., and Brent Begley, also of Danton, were arrested and charged with arson of a building in the fire, last Sunday, of the Mission Community Church in Charlestown. Officials expected to charge the pair with three burnings here, three in nearby Corinth and one other in Charlestown, as well as two more that fit the same pattern.

Because the building was a church, the charges were elevated to a first-degree felony, said Dan Breslin, a spokesman for the Bureau of Alcohol, Tobacco, Firearms and Explosives. That felony carries a sentence ranging from probation to 99 years to life in prison, Breslin said.

"We've been looking at these two guys for a while," the spokesman said. "But we had to paste together information. By working closely with our local partners, we brought tremendous resources to this investigation, working around the clock for over a month."

Also deployed in the investigation was a three-year-old black Labrador female with a super snout by the name of Mina. Her human escort was Mike Maloney, a member of the Missouri State arson task force, based in Jefferson City.

"She's an accelerate detection canine," Maloney said.

Without elaborating on details of the investigation, he said the hound, who has her own badge, played a role in the capture of the suspects, too.

Law enforcement officials at yesterday's news briefing praised just about everyone, from the church volunteers who guarded their own parishes night and day, to a cooperative news media that would not let the story die, to numerous individuals who provided tips to different agencies.

Bond for the men was set at $10 million apiece. They were being held at the Charles County Jail in Charlestown, pending a court appearance set for next week.

Investigators have said that the fires have followed a loose pattern. Different types of congregations, including Baptist, Methodist, Christian Scientist and nondenominational churches, have been hit. The fires have broken out at different hours, but all occurred at night.

Carl Turner, said to be the "mastermind" of the arson scheme, grew up in his grandparents' home and attended church regularly until the last year when his attendance became erratic, for the first time in his life.

"This is not his character. He was raised to be a good Christian," his grandmother, Agnes Turner said. "Our house is full of crosses and pictures of Jesus, our savior," she added.

Looking back, relatives and acquaintances note several signs that Turner, described by many as a bright student and an avid reader in high school, was rebelling against the strict Christian upbringing by his grandparents.

Begley, the suspected "follower" of his lifelong friend, meanwhile, seemed to have become disenchanted with religion after his mother died of a heart disease on Christmas Day two years ago. He was also unemployed, with no prospects for work.

Begley's late mother had been extremely devout and had operated the nursery at the First Baptist Church for many years. His father, also deceased, had been a carpenter.

"Brent was always a quiet, shy kid," a next-door neighbor said. "Carl was more outgoing, more of a personality, always the prankster—and very, very intelligent. I always thought he had a little bit of the devil in him."

On his Facebook page, Turner said he was a fan of bonfires and listed his religion as "anti-Christian." He also posted a quote from the philosopher Friedrich Nietzsche that said remorse for wrongdoing was useless: "Never give way to remorse, but immediately say to yourself, that would merely mean adding a second stupidity to the first."

CHAPTER
43

Waiting in the green room, Dawson Rask looked down at the cover of his latest book as he sipped a cup of tea. He listened to the banal voice of Jim Mayer, the radio host. *The Chat* was a popular talk show that was carried by stations all over Australia. It was, he was assured, quite a coup to be booked on the show.

The show concept built upon each previous segment to be inclusive of all topics. It was an interactive show in which listeners responded by phone and via email.

"Our next guest is the American author, Dawson Alexander Rask," Dawson heard Mayer say. "Have you read any of his books?"

"I'm sorry to say that I have not," the guest replied. "Though I have certainly heard of him, and he does seem to be quite popular now."

"Yes, doesn't he?" Mayer replied.

"Mr. Rask?" an attractive young female assistant said, stepping into the green room. "You will be on when we come back after the break."

"Thank you," Dawson said. He followed her into the broadcast room. Here, there was an L-shaped desk, over which hung two enormous microphones. Dawson wondered why the radio stations couldn't just use the lavalier mikes like they did in TV studios, but figured that perhaps the large microphones were as much for symbolism as they were for operation. After all, radio was entirely acoustic.

Mayer was tall and slender, with very black hair and a black Vandyke beard. His face was ruddy, and the skin was drawn tightly over his cheekbones. He reminded Dawson of the old character actor, John Carradine, and except for the Australian accent, his voice was similar.

Mayer had a computer monitor in front of him, as well as microphone control switches. He didn't look up as the production assistant helped Dawson into his chair, then handed him a headset. He could hear announcements in the headset.

". . . at Mercedes, Melbourne. Politics, sports, the arts, all on the 3WA3 station. And now, back to *The Chat* with your host, Jim Mayer."

"My guest for this segment is American author Dawson Alexander Rask. Welcome to the show, Mr. Rask."

"Thank you. And thank you for allowing me this opportunity to visit with your listeners."

"Six million," Mayer said.

"I beg your pardon?"

"My listeners," Mayer said. "Six million, the largest number in this time slot in Australia."

"That's quite impressive," Dawson replied, not certain where Mayer was going with this.

"So you can see that, with this many listeners, I have an obligation to keep the standards of this show very high."

"I'm sure you do."

"How do you rate yourself as a writer, Mr. Rask?"

"I beg your pardon?"

"Would you compare yourself with someone like John Cheever, Toni Morrison, Cormac McCarthy, for example?"

"I'm not sure what you are getting at, Mr. Mayer. The writers you just named have all won the Pulitzer Prize for fiction. I have not."

"No, you haven't, Mr. Rask. Nor are you ever likely to."

"I wasn't aware than one had to be a Pulitzer Prize winner to be a guest on your show," Dawson said.

"Mr. Rask—I have to tell you, in all candor, that I see your type of writing as being nothing more than drivel."

Dawson stared across the L-shaped table at the radio host, and at the smug, *I gotcha* look on his skeletal face. Was this guy for real? All right, maybe he wasn't Shakespeare or Twain, or even Hemingway. He knew that he could write well and tell a damn good story, and what else did a novelist owe his reader?

He was about to walk out of the broadcast room when it happened again. Disconnected words from the posters in the room, including a movie ad for *The Chronicles of Narnia*, from CD covers, even memos, but in a non-obvious way—everything around him started flying through the air toward him: words and letters that spelled the name of the famous author C. S. Lewis. He felt as if he should duck. His hands got clammy, and he felt nauseous without understanding exactly why.

What did he have for dinner last night? He had to think for a minute before he recalled. He had prawns, huge, broiled prawns. He knew that sometimes people reacted badly to shellfish, but nothing like that had ever happened to him before.

Was he having a reaction now? Something was definitely happening.

"No response, Mr. Rask? You have come to Australia, to my radio show in particular, so you can pimp your book. The least you can do is carry on a conversation with me. That is what 'chat' means, you know."

"You seem to be doing a pretty good job of carrying on a conversation with yourself," Dawson said, trying to control the anger welling up inside.

"This is Jim Mayer, and you are listening to *The Chat*," Mayer said softly—caressingly almost, it seemed to Dawson, as if he were making love to the microphone. "The American popular author Mr. Dawson Alexander Rask is my guest, and I have been trying—without success, I hasten to add—to get some sort of vocal response from him. You do speak English in America, do you not?"

"We do."

"Ah, good, then we can communicate. Mr. Rask, and again, I mean no disrespect to you, as you have made a fine living at writing bubblegum fiction . . . but what is the point?"

"Mr. Mayer, is it?"

"I'm sure you know my name by now."

"How can I put this in a more literary, erudite manner? I'm going to use a word once made famous by Norman Mailer. Go fug yourself!"

"We'll be back right after this message," Mayer said quickly; then he killed both his microphone and Dawson's. He looked across the desk at Dawson as he was taking off his headset. There was not one sound on his headset, since this obviously was not a programmed break. Through the plate glass window that opened onto the control room, he could see that the producers were scrambling to fill the dead air.

Dawson had the irrational thought that Mayer might take a punch at him, but since he had Mayer by at least forty pounds and three inches, none of it fat, he knew that wasn't going to happen.

"Have you read any of my books, Mr. Mayer?" Dawson asked.

"No, why in Heaven's name would I want to?"

"I take it, then, that you aren't one of my fans. I'll just put you down as undecided."

No, sir. At least, it's not a place that I know of. And if it's a person,
n't think I would be able to tell you that. But I have an iPhone.
ld you like me to look it up, see if there is such a person, or place?"

No, that's okay, I was just wondering. Oh, earlier when we driving to
station, back a few blocks before we got there, I noticed a large statue
lion. What is that for, do you know?"

A large statue of a lion?" The driver shook his head. "No, sir, we didn't
a lion statue. But there is one on Spring Street, if you would like to see
was I believe a gift of some sort from China, I think. Anyway, it is in
of Tinian Garden. It is at the beginning to our Chinatown."

You had to have seen the lion," Dawson said, exasperated by the
r's response. "How could you miss it? It was huge!"

Mr. Rask, we didn't pass any lion," the driver repeated. "I been liv-
ere all my life, and the only lion we have is the one I just told you
t down at Chinatown. Would you like me to drive you by there on
ay to the TV station? It's not that much of a detour, and we've got
"

No," Dawson said, speaking more harshly than he intended. He soft-
the tone of his voice. "No, thank you. That's all right, just go on to the
tation."

es, sir," the driver said.

ot only was Dawson confused, but he was beginning to get a little
ened, too. He was absolutely certain that he'd seen a large oversized
sculpture of a lion. And not just any ordinary sculpture but an ani-
sculpture. But the driver insisted that there was no lion there.
as he becoming unhinged? Schizophrenic? He closed his eyes in the
of the car and just breathed deeply. What would his character Matt
hews do?

rst of all, Matt would not be frightened. He would be calm and me-
cal. He would go over all details of the situation and take stock of
hat was happening.

s, that was it. Be calm and methodical.

wson took out his ballpoint pen and the sheet of paper that gave
is schedule. Punching the point out of the pen, he began to write
and isolate all the images and words that he could remember.
was just finishing when he felt the car turn off the street and into
e.

ere we are, Mr. Rask. I'll be waiting here in the car for you."

hank you."

When Dawson returned to the control room, he was met by the same
attractive young woman who had led him into the broadcast booth. To
his surprise, she had a broad smile on her face.

"You were wonderful!" she said.

"I don't think Mr. Mayer thinks so," Dawson said.

"No, but his listeners do. The telephone lines are all lit up, email is flying in, and they are all on your side. I am, too, by the way, and I want to
apologize to you for the way he acted. Please don't think that we are all
like that."

Dawson smiled back at her. "I'd rather think everyone is like you," he
said.

CHAPTER
44

As Dawson walked through the lobby of the station, there were at least three television monitors glowing in brilliant HD color. Each one was on a different channel, and breaking news of the Viva Domingo slayings scrolled across the bottom of every broadcast and cable network, including one showing Dave Hampton's broadcast.

He caught snatches of news—another Viva Domingo murder in Ireland, Hampton speaking of dark matter, gossip about Charlene St. John collapsing at a seminar. Local accidents. A burning building. He could hear every one of the programs, and the words flying at him were dizzying and mystifying, this time with pictures and extreme close-ups of talking heads. A smiling woman holding up some detergent . . .

"Look for the logo, a big C," the woman holding the detergent said.

"Of course, there is a rather sweeping S-curve just before you get there," one of the talking heads was saying.

"The burning warehouse is on *Lewis* Street," a voice over the picture of the fire said in an excited voice.

Now the words were repeated so that they stood out.

"C."

"S."

"Lewis."

"C. S. Lewis."

What was this? Why was he getting these bits and pieces about C. S. Lewis?

Dawson missed a step, fell, and landed facedown. When he looked up, he saw a delivery truck with the letters cs painted on the side. The driver, who was signing in, was wearing a name tag that read LEWIS.

"Are you all right, sir?" the station security guar[d]
stood up again.

"Yes, yes." Embarrassed and bruised, Dawson star[ted]

The publicist came toward him. She was a well [put-together woman]
in her forties with an air of efficiency about her. "You[r interview is at]
Channel Ten," she said. "The driver knows the way, b[ut]
are you up to it? You seem distracted."

"I'm fine," Dawson said.

"Perry Landers."

"What? What did you say?" Dawson asked, almost [shouting]

"I said I will meet you there," the publicist said, co[ncerned at his]
strange reaction. "Listen, are you sure you are all righ[t?]

"Yes, yes, I'm fine." He felt impatient and distract[ed, not wanting]
to offend someone who was trying to help him.

"All right, if you say so." The publicist gave him one [last look and]
moved quickly to her car, a silver Porsche. By the time [he and the driver got]
their car started, the publicist had already pulled int[o traffic,]
maneuvering her nimble little sports car quickly thro[ugh the cars. She]
would be there minutes ahead of him.

"Perry Landers?" the driver asked. Except this tim[e the driver]
hadn't said a word, because he could see the driver's [mouth was closed—]
he was checking the traffic prior to pulling away fro[m the curb.]

He hadn't said the words earlier, either, nor had the [publicist. Wherever]
the words came from, it was playing over and over in [his head, an ag-]
gravating tune that would sometimes get stuck in [his head, repeating]
repeatedly as if in some kind of exasperating comic[—like Whoopi]
Goldberg in *Ghost*, when she was running around th[e apartment]
away from the ever-present spirit—except in this case, [the ghost]
was not "Sam Wheat," but "Perry Landers."

Dawson Rask was caught in just such a loop, but it [was so aggrav-]
ating, it was verging on madness. Dawson had exper[ienced times]
where he felt dizzy, but never had he heard voices in [his head. He]
hadn't read his work, he knew C. S. Lewis's name—[but what did it have]
to do with Dawson Rask?

"Excuse me," Dawson said to the driver.

"Yes, sir?"

"Is there a person or a place called 'Perry Lander[s'?]
Does that mean anything to you?"

"I'm sorry I couldn't help you with that Perry Landers thing," he said. "That's all right."

The driver got out of the car then hurried around to open the door for him. He saw the little Porsche parked in front of them, and the publicist came back to meet him.

"We will try not to curse out the hosts of this show, won't we, Mr. Rask?" she chastised.

"I will make a concerted effort," he replied with a smile.

The show was *The Circle*, which very much reminded Dawson of an American talk show, *The View*.

It started with what could have been an awkward moment, when one of the women said, "Mr. Rask, I do hope that you are more comfortable with us than you were with Mr. Mayer. I wouldn't want to be told to—uh—well, do what you told Jim Mayer."

"I'm sorry about that," Dawson said.

"Don't be," one of the other women said. "Do you have any idea how much I would like to tell him the same thing? And I'm not the only one—I'm sure that half of Australia would like to as well."

"Bully for you," another woman said, and their laughter made him feel quite welcome.

It helped that all the women on the show had read not only this book, but his previous two novels as well. And they were quick to tell him that they were all fans of his writing.

This was such a change, and such a relief, not only from his previous show this morning, but many other shows that he had done, that he was able to relax and actually discuss his book with them.

The questions were rapid fire and interesting. Better than that, they were germane to the story. Dawson was a seasoned pro by now, having done the media rounds over the last few years, but he was very impressed by the chemistry the ladies of *The Circle* had. They laughed and joked throughout the show and evidenced a great respect for each other's energy and intelligence, as well as Dawson's writing talent.

Chrissy Swan was young, with cobalt blue eyes and a vivacious personality. She was doing the interview for his segment, with cohosts Umi and Giorgi listening to cues coming in from their earbuds.

Dawson had just launched into an explanation of his motivation for *The Moses Mosaic*, when he realized something was wrong. All the women's faces reflected shock, horror, and sorrow.

He hesitated a moment in his response to the question, and Chrissy held out her hand as if asking him to be quiet for a moment. The others looked at her.

There was breaking news coming into the studio that would forever change the world.

Suddenly, the interview was terminated, and Dawson not only understood, he was glad. This was no time to be talking about a novel. Returning to his hotel room, he spent the rest of the morning watching the coverage and feeling a sense of helplessness and vulnerability. He couldn't help but remember the events of 9/11 and his last telephone conversation with Mary Beth.

Part
·TWO·

TWO

CHAPTER
45

At Parkland Hospital in Dallas, Texas, John F. Kennedy, the 35th President of the United States, was pronounced dead at 1 P.M. on November 22, 1963. At that exact moment, Marcus L. Jackson was born to a black mother and white father at the University of Chicago Medical Center on the city's South Side. Jackson's mother was a schoolteacher, and his father a policeman.

Marcus had gotten his first indoctrination to how his life was different from those of his friends when he was still in grade school. Because of his mixed heritage, he literally saw no difference in skin color. Then one day as he was on the playground with two of his white friends, the father of one of them came over and pulled his son away.

"Can't you find some white kids to play with?" the father asked his son. Then he turned to Marcus. "You would be better off to play with your own kind," he said.

Later that evening, Marcus asked his father what his "own kind" meant.

"What do you mean?" Lieutenant Matt Jackson asked.

"I was playing with Terry and his father came and took Terry away, then told me I should play with my own kind. What's that?"

"Romulans are not your own kind. Vulcans are not your own kind."

Marcus laughed. "Those aren't real. Those are people from other galaxies on *Star Trek*."

"Oh, well then, you aren't likely to run into any of them then, are you?"

"No."

"That leaves everybody else," Lieutenant Jackson said. "And everybody else *is* your own kind."

Matt Jackson's definition of who was his own kind resonated with

Marcus, and as he grew older he moved with equal ease among white and black classmates.

By the time Marcus was a sophomore he was a starting offensive lineman for his high school football team, and when he was a junior, he made All-Conference.

Then, one week before school was out for the summer of his junior year, he stepped down from the school bus and saw three police cars in front of his house. Because his father was a lieutenant in the police department, it wasn't unusual to see a police car in front of his house from time to time. He had even seen two cars there on occasion, but he had never seen three cars.

Marcus ran to the house, then burst in through the front door. "Mom!" he shouted.

His mother sat on the sofa, crying. Sergeant Golda Bernstein was sitting beside his mother, holding her hand. In addition, there were at least two more officers, including a captain and the police chaplain.

"Mom, what is it? What happened? Where is Dad?"

"Your father was a hero, son," Captain Ken Watson said.

Marcus still had the front page of the *Chicago Tribune* that told about his father.

CHICAGO POLICE OFFICER KILLED
IN LINE OF DUTY

Hunting a violent career criminal wanted for murder, Chicago police detectives knocked on the door of a South Side apartment building Thursday morning. When the man's mother let them in, the police saw that there were two small children present in the room.

Lieutenant Jackson asked if Corey Draper was present, but before his mother could answer, Corey Draper suddenly appeared from another room with his pistol blazing at point-blank range.

Realizing the danger the children were in, Lieutenant Matthew Jackson threw himself in front of them, taking three bullets as he did so. He returned fire and with one, well placed shot killed Draper. The other officers on the scene attempted to give emergency medical treatment to Lieutenant Jackson, but he died before the ambulance arrived.

Lieutenant Jackson's name has been submitted for the

Carter Harrison Award, the Chicago Police Department's
highest award for bravery.

When he graduated from high school, Jackson received an appointment
to West Point, graduating with the class of 1985. While at the Academy,
he played football, an offensive lineman who, as a pulling guard, helped
the Army's Wishbone attack achieve a record of eight wins, three losses,
and one tie, including beating Navy 28-11 in the 1984 classic.

Not bad for a kid from a "mixed" background on the South Side . . .

By 2006, as a Lieutenant Colonel, Jackson was serving as an infantry
battalion commander in Iraq.

·Saba al Bor, Iraq·

Looks like we've got something here, Colonel," Sergeant Steve Hoeler
said as he looked through the thermal sight of the Long Range Ac-
quisition System that was mounted on the command Humvee.

"What do you have?" Colonel Jackson asked.

"I've got six targets with weapons," Sergeant Hoeler answered.

It was pitch dark and the insurgents, dressed in black and blending
into the night, thought they were safe. But thermal imaging enabled the
Americans to see them as clearly as if they were standing in the middle of
the street in broad daylight.

"Paint the target and call in the fire mission, Sergeant," Colonel Jackson ordered.

"Yes, sir."

Less than a minute later, a half-dozen loud booms rattled the neighborhood as great balls of flame erupted at the target building. The flame
was followed by a huge, billowing cloud of smoke and dust.

Jackson almost felt sorry for the insurgents who had just died. They
died from misguided zeal and ignorance. They were unable to even imagine a technology that could not only find them in the dark but could also
bring death and destruction down from the sky without warning.

The next morning Colonel Jackson perched on an overturned bucket
behind a free-standing wall at the battalion command post. At the moment he was eating MREs and staring at images on a TV monitor, the
images being projected from an unmanned aerial vehicle that was circling, unchallenged, over the city. A gray-painted Ford Expedition
marked with the word "Press" on each door drove up behind him.

The two men who got out were both wearing sleeve flashes that identified them as TV reporters. One carried a camera. The other man Jackson recognized.

"I'm looking for the CO," the reporter announced.

"I'm Colonel Jackson," Jackson said without interrupting his eating.

"Colonel, I'm John Corrigan with Satellite World News." Corrigan was somewhat shorter than average, with dark hair, dark eyes, and a deeply tanned face. "I came here to be imbedded with your battalion. I already have authorization from the division commanding general."

"All right," Jackson said abruptly, standing up and discarding the residue of his breakfast. "What do you say, Captain Lindell? Are you ready?"

"Battalion strength, sir?"

"No, one company only. Get Captain Crawford up here."

A moment later Captain Charley Crawford, CO of Charley Company showed up at the command post.

"What's up, Colonel?" Crawford said.

"We're going to do a company strength reconnaissance. You take the number two spot, Charley. I'll take the lead," Jackson said.

"Yes, sir."

"And, take these august members of the press with you," he said.

Five minutes later Colonel Jackson saw a stream of smoke coming toward them from the tower of a mosque. A rocket-propelled grenade passed over his Humvee and slammed into Captain Crawford's vehicle, just behind him. The powerful blast ripped into the Charley Company CO's Humvee sending up a flash of fire and billowing cloud of smoke.

When Colonel Jackson looked back, he saw Captain Crawford's gunner hanging face down on the gun ring in the burning Humvee. The impact of the grenade had not only set fire to the Humvee, it also caused it to turn broadside across the road, effectively blocking off all the vehicles behind it.

Colonel Jackson ran toward the fallen soldier and saw that he had been hit between the eyes. His body lay motionless on the street. Jackson then ran to the burning Humvee. Captain Crawford was still alive, but it was obvious he couldn't move on his own, because his left leg was badly lacerated.

Captain Crawford looked at Jackson and tried to speak, but though his lips moved, nothing came from his mouth.

"Don't try to speak, Charley. I'm going to get you out of there," Colonel Jackson said.

"No," Crawford said, weakly. "Go, while you can."

"At ease, Charley, and that's an order," Colonel Jackson said as he took the belt off the dead driver then put it around Crawford's left leg. He cinched it up as tight as he could, so he could use it as a tourniquet.

Then he pulled Crawford from his seat, and with the Captain draped across his shoulder, started running back up the street. Bullets whizzed and popped by him as he ran, many of them hitting the pavement close to him, then whining as they ricocheted away.

"Come on! Hurry, hurry!" one of the men from the edge shouted, as Jackson started back.

"Damn! Look at him go! Who would've thought the old man could run like that?"

"Well, he played football at West Point."

Almost as if he had no weight at all to deal with, Colonel Jackson dashed back through the machine gun fire until he was finally out of the kill zone. Then, on the sidewalk and out of the line of fire from the mosque, he lay Captain Crawford down as the medic came over to take a look at him.

"Let's get a med evac for Captain Crawford."

Ten minutes later they heard the distinctive sound of an Abrams tank, the growl of the engine, the clatter of track on pavement, and the squeaking of the track wheels. The tank pushed through the burning Humvee. Captain Lindell was on the radio with the tank driver.

"What have you got for us?" the tank commander asked.

"Colonel, he wants to know his target," Lindell said.

"Tell him it's the mosque," Colonel Jackson replied.

Captain Lindell repeated the order.

"I'm going to need some authority higher than a company commander to do that," the tank commander replied.

"Colonel, he wants higher authorization," Captain Lindell said.

"Give me the horn," Colonel Jackson said. "Who am I talking to?" he asked.

"This is Vexation."

"Well, Vexation, this is Turtle Six. Do you copy that? Turtle Six."

Six denoted commanding officer, and Turtle was the call sign for the battalion.

"Roger, Turtle Six. I understand you are personally authorizing this mission?" Vexation said.

Several minutes later, a Blackhawk medical evacuation helicopter landed in the square in front of the mosque. Colonel Jackson was there, holding Captain Crawford's hand as he was loaded onto the aircraft.

"You take damn good care of him," Colonel Jackson said to the flight medic. "Do you hear me, soldier? You take good care of him."

"Colonel, I take good care of all my boys," the flight medic, a specialist, said.

"I know you do, son. God bless you," Colonel Jackson said.

At a court-martial back in Fort Benning, Georgia, Colonel Jackson was found not guilty on all charges of conduct unbecoming and assault on the insurgents in the mosque—but he was strongly advised by his superiors to submit his retirement papers.

"Even though you were found innocent—this court-martial will be a permanent part of your file and future promotions, as well as command assignments, will be affected," Jackson's commanding general told him.

Jackson agreed, and he submitted his papers for retirement.

Marcus Jackson's wife, Win, did what she could to help him through the transition. Her real name was Ngyuen, but she changed it so that her name was spelled just the way it was pronounced. Win's father had been a colonel in the South Vietnamese Army. After the fall of Saigon, he was sent to a "re-education" camp, but escaped three years later, then organized a group to leave Vietnam by sea. Win was nine years old when she became one of the "boat people."

Marcus and Win were married in 1990, and after almost giving up hope of ever having a child, ten years later, in 2000, their son, Marcus Jr., was born.

They moved to Savannah, Georgia, after Jackson got out of the army, and for the first six months he augmented his retirement pay by making speeches around the country. He was a gifted speaker, and despite the attacks on him from a sensationalizing press, a popularity poll taken by CNN showed that 83% of Americans approved of what he had done in Iraq. His popularity grew until one morning three people showed up at his house and asked him to run for the U.S. Senate. Running on a campaign of, "Doing what it takes to get the job done," Marcus L. Jackson became the first black senator from the state of Georgia since Reconstruction.

Four years later he ran for and was elected President of the United States.

Then time turned once more on its eternal wheel . . .

M r. President . . . how are you feeling, sir?"
POTUS opened his eyes slowly and tried to focus, but the lights in the room seemed overly bright and somewhat painful.

"I was tackled, pinned down. . . ." He remembered a more grotesque pain that seemed never to end. Then nothing. Then this. What *was* this?

"I might feel better if you could turn down the lights just a bit. I think I might be having a migraine. Or—maybe it is something else. I have a feeling it was something more, something worse than a migraine, but I don't know what it is. I also have no idea where I am, and worse, I don't even know when or how I got here."

"Sir. I need you to just lie still." The voice was still disembodied, and had a somewhat metallic quality to it, as if coming from a speaker.

"You need me to lie still? Who are you? Where are you?"

"I'm right here, sir. Please stay as still as you can. You were shot."

"Shot? My wife, my son? Where are they? Are they all right?"

"Your family is safe and fine. They were proceeding to another part of the auditorium when it happened, and they were evacuated swiftly from the premises. There was only one casualty."

"Good. Did they get the person who shot me?"

"Yes, sir . . . they did. He got a few rounds off before Secret Service brought him down."

"Who was he?"

"His name was Lee Timothy. He was a nobody, an antiwar protester who somehow managed to be on the honor guard detail. It seems he lost his father and two brothers in the line of duty in the Middle East and Africa."

"Then he wasn't a nobody," POTUS said. "He was an American who has paid a great price for our freedom. I know how painful that must have been for him. But I am happy to hear you report there were no casualities."

"But there was a casualty. One casualty, as I said before."

"Dammit! Please tell me it wasn't Freddy! He must have told me a hundred times that nothing would happen to me on his watch . . . that he would take a bullet for me if he had to. Was it Freddy?"

"No, it was not."

"Who, then?"

"Sir. It was you."

"Me?"

"Yes, sir."

"How badly am I hurt?"

"You haven't figured it out yet?"

"No. I don't feel any particular pain." POTUS made a quick pass over his body with his hands. "I can't find any wounds."

"In truth, sir, you can't even find your body."

"What? That's a strange thing to say."

"Think about it."

The person speaking to him was standing right over him, looking down at him.

"Damn. Martin Sheen!"

"I beg your pardon, sir?"

"You look exactly like Martin Sheen. He's one of my all-time favorite actors. He played the President on TV."

"I look exactly like you want me to look."

"Really? That's a strange comment. And this is one strange debrief. What am I doing here? And where is *here*?"

Whoever it was that had been talking to him disappeared as memories of the event began coming back. He remembered now, exiting the car and starting through the corridor provided by the honor guard, returning their salutes. He could see the men, from eighty-six-year-old Clyde Barnes, the World War II vet (how did he know Clyde Barnes's name—and how did he know that Sergeant Barnes had landed on D-Day?), to twenty-one-year-old Logan McMurtry, who had been to Afghanistan twice (and how did he know that?). He couldn't remember meeting either of them.

Then he remembered seeing Lee Timothy, who was second from the far end on the left side. He brought his M1 rifle from the present arms position to a firing position. He fired twice, and POTUS could clearly remember the .30-caliber bullets going into his chest. He had not worn his bulletproof vest. He hated the damn things.

Wait a minute. If the bullets hit me in the chest, why am I not wounded?

Again he ran his hands over his chest, but this time, he wasn't sure he felt anything at all, including his chest. What was it the man who sounded like a movie star—he couldn't place exactly which one—had said to him? That he couldn't even find his body?

Wait a minute. If I am the casualty, then that clearly means that I am— what? Injured? Dead? Is that possible? Am I dead!

Wow! I thought you didn't feel anything when you were dead. But that's not true. Dead feels like a headache. And a powerful one, at that. Have I been shot in the head? I will need some heavenly Advil ASAP!

POTUS sat up and started to look around, but everywhere he looked, all he saw were rays and shafts of light around him like swords from the sky.

Hmmmm. Sky? Does here—Heaven—the hereafter—even have a sky? Am I in the sky? I have a lot of questions for a dead guy. As soon as my adviser returns, I am going—

"Yes?" Without even a millisecond passing after he had this thought his guide was standing there again.

"You don't look like Martin Sheen anymore."

"Who do I look like now?"

"You don't look like anything. At least, nothing that I can describe. Are you an angel? Are you a ghost? What do I call you?"

"Call me IRA."

"IRA?"

"Yes. *I-R-A*. Intellectual Research Adviser. I appeared to you in the form that you would find acceptable. You would expect a senior member of the Secret Service detail to be with you, so I assumed the role. You are the one who projected the Martin Sheen image on me. You have many questions, I know—and I will answer some of them immediately, and others not quite yet. But there is much work to do."

"Work? I have work to do here?"

"Absolutely. What do you think happens when you die? You think it's all milk and honey from now on? Well, that, goddamn it, isn't going to happen." IRA winced. "Oops, sorry, sir! Not you, sir," he said to POTUS.

"The Big Boss, sir. I mean the Creator. He asks that the name not be used in vain."

"So I've always heard," POTUS said.

"Right. All right, let me try this again. When you die, you don't get a harp, you don't get a halo, and you don't get the universal book of knowledge. You've always heard that dying is a natural part of life, haven't you?"

"I've heard that, yes."

"It's true. And that means that, even after you die, you still have to work at being you."

"IRA, are you telling me that I am going to run the United States of America from the afterlife?"

"Not exactly. You will have a little bit of help. In fact, you will have quite a bit of help. Come with me to the Hall of Governing Wisdom."

There was a flash of light. Or was there really a flash of light? Did POTUS just imagine it? For that matter, was he imagining all of this?

He found himself walking—yes, walking, not gliding—down a great, wide hall with floors of glistening marble, flanked on either side by beautiful Corinthian columns. POTUS had never seen anything close to this; even Saddam Hussein's most elaborate palaces seemed like chicken coops compared to this. He wished he could call Steven Spielberg or George Lucas to make a special effects film of the place, but even that would not be able to capture the beauty all around him. . . .

Without consciously walking toward them, POTUS found himself standing beside one of the columns. Was he standing? When he reached out to touch one of the columns, he perceived no physical denseness to it. Yet this column, and all the other columns, had shape and structure. And something else. They seemed to vibrate, and to give off a beautiful musical chord, like a bridge written by Bach, or Beethoven, or Vivaldi.

"These columns aren't really here, are they?" POTUS asked.

"They are here because you put them here. Everything here is thought and energy."

"Wait a minute. Are you telling me I know enough about architectural design to imagine something like this?"

"Not exactly."

"IRA, I haven't been this confused by something someone is supposed to be teaching me since my first week of calculus in the Academy. You aren't making, if you will excuse the language, a hell of a lot of sense."

"I'll try to do better," IRA said. "Everything here has shape and design, and there is a grand architecture for all the archetypes."

"Right," POTUS said, the expression in his voice clearly showing that he still had no idea what IRA was talking about. It would take him a while to absorb all that was happening. He felt rushed, pushed, propelled—but to what end? He could not even guess.

"Come, they are gathering now."

"They? Who are they?"

"To put it in a form you can understand, I'll say that they are the Council of Elders. Think Parliament, or your Congress."

"Ahh, so there is some structure to this place."

"Yes. But you cannot contribute just yet. They will be expecting you when you are ready—but for now, all you can do—all you will do, is observe."

The members of the Council, men and women, were sitting at a great round table. They were meeting in a room that had textured white wainscoting halfway up the walls, then marble above. An unbelievably large chandelier hung over the table. All the men had silver hair and were dignified looking, the women had brindled hair and possessed an aura of beauty. There was an appropriate racial mixture to the group, and even as POTUS looked at them, he realized that he wasn't "seeing" them at all.

This room, the chandelier, the table, and the members of the council had all been created in his own mind. Somehow, he understood that, that didn't mean they weren't there. They were *there;* he just needed a frame of reference for them, and his mind had created that frame of reference.

Slowly—all too slowly from POTUS's perspective—he was learning and experiencing some amazing things. How had all this come into existence? It wasn't all just in his mind, though his mind—his soul, really—was forming "sights" and "sounds" to fill his consciousness with images and ideas. It was all still very foreign to him, yet somehow familiar . . . he wondered whether this was what *eternity* meant: Experiences and images that were always and everywhere present, the same yet constantly changing, always had been and always would be. And he had been invited to step into the stream of eternal consciousness at this time—as measured in earthly time, that is—and for all time. This was his new home, he realized, and he was being called upon to make new choices, each and every moment of his new existence. When would it end? Probably never, he thought. Nor did he want it to.

CHAPTER
47

There was a barely perceptible and unintelligible murmur among the Council members; then Mr. Pennington held up his finger to call for attention.

Mr. Pennington?

Suddenly he was no longer POTUS; he was six-year-old Marcus Jackson on the way home from school on Chicago's South Side when three older and much larger white boys stepped out in front of him.

"Where are you going, colored boy?" one of them taunted.

"I'm going home."

"Not before you shine my shoes—boy." He stuck his foot out and the other two boys laughed.

Young Marcus did nothing.

"Shine my shoes, or we're goin' hurt you, bad."

Marcus got down on one knee, and with a broad smile, the bully lifted his foot. He took the bully's foot, then jerked it up quickly, throwing the bully on his back. The other two boys attacked him then, but like an avenging angel, a gray-haired white man who lived on the corner was on them. He pulled the two bullies off the Marcus, then helped him back to his feet. The three bullies ran off.

"That's right, run!" Mr. Pennington said. "Every time you little punks come by my house, you had better run!"

Marcus Jackson was wearing shorts, and Pennington brushed the dirt away from Marcus's knees. "That was a brave thing you did, son," he said. He invited the child in for milk and cookies, and he visited him often after that.

Pennington was a retired army master sergeant who had won the Silver Star in Korea. It was Pennington who persuaded the young man to go to West Point, and ultimately came to stand proudly in the audience with his mother to watch his graduation and commissioning. Captain Jackson was in Germany when Pennington died, but as soon as he returned to the States, he visited Pennington's grave.

But even as POTUS stood there remembering Pennington, he realized that the Governor of the Council was not Pennington, and now he no longer even looked like him.

He looked around and recognized no one. What he did not yet realize was that these Council elders had not been incarnate for centuries . . . so he would have no way of knowing them.

"Ladies and gentlemen of the Council," the Governor said. "We are gathered here today to discuss the territories for which we are responsible. The Dark Forces are gathering in their uniformity, and they are orchestrating the masses to bond and unite against the Light."

Echoes of frustration were heard from the other members of the assembly.

"That's not good."

"We need to do something."

"What can we do? Our options are very limited."

"We have to do something."

"There is very little we can do," the Governor said. "We are bound by the rules of our Divine Creator and Source, and we cannot interfere and actually do things for mankind. We can only interface with them, and inspire them to make more positive choices. How many times do we need to go over this?"

POTUS chuckled. Had the Governor actually said *interface*?

"You do understand, don't you, that this is cognition only, that nobody is actually speaking?" IRA said. "You are creating the language you think you hear, and thus you are responsible for the vocabulary."

"OMG! That's like Doctor Who's Tardis. It translates the alien languages so it all sounds like English. Oh, and how does the Big Guy feel about the OMG reference?" POTUS asked.

"Touché. Well, I didn't vocalize my thought just now, but your interpretation of it was accurate."

The Council had interrupted its conversation during the exchange between POTUS and IRA, and for the moment there was not only no sound, but no motion either. It was as if a hold button had been pushed.

"Do they know we are here?" POTUS asked, nodding toward the Council in freeze-frame.

"We aren't here," IRA said.

"What? Well, if we aren't here, where are we?"

"We are nowhere and everywhere," IRA said. "Think of it as electricity. The electricity is everywhere in the grid, but not until you close a switch is it 'there.' We will be here when we need to be here."

"Fascinating," POTUS said in his best Spock imitation. Now, with his attention returning to the assembly, they resumed their discussion.

One of the other members spoke. "Brothers and sisters, I know that we are all terribly concerned with the planetary shifts that are coming and what will befall humankind. But I agree with the Governor of our Council as he states the rules that we cannot interfere with their destinies."

"The Dark Forces can," another entity said.

"That is because they are fallen energies from the Light and are no longer bound to our treaties and covenants," the Governor said. "They can create chaos and prey on the fears of man, enable their jealousies and torment them to react. They seek out the meek and vulnerable, the emotionally and spiritually void persons, and strike like a rattlesnake."

The next voice was that of one of the female members of the Council. Her voice was soothing and well modulated. "And all of this while we and our forces of Light watch, with only the hope that our inspirational energies will assist mankind in making more positive choices. But obviously, that isn't enough. Something, I don't know what, but something has to be done."

"Something must be done, yes," the Governor said. "Where is IRA? Is he here?"

"I am here, Excellencies of the Council," IRA said. "And I have with me our newest arrival. He is not ready yet, as he just woke up from his second sleep and learned of his humanity."

The Governor of the Council looked over toward POTUS and welcomed him with a nod and warm, energetic gesture. Then the Governor turned his attention back to the council.

"I would like to take a vote of all Council members and suggest that the time has come for us to fall back to the earthly plane to assist our children. We need them to express more strongly our energetic principles so that man may be able to make the right choices. We can provide reminders and gentle nods that they are not alone."

POTUS realized now that the Hall of Governing Wisdom was considerably larger than he had at first perceived, and many more people were present than he had previously thought. The round table of the Council sat on a raised floor in the middle of the great hall, while around the Council all the others sat in concentric circles.

The presence of the others, not as mere spectators, but as participants in the deliberations, reminded POTUS in form, if not in appearance, of the joint sessions of congress when such were assembled. Except this was a room he didn't mind being in—even under the circumstances of death.

The Governor continued:

"We will have but a small window of opportunity to do this, because the veil between their world and ours is diminishing and we will not be able to lower our vibrations. I suggest that dynamic teams be put together. These masters of love and insight will 'fall' down, and their lower vibration waves must work strategically with other human beings in making great changes."

"Do we have a list of the people who will be our voices?"

"All this 'Dark Forces' talk is rather disconcerting," POTUS said. "Tell me, can the Council actually do something to help combat the spiritual terrorism we see today?"

As before, the Council and indeed every representative in the chamber, for POTUS thought of the others as representatives—went into freeze-frame as he and IRA carried on their discussion.

"The Governor and the Council of Elders are attempting to make things better," IRA said.

"But I just heard them say that they can't interfere."

"They can't interfere directly, that is true," IRA said. "But what they can do, and what it is their job to do, is to inspire people who are living on the planet now to make a difference and to consciously abandon evil and darkness. The Council will encourage people to use their free will to choose the Light."

"Can they do it?" POTUS asked.

"I don't know," IRA replied.

"What do you mean you don't know? Aren't you my Intellectual Research Adviser? I thought you knew everything."

"What the Governor and the Council of Elders have set out for themselves is no easy task," IRA said. "Sadly, Heaven will more than likely not succeed because, I regret to tell you, the Dark Forces are flowing in abundance."

"How much power do these Dark Forces have?"

"Their power is considerable."

"But good will always overcome evil, will it not?" POTUS asked.

A sad smile spread across IRA's non-corporeal face, that is, across the face that POTUS was perceiving. He wondered now, why he had ever thought it might be Martin Sheen. IRA didn't look anything at all like Martin Sheen.

"Yes, good triumphs over evil," IRA said. "That was one of the earliest precepts we were able to inculcate in the human experience. An oldie but goodie to be sure. Unfortunately, it is not necessarily true. You heard what the Governor said. They are fallen energies from the Light, which means they have as much power as any angel of good. More, when you consider that they are no longer bound to any code of ethics."

"I spent my entire life believing in the concept of good over evil," POTUS said.

"Ah, yes, your Mr. Pennington."

"You know about Mr. Pennington?"

"I know all there is to know about you. What about your own situation in Iraq? You were certainly representing good when you ordered a counterstrike on those insurgents in the mosque who launched bombs at Charley's Humvee. You saved lives. Yet you were punished for that. Did evil not overturn good?"

"Aha!" POTUS said as if scoring a point in a debate. "But the charges were dismissed. And didn't the American people respond to that—and elect me president?"

"And were you not assassinated?" IRA replied.

"Yes, but . . . I am so confused."

"It is a very natural thing. Since you have not yet divested yourself of all your earthly trappings and involvements, I suppose you are still thinking of your family," IRA said.

"Yes, I am, very much. Is there some way I could see them? I just need to know that they are all right."

"You'll see them at your funeral."

"I'm going to my own funeral?"

"Nearly everyone does. Of course, you don't have to go if you don't want to."

"No, I want to go. How do I do it?"

"You just will yourself there."

"When is the funeral?"

"Yesterday, now, tomorrow, one year ago, one year from now."

"Now, that doesn't make one lick of sense."

"Sure it does, if you realize there is no such thing as time here. At least, not as you are used to it. Now is when you choose now to be. Do you want to go to the funeral now?"

"Yes."

IRA raised his hand, or, he would have raised it if he had a hand. POTUS was beginning to understand that he was constructing the visuals in his own mind, like lifting a needle on a phonograph record and dropping it on a specific song—to put it in old-fashioned terms that PO-TUS as a youngster in the 1960s would understand. "Will yourself there."

CHAPTER
48

Half a million people were watching as the same horse-drawn caisson that had borne the body of JFK, Franklin Roosevelt, and the Unknown Soldier carried the assassinated President's polished bronze casket down Pennsylvania Avenue. Muffled drums and the clacking hooves of the horses pulling the caisson were the only sounds to be heard on Pennsylvania Avenue. Those gathered along either side of the street watched in stunned and saddened silence as the cortège made its way to the Capitol, where the body would lie in state.

POTUS watched the funeral cortège from several different angles, sometimes looking down on it, sometimes from the caisson looking out toward the people paying their respects, and sometimes from the crowd itself, standing next to someone—or assuming the illusion of standing next to someone.

"He was a good man. He was a good president. What's gotten into people that they are so quick to kill, anymore?"

"Killing is the natural order of things," another said. "It thins out the herd and allows only the strong to survive."

From this speaker, POTUS felt a wave of cold, and as he looked at him, it was almost as if he was surrounded by a black cloud. POTUS found that very strange, and he would have to remember to ask IRA about it.

He willed himself to the Rotunda.

In the Rotunda, Win Jackson managed to hold back her tears, as did her son, Marcus Jr. POTUS stood beside them. He leaned over and kissed Win on the cheek and smiled, or imagined himself smiling, when Win reached up to put her fingers on the exact spot he had kissed. He would have to remember that on future visits.

During the public viewing, hundreds of thousands of mourners waited for hours in a line that stretched for four miles, fifteen persons wide, for the opportunity to view the casket. Inside the Rotunda, the closed and flag-draped coffin was guarded at each of its four corners by members of the military.

After the viewing, the body was transported to the National Cathedral, and though there were only one thousand invited guests inside, millions around the world watched the funeral on television. Major General Ken Coats, Chief of Chaplains, conducted the funeral, and Charles Crawford delivered the eulogy.

"The world knew Marcus L. Jackson Sr. in many ways. Many of the world's leaders knew him as a man who was quick to offer support to allies when such support was needed. Other leaders, those who would do harm to the United States, knew him as a fierce enemy who would stand up for the freedom of his country.

"Nations in strife, suffering from floods, hurricanes, earthquakes, fires, and famine, knew Marcus Jackson as a man of compassion, one who reacted quickly to provide assistance where assistance was needed.

"Historians will know him as a black president, an inspiring speaker, and a great motivator. Win knew him as her husband, and Marcus Jr. knew him as his father.

"I come from a slightly different perspective. In the army I knew him as my commanding officer. In my professional life, I knew him as my boss. But on a personal level, I knew him as the closest friend I will ever have, and I know him as the man who braved enemy fire to throw me over his shoulder and save my life."

It was difficult for Charley Crawford to get through the eulogy—he choked up at least three times and had to stop to regain his composure.

Then Charlene St. John sang her most beautiful and heartfelt song: "Someone, Somewhere."

> *Do you see the light*
> *Of all creation: the day, the night?*
> *A universe of peace and love*
> *Of goodness that comes down from above*
> *Take his hand*

And you will understand
That we are one
We are one
We are one

Never had she sung it more beautifully, and never had POTUS heard more beautiful music.

"It is truly the voice of an angel," POTUS said on the Other Side. "And though I have heard this song before, I don't think I ever heard the words, I mean truly heard the words, before now." It was as if the notes didn't just form chords; they created intentions as well. Inspiration held a whole new meaning for him.

Instantaneously, POTUS found himself standing in the private garden of the White House. This memorial was not for the nation, but for his immediate family and close friends. From POTUS's perspective, there was absolutely no time between the public funeral and the private memorial, but POTUS was learning to deal with that. It was here that POTUS felt love in a way that he had never experienced before. Love, joy, and fulfillment were all wrapped up into one feeling, and when he looked at Win, his beautiful wife, he knew immediately that somehow she would be all right and manage to move on. He didn't know how he knew this, but it was something that he just knew.

POTUS and Win had never really discussed a potential future without him in it, with her having to take care of their only child, fifteen-year-old Marcus. He knew that she would be fine financially, and security was a way of life for all of them. He looked at his son and couldn't be more proud. Marcus Jr. was standing way off to one corner of the garden, separated from the others. He was grieving, yes; it showed clearly on his face. But that same face, even as it showed grief, was also showing strength and maturity, more strength and maturity than POTUS ever would have imagined a young teenager could exhibit.

IRA looked over at POTUS and said, "Go ahead."

Go ahead? How did IRA know what he wanted to do?

Then, even as he was thinking that, IRA reminded him that now, everything was thought form, without boundaries, which meant that his thoughts were as audible here, as the spoken word had been in the before life. It was also part of IRA's job to assist.

IRA handed POTUS a TiVo remote. "This is to help you deal with the concept of time," IRA said. "You have to understand that in the ribbon of time, everything that has ever happened is still happening, and that means you can move forward or backwards at will."

"With a TiVo remote control?"

IRA said, "Admittedly, that is a gimmick. But do you remember how I told you that I appeared to you in the form of a secret service agent so you would not freak out? You saw me as the actor Martin Sheen, because that was your frame of reference. This, too, is part of your frame of reference. I have seen the commercials about how you can fast forward through the commercial, rewind, and pause . . . so hit the pause button."

"Hit the pause button? What is that supposed to do?" POTUS asked.

"Why don't you hit it, and find out?"

POTUS hit the pause button and watched the action in front of him freeze as if the world was a large movie screen with 3D HD images that no longer moved. POTUS hit play, and it moved again. He then hit reverse frame and the whole scene shifted. This moment was really starting to feel like *It's a Wonderful Life*, with Jimmy Stewart and his guardian angel standing next to him.

IRA looked at him. "Do you understand the concept now?"

"Yes, I think I do."

"Good. Are you ready?"

"I am."

POTUS realized that he was actually looking forward to it, even to the scene at the end where he would watch himself get shot.

"Once you thoroughly embrace the concept, you won't need the remote. You can go anywhere within your lifetime quite easily; in fact, you will discover that you can go anywhere in the history of the world. And, as I told you, time is a ribbon so everything that has ever happened is still happening. That means you can move forward or backwards at will."

"What about going into the future?" POTUS asked.

"We can proceed forward along the line of probable events based on today's actions, but there is a problem with that, in that the timeline comes to an end in the not-too-distant future."

"You mean they are right? All these crazy 'end-of-the-world kooks,' who spout off the doomsday scenarios, the third secret of Fatima, the Y2K, and the Mayan 2012 conspiracies?"

"You didn't really just call the entire Mayan people crazy, did you, sir?"

"What? You mean the 2012 thing isn't just a kooky idea? It has to be. It's past 2012, and we are still here, aren't we?"

"Yes, and no. Clearly, the date is not 2012, and quite sincerely, we don't know the actual date, because so much depends on the acceleration of the negative tsunami of energy blanketing your world. We can't see the end, as the negative forces want that edge. That is why so many are going back."

"Going back? Wait a minute, you mean reincarnation is real?"

"Sir, oh . . . all these questions . . . it is almost not fair that I am only one packet of conscious energy, and yet they want me to assist one of the greatest minds ever to incarnate."

POTUS felt himself beaming and flattered at IRA's remark. He let himself embrace the ego of IRA's statement. "IRA, are you telling me that I am seen here as one of the greatest minds?"

Suddenly the Governor of the Council of Elders appeared before them. "No," he said in a voice that showed his irritation. "You were seen as one of the greatest minds there, though I'm not sure I know why. Here, you have to participate in your own transition and learning. God has a plan for all of us, and he needs your help."

The Governor was gone as quickly as he had appeared.

"I wish he wouldn't do that!" POTUS said.

"Yes, sir, that is quite annoying to me as well, the way he just pops up like that. Now, where were we? I lost my train of—"

"We were talking about reincarnation," POTUS said.

"No, *you* were talking about reincarnation. Now, please pay attention. There is much to do and I don't have all eternity." IRA laughed then, a cackling, high-pitched, and discordant laugh. "Actually, I do have all eternity, but I would rather not spend it acting as a guide to your Walt Disney Dead World experience. So, may we just focus on your funeral, sir?"

When POTUS didn't respond, IRA heaved a big sigh.

"Hit the button, sir," he said. "Hit the button."

When POTUS returned to the funeral, he focused on his son. Marcus Jr. was holding back his tears and trying to be strong. POTUS thought he was a perfect blend of his mother and himself. Marcus had beautiful eyes with just the suggestion of an epicanthic fold, light brown with gold specks that complemented his light brown skin.

Like his father, young Marcus kept his hair cropped close to his head. POTUS had never allowed it to grow into a full Afro. This was a personal choice that became a professional mandate. It was nice to know that America had come so far as to elect a black man who was married to a Vietnamese woman to the office of President of the United States. Yet, here IRA and his seemingly vast army were ready to march onto Earth to battle the bad guys.

Could it be that this whole thing was no more than a weird hallucinatory dream? Could it be that he wasn't dead at all, that someone had just slipped him something at a cocktail party?

"Sir, would you keep this moving, please?" IRA said irritably. "Having to follow your thoughts has become tedious, almost beyond endurance. Eternity, sir. Eternity?"

Metaphorically "hitting the pause button" on his life remote, everything stopped. POTUS moved closer to Marcus, and as he did so, he could feel his pain. Everything in his being wanted to take the pain away from his son.

"No," IRA said, reading POTUS's emotional response, even before he formulated the thought.

"What would it hurt to assuage his grief?" POTUS asked.

"Do you think there is any emotion without cause or consequence?

Grief is planting seeds in the garden of his life, and it could help inspire him to be great. You will have the opportunity to help him, though."

"How? When?"

"Now," IRA said. With that one word, they were no longer in the garden. Instead, they were in Marcus's bedroom, and Marcus was asleep. This moving back and forth on the ribbon of time no longer surprised POTUS, and it seemed as natural as breathing to have gone within the blink of an eye from a beautiful sunny afternoon to the middle of night. The darkness of the bedroom was illuminated only by the green glowing digits of the clock—*2:23*—and the blue light of the TV satellite box.

"You can communicate with him now," IRA said.

"How?"

"By joining him in his sleep. All you have to do is think about him and it will be like tuning in to a radio frequency."

POTUS found it almost ridiculously easy to do as IRA suggested. He thought of his son, and the next thing he knew he was walking toward the back part of the three-level brick manor house that was their private home in Savannah, Georgia. It was midafternoon, and the lawn had just been cut. The gardens were in full bloom with a myriad of flowers of all sizes and types. They exploded in a profusion of color, their scent perfuming the air.

POTUS heard the bouncing of a basketball on the cement pad that had been poured alongside the house, and he projected himself there in time to see Marcus make a long jump shot, his right arm extended as the ball started its arc, his hand pointing as if willing the ball to get all net. It swished through cleanly.

"A three-pointer," POTUS said. "Impressive."

As he hoped would happen, when the boy turned toward him, POTUS felt an explosion of energy from his son. "Daddeeeeeeeeeee! Is this real? Are you here, or are you a ghost? It doesn't matter, I see you, that makes you real to me. I love you, Daddy. I love you."

"How is your mom doing, son? I miss her so much."

"I guess she's doing okay." It was difficult for the fifteen-year-old to process that he was talking to his dad, let alone answer questions. But he pulled together all his strength and concentration, for he sensed this was a unique moment.

"And how about Charley?"

"Uncle Charley is really sad. Everyone is sad—Mama and me the most, then Uncle Charley. Can I still call him uncle? I mean, I know he isn't my real uncle, but now that you are gone, can I still call him uncle?"

"Yes, of course you can."

"Miss St. John came to sing at your funeral. And the writer that I like? Dawson Rask? He sent me an autographed book."

"You are going to have to be very grown up now, Marcus. You are the man of the house."

"That's what Mama says. Daddy, how is it that we are talking, but there aren't any words being spoken?"

"It is because this is a conversation between our souls."

"Does that mean this isn't real?"

"How does it feel to you?"

"It feels real."

"Then it is real."

"Is it real enough that I can give you a hug?"

POTUS looked over toward IRA, who had been hanging to one side, watching with complete dispassion. IRA nodded yes.

"What are you looking at?" Marcus asked. "Is someone there? Someone that I can't see?"

"Can you see me?"

"Yes."

"That's all that matters. Do you still want the hug?"

POTUS opened his arms and his son came to him, filling his arms like a hand filling a glove. POTUS sensed that the connection between them wasn't actually physical, but the embrace was one of the most powerful feelings he had ever experienced.

Marcus pulled away from him, and when he looked up, POTUS could see tears streaming down his son's cheeks. They were also streaming down POTUS's right arm. That didn't upset him as much as perplex him.

"IRA, how could—?"

IRA interrupted his question. "Later, sir. Be in the moment. We will have to leave soon."

Marcus looked to see whom POTUS was speaking to, but could not see IRA. "There is someone else here, isn't there? Who is here?"

"It doesn't matter. Marcus, I need you to do something for me. I need you to tell your mama that I came to you and that I am okay. I just have some things to take care of, and when I do, I will come back. Can you do that for me, son?"

"Yes, Daddy, I can. Daddy . . . Can I help you? Do you need me?"

"No! Absolutely not!" IRA blurted out.

By now POTUS was beginning to realize that while IRA was his guide, the adviser wasn't his superior. So he responded to his son as he wanted to, without regard to IRA's negativity.

"Marcus, I will always need your help. I need you to tell your mama that I am all right. Remember, I will be with you—and the family— remember what I always told you. When you miss me . . ."

In a ritual they had followed when POTUS was alive, each of them put their hands over their hearts, pointed to each other, then put their hands over their hearts again. By doing this, they were saying that no matter where the other went, their hearts would always be together.

"Tell him you need to go now," IRA said. IRA's voice was completely unmoved.

"Marcus, I need to go now," POTUS said to his son. "I love you."

"I love you, too, Daddy. I love you, and I miss you so much."

In an instant, Marcus was gone. So were the flowers, the lawn, the house, and the beautiful day. POTUS and IRA were in a sort of void, which was something new for Marcus.

"Stop thinking of him," IRA said. "You are creating a confusing conflux of energy."

"IRA, how is it that you are so devoid of compassion?" Marcus asked.

"I have work to do," IRA said. "There is no room for what humans call sentiment. On this side, what you would call the Other Side, there is no attachment to ego."

Did that leave no room for individuality in the spirit realm? Or was ego a burden for human beings on Earth? POTUS had never reflected on this notion before . . . had never been called upon to do so or felt the need within himself. In this place, all kinds of ideas were bombarding him, like questions at a press conference. But he had fewer answers here than he ever did in the White House. In fact, he was equipped with far less knowledge for the situation in which he found himself than he had been since kindergarten. The thought amused him—but just for a brief moment.

CHAPTER
50

Mama G brewed herself a cup of tea, sweetened it with a bit of honey, then sat in her rocking chair and picked up her remote to turn on the TV. She could see the carriage being drawn through the streets, a flag-draped coffin on the back. The crowd was absolutely quiet, the only sound being the muffled drums, the hollow clop of the horses' hooves, and the ring of the steel-rimmed wheels rolling on the pavement. The carriage was being drawn by six white horses with three soldiers mounted on each of the three nigh horses and was flanked by marching members of the military—army, air force, marine corps, and navy. One soldier was leading a saddled but riderless horse with a pair of boots reversed in the stirrups.

"The riderless horse you see behind the caisson is named Sergeant York for the famous hero of the First World War. The same magnificent horse was used for President Ronald Reagan's funeral in 2004," the announcer said in a quiet and somber voice.

The camera moved in for a close-up of the front row of spectators, found an old man with tears sliding down his cheeks, and held that picture for a long moment before moving out to follow the caisson.

Mama G was watching the funeral on television; then the picture, the TV, the room itself faded out, and she found herself watching the tender scene between the president and his son. She watched the entire thing knowing exactly what she was seeing, and not questioning what it was or how she got here.

"We needed him," a voice said. "The world needs him."

"Yes, he was a wonderful man and a fine president. It is a shame that he was assassinated," Mama G answered.

"It was necessary."

Now Mama G was confused.

"What was necessary?"

"It was necessary that he be assassinated. We needed him."

"Are you saying it was all part of the plan that he be assassinated? That this wasn't just some insane act?"

No answer.

Mama G wondered where the universal plans ended and individual actions—good or evil—began.

Whatever psychic, cosmic connection Mama G was enjoying was broken, and once again she found herself sitting in her rocking chair, watching the images of the President's funeral play out on her television screen.

·Europa, Belgium·

He was proud that he was not a native Belgian, but an Austrian. It made him kind of exotic to people in the small town in the far western Flemish region where he had lived for the past ten years. His name was simple, spelled the way he preferred it: Hans Smit. He was a man without a country but with an idea. He would make them all sit up and take notice. Soon.

The children. He would take the children. The parents were corrupt and soft. They had chosen the easy way, but Hans Smit had chosen the *right* way.

On the outside, he smiled and was unfailingly polite.

He worked at a café next door to the bus and train station that saw daily traffic to and from the city and the countryside. Hans stood behind the counter and served coffee and ran the cash register. One day he counted over five hundred transactions. Somebody was certainly making money on this deal—but not him.

Hans heard many languages spoken in the station, including Arabic and African tongues, and he thought it might drive him insane. These strange foreigners and immigrants—so-called minorities—were responsible for the decline in the standards of living in his adopted country. The times called for a leader, a führer to lift the true people to their true position of ultimate superiority over all others.

The true people, who had no children, lived somewhere nearby. Hans did not know where, exactly, but he did know he could hear them speaking, and they spoke to him. They told him he must take the children from their families.

He lived on a minimum wage, occasionally supplemented by small tips. And he slept in a room behind the café and drew pictures incessantly.

The school bus stopped at the café each afternoon, and the driver came in to go to the bathroom. Like clockwork, the driver came into the station for his "pit stop." Hans watched him from behind the counter.

He knew the driver left the keys in the bus because he blabbed about it one day and Hans had overheard him. Now he acted. He ran outside and hopped into the bus. The key was there, in the ignition. He turned it and the bus roared to life.

Hans Smit looked into the mirror to see all the kids in their seats, paying no attention to him. He counted them once, then recounted. There were forty-seven kids on the bus. Hans smiled silently. This was perfect.

He drove toward the river, less than one kilometer outside the town's border. The children began to notice something amiss. They were being driven somewhere they had never been before. They shouted at the new bus driver.

Hans drove on for another few minutes. As he approached the river, he slowed and then shifted the vehicle into neutral. It kept moving. He opened the door and rose from the driver's seat. Timing it to the best of his ability, he steered the bus directly at the river.

With one fluid motion, he jumped out the open door.

He had accomplished his mission: He had delivered the children. Now they would never return to their parents. Hans stood aside and watched the bus and its human contents slowly move closer, then over the edge of the bank.

The yellow and blue school bus bounced once. A second later it had disappeared from view, and a loud splash, followed by a low rumbling sound, indicated that the vehicle had crashed into the river.

Hans Smit walked away. He wouldn't be gone from his workplace for more than a half hour. He would finish up there and close up the café, and then he would return to his small apartment room for the rest of the evening. He had some interesting pictures to draw.

He heard the voice of his master and guide congratulating him on a successful execution of their plan. Whose plan? "Our plan," the now-familiar voice in his head chided him. He felt the presence beside him as well as within him as he walked.

Soon, many others around the world would join Hans and his guide in taking action to fulfill the promise of a new life beyond moral constraints and mere laws. This was but a first step—an important one, yes—by one man to lead the way for others. For millions of others who would hear their own call to action and respond as he had.

A whole new world awaited Hans Smit, promised to him by his guide if he would follow the instructions laid down at the appointed time. That time had come. Hans smiled. He was ready to answer the call.

Marcus Jackson Jr. was sad when his father left him, but he was happy, too—happy that he had been able to see him. He wondered if he should tell his mother about it. His father had told him to tell—to tell her that he was fine. But he hadn't appeared to her, and Marcus didn't know if she would believe it. And if she did believe it, would she be hurt that he came to Marcus, and not to her?

No. He knew she wouldn't feel that. He knew about good and evil, and he had never met anyone with more good in her heart than his mother. He would tell her.

Marcus took one more shot, this time on the real basketball court on the presidential grounds. He came out here after the strange dream he had, partly in an effort to feel closer to his father. He felt a sense of satisfaction as the ball whisked through the net, then started toward the house. Marcus knew that he wouldn't have too many additional chances to play on this court, as he and his mother would soon be moving out in order for the new sitting president and his family to take up residence.

He felt he was being watched, but shook off the paranoia. Soon he would return to school and try to carry on with the rest of his life. He wasn't certain that he wanted to.

He went inside and told his mother he was going out to meet a friend for a cup of hot chocolate at his favorite Starbucks in Georgetown. The Secret Service was notified and, with the First Lady's permission, several agents accompanied the teenager to the coffee shop.

None of them could adequately explain what happened next. They could not know that the Army of Darkness that planned this excursion had forces in place, standing by to create a chaos of dark energy, a negative miasma that covered up a shocking crime perpetrated on their watch.

All they knew was that the President's son was suddenly gone, and it was their fault. . . .

He awoke in total darkness. His senses had been shut down for twelve hours and now were revived as he emerged from a drug-induced coma. He knew immediately that he had been kidnapped and drugged—and he knew without any doubts that he had been abducted by enemies of his late father. Beyond that, he had no clue as to where he was or when and how he had gotten there.

It had happened with a swiftness that nearly scared the life out of him . . .

The men—he assumed they were men, though there had been something not quite human about them—had taken him when he was out of sight of the Secret Service detachment assigned to guard him. After telling his mom he was going to meet a friend, he had gone into a Starbucks coffee shop in Georgetown to grab a hot chocolate. The agent who came inside with him had to go to the bathroom and didn't signal for backup. A big mistake. Or was it?

The moment he had been touched by his kidnappers, he had gone limp and fallen asleep. How that happened, he was never to know. Nor could he figure out how he could have been carried past the Secret Service, either via the front door or back door of the Starbucks.

Within minutes the rest of the world learned that the late President's son had been abducted; meanwhile Marcus himself was in a half-coma, half-dreaming state during which he was convinced he had been put on an airplane for several hours. But where was he now? Who were these people? Why was this happening?

Inside his head, and in his heart, he clearly heard his father's familiar voice. Strange. His father, the President of the United States, had been assassinated less than a week ago . . . Marcus and his mother, the grieving First Lady, had walked through the ceremonies and tributes, the seemingly endless hours of a state funeral being played out before the entire world, when all he and his mother wanted to do was go home and cry. Never had he known the true meaning of loss—not before now. So, as he sat upright and held his throbbing head in his hands, he felt only numbness—and an empty void within.

Yet the *voice* was with him.

And more than that—he felt his dead father's presence in the black room, or wherever he was. Indistinct . . . he could not make out individual words or thoughts, but his heart was full of his father. *How can this be?* He asked the universe in silence.

Marcus had grown up in a supercharged atmosphere of politics and publicity. His parents, however, had protected him to the best of their abilities from the egregious intrusions of the press. They were not perfect parents, but there was a strong bond among the three—a bond of love and trust that had survived two long years of a presidential campaign and three years under the media microscope in the White House. He had not been a perfect kid, but through it all, despite some teenage rebelliousness, he had remained a "good kid." He was proud of his mother and father. Proud to be their son.

A chill descended on Marcus. He opened his eyes as widely as he could—but still he saw nothing. He listened intently, but there was nothing to hear. He realized that he was in a soundproofed room.

At least I'm not handcuffed or tied down, he thought.

His head ached, and he felt tired from the aftereffects of whatever drug he had been given. He was confused; his mind raced. Listen, listen . . . Nothing. The son of the President was alone in total darkness, and he could not know what his fate would be—or if he would live another day.

CHAPTER
52

In the hall, the Governor was speaking to the Council of Elders: "Ladies and gentlemen of the Council, we are gathered here today to discuss the gravity of the decline of the territories for which we are responsible. The Dark Forces are gathering in their uniformity and purpose, and they are orchestrating the behavior of the masses to unite against the Light Energies." The Governor paused as echoes of frustration were heard among the elders who stood or sat before him.

"We are bound by the rules of our divine Creator and Source and cannot interfere and do things *for* mankind, only inspire them to make more positive choices. How many times must I repeat that cardinal principle."

Another voice spoke up: "Brothers and sisters, I know that we are all terribly concerned with the planetary shifts that are coming—that will befall humankind. But must I agree with the Governor of our Council as he reiterates the rules that we cannot interfere with their destinies like the negative tides can?"

The Governor replied, "It is true that, as energies fallen from the Light, our enemies are no longer bound to our treaties and covenants. Yet we are bound and must remain so for all of eternity. To abandon the rules, as you call them, denies our very purpose and reason for existence. Even in times of emergency, such as this."

The Governor paused. "We must discuss the new soul that is among us, a soul that could greatly impact all the souls both here and on the Earthly plane."

"What must we do, Governor? Would you suggest that we stop the evolutionary process of his soul?" the Ambassador, one of the most senior and most trusted elders, asked.

"The longer we allow him to evolve, more the chance that he will choose the dark side."

"What is driving him in this direction?"

"That is an easy enough question to answer," the Governor responded. "He is used to power. He has wielded so much power in 'his' world that he feels a sense of entitlement, and being here, he is being presented with temptations that might undermine the process and progress we are attempting to achieve on the Earth level."

"I fear you are right, Governor," the Ambassador said. "We must monitor him closely and hope for the best. His negative spiral has begun and the evolution away from the Light is growing. We can but put the good in front of him and hope he realizes it in time. But our task will not be easy, not when they have spent so much time together."

"The manipulations and trickery that have been born here should not be tolerated," a female member of the Council said. "I say it should be banished now."

"My fellow members of the Council, the situation is becoming critical. We must all keep our eyes and souls open to learning from this. We can no longer deny the fact that evil has found its way here, here in this place that, for eons, we have considered our sanctuary. And, sad to say, it is spreading like a virus within the very hearts of those here we are choosing to assist and protect."

As IRA and POTUS moved toward the realm of the Spirit World, the sensation of motion, of moving away from one place and to another, was suddenly interrupted.

"Why have we stopped?" POTUS asked.

"I want you to observe this place," IRA said. "Really observe. Take a moment and look at the beauty of all that you can see, hear, and feel."

"Yes, I have seen it," POTUS said. "IRA, you have not told me what this place is. Or where it is. Is this Heaven? Because if it is, I have to tell you that it doesn't quite fit the pattern I had pictured for it."

"Forget all your worldly notions of what or where this place is. Your reason for being here is so I can assist you to once again see that there is a plan and order. And if you attempt to label it anyway, you will hinder your ability to see it.

"Now, turn around, sir."

POTUS turned around as directed, and found himself standing on the marble steps of a huge columned building. It could have been a building in Ancient Greece or modern Washington, D.C. There was a familiarity to it, yet he was certain he had never seen it, or even a picture of it.

"This is the Great Hall of Memory," IRA said. "But before you go inside, I want you to take a long look around and tell me what you see."

POTUS looked around as directed, and saw only the greenest grass and rolling hills, with trees and flowers that vibrated and hummed with color. POTUS was a man of words, noted for the expressiveness of his public speeches, even before he got into politics. He had a knack for choosing powerful words and colorful phrases to elevate his speeches to heights of eloquence that, according to one review, had his words "soaring with the eagles."

But despite his fluency with the language, he knew that there were no words in English, or any language to describe the exotic beauty of this scene.

"It is beautiful," POTUS said, knowing even as he spoke that the words were woefully inadequate.

"Look again," IRA said. "Look beyond the beauty."

POTUS did look again, and as he did so, he opened his heart to see a road develop, the road flanked by more structures as magnificent as the one he was standing before. The new buildings seemed to be edifices of every type of architecture through the history of mankind, including some that had not yet been developed or created. In an instant, POTUS could identify every building and its purpose. He knew that as clearly as if there had been a descriptive sign in front of each one, yet no such signs were in existence.

"It's funny," POTUS said. "I know what all these buildings are, even though there are no signs."

"Here, signs are not necessary," IRA said.

They stepped into the Hall of Memory.

"You know, if all the world leaders could have access to this great hall and see the history and issues mankind has experienced, the world would get along in a much more harmonious way. Why doesn't God—?"

"Please don't call it by that name!" IRA said.

"So, why doesn't . . . who, what?"

"The Source," IRA replied.

"All right, the Source. So, why doesn't the Source allow man to see and feel this? I mean, when I became President of the United States, I was briefed about so many mysterious and unique things that the public has no clue about. Why is there no public record?"

"There are such records, sir. They are ignored."

"What are you talking about? There are no such records of all the worlds' memories like this."

"It's called a history book, sir. People just tend to ignore what they read and treat it as a mere story. Something that doesn't affect them, doesn't apply to them. Or so they believe. Lessons that were taught, and experienced, are only learned by a small few who try to teach them. The sad truth of humankind is that most ignore those lessons."

"Why doesn't someone tell us? Why must we wait until we get here before we find out?"

"You have been told, many times. This is how malevolence infiltrates.

Mankind likes to play the game of God, play the role of being spiritual, while all the while ignoring their history. It's only been a few short Earth years since some of the greatest cycles of human destruction in your world . . . some in the same span of human lifetimes—yet—history repeats itself—stupidity is what the Governor calls it. The last century of your earthly lifetime saw the most amount of genocide at the hands of each other in the history of mankind. And now the potential for death and destruction is even greater. That kind of energy fuels the Dark Forces to grow in its power and strength."

"Again, IRA, how can He—sorry, the Source—or anyone else here pass judgment?"

"That is my point, sir. Someone who is here in this place—*if they are pure of heart*—cannot."

"Wait a minute. Are you telling me you think that the Governor of the Council is corrupt?"

"I am saying that I am telling you the rules of this place."

"That isn't right," POTUS said. "Something has to be done. There must be a private committee meeting or group to create a review board—a heavenly democracy."

"Sir, we must be wary of speaking this to anyone here. I am not certain of who sees what. May I dome you so we can speak freely?"

POTUS nodded his assent and he found himself and IRA surrounded by a blue-glowing dome aura. He felt a sense of separation from everyone and everything except IRA who was inside this bubble with him.

"I wasn't sure I could share this with you before," IRA said. "I needed to know that you had the principled strength and moral courage to handle it. Especially as it deals with the Council of Elders."

"What are you trying to tell me, IRA?"

"Sir, I think the Dark Forces, a corrupt energy, has infiltrated even this level. I think some on the Council of Elders conspired to bring you here on purpose—had you killed—because if you had stayed in office, you would have been contacted by one of the Fallen Masters to alter the Dark Forces and raise the Light energy."

"What? Are you sure of that?" POTUS asked, putting as much anger into his response as he could, shouting the words, even though it was a shout that was projected and not vocalized.

"I am reasonably certain, yes, sir."

"This is outrageous! It is beyond contempt! Do we not have enough evil on Earth? Does heaven itself has to conspire to kill me, to take me away from my family?"

"It is not all who are here. It is just a corrupt element of the Dark Forces," IRA said.

"I thank you for allowing me to see this, IRA. You have helped me to open my eyes, and with that I can try to heal and evolve. Please help me to do whatever you feel I need to here to make sure that I am not earthbound or led down the wrong path. And I vow to you, that we will work together to reveal the wrongdoer."

"You are doing fine, sir," IRA said. "Now, let me show you what is next."

CHAPTER
54

POTUS looked out at the landscape—or heavenscape, as it were—and nearly gasped in awe at the sight. His vision here was acute, as was his hearing and other senses, though he somehow understood that without a corporeal self he really had no senses at all. Perhaps his memory had been liberated, and his consciousness could recall every smell and touch, every sound and sight, every sensory incident he had experienced in his lifetime. And what he was experiencing here on the Other Side was filtered through those sense-memories in a way that made them now equally as intense as the past—or, more accurately, with the sum of all things past.

Here he stood, apart from his guide and from every other being of this plane, and gazed upon the tiers of time that were arranged like mirrored reflections—and reflections of reflections without end. IRA was somewhere else—he was not sure where.

Images of people, like himself, and angels—very unlike himself—moved in masses without colliding. There was no evidence of chaos, only harmony, no imposed order, yet a unity of movement and purpose.

He felt that he could enter any tier and experience the unique life that it represented. Yet he strongly sensed that to enter one would in no way exclude participation in any other. Whereas on Earth he might find this very thought contradictory and frustrating, here his consciousness did not linger on such seeming absurdity. There were no roadblocks on the path to understanding.

Was this, in fact, heaven? Was this any *place* at all in a dimensional sense?

The President "heard" himself laugh aloud, which resembled the clear, liquid tone of a bell or a pipe of some kind. There was no echo or reverberation—because, of course, he had no eardrums. There was only sound, or the memory of sound.

"If this is the case, I have no voice," he said to no one. "Perhaps I don't need a voice. Perhaps I have nothing to say."

A warmth filled his spirit being. He knew a comfort level with this new self that he had never felt in his life on the earthly plane. Even though he remained uneducated in the newness of his existence and still unacquainted with God, or whatever the Source was that was the Creator of all he beheld, there was no fight in him, no resistance to the unknown that stretched out before him in every direction and in dimensions beyond his ability to count them.

With his family now left behind on Earth, he felt tethered in a way; he could "tune in" to them at will, and on some level he wasn't completely separated from them. He hoped he never would be.

From the steps of the Great Hall where he stood, there was no limit to his vision. He also saw innumerable souls—whether they were people or angels, he could not know—wherever he looked, and he sensed that he could be seen, in turn, by any of them who happened to be looking back in his direction. Their faces were clearly delineated no matter how far or near they stood. Who were they all? What were they thinking? Were they, like him, newcomers to this dimension or beings long departed from Earth? POTUS smiled inwardly at the clichéd but appropriate thought: "Time will tell."

The tour of his new home—or place of residence—continued even as POTUS experienced an odd sense that he had seen some of these "buildings" before, some of them many times. Had it been in the seemingly short time he had already been here . . . ? His tour guide, IRA, reminded him that none of these places were places he was able to gain access to on his own.

"Yet you can *see* virtually everything 'inside' and 'outside,' can you not?" IRA probed.

"I can see the earthly planes in a limited way. Some of my vision is still unclear, as if it were immature. But I can feel them—the earthly planes and the people of Earth—very strongly."

As IRA spoke, POTUS became aware of a new presence.

The being said nothing but hovered so close that the President could almost breathe it in. It seemed like hours, or even days, though it was much less in real time. Then the being was no longer there, leaving POTUS and IRA alone in conversation as they had been before. It became apparent to POTUS that IRA could not see or sense this new presence. A name came into his head, unspoken but as clear as a siren: "I am Caleb."

POTUS accessed the memory of the intoxicating feeling of light and vitality he had known in only moments of being in Caleb's presence. He wondered who Caleb was . . . and why IRA couldn't see him. The one thing that struck POTUS so strongly, however, was the incredible wave of what felt like love wash over him when Caleb "arrived" and he suddenly felt sad that the presence was gone.

Messengers, guardians, and guides—a celestial "workforce"—were arrayed behind the figure who communicated with him now. But they were not idle. POTUS somehow (and he wasn't sure, at this point, just how it could be) knew that their images were available to him, even if they were present elsewhere doing the work they were assigned on Earth. He was beginning to understand that this was less a *place* than a state of being or a dimension that he had entered upon his transition from life on the earthly plane.

If it were physically possible to smile, POTUS would have done so. He was pleased that knowledge was coming to him now consciously and rapidly, as opposed to the struggle he had undergone during the first stage of the transition to the Other Side.

"If I am on the Other Side," he said to IRA, "I want to see my father."

"In due time. You have to trust us to guide you into this new realm. There is much you must absorb first."

"But why can't I—?"

"You can. In fact," IRA said, "you can have it all, when you are ready."

POTUS did not like this answer. It made him angry, which surprised him, because he thought he wasn't supposed to feel anger in this new situation . . . or was he? He was still more than a bit confused about what was and was not expected of him.

Then he felt a warm, reassuring hand on his soul. He knew *that* couldn't be right, because there was no corporeal reality here, no touching of bodies. But it was very real, and he wondered what it could be. Then that voice came into his consciousness. Again, he understood immediately that for some reason IRA could not hear this voice, even though he, the newcomer to this dimension of existence, could—loudly and clearly. Then he knew who it was; it was Caleb again.

"All shall be revealed to you, dear son. Know that your father is here among us—and that your son is safe and alive in the world of humankind. There is no cause for you to be concerned, or to be angry."

He was bathed in a bright, mysterious light in which he could see nothing—and everything. His heart was reassured, even as the newest presence introduced itself to him. Silently, he wondered what this presence was—or who it was. A single word, a name, came to him again: *Caleb*.

He accepted the mysterious element as something that he wasn't meant to understand—yet. And he kept his silence on the subject. Instead, he spoke to IRA: "I don't want it all. I want to reconnect with my kin. I just want to know that they are well, that we will be together in the long run."

The presence known as Caleb planted a new thought within POTUS: "You have the opportunity to get it right—now and in the future. Take your time, and all shall be made known to you when you are ready to receive the fullness of knowledge. Take care to make the right choices. That is the key—here and now and always."

IRA was chattering away, but POTUS was having troubling hearing him, absorbing the guide's words and concepts as his thoughts were diverted by Caleb. Again, he wondered silently why IRA could not see or hear this other presence. It intrigued him. Were there differences and "politics" even here on the Other Side? Were there rivalries and divisions? If so, he must indeed be careful to make the right choices as he progressed on this new path—especially if his goal was to know his own father and to be able to help his son from this side of existence.

This majestic being known to him as Caleb was, he understood as he gained clearer insight, his own true guide. IRA, who had seemed so powerful and clever to him at first, now faded in his estimation to a secondary level, and he began to question IRA's bona fides as a spirit guide and mentor. He always felt more baffled and unsure after a conversation with IRA, rather than more confident in his knowledge of what was happening to and around him.

In the end, what POTUS wanted and needed was to be in contact with his son and with his family who had passed over before him. IRA, he now felt, was keeping him away from them. Caleb, on the other hand, at least held out the promise of a pathway to be with them, with the ones he loved.

Words formed in his mind that the being Caleb put there in his way of communicating with the President: "The choice lies with you. As with all created beings on Earth and in the heavenly realm. This is the essence of our existence: free will. That is something that most human beings simply do not fully understand, despite ample evidence and the spiritual teachings that are available to them."

"What choice? To be with my son and wife, even though I'm dead? To reconnect with my own father and the rest of the family who departed before me? Of course, this is what I choose. I only lack the means to act on that choice."

"But it is so much more than that. Just as you have been selected by the Council of Elders to help bring about change in lives on Earth, you must look inside yourself to see whether you wish to take on this responsibility and to gain the understanding it will take to accomplish it. The end result of your choice—and your action—will bring about what you most desire. Happiness is available to anyone who is willing to take the right action and make the choice that is most beneficial to others. Where humans so often err is when they focus on making the choices that are beneficial to *themselves* first and others secondarily, or not at all."

"Do unto others as you would have them do unto you."

"Very simply put and the core of all wisdom when it comes to human relationships. Could it be more clear than that?"

"The things we were taught as children, then, in school and in religious training, turn out to be the keys to true understanding."

"Yes. There are teachers all around us, for good and ill. In classrooms and places of worship, at home and in the village, and all teachers of good say basically the same thing. And all teachers of evil, too, influence the minds of men and women in the same way."

"But I don't understand what IRA is supposed to teach me and how he is to influence me."

"By questioning, you have your own answer. Ask and you shall be answered. Knock and the door shall be opened to you."

Caleb's message was baffling in its simplicity. And POTUS understood, too, that he, like any human being at whatever stage of life—or after—must be exposed to both good and evil in order to understand the nature of the choices that lay before them.

Unfolding on Earth, at this very moment, was just this juxtaposition, yet the Dark Forces had carefully gathered all their strength and had coordinated their timing so that they would achieve maximum influence on the choices of a maximum number of people in the world—all at the same time. They were not holding back or playing at the margins now . . . It was an all-or-nothing situation with the confluence of natural phenomena and ancient black arts being brought together across the entire globe for all human eyes to see and experience.

"It's like the Garden of Eden being replayed, only at the end of time instead of the beginning," POTUS said. He had not even had the conscious thought, but the words came out in that way.

"You have received the insight you were meant to receive because you are open to it, not closed off by darkness, but opened by light. Happy is the man, such as you, who can see clearly not only in the light of day but in the darkest hour of night."

"But is hope lost for the many who cannot see?"

"Hope is *never* lost. No matter how dark and dangerous the hour. Hope can triumph. Always."

Caleb, whose visual imprint had changed from an awesomely bright and beautiful creature to a small and slender man the same size as IRA or the Governor, stood—or hovered, as it were—close to POTUS. The President could *feel* the spiritual power almost as a physical presence, as warmth and *sense*—even without the human body, which he had shed but which he yet remembered vividly—the nature of pure goodness and light which stood by him. It conveyed a sense of power and energy he had not felt since he had passed over from one realm to the other at his own death. The President was pulled out of the encounter with Caleb by IRA's sharp words.

"Focus on what I am trying to teach you!" IRA cautioned, in response to his unspoken thoughts. He saw that POTUS was distracted but was not able to identify the cause.

"I am sorry if I seem distracted. It's just that I have many questions, and you are trying to teach me so much. I feel as if I am starting to read too many different books and not finishing any of them." POTUS's mind continued to reel, and he struggled to get a handle on his thoughts, so many new and conflicting images and ideas. "The overwhelming feeling of purpose and need seems to be growing stronger within me. And I know that you are helping me as quickly as you can, but I feel like the people and energies here—the Council—they just don't *like* me. It is so clear by the wave of feelings that are directed at me every time they are near me."

The equivalent of tears, whatever that might be called on this side, formed in POTUS's vision, blurring it temporarily.

IRA smirked invisibly, pleased that POTUS was still so ego-bound, then shifted his own thoughts back to POTUS. "We have much work to do," he said. "Do not let your earthly ego get in the way of the spiritual achievements on our journey. I want to show you something else. There."

He brought the President into a structure that resembled the Colosseum, a façade that hummed and vibrated like the rest of this spiritual city they inhabited. Everywhere he looked, he saw waterfalls. The sight didn't make any logical sense, but there they were, countless waterfalls and waterfalls upon waterfalls flowing from—he could not see where. Each waterfall formed a swirling pool, of which there seemed to be thousands all contained in this enclosed arena.

"How is all of *this* able to fit inside of the edifice we just walked into?" The awe and confusion was evident in POTUS's question.

"Ah, you are still employing an earthly point of view and definition to our world of energy, I see," IRA commented, somewhat sarcastically.

POTUS winced at the implied criticism. He still had so much to learn. It was uncomfortable to be so naïve and incompetent. I should feel *good* in the light, but I don't, he chided himself.

IRA pointed out what all the other energies were doing. They were looking in on the earthly planes of existence, the levels of spiritual evolution that humans on Earth materialized into—or incarnated into.

"So—all these waterfalls represent one person?"

"No. They represent millions of people."

POTUS looked around at what felt like thousands of football fields for miles with thousands, perhaps tens of thousands of waterfalls as large as Niagra Falls and as small as a water feature in someone's garden.

"Listen to the music."

POTUS did not hear any music. But what he felt was the thoughts and feelings of millions of conversations. It was as if he was able to hear all of them, and focus on no particular one at the same time. Still, he was able to absorb the sounds—the "music," as IRA called it—not as a cacophony, but as individual bits of data. However, he could not know whether he would be able to retrieve any of it or make any sense of it at a future moment.

"Why doesn't this sound like noise in a cafeteria or marketplace?" he asked. "All these people's thoughts that I am listening to—"

"Wait! First of all, you cannot read anyone's thoughts. The Divine Source has made it so that remains the private space for all created beings. You are only able to read the projected thoughts of all living creatures." IRA was beginning to sound slightly impatient, which POTUS thought a little odd for an "angelic" being.

"You mean, I am hearing animals, as well?"

"If it is living, you are experiencing it. Can we please start to use the terminology of this world and not your former world? How can I help you move away from it if you remain trapped there?"

"Sorry," POTUS said, perplexed and somewhat sheepish.

This place took his breath away, figuratively. He was overwhelmed by pictures and scenes of what was happening all around the world revealed whenever he looked closely into the falls. At the same time he heard the conversations that, after a time, did start to resemble a kind of music, as IRA had called it. The falls created the most beautiful lakes and pools of various shades of blue, each one correlating to notes on a scale. And the light that shone on all these colors emanated from the Source! . . . How did he know that?

These things are being revealed to me, so I must keep my mind open to receive the messages that are constantly bombarding my now nonexistent brain! Again and again he felt reduced to the status of a youngster attending his first day of school. How long ago had *that* been?

He had to ask another question: "IRA, why can't I connect with Caleb—or with my father?" He suddenly felt a deep need to communicate with his father, yet he was uncertain as to why he included the new being whom he had just encountered only once and only a brief time ago . . .

IRA winced. POTUS was seeing things that he, IRA, had tried to block him from. He should not be experiencing anything but what his guide and mentor was allowing to be visible. Not his father—and certainly not Caleb. This was IRA's primary responsibility. POTUS was resisting, not accepting the guidance IRA was supposed to provide. How would POTUS know about Caleb in the first place? Caleb would lead the newcomer down the *wrong* path, the one that the Governor and his minions intended.

It dawned on POTUS that Caleb had been there all along, present and available to him as his guide, even as IRA had done his best to lead him in the direction that *he*, IRA, had selected. Then the question became, *Why?*

The apparent shift when Caleb's name came up darkened the space between POTUS and IRA. Smiling, despite his not-so-hidden agitation, IRA said, "I guess when you are ready to see them, you will."

"But where are they?" the newcomer demanded.

IRA sighed. "They're here already. You just can't see them yet. This place has many levels and dimensions that you don't gain access to just because you died physically. Sir, you need to understand that just as in life, you are working on the evolution of your soul. You need to finish some lessons in order to advance to others. You may be here for a while."

"How is that possible? You already told me that there is no time here. How can you say, 'a while'? *What does that mean here?*"

IRA was trying hard not to be flummoxed by POTUS's repeated, nagging questions but was starting to find it blocking his plan. Then a shaft of crimson light flashed around IRA. He heard the words, "Stop this now!" and responded nervously, looking down.

POTUS looked around at what could have caused IRA to react so uncomfortably. Surely, it was not solely his questions. But he could sense nothing visually or aurally and was mystified.

IRA, however, looked to his left, and standing there were a number of the Council of Elders members, including the Governor.

In that moment, POTUS felt protective toward IRA, his guide through this wondrous land of afterlife, and he sent out a thought wave of energy for the Council to step back and allow him the space to deal with IRA—and to learn what the guide was teaching him. At the same time, his natural skepticism gnawed at his spirit and he wondered just who Caleb was in the order of the universe, and he tried to tamp down his doubts and too-numerous questions.

A return thought from the Governor stated simply: "So be it."

POTUS was pleased that the Governor trusted his judgment, in contrast to his mixed—or mixed-up—feelings about IRA.

IRA looked down and smiled. He looked back up and said, "Thank you. I am trying to help you. I want to answer all your questions, but these distractions just seem to be creating new questions for you, ones designed to stop you from achieving the greatness that I know to be your destiny."

POTUS merely nodded and said, "What's next on the tour?"

When he reconnected with IRA, it seemed as if many of the other energies that were in their immediate presence became invisible. POTUS was brought to another level, and IRA was firmly imbedded into the psyche of POTUS with less "competition" for his attention.

"May I show you something that we are not supposed to do?"

POTUS laughed and said, "Sure, why not?" He felt that IRA was pushing him hard, getting ahead of where he was ready to be, but he went along.

IRA pointed to a waterfall that flowed in all shades of red. IRA instructed him to bathe in it. POTUS immediately had a feeling deep inside that this direction was misguided and wrong, and that he was being led in a direction that was not healthy or correct for him. But IRA had gained his trust, more or less, and POTUS was still uncertain if he was even supposed to have "feelings."

When he stepped toward the magnificent red waterfall, he experienced a quick visual image of the Governor looking at him as if he were the family dog about to relieve himself on the living room carpet. Then he heard the unseen Caleb tell him to trust himself. But the next thing he knew, IRA had led him right to the pool of illuminated red energy.

"I feel amazing! What is this?" POTUS exclaimed.

IRA coyly told him that the energy of the physical world can be used as a form of currency or fuel for these dimensions. "It is something that you are not really allowed to do, but from time to time, to fully understand the human experience, we bathe in this energy to reconnect and recharge."

"I feel like Superman—for real! The vitality and force of raw energy are unbelievable. Can we do this every day?"

IRA's eyes lit up at this question, pleased at the direction POTUS was moving—toward him, like Eve eyeing the apple in Eden. Finally, this was something that he could answer to achieve the result he wanted. He said, "The reality is you can come here any time you like. I have created access to this place for you. This vortex of light and energy will fuel our relationship and help us to move forward in a large way to accomplish our goals."

The President stood in the humming pool of red energy, not listening to IRA's words, which were intended to entice and confuse in any case, programming himself and recharging his essence and feeling like a child who doesn't want to leave the amusement park.

Meanwhile, IRA stood on the sidelines like a proud parent who had taken his child out of school to treat him to a day of fun instead of fulfilling his responsibility for the education of the child. He laughed out loud as he knew that POTUS was now fueled with a newfound allegiance to the teachings of his guide, IRA.

Angels and ghosts, POTUS realized, are images that human beings use to process what they do not understand about contact between the two realms of Earth and Heaven. Our knowledge is severely limited, circumscribed by lack of spiritual preparedness and, often, willful ignorance of greater and deeper forms of learning. The reality, he could now see, was more spectacular than the human mind could imagine. On Earth, we are weighed down by cares and obsessions and fear; our eyes are heavily lidded of our own making. Very few are willing to step out of what they know into the unknown—most because they are held down by poverty or fear. And those who have means become tied to their wealth and unable or unwilling to let go, for fear of losing all.

Fear. Fear. Fear. Always that was at the root of inaction or wrong choices. Fear keeps human beings locked in their own minds and impotent to change. Fear, then, is the weapon of those who wish to keep them in that place and to control their world . . . fear is the tool of the forces of darkness. And at that moment the one emotion that POTUS wasn't feeling was fear.

CHAPTER
56

In the same dimension, standing right next to IRA and watching PO-TUS become intoxicated by the red waterfall, Caleb turned to the Governor and said, "We are losing him more quickly than I thought we would."

"I know we are," the Governor responded. "I have tried since he arrived to indicate that he should not trust IRA, but I have perhaps been too subtle." He now regretted that he had not been more overt, rather than transmitting signals and images that IRA had effectively countered. The Governor went on: "He has not allowed himself yet to trust his own instincts on a soul level. He is so used to ruling by committee and listening to a political cabinet of advisers. It was the one vulnerability we knew of in this fight for his soul's decisions."

Caleb turned to look again at POTUS with his eyes closed. "We need permission to show him some more answers to the questions he does possess, the ones IRA is blocking. IRA is playing to his trust and manipulating him. He has to choose *good* and *light* over *evil*. That is his purpose and his true destiny. But he has to make the choices for himself, as all men do. Somehow he has to allow us into his thoughts and his soul's energy so that we can show him more of this plane."

The Governor had long known how smart IRA was, how well trained by the Dark Forces. IRA was an expert on using the fear principles of the earthly realm to create the illusion of truth and achieve the desires of his masters. But the Governor also understood that the Source allowed *all* souls to experience evolution, in whatever realm they may exist. For IRA to be here presented an opportunity for the Forces of Light to try and shift IRA himself back to the way of the good and away from the dark. It had happened before.

Neither could the Governor or anyone else stop him from being there, no differently than humans can stop the negative people or negative forces in their lives. What people *can* do, the Governor knew, is control the choices they make. . . . The alternative, upon which the Dark Forces based their actions, was to surrender free will and blame God for the evil that happens in human existence.

There had been moments after POTUS first arrived and was waking up to the new reality, the Forces of Light had tried to show him the truth of IRA's intentions.

Caleb looked at the Governor, and they knew that the reality of losing the soul of POTUS to this trickster energy was in the balance. Caleb would make a quick attempt to "wake him at this moment. . . ."

He spread his arms, wings of light, which illuminating the dimension that the POTUS now occupied. IRA reacted angrily, knowing he had no control over this maneuver, which was as simple for Caleb as making a casual gesture at a tea party.

The Governor emitted a cosmic chuckle, which distracted IRA enough to loosen some of his mental control over and connection with the free will of POTUS.

Marcus opened his eyes to connect with the brilliant light Caleb emanated. He suddenly recognized his circumstance—seeing for a brief second the earthly illustrations of the energy he was standing in: Hundreds of thousands of images of people having sex and situations of intense fear processed through his consciousness—it was as if *The Gates of Hell* by Rodin had been awakened—overwhelming and embarrassing him as he stood in the red pool. Horrified, he removed himself from being the receptacle for these experiences, even as he began to glimpse the implications of his predicament.

Feeling humiliated at participating in the most intimate moments of people's earthly experiences and having a hard time shaking the images and feelings, POTUS turned to IRA in a rage.

"Why the hell did you do that to me?" he screamed at IRA.

Without skipping a beat, IRA had his reply at the ready: "Why did *I* do that to *you?* I recall you walking into that pool of energy of your own free will. I did not make you do anything. I would like to tell you that I do not appreciate the fact you are accusing me of having intentions that are not to show and teach you of this dimension. You are showing a sense of human entitlement and lacking appreciation."

IRA turned and began to move away from POTUS. "Perhaps I am not the person to be assisting your transition."

Confused, dripping with angry emotions like water from the pool, isolated and alone, POTUS wanted to allow IRA to go. Yet there was no one else here for him. Where was his family, who had died so many years ago? Why was this experience so lonely and non-God-like? This was not what his Sunday School teachers had taught him. Isolated and alone, but yet he was feeling a willingness to stay that way and let IRA walk away from him. Why was that? There seemed to be more confusion than clarity.

Just as he was going to thank IRA and allow him to leave, he heard a projection, a thought that emanated from IRA.

"I understand you want me to go. I cannot stop your feelings but must honor them. But I was hoping to bring you here to energize you and reconnect you with yourself—to make you feel something. The energy of the Earth World, fueled by the base energy of sex and physical energy, does just that. And think about how you feel energy-wise right now. I know you feel what we just did was voyeuristic and wrong, but *you* were the one who walked into it—and stayed there—because you know you felt *something*. Am I right?"

"Yes," POTUS said.

"We have much work to do, and I want to talk to you about your son."

"Finally! My boy! I miss him so much. Take me to see him. I must speak to him one more time. Please make this experience worth it by showing me my son."

"I cannot take you to him now, but I *can* show him to you," IRA said.

"Now?"

"Yes, now that you reconnected so strongly with the earthly energy of lust and human emotion, you will be able to use that to see him again."

POTUS was rocked to the core of his soul for the second time.

IRA looked past him to see the Governor and an invisible Caleb turn to walk away, hoping they had not completely lost the POTUS to IRA and the Dark Forces for all eternity. . . . This Fallen Master in training would never be ready to help them—or the energy of the whole planet.

IRA knew that he was now permanently in control over the programming of the President of the United States. Revealing to him that his son was still alive and on that side of the veil would only secure more of his desire and interest to reconnect with him and *it*. This would act as the complete distraction and conduit that IRA and his dark masters would need to keep their overall plan of sweeping the earthly plane with fear and negativity and fueling their tanks to control and create more of the same energy. It was a beautiful plan—a very efficient system of energetic resource: control the source of energy and dominate the actions and currency of every living thing

"Sounds like someone from your side of this equation is controlling the oil industry down there, IRA," Caleb said as he manifested himself fully before his enemy.

IRA did not need to play any role or assume any form other than his own in front of Caleb. So he, too, stood at his full, majestic height and spread his light in the same gorgeous shades of red that POTUS had bathed in earlier. Caleb's aura, in contrast was a milky white-gold.

IRA challenged Caleb with a furor: "Just surrender. Recognize that the Dark Forces have finally tipped the balance, and the pendulum of the Earth and its weak and miserable inhabitants is no longer under the control of the Divine Plan. For billions of years this autocratic dynasty of 'His' love and light have inspired and controlled the fates of their world. And now, with just a bit of simple strategic centuries of planning, technology, sex, and ego, our side—the *right side*—will take over the design of structure and community on Earth. Thank you very much." IRA spat his words. "You will watch helplessly as mankind succumbs to its own issues of fear, greed, power, ambition, ego, and lust as their main goal and source of all human energy."

Caleb smiled and acknowledged the words and energy that IRA conveyed. He validated the triumphs and dedication that the Dark Forces had worked with and applauded their patience.

Caleb was calm in his response. "You are only counting on what you project onto them. You do not credit them for being able to decide and choose. That is going to be your downfall, my brother." Caleb turned to leave and started to vibrate and illuminate ever more brightly. His parting thoughts to IRA could be heard echoing as he left:

"Do not discount the power of love, IRA. I know it has been a long time since experiencing the light of that Word and the power of that Source, but it is the Divine Plan's ultimate gift to mankind. Like it or not, it is in their cellular structure—something you can mask, but never destroy."

IRA's auric field blazed a fiery red-orange glow as he heard this. Then he regained his composure and smiled evilly to himself. "I have not forgotten that at all, Caleb. I am actually counting on it." Then he dematerialized into a mist of gray.

CHAPTER
57

POTUS stood on the edge of the pool of passion, as he now referred to it. Gazing at the beauty of this place, he walked over and sat on a large boulderlike seat and started to reflect on his earthly life.

This place, or dimension, enabled him to view his life and moments from his earthly family like watching a videotape or film of his soul. It was all recorded and retrievable. He was able to watch events that he had not been able to remember before: events and conversations that came back as clearly as if they had occurred just moments ago.

He watched his father hold him and speak to him, rocking him in his arms as a newborn. He saw his mother come into the nursery to tell his father that he needed to put the baby down so that both could get some needed sleep. Deep in thought about his father and his mother, "It doesn't make any sense," he murmured, thinking back on the course of his life—and theirs.

While growing up, before his dad passed, his dad had been there for him every second of every day, answering questions and drying tears, cheering for the young Marcus when he achieved even the smallest thing in the classroom or on the playing field. His mom, God bless her, had tried her best after she lost her spouse and best friend, but grief had scored the rest of her life, and she had never been the same. Still, the love was there. The energy of the father had continued to pass through the mother to the son. He had felt it then, even though he had not had the vocabulary to express it. His father was there. *He was always there*, POTUS knew.

But where was his father now? Why had he not been the person that had come to welcome him? This thought gnawed at POTUS. Maybe there had been something that *he* had done wrong on Earth. But looking back on their time together, he couldn't think of anything. He had been a good kid, for the most part, always eager to please his parents. He could not remember a single time his dad had raised his hand in punishment, nor his mom.

Feeling dejected and defeated, and still more than a bit confused, POTUS looked up and saw IRA standing knee-deep in the pool of passion, absorbing energy from that place. POTUS wondered why he had not seen him there before. They were only some thirty feet apart. Again, something struck POTUS as "odd." Although everything was incredibly odd, this still didn't "feel" right.

This other realm or dimension was so complicated. There were multiple levels of access that some of the more evolved energies could experience and some from which he and others were shut out from because of their lack of evolution on this side. So complicated . . . All those years of Sunday school teaching that there was this good place called Heaven and the bad place called Hell—you either went *up* to Heaven or *down* to Hell. They didn't tell you that you just *went*.

Then, within his mind and with a physical sensation, POTUS felt he was being pulled toward another pool. It seemed the more questions he asked the stronger the pull became. He looked around, beyond IRA in the red pool, and realized he was being summoned to appear before the Governor and the Council of Elders.

POTUS sensed the pull rapidly growing in intensity. He wanted to reach out to IRA to stop this, to seek his guidance on how he should respond. . . . But IRA was totally caught up in the ecstasy of the pool of passion and was apparently not able to feel or see POTUS or accept his thought-energy. The President felt that he was now completely on his own, that this was a moment of reckoning—perhaps a showdown with the Governor once and for all.

He had thought, hoped, that he was beyond such struggles now, on *this* side of existence. But he was still frustrated, disappointed in himself and his situation. He had to get up to speed on this new form of existence. His old impatience reared its head within him. He knew so little, needed to know more. But he did know without a doubt that his soul was hanging in the balance.

The President had been summoned to the chamber of the Council of Elders once again. This time he did not feel the sense of awe and mystery he had previously experienced. Instead, he had an odd sensation of *belonging*, of being home. He had undergone not only physical and metaphysical transformations but a shift of knowledge as if he had taken on a new mantle over his shoulders and a new pair of shoes that fit him perfectly. Almost imperceptible, yet all too real . . .

"I was sent here for a purpose," he said as he reached the center of the circle, addressing all the Elders but looking at no one in particular. He stood beside the Governor, feeling a great serenity through his entire being.

The Governor addressed the Council: "Wise men and women, angels and beings of this higher realm, I speak for you and in your voice as the elected leader. And in that role I have been empowered to speak the meanings that the Source has given to our minds. That One who created us and conceived of this world for our benefit and grace selected each of us to play a role in the earthly order and beyond—in this, the purely spiritual plane that opens to us after release from the physical limitations we once knew."

"I am beginning to understand," POTUS said.

"That is why you were chosen, not only because you achieved a unique status on Earth but also because your heart was tested and found worthy of true leadership and service."

"I now know there is really no such thing as power on an individual basis. As the so-called leader of the free world and the mightiest military force in existence, even I could not do everything I wanted or implement changes that would improve people's lives. I truly intended to do good and to institute reforms in government and international policy. At every turn I faced frustration by political forces beyond my control. And the harder I worked, the less I seemed to be able to accomplish."

"That is the way of the realm on Earth. You confronted the Dark Energies every day of your life. It is true that you did not defeat them. But the crucial fact is, you never gave up the struggle against evil and injustice. If you had lived longer on that side, the result would not have been materially different."

"Do you mean there is no hope for victory over evil on Earth?"

"Oh, there is always hope, as long as we remain close to the Creator of all that is good and tap into that infinite Source of power. Look around at this Council, and you will see many who never abandoned hope and constantly engaged in the eternal struggle."

POTUS trained his vision on the faces of the spirits gathered in the Council of Elders. Many were, in fact familiar, from his own earthly life span in the late twentieth and early twenty-first centuries, and from the annals of history. Mother Teresa of Calcutta was one he could not help but recognize immediately—others such as the patriarch Joseph, son of Jacob; Pericles of ancient Athens; the philosopher Lao Tzu; and the French scientist Marie Curie he somehow recognized through instinct or unspoken knowledge. One figure stepped from among the others and walked with great dignity toward the President and the Governor.

The American leader studied the face—that is, the reflection of the earthly face that each of the entities in the assembly carried as a mark of his or her former existence on Earth—and did not recognize it. The male being manifested great strength, power beyond the merely physical. He had a dark complexion, and when he spoke, his voice held a surprising musical quality.

"My respected friend," he began, addressing POTUS. "My birth name is Abu I-Hasan, but those who knew me during my lifetime called me Ziryab. That name means 'blackbird.' Perhaps you can allow me a few moments out of eternity, to visit with you."

"But of course," POTUS replied.

Ziryab was speaking in classical Arabic, but the now-deceased President of the United States absorbed and understood every word spoken to him, as, he assumed, did each member of the Council of Elders. *So this is how human beings were meant to communicate with and to relate to one another . . . across barriers of time, space, and language. Why is it only possible here and not on Earth?*

POTUS thought of the story of the Tower of Babel. Men—humankind—had thought so well of their own powers that they chose to build a tower to heaven, without considering what greater power and spiritual foundation might underlie their earthly achievements. Well, that higher power (Creator, God, Allah, whomever he or she would turn out to be) had confounded the humans by screwing up their communications, making each speak a distinct language not understood by the others. . . . That was then. Is it so different now? he wondered.

"In my time, I was a slave, a musician, and a scholar. More important—in my time, I was a human being with a soul and aspirations to please Allah, the God of Abraham who revealed Himself to the righteous," the remarkable figure said. He held up a lute, which POTUS had not noticed him carrying, and the entire Great Hall of the Elders was filled with an unreal, magical music that touched every soul within its reach. "Such music was the great love of my seventy years of life among men in Baghdad, Syria, Tunisia, Africa, and Spain. It was not the custom for one born a slave to see so much of the world, but God granted the privilege to me most generously. God is good, in all times and places.

"What I saw and experienced moved me to apply all my powers and talents, which I learned from many masters, to help improve conditions for fellow men and women in those distant lands. This I did, to the best of my abilities, and lived in many glittering capitals and many a hovel. I slept in soft beds and along hard roadsides in the desert. Something moved me to expend the energies I was given to serve others who had not my gifts. That *something* is what motivates and sustains us today. That *something* is Allah, God, Creator, Way. God wishes us to share at our maximum level with the other creatures we encounter in our travels.

"Not all will travel to faraway cities. Some of us remain in one place our entire lives. But you and I—and most in this chamber of the Elders—saw many faces in our lifetimes. Those faces are now turned to you. What will you say to them? What will you do to relieve their suffering and that of their children?"

The powerful message washed over the President like a tsunami, sweeping all other thoughts aside and leaving him staggered.

He had never before heard of Ziryab, who had lived from 789 to 857 and had been revered and applauded by all who knew him from Spain to Mesopotamia, in royal courts and caravans of poor travelers. But the spiritual and cultural achievements of this one man of humble birth all became known to POTUS in this moment, opening his mind to a previously dark period in human history.

Why had I never read about this man? What are the true depths of my ignorance?

Murmurs arose from among the Council, and Ziryab stepped back among the others with a courteous bow to the newcomer and the Governor. With a smile, the Governor said simply, "So it is with the Source—all things are possible in goodness. Revelation is all around us, if we are open to receive the word that is spoken in many tongues and understood by all."

POTUS had been fairly conscientious in going to church and understanding his religious faith as a younger man, but upon becoming President, he had begun to see such matters in a much different light. He had prayed more often and with greater purpose than ever before in his life. His wife had noticed the difference and appreciated it. She encouraged him to pray and sometimes joined him in the evening before bed in quiet, private moments.

As he listened to the words of Ziryab and the Governor, he could suddenly and quite clearly remember every prayer he had ever uttered and every Bible passage he had ever read or heard proclaimed at whatever church service he had attended. Remarkable. This transformation was opening him up not unlike a flower responding to rain or sunlight.

"So I have been directly called, as have all who are present, for a distinct purpose," said Marcus.

"Yes," the Governor of the Elders said.

"As have all the members of this Council? It is no accident that any are here."

"There are no accidents in the movements of the Source. There are accidents and mistakes in the realm of the humans and in the flailings of the Dark Energies. That does not mean we are perfect—not by any means."

Another figure appeared in Marcus's vision, a strange and ugly figure in sharp contrast to the handsome, vigorous form that had spoken a moment before. This one moved with a slouch, holding his hands crossed in front of him.

The President reacted with disgust at the sight: It was Adolf Hitler, the definition of evil.

What is this!" POTUS exclaimed. "Who is this man?"

"It is what you know it is," the Governor answered.

The loathsome figure said nothing but gazed at the President with a bottomless sadness and despair in his black eyes. POTUS could conceive of nothing more repellent or out of place.

POTUS shouted, or conceived and projected the words as loudly as he could to express the outrage he felt over seeing Hitler here. Hitler started toward him, and POTUS raised his hand and pointed at him. "Don't you even come close to me, you perverted piece of shit!"

At that moment, everyone in the Hall of Governing Wisdom turned to look at the new arrival as if he were a child in church who had dropped the F-bomb. The Governor of the Council of Elders addressed this outburst interacting directly with POTUS for the first time, chastising POTUS for making a judgment.

"You are new here, so we will allow your indiscretion, brother. All of the people who are in this room are here for a purpose. In the physical world they played a role, acted as a character, and in some cases were inspired by the Dark Forces. But in the Divine Light of the Source, the Universal Oneness that we are all a part of, there is no judgment, only justness. The man you see as the iconic ambassador of evil is no more that monster here than you are in one of your past incarnations. The longer you are here, the less you will judge and react to things in your earthly frame of reference, and the more you will learn to view things with a loving heart and soul."

POTUS reacted immediately, and involuntarily from the earthly perspective that still clung to him. "That is the biggest crock of bullshit I have ever heard, and believe me, with twenty years in the army and seven years in

Washington, I have heard my share. That monster was responsible for one of the greatest genocides in the history of mankind! How could you—?"

In the middle of his rant, POTUS suddenly discovered that Hitler was no longer there. Neither was the Governor nor the Council nor even the Hall of Governing Wisdom. IRA had instantly phased or transitioned them to another place.

"I see that we are in another place," POTUS said. "Are we in another time as well?"

"What is time?" Abraham Lincoln asked. "It is merely a device to keep everything from happening all at once. The best thing about the future is that it doesn't all happen at once."

POTUS started to respond to Lincoln, but he was gone as quickly as he had appeared.

"You don't understand," IRA said.

"Apparently I don't. Not if someone like Hitler can be here. Who else is here? Stalin? Attila the Hun? Jeffrey Dahmer?"

"Hitler's soul is in transition," IRA explained. "He needs to feel, and to experience the pain and suffering of the people's lives he destroyed in the name of his plan."

"His plan?

"Well, it is a plan more of Ego than God. The Council needs Hitler to see and understand the process of spiritual evolution in a much larger perspective."

"How do you do that?" POTUS asked.

"I'm not a member of the Council," IRA said. "But the way it works is that everyone has to do something called a Life Review, where they unpack their last life."

"I see."

"I'm not sure that you do see, but I will try to explain it to you. Hitler has to take full responsibility for the actions of his soul while he was alive. He can't just cross over to the kingdom of God and stand in that light and yell out, 'I am sorry' and all is forgiven. All may be forgiven here, but all is certainly not forgotten. He lives in an eternal state of pain for all the countless lives he took, and he must now serve the greater good in a way he never did on Earth."

"It damn sure isn't forgotten," POTUS said. "It will be remembered on Earth for one million years, if the Earth is around that long."

"Mr. President, sir, do you understand now?" IRA asked, showing the patience of a first grade teacher teaching someone how to read.

"I do. I got it," POTUS replied.

POTUS said that he understood, but now he was actually trying to work it out in his mind. He could understand the level of pain and grief and suffering that one family feels, but to multiply that by the millions of lives that Hitler was responsible for ending, then that pain had to be enormous.

As he was considering this, he suddenly found himself back in the Governing Hall of Wisdom, though whether he returned of his own volition, or was brought back by IRA he didn't know.

Hitler was still there, but he no longer even looked like Hitler to him. Now he looked like a soul in torment. Earlier, POTUS had recognized him as he was, so he could reconnect with his earthly historical perspective and human judgment. Only in this way, could he grow.

"He has no voice here," the Governor went on. "At his death he made a choice not to join the Dark Forces for whom he had worked throughout his earthly life. His power died with him, and it will take an eternity for him to regain his voice, if he ever does, and to be accepted in the company of the good, if he ever is. His presence at this Council is the ultimate caution to any who would presume to act in a way contrary to the will of the Source."

The President, who had now received more knowledge and revelation than he could possibly absorb, stared at the apparition of Hitler even as he heard the strange words spoken by the Governor. "So he, too, is here for a greater purpose. But the pure evil he unleashed upon so many innocent people during his lifetime . . . How can that ever be forgiven, even by a loving Creator? Is there no limit to the evil that the Source can tolerate?"

"There is no question of toleration. Every small act that opposes the good and every global act of darkness that destroys men, women, and children on the planet Earth is abhorrent to the divine. Yes, great evil must be punished on a grand scale, more than a little lie or bad act. Look at him and you will see the price that can be—and must be—paid. There is a divine scale in Heaven. It has less to do with the so-called wrath of God and more a system of checks and balances."

The pitiful creature, so out of place in the company of saints and sages.

"And is it not better that he is here for now, rather than among his onetime dark allies? He is, in fact, free at any time to join them, to leave us. It is his choice, so his own free will is now the means by which he suffers the eternal fires of hell."

"It is very difficult for me to accept this," the President replied.

He could not unlock his eyes from those of the pitiful remnant of a man who stood before him with crossed hands.

"We require that you first accept your own situation. You understand that you have been chosen to be here at this time, and that we seek your help in the fight that lies ahead. There is no time, in this reality, to hesitate or to doubt."

"I am here to effect the change I was not able to accomplish in my lifetime. The Source has a new purpose for me." POTUS did not speak these words, but he heard them, none the less. As did the Governor and the Council of Elders.

Then a curtain fell between him and the Council, and suddenly, unexpectedly, IRA appeared at his side. POTUS now felt less startled at the phenomenon of rapid change in his environment. It seemed to happen with increasing frequency on the Other Side. He was quickly getting used to these swift comings and goings and changes in perspective in this still-new place.

He could tell by IRA's quick, jerky movements that he was prompting POTUS to move to another place.

Where? What is happening now? What am I supposed to be doing?

Then his vision cleared all too sharply and suddenly. It was night . . . and he no longer knew sleep. Constant wakefulness and never a moment of tiredness in this realm.

He saw it happening and was absolutely helpless to prevent it. He did not know who was perpetrating the crime against his own son, his family, or why. He could see his wife going about her business in the aftermath of his death, not yet knowing what was happening to their son. Every emotion he had ever experienced as father and husband came flooding back into his consciousness. If he could shed tears . . . but he could not.

Marcus Jackson, Jr. was being abducted at this moment in time, in this segment of eternity.

Part

·THREE·

CHAPTER
60

Singers, dancers, actors who could not go out in public without being inundated by that public, could come to the rehearsal hall and prepare for their appearances without being bothered by unwanted attention. That is because the people who worked at the rehearsal hall, the janitors, the plumbers and electricians, the manager and the secretaries were accustomed to famous performers rehearsing for an upcoming show.

But it was different with Charlene. Her voice had never been better, sweeter, purer, or more powerful. As she sang the songs she would sing during her show in Mexico City, the rehearsal hall employees, jaded though they were, would gather in the dark shadows of the far corner of the hall, just to listen.

Tom Colandrea, a tough-as-nails, sixty-two-year-old marine vet, who had held his friends as their life bled away in far-off wars, found his throat choked up, and his eyes welled with tears, as he listened to the music. Melinda Peterson, a secretary whose father had died one month earlier, could actually feel his presence. There were no jokes, no conversation, but there was a mutual sharing, and understanding of the feelings that washed over them as they listened. It wasn't just the purity and sweetness of the music. It was the lyrics, words that unlocked a secret longing in everyone's soul.

> *I dreamed a dream that day*
> *Of lost love on a beach so far away*
> *A time and place that I can feel*
> *Oh please tell me that it is real*

Charlene would be introducing the song for the first time at her show in Mexico City. The words and melody had poured out in a long, unbroken stream of consciousness—not one word changed or altered, not one note rearranged.

It had been six weeks since she left the hospital, and Pam had moved in with her, to help her prepare for the show. The preparations weren't physical, Pam would be the first to say that she had no musical talent. Nor did she have an idea of the type of costumes Charlene should wear— that was Sue's purview—or how the stage should be set, or the mechanics of the show, that came under Paul's bailiwick. Pam had taken upon herself to get Charlene mentally, and even more importantly, spiritually prepared for what was to be her farewell performance.

"I have always thought that God manifested Himself through the art of His people," Pam said. "And from the first time I heard you sing, I knew that you were channeling His love. But never, ever, have I felt more of God's presence than I do now, listening to you sing. And your new song, 'Time in a Dream,' is unbelievably moving. I can't explain how, but there is no doubt in my mind that when you had that attack, you actually did stand in the presence of God."

Charlene had told Pam, Sue, and Paul about her unique experience standing on a beach somewhere, talking with her father and with Ryan.

"There is no God," Charlene said.

"Charlene!" Pam gasped. "How can you, of all people, say such a thing? You stood before Him. You saw Ryan, you spoke with him. And you saw your father again."

"I dreamed of Ryan, and of Daddy," Charlene said. "And that wasn't the first time I ever dreamed about them. I have dreamed of them many times."

"Let me ask you something. Have any of your dreams ever been as intense as the experience you described to me?"

"No, but then I've never had a heart attack before, either."

"Where did 'Time in a Dream' come from?"

"What do you mean where did it come from? I wrote it," Charlene said. "It certainly isn't the only song I've ever written."

"No, it isn't. But you have always had to struggle before, changing words, changing notes, often abandoning one idea to go off on another entirely different tangent. But this one, you said yourself, came streaming from your mind as quickly as you could put the words on paper."

"It just happened that way," Charlene said.

"No, it didn't 'just happen that way.' That song was inspired."

"If you say so," Charlene said.

"Charlene, I don't know why you, of all people, can't believe."

"If it was true, Pam, I would have stayed there, on that beach, with Ryan and my father. Don't you understand? I didn't want to come back!"

"Didn't you say Ryan told you that God had work for you to do? That's why you came back."

"Right," Charlene said sarcastically. "Some work. I have a growing tumor behind my heart that is killing me. Whatever work you think God has for me will have to be done pretty darn fast."

"I wish I could make you understand," Pam said. "But true understanding, like true faith, has to come from within. I think the time will come when you will know."

"When will I know? And just what am I gonna know? I don't have much time left."

"You will know when you know," Pam said.

Charlene laughed. "That's very profound, Pam."

Despite herself, Pam laughed with her.

Charlene heard the phone ring, and heard her mother answer it. Like Pam, her mother would not take no for an answer and had insisted on moving in with her.

"Charlene, honey," Louise said, bringing the phone to her. "It's Paul."

Paul was already in Mexico City, having gone ahead to make all the arrangements, and make sure that the hotels and venues were ready and secure.

"Hello, Paul," Charlene said. "How is it going down there?"

"I'm doing what has to be done," Paul replied. "But how do you feel? Do you still feel up to it? The reason I ask is because it's not too late to cancel."

"I feel fine, Paul."

Louise reached out. "Charlene, let me talk to Paul."

"Mama wants to talk to you," Charlene said.

"Paul," Louise said. "Are you sure you can keep my little girl safe down there? I've been reading about Mexico, and Mexico City in the papers, and seeing stories about it on the TV. All those killin's, and the kidnappings and everything. You know those drug cartel people would love nothing better than to get hold of someone like Charlene. That place is pure evil. I don't know why you ever booked a show there in the first place."

"Louise, don't worry. The President of the United States wouldn't have more security than I'm arranging for Charlene."

"Forgive me, but I am not all that impressed, given the fact that we are right now mourning the death of our President. How do you know that the Mexicans that are supposed to be guarding Charlene won't kidnap her themselves? I've read about all the corruption in their police force. And you know that any private security force you might hire there would be even more corrupt."

"Okay, the presidential analogy may not have been the best. But we aren't using Mexican security," Paul said. "I've already arranged for our own security. Trust me, nothing is going to happen to her while she is here."

"I don't like it, but I am going to trust you, Paul," Louise said. "What other choice do I have?"

After discussing a few more last minute details with Charlene, she punched the call off and handed the phone back to her mother.

"I wish I could go with you," Pam said. "I would go, if I hadn't agreed, six months ago, to a seminar at Georgetown. . . but maybe I could get out of it."

"Don't be ridiculous, Pam," Charlene said. "You signed on to do that seminar six months ago. You know that the school has made all the arrangements for it already. If you backed out now, it could be disastrous for any future speaking engagements."

"You just be careful, Charlene. You hear me? You be very careful while you are down there."

Sue called Pam and asked her to come help her for a moment. Louise went into the kitchen to help Lucien, and Charlene found herself alone. It was funny, before her—Paul called it an "incident"—Charlene had spent a lot of time alone. Now, it seemed, there was someone with her all the time and she found this unexpected and brief period of solitude welcome.

She went over to sit on the window box seat and looked out over the expanse of her lawn. She looked for her furry, gray-tailed Mr. Fitzpatrick, but didn't see him.

R*yan, what is this all about?" Charlene asked. "You said God wants a favor. What kind of favor?"*

"I will try and explain it to you," Ryan said. "But I will only be able to open the window a tiny crack. You will have to open the door to understanding yourself.

"There are positive and negative forces in the Universe, and the veil between those forces is weakening as the Dark Forces are gaining strength. We are all a blank slate when we come into our physical form, and our ability to make choices, our free will as it were, is being lobbied by these positive and negative political forces."

"Ryan, you are saying things like positive and negative forces, but what you are talking about is simply good and evil, isn't it?" Charlene asked.

"Yes."

"I don't understand. Oh, I understand good and evil all right. But I don't understand what role I can play."

"There is a war brewing, a war of Armageddon proportions, and souls are at stake. Believe me, Charlene. You can make a difference."

Charlene was startled back to the present. Had she just now dozed off for a moment and dreamed that? Had she just experienced a vivid memory? No, it was much too vibrant, much too real to simply have been a dream, a memory, or even a hallucination. She had actually gone back, had actually revisited that moment! But how? How could that be? Is there really a God who moves in such mysterious ways?

That reminded her of the hymn by William Cowper. She had sung it in church when she was twelve years old, her very first public performance.

> *God moves in a mysterious way*
> *His wonders to perform;*
> *He plants His footsteps in the sea*
> *And rides upon the storm.*

She remembered a story she had read about Cowper, how he was often depressed, and once became so depressed that he decided to throw himself into the Thames River. He hired a cab and told the driver to take him to the river, but a heavy fog moved in, and the driver couldn't find his way. He wandered around lost until, in a pique, Cowper told him to just let him out and he would find his own way. He was surprised to find that after the aimless wandering around in the fog, the driver had let him out in front of his own doorstep. He believed then that God had sent the fog to help him find his way home, to safety, a changed and renewed man.

On the day Charlene was to leave for Mexico City, she stood in front of a small table in the bedroom she had shared with Ryan. The table was her own little shrine to him: a picture of him, their wedding picture, one of the footballs that had been used in that Super Bowl game, signed by all the players (Ryan had paid a fortune for that), and most treasured by her, the dried blue rose he had given her.

She took off her wedding and engagement ring and placed them next to the rose. It had been reported in every newspaper, magazine, and on every talk show that Charlene had never removed her rings. Now it was done. So she thought. Now it was time to move on. She didn't have much time left.

CHAPTER
61

I *have dealt with these syndromes before,*" one pop-psychiatrist guest on a highly rated, afternoon talk show said. "*She is showing classic traits of defense mechanism, arising due to traumatic loss. In other words, she is in a state of denial, and as long as she continues to wear the rings, she will be able to convince herself that her husband is still alive.*"

"*Is that bad, Doctor?*" the host asked, the expression on her face one of sympathy and concern, shared with the millions of regular viewers of her afternoon show.

"*Yes, it is very bad,*" the psychiatrist replied. "*It is a failure to grasp reality, and I fear that if she does not get therapy soon, she may never recover.*"

She knew that as soon as she hit the airport terminal, someone in the popular press would see that she had removed her rings and was ready to move on. They should only know.

When Charlene got to the airport, the car was stopped by security guards. Because the rear windows were tinted, they made Raymond put them down. They looked inside the car from both sides. Charlene stared straight ahead, not wanting to get into any conversation with a fan, but to her surprise, and if she were honest with herself, her chagrin, they did not seem to recognize her. Instead they went about their duty, mechanically, and professionally.

They made Raymond open the hood so they could look at the engine. Then they held mirrors attached to long sticks under the car. A dog sniffed all around the car before they were allowed to proceed. Charlene noticed they were doing the same screening to every car that came onto the airport grounds.

Raymond passed by the passenger terminals and drove straight to the general aviation hangar. Ryan had always had a private jet complete with crew, and after his death Charlene had kept them on. That was one of the things she most appreciated. Because of that, she was able to avoid flying commercially. In addition to the general hassle of commercial flying, she found it impossible to fly commercially without being recognized. Then she would have to undergo a flight-long dissertation on how her music had changed the passenger's life, allowed them to find love, or to cope with the death of a loved one.

Well, she had lost a loved one, and now she was dying, so she had no desire to listen to their heart-felt stories, thank you very much.

Raymond parked the car, then got her luggage out, and they walked to the general terminal where they were met by their pilot.

"I'm sorry, Mrs. McAvoy," Biff Jamison said. "But all noncommercial aviation in and out of LaGuardia is prohibited."

"What? Why?"

"I don't know, I just called operations to file my flight plan and was told that all personal aircraft were grounded. I'm on my way to operations now to see what is going on."

"Did they give you any idea how long it would be?"

"The word I got was indefinite."

As soon as Biff had told Charlene that all noncommercial aircraft were grounded, Sue had gotten on the phone. It was like Sue, Charlene thought, to stay ahead of the situation.

"I just booked you first class on American Airlines. You will connect through Dallas to Mexico City. I was able to secure you one first class ticket."

"I hate flying commercial," Charlene said.

"Well, you can't take your private jet, and it's a long way to drive," Sue said.

Charlene laughed. "You're right about that. And I thank you for being so efficient. All right, let's get over to the terminal."

When they got to the airport there was chaos everywhere. People were angry and some were crying. Something had definitely happened, but Charlene had no idea what it might have been.

"I'll find out," Sue said. She went over to talk to one of the airport officials, then came back. There were tears in her eyes.

"Sue!" Charlene said, shocked at her appearance. "What is it? What has happened?"

"It seems that three airplanes coming from Europe and bound for the States crashed into the Atlantic."

"Three crashes? But that's impossible!" Charlene said.

"Improbable, not impossible. Especially given the last transmission from each of the three planes."

"What was it?"

"Viva Domingo."

"They were hijacked, clearly," Raymond said. "But why? What does that mean?"

Sue offered only what came to her mind: "No survivors. Six hundred people killed. I don't know—" She could not hold back the tears. "Six hundred innocent people murdered," she said, her voice breaking on the words.

Charlene felt an odd sense of disconnection to terrible news. She wished that she could muster some sense of sympathy, but she could not. It was as if it never happened.

She waited for what she assumed was an appropriate length of time before she asked a question. It was a practical question, though its very practicality made it seem cold and uncaring about the lives of the six hundred who had just died.

"What time is my flight, and is it leaving on time?" she asked.

Sue looked at Raymond in a way that indicated disbelief to the question, but she bucked up to answer it professionally.

"Your flight leaves in thirty minutes. By the way, it cost a fortune to book you this late. And only because of who you are was I was able to book a seat at all. I know that doesn't matter to you, but I just thought I would tell you," Sue said.

"Is it on time?"

Sue looked up at one of the departure monitors. "It is on time," she said. "I am amazed that all travel isn't completely shut down but I suppose we have to live with horror and commerce must go on. Come on, there is someone at the concourse who will escort you to the VIP lounge. This is as far as Raymond and I can go."

Charlene looked at Sue and saw genuine sadness over the fate of those passengers who had perished in the three ill-fated flights, as well as a sense of disappointment in Charlene's cold reaction to the news.

"Sue," Charlene said. "My dear and wonderful friend. How like you it is, to be moved by such tragedy. Please don't think I am insensitive to it. It's just that—so much has happened—and I've so much on my mind now. It's almost impossible for me to comprehend such evil. There are positive and negative forces in the Universe, and the veil between those forces is weakening as the Dark Forces are gaining strength." It was as if she were compelled to say these words, as if she were hearing them just as she was speaking them. But she did not know why. . . .

"Yes," Sue said. "Yes, that is it exactly. You do understand."

Those words had come from Charlene's mouth without any conscious thought on her part—and with surprising confidence, given the lack of compassion she had felt moments earlier. Then she knew: they were Ryan's words.

Charlene embraced Sue, a long, heartfelt embrace. She also hugged Raymond then he took her luggage to one of the two agents who were waiting to escort Charlene to the VIP lounge for her brief wait before boarding.

In less than six hours, Charlene thought, she would be relaxing at the Four Seasons Hotel in the Zona Rosa of Mexico City. Hopefully, her seatmate would not recognize her and would not be chatty.

She got her wish . . . at least one of them.

In the VIP lounge, the large screen HDTV was tuned to one of the cable news channels, and a grim-looking male reporter was talking about the hijacked airliners. Even as he talked, the running scroll on the bottom of the screen was providing even more details.

. . . *Number of passengers in the Lufthansa plane was 212, including thirty nuns from the order of Our Lady of Penance Convent in Schweinfurt, coming to America in an exchange program . . .*

Charlene was the only passenger in the VIP lounge at the moment, so when she asked one of the attendants to please turn to another channel, he did so. It was a documentary of the pioneers of computer software, and at the moment, it featured a much younger Ryan McAvoy. *From the fat to the fire*, Charlene mused. But she could stand heartache as she contemplated all the families who had lost a loved one this day.

CHAPTER
62

"Hello, Miss St. John," the flight attendant said, smiling broadly. "For your information, your seatmate will be Mr. Alejandro Rojas. Do you know him?"

"No, should I?"

"Not necessarily. He is a very successful housing developer. I just thought you may have heard of him."

The other passengers began boarding; then a few moments later Mr. Rojas, with a polite greeting, took his seat beside her. Charlene realized right away that not only did she not know him . . . he didn't know her either.

Rojas slept on the flight from New York to Dallas. As it turned out, they were seatmates on the flight from DFW to Mexico City as well, and that was fine with Charlene. He hadn't been a bother so far and that is the way she liked it.

Forty-five minutes after departing DFW, the FASTEN SEAT BELTS sign came on, followed by the cabin speakers. The captain had already given his usual departure spiel: altitude, length of flight, et cetera. This, concurrent with the seat belt sign coming on, couldn't be good.

"Uh . . . ladies and gentlemen, this is the captain. We've been given permission to make a slight deviation in our flight path in order to go around a rather severe storm cell that is in front of us. I'm going to give you as comfortable a ride as possible, but we are going to experience some moderate to sometimes heavy chop. Please keep your seat belts fastened, and I'll get us through this as quickly as I can."

Within moments of the announcement, they experienced the turbulence the captain had warned of. Most of the chop felt like a car going over a very rough road, but some of it was quite severe, a long enough drop that Charlene was actually experiencing weightlessness, and if it had not been for the seat belt, she surely would have come up from her seat.

Señor Rojas started to pray and was using a rosary. Seeing Rojas with the rosary reminded her of her father's rosary, that had been with him, but was given to her just before the coffin was closed. That rosary was now in a jewelry box back home. Charlene's mother, on the other hand, had been Baptist before she married her father, who was Catholic, and after her father died, her mother went back to the Baptist church, which was primarily Charlene's experience when she went to church.

Rojas continued praying until the plane passed through the turbulence and the seat belt light was turned off again. There were a few audible sighs of relief among the other passengers in first class. Rojas put his rosary back in his pocket, then perhaps from embarrassment, or relief, or just a sense of having come so far with her, he turned to talk to her.

"Is this your first time to Mexico City?" he asked.

"No, I was here once, many years ago," Charlene said. "How about you? Have you been here before?"

"I've been here many times," Rojas said. "In fact, this marks my fiftieth year of promissory trips to the Basilica."

"The Basilica? What is that? Is that a special Mexican team or group, or something?" Charlene asked. "And what's a promissory trip?"

Mr. Rojas laughed. "So many questions. You will excuse me for asking this, but you aren't a woman of faith, are you?"

She started to say no, but she held the answer. Could she really say no? Considering all that had happened to her lately? She decided that she could say no. After all, the only thing that had happened to her that she knew, without doubt, was true was the death sentence she had received from the doctor when he told her about the tumor behind her heart.

"I guess I would have to say that I am not a person of faith," she replied. "Please tell me about this Basilica and why it is so important."

"It deals with the miracle of Our Lady of Guadalupe. Have you not heard of that?"

"No, I'm afraid I haven't," Charlene replied.

"Would you like to hear the story?"

Charlene's first thought was to answer, "No, thank you." But even as she opened her mouth, she was almost surprised to hear herself say, "Yes, please do tell it. I would love to hear the story."

Rojas began to talk. His voice was low and soothing, not the kind that would lull her to sleep, but one that, strangely, seemed to comfort her.

"Once, long ago—in 1531, actually, on December ninth—a poor man, a fifty-seven-year-old widower by the name of Juan Diego, lived in a small village near Mexico City. He was on his way to a nearby barrio to attend Mass in honor of Our Lady, and as he walked by a hill called Tepeyac, he heard beautiful music.

"Then a cloud appeared, and within the cloud he saw a young woman dressed like an Aztec princess. The young woman told him to speak to the bishop of Mexico, a Franciscan named Juan de Zumarraga, and to tell the bishop that a chapel was to be built there, in that place where she had appeared.

"Juan Diego went to the bishop, and the bishop told him that the lady would have to give him a sign. But at that same time, Juan Diego's uncle became seriously ill, so Diego forgot all about the lady. She didn't forget him, though, and she told him that his uncle would recover. She also provided fresh roses for Juan to carry to the bishop in his *tilma*, or peasant's cloak. Now this, in itself, was a sign, you see, because it wasn't the season for roses, and of course, in those days, there were no florist shops or greenhouses. When Juan Diego told the bishop about the fresh roses, and he opened his cape in the bishop's presence, the roses fell to the ground and the bishop sank to his knees. But it wasn't the roses that startled the bishop. It seems that on Diego's cape appeared an image of Mary exactly as she had appeared at the hill of Tepeyac. That was December 12, 1531, and that day is now celebrated as the day of Our Lady of Guadalupe."

"That is a beautiful story," Charlene said.

"But you think it is only a story," Rojas replied.

Charlene smiled. "I—I envy you your faith," she said.

"Would the story be more meaningful to you if I told you that some of the roses were blue?"

"What?" Charlene gasped.

"Blue roses have some meaning to you, don't they?"

"You—you know who I am."

"Only what the flight attendant told me. She said you were a famous singer. I must confess that I don't listen much to popular music, I don't know anything about you."

"Then how did you know about the blue rose?"

Rojas looked surprised. "I don't know," he answered truthfully. "I just had the idea that if the roses were blue, it would mean something to you. Does it?"

"Yes," Charlene replied without further explanation. "You said you were making a promissory trip to the Basilica. Your fiftieth, I think you said. Does that mean you go every year?"

"Yes," Rojas said. "I have a daughter—she is fifty now. When she was a baby, she was diagnosed with a rare form of cancer. This was fifty years ago, remember, and the treatment for cancer was not as advanced as it is now. The doctors told me that there was no hope.

"But I prayed to God, and I made a promise that if my daughter was cured, I would make this pilgrimage on the anniversary of her healing every year that she was alive, no matter what."

Unable to let herself believe that there was any correlation to his daughter's healing and his faith, nevertheless, slightly envious of it, she smiled indulgently.

Rojas showed a picture of his daughter, her children, and her grandchildren.

"I am glad you have such faith, Señor Rojas. And I am glad your daughter lived to provide you with such beautiful grandchildren and great-grandchildren."

"Faith is a privilege to be shared, my dear. And God gives gifts all the times . . . *Milagros,* miracles are his calling card."

Rojas grew quiet then, but his simple declaration of faith had left her feeling moved. She was also aware that there was something in great opposition happening inside her. Part of her wanted to hug this complete stranger for sharing his personal and intimate story with a complete stranger, but there was this weird swirling of hate and envy being nurtured inside her. She was in tune with her own feelings and she felt anger and hostility toward this man who, unlike her, had been given such a happy ending. She had been to more specialists and all concurred that her cancer was incurable. There was no happy ending for her. She was also acutely aware that for all the money in the world, success, and fame, none of it could give her that sense of peace, nor did it save her father or her husband. *What about me?* she wanted to cry out. *What about* my *life?*

CHAPTER
63

· Mexico City ·

When the door to the plane opened, Paul was standing there in the Jetway with a team of private security agents, waiting for her. Most people can't even come to the gate anymore, and Paul was actually standing in the Jetway. She wondered how he'd gotten access until she saw some uniformed airline executives standing there with him, waiting to whisk Charlene off the plane. She couldn't help but wonder if there was any limit to Paul's ability to get things done.

Mr. Rojas was coming behind her, and because he was old and lamed by ancient knees and protesting joints, he needed assistance. She crooked her arm to let him walk with her.

"What are you doing, Charlene?" Paul asked. "We are going to be late."

"Late for what, Paul?" Charlene asked. "Mr. Rojas was very helpful to me during the flight down, and the least we can do is help him off the plane."

"Helpful in what way?" Paul asked, clearly irritated by the situation.

"Not in any way you would understand," Charlene said. "In fact, I'm not sure I understand it myself. Come along, Mr. Rojas, just hold on to my arm and we'll get down all right."

"Thank you, Miss St. John," Rojas said as the two of them moved slowly down the Jetway. There was a wheelchair waiting for Rojas when they reached the gate, and Charlene wished him well, then left the airport with Paul.

She was used to checking into hotels under assumed names, but she was quite surprised when she saw how Paul had registered her.

"Eva Perón?" she said. "Paul, you actually checked me in under the name of one of the most famous women in all of Latin America?"

"Yeah, well, that's the only name I could think of," Paul replied.

Charlene laughed.

Five minutes after unpacking and appreciating the courtyard of the Four Seasons Hotel, Charlene picked up the phone and dialed Paul's number.

"This is Paul Maxwell."

"Paul, I'm going to take a drive."

"I can't go right now, Charlene. I'm waiting on a call to confirm some details of the show."

"I don't mean to sound put-offish, Paul, but I didn't phone you to ask you to join me. I'm going for a drive, by myself."

"I don't think that's such a good idea," Paul said.

"Paul, my father is dead. I don't need a surrogate father."

Paul sighed, indicating that he knew he had been beaten. "All right, I'll have one of the security men bring the SUV around."

"Thank you."

Charlene didn't tell Paul, but she had no intention of going with one of the security men, so she didn't even approach the SUV she saw parked at the far end of the curved driveway. Instead, she got into one of the hotel's town cars that was parked around on the side. She felt she just needed to get away from the "madness" that always accompanied major tours and public events, despite Paul's and the others' genuine concern for her safety.

"*Señora?*" the driver said.

"I would like you to take me to the Basilica, please."

"*Señora*, it is nighttime. The Basilica is closed," the driver said. Charlene knew that if she didn't go now, she never would get up enough nerve to do this again.

"I know, but please take me there. I would like to see it, even from the outside."

"*Sí, señora.*" The man behind the wheel was more than accommodating to Charlene. After all, she was an American and she would tip him well.

"How far is it?" Charlene asked as the car pulled away from the hotel.

"*Cinco minutos, señora,*" he replied. Then he translated. "Five minutes."

As they rode through the Zona Rosa, Charlene looked around at the busy street, taking in all the buildings and apartment complexes. She recognized many of the American chains like 7-Eleven, Burger King, and McDonald's . . . but so many signs were in Spanish and she had no idea what they were advertising.

The driver turned down a dark street and pulled in between two buildings and stopped the car. Charlene immediately sensed that something wasn't right about this.

"What are you doing?" she asked. "Why have we stopped? Why are we in this alley?"

The driver started honking his horn, and five men appeared from behind one of the metal doors onto the alley. The door was marked with graffiti that read, VIVA DOMINGO, and Charlene thought to herself that there might not be a "Viva Charleno" if this played out the way that she was seeing it.

"Get your famous *gringa* ass out of my car," the driver said.

"What is this about?" Charlene asked. "Why are you doing this?"

"You think I do not know who you are? You are Charlene St. John, the famous American singer. And you are worth much money to my friends and me."

When Charlene exited the car, she found herself standing in the middle of what seemed to be a very long, narrow alley that would only fit one car. There were two people guarding her behind the car, and four others in front. They were arguing in Spanish about what they should do with her. She knew the word meaning "to kill" was *matar,* and that was definitely used a few times. It was at that moment she realized how tall the buildings were on both sides and that they went straight up and formed great columns.

She smelled something very familiar and realized that it was McDonald's french fries, a universal smell. Where there were McDonald's, there were people, at all hours of the night. If she could get their attention, maybe they would help her.

But yelling for help would do nothing, this she knew instinctively. And though she knew the word for "help me" in Spanish, *ayudame,* she didn't think shouting that would accomplish anything either.

She could scream. But, too often now, with the violence and evil—the Dark Forces—in the world, a scream would simply send people running in the opposite direction.

"Sing, girl, sing." She heard her father's voice. . . . "You know what to do."

Did she actually hear this? Or did she imagine it? Whatever it was, it was inspired. She was told that the entire world recognized her voice, so that is exactly what she began to do. She sang an aria, her voice rising to magnificent heights of volume and power.

Charlene St. John might have been able to navigate a crowd without being recognized, but there was one thing that was undeniable and recognizable and that was her voice. When Charlene opened her mouth, her would-be captors were stunned, and by the time they were thinking on their feet again, a crowd of people had started to form to hear where her voice was coming from.

Within one minute there were enough people there for Charlene to be signing autographs, taking photos, all while singing as loudly as she could. Charlene grabbed two of her would-be kidnappers and pulled them into a photo with her, kissing one of them on the cheek.

But as she touched him, it felt as if, somehow, the gates of Hell had opened. She couldn't explain it, not even to herself and certainly to no one else, but she felt the swirling pool of evil in his core as a "black force."

She recognized that this feeling was not pure, and it certainly wasn't positive. It was frightening, yes, but much more than frightening. It wasn't just that the man was evil—evil itself became almost sentient.

As the crowd moved her down toward the main drag, she saw Paul standing there with a camera crew from the local affiliate. Her SUV and a security detail were waiting to take her back to her hotel.

"What are you doing here, Charlene, of all places?" Paul asked, surprised to see her coming out of the alley. He had been looking everywhere for her and gotten totally freaked out—nearly ready to call out the national police to find her.

"It just happened," Charlene replied without being more specific.

"Come on. I'm going to get you back to the hotel."

"No, not yet," Charlene said. "I still have one more stop to make."

"Charlene, don't be silly," Paul said. "I don't know what you were doing here in this alley, but I have a feeling it wasn't something you had planned."

Charlene was not used to hearing the word no. She just found out she was dying a few weeks ago and she had just foiled a plot to kidnap her; she felt she was entitled to do what she wanted.

"Paul, I am going to do this," Charlene said. "And I can either do this with you as my manager, making all the arrangements for the concert coming up, or . . ." She let the sentence hang.

"Or what?" Paul asked, concern in his voice.

"Or I can do it without you as my manager. It's your call."

"All right, all right," Paul said. "I won't try to stop you. But, there's something I must insist upon—meaning that if you don't agree, then you really will have to do it without me as your manager, because I will quit."

Despite the intensity of the moment, or perhaps because of it, Charlene smiled. "All right, Paul, what it is that you insist upon?"

"You will take the SUV and a security guard."

Charlene stepped up to Paul and kissed him on the cheek. "Isn't it fun when we threaten each other and neither of us mean it?" she asked. "I'll take the SUV and the security guard."

"And call me when you get back."

"Yes, Mama G," Charlene said with a little laugh as she slipped into the backseat of the SUV.

Mama G? Where did that *come from?* she wondered. . . . She had only meant to say *Mama.*

· Mexico City ·

As Charlene and her bodyguard walked toward the Basilica—which reminded her of the Space Mountain ride at Disney World—she noticed a church to its left that seemed to be lopsided and sinking. She had been told that the Basilica was closed, and pulling on a few locked doors seemed to confirm that. Not ready to give up, she approached yet another door where she saw a young Mexican priest who could not have been more than thirty years old. He was startled when he saw her, not because he was afraid, but because of who she was—or at least who she appeared to be.

"You?" the priest said. "Are you Charlene St. John McAvoy?"

Charlene started to deny it, but she was standing in front of a church, and he was a priest—so she couldn't do it.

"Yes," she said.

"Encantado. Que gran privilegio," he said.

"I'm sorry, I don't speak Spanish."

"I am privileged to see you," the priest translated. "Why have you come?"

"I'm not sure why I came," Charlene admitted. "I am afraid that I have no faith. I have no particular belief. But I met a man on the plane. His name was Mr. Rojas, and he has come here every year for fifty years on what he calls a 'promissory trip.' It has something to do with his belief that prayer saved his daughter when she was a little girl."

"There have been many miracles worked by Our Lady of Guadalupe," the young priest said. "God has worked miracles through you, through your music, though you may not know it."

"I've been told that," Charlene said.

"And how does that make you feel?"

"It makes me feel uncomfortable. I'm not a miracle worker, Padre." Somewhere she had heard that priests in Mexico were called padres. "I am merely a woman with a good voice."

"And where do you think you got that voice?"

"I was born with it."

"Does everyone have a voice so beautiful?"

Charlene smiled as she thought of Anna York in the Baptist church, back when she used to attend. Anna York had the worst voice she had ever heard, but seemed, somehow, to sing the loudest.

"No," she admitted. "Not everyone."

"God grants such gifts only to a few people," the priest said. "And accepting that gift means also accepting the obligation to use it for His glory."

"If you say so," Charlene replied. The conversation was making her uncomfortable, and she was wondering now why she had come here in the first place.

"Do you want to go inside?" the priest asked.

"You can let me in?"

"Yes." He opened the door just wide enough for her to enter. "Please remember to close the door when you leave."

"I will, Padre, and thank you," Charlene said.

CHAPTER
65

The priest walked away and Charlene went inside, thankful for this moment of privacy.

The church wasn't completely dark, but very dimly lit by dozens of flickering candles. She stood just inside the door for a moment, awed by the silence and majesty of the enormous church. She had played in large auditoriums many times and was fairly good at estimating the number of people a particular venue could accommodate. Ten thousand could be seated here, easily.

Awkwardly, she walked up to the framed likeness of Our Lady of Guadalupe. There was something beatific about the image of the standing, robed woman. The frame was gold, and above the picture was a crown.

She thought about this place, a house of worship where so many of the faithful come to ask for help and favors.

Looking down, she saw the bloodstained lines that formed near the four moving sidewalks that people would stand on to gaze upward at the Lady in the frame. Bloodstained because so many had gotten there on their knees to pray and ask for help. Before leaving the hotel today, Charlene had gone online to look up this iconic place. She learned that there had been an attempt to destroy it by bomb, and though the bomb did some damage, the cloak was undamaged.

She also knew that, as with the Shroud of Turin, there had been various scientific studies to either authenticate or discredit the miracle of the cloak. They had been unable to discredit it, which meant that the believers still had their faith to support its authenticity.

As Charlene stood there, she felt somewhat hypocritical and quite foolish asking for a healing when she didn't really believe it was possible. She was dying, but death was not a fear of hers. If there was an afterlife, then perhaps she would see her beloved Ryan and father again. If death was all there was . . . so be it. At least all this pain would be no more.

Charlene heard someone sniffing behind her, which startled her because she had been certain she was alone. Turning, she saw a woman dressed in black and wearing a veil. The woman was weeping.

"I'm sorry, I didn't see you when I came in," Charlene said. Charlene must have left the door open enough for the woman to come in after her.

The woman didn't respond, but continued to weep quietly.

Charlene walked over to her. "Are you okay?" she asked. "Do you speak English? Is there anything I can do for you? I want to help."

"There is nothing you can do," the woman said. "I lost my only son. He was murdered brutally."

Charlene knew of the brutal slayings that were taking place in Mexico's drug war. "I'm so sorry," Charlene said.

"I have come here to find peace," the woman said.

This made her feel awkward, and she groped for the right words, not really finding them: "Look, my name is Charlene St. John. I'm a singer. Maybe you have heard of me?" she added somewhat sheepishly. Charlene reached into her purse and pulled out Paul's card with his cell phone number printed on it. "I'm giving a concert here. Perhaps you would like to come. I'm told that the tickets are very hard to come by. I'd love to see you there. If you'd like to—"

The woman stopped weeping and looked up with an expression that startled Charlene. It was an expression of disbelief and displeasure. "Did you not hear me? I just told you I lost my son. *And you respond by inviting me to a concert?*"

"I'm sorry," Charlene mumbled. "I meant only to—well, I'm sorry," she repeated. Charlene, clearly feeling like an idiot, and not comfortable in this place to begin with, hurried out of the church.

CHAPTER
66

When Charlene returned to her hotel room that evening, she felt the words of a song nearly bursting from her. Sitting down at the desk, she used hotel stationery and pen to write the new words, which she set to the tune of her signature song, "Someone, Somewhere."

> *This time and this place*
> *Are ours by a certain grace*
> *A gift from one loving Source*
> *That guides us on our course*
> *Somewhere is here*
> *Sometime is now*
> *Take my hand, dear*
> *Let me show you how*
> *We are one*
> *We are one*
> *We are one*

She had just finished writing the song when the phone in her room rang. "Hello?"

"Charlene, turn on the TV," Paul said.

"Why? I don't speak Spanish."

"Turn to channel 360. It's one of the satellite news networks from the U.S."

"What am I looking for?"

"You'll see as soon as you turn it on."

Charlene picked up the remote, then clicked on the TV. It was showing the replay of a soccer match and the announcer was shouting in excitement as one of the players scored: *"Bustamante es exitoso!"*

She punched in channel 360.

"We are bringing you breaking news about the latest earthquake, this time affecting the lower half of the Indian subcontinent. The unusual thing about the earthquake is the area that it covers," the announcer was saying. "Like the earthquake in Turkey that has taken place recently, the area covered by this earthquake is unprecedented. Equally unprecedented is the strength of the earthquake, which, like the Turkey quake, registered at 9.5 on Richter scale. One third of the subcontinent appears to have been flattened. There is no historical record of two such large events occurring so closely together in time. We've entered new territory here. We have no way of determining yet the extent of casualties from the earthquake, but early estimates indicate that millions have already perished," the announcer said in somber tones.

The screen was filled with pictures of the devastation, cities reduced to rubble, dazed survivors walking around as if they were lost ants whose colonies had been decimated.

For the next several minutes Charlene watched the pictures and listened to the descriptions of the destruction, almost unaware of the tears streaming down her face. Everything seemed to be flooding into her—flashing into focus. The lecture, her dreamlike reunion with Ryan, and her day, starting with planes crashes, meeting with Mr. Rojas, the Basilica, and the strange encounter with the woman at the church.

Then she got an idea, and she picked up the phone and dialed Paul's room.

"Are you watching this?" Paul asked. He sat on the edge of his hotel bed watching the scenes of destruction and chaos in India. He had to force himself back to the present reality to hear what Charlene was saying to him.

"Paul, I want this concert to be a pay-per-view. Just like we did before." She smiled slyly, knowing what kind of response she would get from him. "I've already announced I want all the ticket proceeds to go to Turkey for the relief of all those injured and displaced people, and this would be the perfect time to try to raise funds for this new horrific event."

"Impossible," Paul replied, sputtering in surprise at her request. "We can't possibly make the broadcast arrangements for pay-per-view at this late date."

"Make it happen, Paul," Charlene said. She didn't often "pull rank" with him, but she felt she had to see this through. There was so little time left—for anything.

"How am I supposed to pull this off?" Paul asked, clearly frustrated by her impossible request.

"You can announce to the world that this is to be my farewell concert, and my farewell gift to the world."

"Even so, it would take a miracle," Paul said.

Charlene smiled. "Do you know anything about Our Lady of Guadalupe?" She had been learning a lot herself—and very quickly—about the Lady and what she represented. Millions of people believed this was a sacred place, where miracles occurred for those who had faith. "This might just be the right place to help a miracle come true," she said. Suddenly, she knew—she really understood—what she was here to do.

"I'll do what I can," Paul promised.

Over the next few days, the earthquake in India, and the announcement that Charlene St. John was giving the proceeds of her farewell concert to benefit not only the earthquake victims in Turkey but also the victims of the Indian subcontinent became symbiotic news stories, creating a frenzy of subscribers to the concert show, raising millions of dollars.

Charlene did a round of publicity while in Mexico City, promoting both the live concert and the pay-per-view show. She did several television interviews, not only for Mexican TV but satellite TV networks from around the world, speaking, when necessary, through translators.

"How much money do you think you will raise?" a German television station wanted to know. "I mean how much of what you raise will actually go to the victims of the recent earthquakes?"

"Everything it makes will go to help those people," Charlene replied.

The interviewer chuckled condescendingly. "Really, Fraulein St. John? When you subtract your fee, the cost of production, and all other attendant expenses, do you actually think that there will be enough money to amount to anything?"

"I will take no fee," Charlene said. "And I will personally pay for all expenses, so that every dollar raised will go to help those who survived these horrendous earthquakes. And," she added, "I will match whatever is raised, dollar for dollar."

"I do believe you have gone insane," Paul said after the journalist left. "Once the world hears that, tickets are going to sell like salted peanuts. And you not only say that you aren't taking your fee, but you are matching the money raised?"

Charlene laughed. "Don't worry Paul, when I say I am paying all expenses, that includes your commission."

"Now you're hurting my feelings," Paul said. "I get it. I can go without MY commission. I also get that you're so charitable; it's who you are. But somebody around here has to pay our bills, and that somebody happens to be me!"

But in the end, Charlene decided to cover all their bills and expenses from her own pocket. So the staff would get paid, anyway. She wouldn't tell them that, though, until the event had concluded. It would be her secret—and the Lady's.

Paul had no idea how prophetic his comment was about her "insanity" being contagious. The entire production staff at the show venue announced that they would be donating their salaries, and the theater waived the charges.

At the first rehearsal, Charlene sang the new song she had written. The backup musicians did not need to go through it more than once, because it had been written to the same tune and rhythm as "Someone, Somewhere." It was stunning, and all of the stagehands and event personnel who were present gathered around to listen. When she finished, there were tears in the eyes of many, and nearly all crossed themselves.

Paul had the song recorded that very afternoon, and it was released almost immediately. Within three days of its release, the song had gone viral over the Internet, raising over $5 million.

On the day before the show, Charlene was doing her last rehearsal when a couple of Mexican police officers came to present her with a letter of appreciation.

"Thanks to you, Miss St. John, and the photograph that was taken of you kissing the cheek of one of those thugs who attempted to kidnap you, we have captured the six most notorious outlaws in Mexico. They are members of the most evil cartel of drug and human trafficking, responsible for hundreds of murders."

The policeman showed her some of the photos that people in the gathered crowd had taken of her that night, including the one of her kissing the cheek of the outlaw.

"You see here," one of the policemen pointed out, "the words *Viva Domingo*. That was what gave us the clue as to who these men were."

Behind the words VIVA DOMINGO, Charlene saw a graffiti sketch in the alley of the same iconic figure of Our Lady of Guadalupe she had seen in the Basilica.

"That's funny," she said, pointing to the photo. "I remember seeing the words *Viva Domingo*, but I don't remember seeing this sketch behind the words."

"What sketch?" Paul asked.

"This one," Charlene said. "Are you telling me you don't see the drawing of a woman in robes behind the words?"

"I don't see anything but the words," Paul said.

"Do you see it?" Charlene asked one of the policemen.

"I have been there several times in the last few days, Señora McAvoy," the policeman said. "There is nothing there but the words."

"How very strange that I see it, and none of you do," Charlene said. She reached for the picture so she could point it out—but this time she saw nothing but the words. She did see, however, rejoicing in the crowd, the same woman she had seen in the church. But that did not seem possible to her. But something about the woman felt so right. Charlene felt as if a great weight was being lifted from her chest when she looked at the woman and she also felt an overwhelming need to do something positive, an aching to do good came over her. Charlene wondered what this meant and if there was anything she needed to do.

As Charlene made her way to the rehearsal, she reflected upon the strangeness of the last few days. Meeting Mr. Rojas, and experiencing his unwavering faith, had opened her mind and heart to matters that had been closed for so long. The attempted kidnapping had rattled her and the encounter with the woman in black in the Basilica hadn't helped. And then suddenly seeing the same woman in the photo sent a powerful chill up her spine.

Paul had to stay behind at the hotel to arrange for some last-minute details with regard to the concert, so there were just Charlene and her driver in the car. Charlene was sitting in the backseat, humming a little song to herself, when she saw another car come up beside them. They were on the road near the Pyramid of the Sun and the Calle de los Muertos, or "Street of the Dead." The back window of the adjacent car was rolled down, and because the SUV she was riding in did not have tinted windows, the backseat passenger was able to see her. Charlene was stunned by the expression on his face. She was looking into the face of pure evil. She cringed at this image . . . and suddenly the world went black.

When she woke up, she was surprised to see Paul and several others standing around her bed. What were all these people doing in her bedroom? Wait, this wasn't her bedroom.

"Paul, what is this place? Where am I? What has happened?"

"You don't know? You don't remember?" Paul asked.

"No, the last thing I remember is sitting in the car, going to the rehearsal. Oh, the other car. Was I in an accident?"

"It was no accident," Paul said. "The people in the other car were part of the cartel you helped bring down. They ran your car off the road."

"The driver?" Charlene said. "What happened to the man who was driving me?"

"He wasn't hurt."

"Thank God for that," Charlene said.

Paul smiled. "You can thank God for something else as well," he said.

"What?"

"During the x-rays to make certain there were no internal injuries, the doctors made a discovery. At first they weren't sure, so they redid the test four times."

"A discovery of what?" Charlene said.

"Your cancer," Paul said. "Charlene, it is gone. Completely gone!"

"What? How?"

"The doctor says it was a spontaneous healing; a *milagro,* I think he called it."

"A miracle," Charlene interpreted.

"Yes, well, you did tell me this is the place of miracles, didn't you?"

"I did, yes," Charlene said, realizing even as she spoke that the real miracle was not in her spontaneous healing, but in her search for something to explain or perhaps assuage the pain and sadness that she had been feeling so intensely. She knew that not only would she get out of that hospital in time for her concert—it may or may not be her farewell concert, after all—but it was clear to her that she was embarking on a journey that she never would have imagined.

CHAPTER
68

Charlene St. John walked onstage in Mexico City to open her concert on a picture-perfect night. She mixed a bit of Spanish with English as she greeted her fans, some sixty thousand who had packed the outdoor arena that had just been converted from the Olympic Stadium into a state-of-the-art contemporary performance space. Hers was the first musical event to be held there, and she was the first artist to test the marvelous sound system that reached every seat in the house. In this way, she felt she could touch—and be touched by—each and every person in attendance. They had come out to see her perform and to hear her world-famous voice, but she had come to this place with a purpose as well: to put herself in the presence of what she had come to think of as her special guide.

For now Charlene was obsessed, or perhaps consumed was a better word, by Our Lady of Guadalupe. The image of the woman on the cloth haunted her, and the appearance of the same woman in different guises over the last few days unsettled and yet comforted her at the same time. But no longer did she have any doubt that she had been summoned here to receive a message, or perhaps to face the end of her life, if that was the will of the Almighty. She no longer cared. She just wanted to show up where she was supposed to and to open her ears and her mind and her heart to the word she was supposed to receive.

The sound of her own voice startled her as she began the first number of the first set. The orchestra, with whom she had rehearsed diligently over the past few days, followed the tempo they had established and blended with and amplified her astounding vocal range as if every instrument were one voice—her voice. Soon she forgot everything else that had been in her mind and was, simply, the song. One number, then another, then another.

The audience was entranced. They applauded and stomped and cheered during and after each song. It was clear that they loved this slight woman who entertained them so expertly and moved their hearts with each word that she sang. A wave of love swam back and forth between the performer and the audience. Charlene's backup singers, five beautiful voices who probably could have been superstars in their own right, stood in awe between the orchestra and the main act and felt it all come together in a totally unique way.

For a full hour, Charlene St. John sang her heart out. Seven big numbers. It passed for her in the blink of an eye, and then it was time for a break between sets.

She usually did three sets—one long one to begin, then two shorter ones—over a period of three hours. But now she felt so energized and inspired that she did not want to break. She said to the audience, "What if I just continue for a little longer before we take our first break?"

Sixty thousand fans roared their approval. Even the musicians were caught up in the excitement of the moment and wanted to play on. Charlene bowed, then turned around to her supporting groups—the orchestra, backup singers, and crew—and folded her hands as if in prayer, bowed to them, and mouthed the words, "Thank you."

As Charlene sang the next song, she looked out over the audience, visible only as dim faces in the darkness, except for one person. She almost gasped as she saw her. It was the same grieving woman she had seen in the church, no longer in black, but wearing an all-white, two-piece business suit.

No longer weeping, the woman looked relaxed, radiant, and, Charlene had not noticed this before, beautiful—beautiful beyond description.

Charlene could not tell whether the audience saw the same thing she did, nor did she know whether she was supposed to share her vision with them, or with anyone, for that matter. Instead of being startled or confused, Charlene felt a remarkable sense of peace. And she heard the woman speaking to her, not in words that were audible to her ears, but words that resonated in her heart.

Her mind—and her spirit—refocused.

"My Lady, it's you!" She felt the warmth of the unearthly light that emanated from the woman, who suddenly disappeared from the audience and now stood beside her.

"My child," the Lady said, as if continuing a conversation over tea. The voice filled and surrounded Charlene St. John, and she wondered what was happening in the real world. Was she still singing? Was the audience seeing this amazing vision?

"You have been given life by the Creator that you may do good and serve others. This you have done with great love in your heart, and you continue to touch so many people." She extended her arm, pointing to the audience.

Charlene answered with humility. "But how can I sing for the entire world? Does it really matter all that much? My voice is not *that* great."

"Oh, my beautiful one, when the Almighty desires the word to be proclaimed to all the people, He can give voice to the voiceless and sight to the blind. To you He has given the ability to achieve such a task." Charlene felt her other self singing to the audience while conversing with the Lady.

> *Do you see the light*
> *Of all creation: the day, the night?*
> *A universe of peace and love*
> *Of goodness that comes down from above*
> *Take his hand*
> *And you will understand*
> *That we are one*
> *We are one*
> *We are one*

"You are a child of God, in whom He is very pleased. You have accomplished the mission He has set out for you. We are one."

The mysterious lady said the words "we are one," just as Charlene sang the last line of "Someone, Somewhere"—*We are one*—her voice lifting to Heaven in the highest, purest, and most powerful note, causing even the angels to sing in concert with her.

As Charlene held the last note of the song, the mysterious woman rose, ascending high into the heavens. She became more radiant, her light filling the arena, and Charlene realized that she was the only one who could see her.

The pure white two-piece business suit suddenly burst into all the robes and colors of Our Lady of Guadalupe, and in her heart, Charlene heard her say, *"Remember I told you—I lost my son."*

Never had Charlene sung more beautifully, and there was thunderous applause for her from everyone in the auditorium. Just before Charlene left the stage, Paul brought her a note. She read it and smiled.

"Ladies and gentlemen," she said. "The world has been most generous in response to the recent tragedies that have ravaged our world. In sales to this concert, and in sales of the recording, we have raised almost fifteen million dollars. I am going to match that amount, as are three of the world's richest men. As a result, including many other generous individual donations, more than one hundred million dollars for the relief efforts have been raised this very night.

"I am told that $305 million was raised for relief in Haiti after the disastrous earthquake in January 2010, and I feel certain that generous people will surpass that. God bless you all, thank you, and good night!"

I *knew my lassie could do it. Just think how much your love has touched the world!"* Ian's voice was as strong and immediate in her heart as if he were standing beside her. And she was sure now that he was.

"I know, Daddy, and I know that you will be with me for every step on my journey now," she answered from within the dream.

The anger and grief she had felt ever since her diagnosis, her desperate loss of hope for life, seemed to be receding to more distant parts of her soul, to shores of consciousness that were far away from this place and this time. How could this be? Her father's touch . . . the intercession of Our Lady . . . the overwhelming light that had enveloped her in those moments when she had sung her heart out for the people—and their love for her in return. Something that could only be called miraculous had occurred in the here and now of Charlene's life. Something that had transformed her.

She awoke and said a little prayer to ask for some understanding and wisdom from the blessed Lady who had lost a son and gained a new daughter.

CHAPTER
69

E ver since the trip to New York and the encounter with Charlene St. John—followed by the tragic events playing out in the world—Tyler Michaels had felt more emotionally raw than he had ever felt in his life. And through it all, the loss of Karen and Jeremy pierced him like a warrior's lance, penetrating his body and soul. He knew intellectually that he was not the only person in the world who had suffered such grievous personal losses. Around the world, every day, families were torn apart, parents, husbands and wives, children, dearest friends were taken from those who loved them . . . But the hurt was real nonetheless, and the surgeon who had lived for so long on the fastest of fast tracks now felt completely derailed.

What is my purpose? Saving lives? I saved many lives before Charlene St. John, but none since. I am without a destination.

The Swedish-inflected voice returned occasionally to advise him—or haunt him—and he began to listen to it in a different way, trying to understand the messages rather than critique them.

He was expecting Nurse Rae Loona to stop by his home for dinner after the conclusion of the worldwide broadcast of the President's funeral. He didn't necessarily feel up for it, but neither was he going to try to stop her. Never stand between Rae Loona and her need to express love and friendship.

He tried to read a magazine, sitting in his living room with a small fire burning in the fireplace. His heart had never been heavier, yet he was sick of feeling sorry for himself. It was very difficult for Tyler to concentrate on what he was reading or to keep a coherent thought in his head for more than a minute at a time . . . so he sometimes wondered if the messages he heard were coming from some long-ago memories, perhaps university or medical school lectures that he had heard while half-asleep twenty years ago. Who knew?

It was not a particular surprise that he suddenly found himself confronted with a fair-skinned man in a dark blue coat with bright brass buttons and a starched, ruffled white shirt with long, flowing white sleeves poking through at his coat cuffs. His fingers were long and tapered and seemed, oddly, to be ink stained. How could a spirit—if that's what he was—have ink stains on his hands?

"You are seeking, my friend, just as I sought for a lifetime to touch the truth of existence, to understand the very point of creation and all subsequent existence of all creatures great and small, of our human enterprise in this vale of tears. I understand."

"Well, I'm glad you do," Tyler offered, "because I am having a hell of a time understanding what is happening to me—and what is happening to the world. I thought I was so educated, that I was 'in charge' of my own life. That is certainly not the case. Not happenin', as they say."

"Modern man believes himself to be wise and full of knowledge, and it is true that through his hard work and study, the human being has progressed far beyond anything I achieved, and more people today know far more than the average person three centuries ago. However, you have not recovered the lost knowledge that I pursued in my time. No one has—yet."

"What 'lost knowledge'?" Tyler found himself more baffled, yet more intrigued with each passing minute of this bizarre conversation. He almost couldn't believe it was happening. He hoped Rae would show up and see this fellow and hear what they were talking about.

"Since the fall of man and woman in the Garden of Eden—"

"That's all great, but I'm not religious in any way, shape, or form."

"Nor am I," the figure stated. *"Where I am now is beyond religion but is pure spirit."*

"I'm no philosopher. I just want to understand the world around me. But it gets more confusing rather than less so, the older I get. And science is even more complicated, raising more questions than answers, as far as I'm concerned. So where do I look for the answers? How can anyone tell me *why* I lost Karen, or *why* the President of the United States was assassinated?"

"There is always a reason behind every action and reaction. It goes back to the first movement of energy at the first moment of time, if you will. We all are here for a divine purpose and a spiritual end."

"Many people today think the end is near—very near."

"It is always near, and becoming nearer, because the beginning is increasingly far away—but only in time. Time does not really exist, as such, but is a concept of measurement conceived by man. Like an inch in your system of measurement. Does an inch exist, as such? No. But you can certainly measure a tabletop in inches, and if I tell you that a tabletop is thirty-six by forty-eight inches, you have a clear idea of the size of the surface. A real tabletop—that one over there, for instance—" The speaker pointed at a coffee table right in front of Tyler. *"—exists, whether or not there is any way to measure it or to talk about it in terms of its size and shape."*

Tyler wasn't overly impressed; he vaguely remembered his college philosophy courses and some of the systems of thought and logic to which he had been exposed. At the same time, he had not been a philosophical thinker himself ever in his life. And never had he considered how science and philosophy could be—perhaps should be—blended in order to understand the world.

"How does all this relate to what is happening today?" For a change, he was thinking not only of his own life but all that was happening around him and around the world. He sensed that the globe was shifting on its axis and something was about to explode. Did this visitor have the answer for him?

"We are all related to one another as players on an eternal stage, each with his own role in his own time. You, my medical friend, are called to be present at the final confrontation."

Before he could respond to the philosopher, Tyler heard the doorbell. It was Rae. When she came in, she gave him a hard hug and stood back to look at him. "Mikey, you're looking rather peaked. Did you see a ghost or something?"

"Yes," he said.

"Oh, I get it. Hearing voices and seeing visions. Well, I guess that's part of the package."

He told her exactly what he had experienced.

"Any new conclusions? No? Well, let's get some music on, and I'll fix up a bite to eat. You need food in that skinny stomach."

After a late supper, Rae and Tyler watched the eleven o'clock news together. The anchor read a news bulletin from overseas:

"In Tokyo, a Shinto splinter sect is apparently responsible for an attack on the city subway system that has claimed at least sixty-seven lives today.

The terrorists used sarin gas in a coordinated assault on twenty trains throughout the city during the early rush hour. Police officials say it is a near-miracle that more people were not killed, since literally millions use the subway during this time. They fear it is the first of a planned series of gas attacks and have placed the entire city on alert for a repeat of the incident."

"The whole world has gone crazy," Rae intoned.

"Then let's try to stay sane, Nurse Loona. For what it's worth."

"Oh, it's worth a lot, Dr. Michaels. Now you need to go beddy-bye. We'll talk tomorrow."

·New York·

N ow, stay with me on this," Dave Hampton said during the Critical Update segment of his show.

"Camera two, move in," the director said.

The set disappeared and the screen was filled with a close-up of Dave's head and shoulders. This allowed the viewers at home to see the sincerity in his eyes.

"I'm not sure how I know this—to be honest with you, I can't actually say that I do know it. But I feel it. I feel it with every bone in my body.

"There is some connection between the earthquakes in Turkey and India, and the assassination of President Jackson. I know, earthquakes are natural disasters and the assassination was an act of man, yes, but both were influenced by, maybe even created by this Dark Force.

"Think about it, we've always had disasters and there have been wackos aplenty who wanted to take down political leaders. But the level of events are coming fast and furious, folks, and you only have to look at your local news to see how the level of insane crimes has jumped in the last few weeks.

"I have to believe that this is part of a bigger picture, something the likes of which we've never seen. I know I sound like a nut-job, but I have become convinced that we are facing nothing less than a Dark Force.

"What is this Dark Force? Is it something physical and scientific, like dark matter? Dark matter exists, we know this. Is this Dark Force something more metaphysical, such as the religious concept of a dark force of evil?

"What does all this portend? That, my friends, I cannot say, because I do not know. I know only that it is there, and it has caught me up in its whirlpool. But I am determined to keep talking about it, to bring you folks information so that you can think about what this might mean and if we somehow can come up with a plan to combat this force that might very well threaten all our lives."

Dave held his hand up, palm facing the camera.

"This is Dave Hampton saying, good night, America."

· *Leawood, Colorado* ·

I t was so simple, yet so important to do it—and to do it right. Scott Dryer had quit the Boy Scouts after a couple of years because, as he told his mom, he felt they didn't go far enough. It wasn't tough enough for him.

He wanted a challenge. He wanted results. He wanted to make a mark on the world. His mark.

He hated people who didn't try, who had things handed to them, or who whined and complained that they were persecuted. They were a drag on everyone else. Most especially, they were a drag against Scott Dryer's big plans for success. They should be punished.

Scott's world was getting smaller by the day. He was nineteen and had no idea where he was headed. He had dropped out of high school in his senior year and had no plans of going back for his diploma. His parents were at a loss, but they let him stay home because he had nowhere else to go. And he was their only child.

They sent him to therapy, but that had been a disaster. After two sessions, the psychiatrist suggested he seek treatment elsewhere. He never told Scott's parents why.

He was driving his father's car, without permission, and didn't have money for gasoline. But he had enough money for supplies. Black spray paint and kerosene. He didn't know whether kerosene was the best or most efficient fuel, but it sounded right, and he knew it was flammable. He had a book of paper matches that he had found in a kitchen drawer. He also took possession of the matches without permission.

My choice. My decision. My destiny.

After sunset, Scott drove to the B'nai Shalom Temple and pulled around to the rear of the structure. Within just a few minutes, he ignited a pile of linen and blankets soaked in kerosene that he had packed against the back door. Without hesitation, he drove around to the front of the building again and jumped out of the car, leaving it running.

On the concrete front wall he spray-painted a huge swastika under the illumination of a bright streetlight. He didn't particularly care if anyone saw him doing it. It was more important to get the job done, whatever the consequences.

It was more important to send a message that these people must go. And if they did not go of their own volition, Scott Dryer would make sure they were eliminated however he could. It had been a vague idea in the back of his mind, but lately the messages were getting stronger and Scott knew that he had been chosen for something very special. His life would have meaning and his actions would make such an impact as to change the world.

He tossed the spray can into his dad's car and drove home. He got there by nine o'clock and hoped he would see the results of his handiwork on the ten o'clock news that night.

· Constitution City, South Carolina ·

Emmaline Dixon never got to bed before three o'clock, but she never got up later than six o'clock in the morning. Most days, as a matter of fact, she rose before that hour, refreshed after no more than two or three hours' sleep.

At eighty, it was what she knew and how she had lived her life. Her twenty-seven grandkids were all nearly grown, and seven great-grandkids were already big fans of Grandmom Emma. Her best friend, a younger white lady named Genevieve Farley (just plain Jenny to Emmaline), could barely keep up with her, though she tried valiantly.

After midnight, Emmaline and ten or twenty volunteers drove around the city in donated Dodge vans and collected uneaten, unsold food from behind restaurants and supermarkets and delivered their bounty to kitchens and homeless shelters for the poor.

Over the years, since the idea had first occurred to the widow lady in the 1990s, the restaurants and stores had gotten on board with her. So she and her friends no longer had to climb in and out of Dumpsters the way they did early on. The restaurants even contributed a nominal percentage of their profits to Emmaline for gasoline and transportation expenses. A few delivered the excess food themselves. And the stores offered special coupons and supplies to food pantries and other charitable organizations who signed on to the loosely organized effort Emmaline Dixon had founded.

This was what she had been called to do. Anyone would say that she had earned her rest and that she should let others carry this load. But Emmaline knew in her heart that this was the right thing to do. It was something that she would do until the day she died, God willing.

CHAPTER
71

The eleventh body had just been discovered when the director summoned Special Agent Bobby Anderson to a one-on-one meeting at FBI Headquarters in Washington, D.C. Bobby held an unusual at-large status within the Bureau that did not tie him to one office or city but allowed him to take on important investigative assignments on an ad hoc basis anywhere in the world.

He and the director had served together for more than twenty years and knew each other well. More important, they trusted each other.

"Bobby, sit here," the director said when the agent entered his vast office—the same one that had been occupied by the legendary and notorious J. Edgar Hoover for a few years after the headquarters building had been constructed.

"Thank you, sir," Anderson said, shaking hands with his boss.

"I've been following the serial murder case in Belfast." He gestured in the direction of a stack of files on his desk. "Update me on the latest in that case, if you would, Bobby. I want to know what's in your gut—not just on paper."

"Well, sir, it's pretty complicated."

"I've got time," the director said.

Anderson held nothing back in his verbal report to the director. "I have never been part of an investigation like this one." From the discovery of the first few bodies and the embedded messages to the arrangement of the victims in the open field in a near-perfect circle to the careful gruesome mutilations of the corpses and removal of "souvenirs"—the details were numbing to recite and equally numbing to hear.

"The message of the killer—and I believe it is a single killer, or a single mind and motivation behind the murders—is sourced to ancient superstition and prophecies about the end of time and a final war between good and evil. He is telling us that the war is at hand."

"Another end-of-the-world prophecy, eh? The last several haven't borne out. Is this one linked to any particular religious group? Every day there's some new prediction from this sect or the other. I happen to believe the Mayan calendar. Now *there* was a smart group of people." The director smiled wanly at his own poor joke.

"We've just begun analyzing the eleventh corpse on the wheel. We're close to cracking the code and understanding what the murderer is telling us. If we can solve the riddle, we may be able to prevent the twelfth killing—and the ultimate cataclysm the killer or killers plan to unleash."

The FBI director leaned back in his chair and regarded his colleague and friend. "You've got to solve this one. Our opposite numbers in Scotland Yard are stumped just as we are."

"Believe me, I know they are. I talk to them every day, as well as the local homicide people. Even the most experienced cop on the ground there is baffled. But all of us know one thing: There is more to come, and it's only going to get worse."

The director furrowed his brow and closed his eyes momentarily. Then he said, "Well, as if you don't have enough on your plate right now, Bobby, I have another investigation that needs your immediate attention." He retrieved a thin file from his desk. It was clearly a brand-new case. He handed it to Anderson. "Highly sensitive. You'll see why."

Bobby quickly opened the file and saw immediately that "sensitive" didn't come close to describing this one. The son of the late President had disappeared. He looked at the director, who said, "This is a screwup of major proportions. It is unclear just how this took place, and we have been scrambling ever since the event happened."

"Director, I can't take this on top of the Belfast case. Either one is all-consuming. Both are impossible. Besides, I know the boy and his family. We were close at one time. There could be a conflict of interest."

"I know you can't be in two places at once, but we have to put our best in the field to find the President's son. We don't have any time with Marcus Jackson. And I've already decided there is no conflict of interest. The other case, while horrific, is now months old. That's harsh but true. We have to resolve this one ASAP. The nation is still reeling from the president's death, and this abduction is likely to cause even more distress, and maybe even panic. We need to find the boy. Now. And do everything in our power to make sure that when he is found he's alive."

Bobby Anderson's mind raced ahead. Over his many years as a cop he had developed a sixth sense, which he actually called his "seventh sense," about crime patterns. He scanned the file on the Marcus Jackson abduction. There was no ransom demand and there had been no physical evidence at the scene of the abduction.

A deep doubt or instinct nagged at Bobby. Something told him that he should have anticipated this. That it was not a random act, and that it had less to do with the President or with politics than with . . . something else. *What? What?*

He scanned the documents in the file again. The few facts were there, but they added up to a whole lot of nothing. He would have to go to the scene and start interviewing witnesses. Except that there were no witnesses. At least none that had been identified so far. *Damn!*

"Director, you've got me in a box. You know I can't abandon the Belfast investigation. But this—there's something very strange going on here. It's not a simple political kidnapping or a terrorist act. It seems very personal, and at the same time . . . very global."

The director smiled wryly. "You see, that's why I need you on this, Bobby. For your golden gut."

"My golden gut is going to get sick in a minute."

"Don't go soft on me now. I have to trust you. In fact, you're the only one I can trust."

"You shouldn't put yourself in that position, Dave. What if something happens to me?" Even though he was a good friend of long-standing, Bobby rarely called the director by his first name, unless they were out together socially, having a drink or hunting—increasingly rare occurrences.

The director said: "Nothing's going to happen to you, Bobby. The only credible lead we have is this: a possible witness sighting in Los Angeles, by one of our informers. I want you to get out to Los Angeles and find that kid. You know the First Family better than anyone. You can still work on the Belfast thing remotely—that's what we have computers for these days, eh? Will you do this for me?"

"Of course, Director. That's why you sign my paycheck, I suppose." He gave his friend and boss a lopsided grin.

"There's one more thing. And this is something I will deny having said to you if I am ever asked. I suspect there may be an element within the FBI or CIA, or both, behind this abduction. Just as I am seeing more strands of evidence that the same bunch may be responsible for the assassination of the President. It may sound far-fetched to you now, but I want you to be aware of this theory—just between you and me—as you follow the facts here."

Bobby Anderson had no response to the director's final statement. He could think of nothing to say.

Within three hours, he was on a flight to LAX, during which he slept and dreamed of confronting the mad killer who had slaughtered eleven innocents and would kill who knew how many more if he failed. And in his dream state he already was trying to find a way somehow to rescue a young man who had already lost his father and was thrust into new danger just because of that relationship.

They were more nightmares than dreams.

· Los Angeles ·

Special Agent Bobby Anderson's flight landed in Los Angeles, and he received a special escort from the aircraft to the FBI office downtown, where an office had been arranged for him. Two agents and a secretary also were given to him by order of the FBI director through the Special Agent in Charge. He slumped in the chair and scanned through the text messages on his mobile telephone pad. There were a dozen from Belfast and one from the director. He read his boss's first:

"Personnel in L.A. office are clean, in my estimation. However, I advise you to suspect everyone and everything you encounter, as discussed between us. Solve this case."

Not that he needed any further encouragement . . . Anderson stifled a smile. His old friend was deathly afraid that the solution to the Marcus Jackson kidnapping would damage the agency and lead to further questions about the President's killing. The entire intelligence community of the United States—and around the world, for that matter—were being publicly challenged to prove they were not involved. Difficult to prove a negative, but a professional proactive investigation by Agent Bobby Anderson would go a long way to winning back some credibility for the Federal Bureau of Investigation.

But even with a new and overwhelming challenge, he couldn't get the serial killing investigation out of his mind. The evidence at the bizarre crime scene in Belfast had pointed to an international scope of conspiracy, and his personal instinct—almost from the very beginning of his involvement—was that it somehow tied back to the United States, as well as other countries. But how? Why? Could there somehow be a link to the abduction of the late President's son?

He did not want to speak of his questions to anyone. He kept it all in his gut and in his mind. He would follow the evidence, and right now the evidence and his FBI superiors wanted him to follow up persistent rumors that Marcus's kidnappers were from L.A.—or might have transported the boy to L.A.

The hair on the back of Bobby's head stood up when Los Angeles had been mentioned in the first briefing on the abduction case. Making connections . . . this was what Agent Anderson did. But connect what to what? He smiled inwardly at the thought. More would be revealed, as Dawson Rask might say.

Which brought Bobby back to the memory of his days in NYPD. That had been an education and a half. Something he'd never forget. His rookie assignment had been to the homicide squad, and his very first case a suspected serial killer operating in the five boroughs of the city. Those were the days of HEADLESS BODY IN TOPLESS BAR tabloid headlines and Mob hits seemingly every Thursday and the days before routine DNA testing. But Officer Anderson caught a juicy one they called the Bridge Man, who killed and mutilated prostitutes beneath some of New York's famous bridges. Nine months of his life were devoted to meticulous follow-up of evidence and interviews with witnesses.

He made himself go to church every Sunday and showered twice a day—and he didn't have a drop to drink, not even a single beer, during the investigation. He barely kept his sanity. Finally, he and his boss, a thirty-year sergeant, cracked the case together, based largely on a half thumbprint and a drug-addled witness at one of the crime scenes. And since then, during every day of his work in the FBI, he carried with him the lessons learned on the streets of the Big Apple—one of the chief of which was, he would follow his investigative instincts. Always.

So far, Anderson was drawing a complete blank on the Jackson case, and in frustration, he sat at his desk looking over the Belfast material again. How many times had he struggled with these case notes, and he still was left with more questions than answers.

Five of the first six victims had all been women, which had caused the police to conclude, at that stage of the investigation, that the motivation was, at least in part, sexual. The elaborate tattoos, the removal of the hearts, were perhaps no more than a smoke screen thrown up by the murderer to confuse investigators and throw them off the killer's trail.

Then, the next victims, men of different backgrounds, diverted from the profile wildly. The only thing that seemed to emerge from the deaths was that in addition to the mutilations, the placement of the bodies seemed to show an ever-widening circle. The damnable thing was that in spite of the twenty-four-hour surveillance of the crime scene, bodies continued to pop up as if by magic.

Instinctively, Bobby Anderson, who was focusing more and more on the cultist dimensions of the crime, believed that the key lay before him—not only to solving these murders but to something else, something of greater dimensions. Once he found that key, it would unlock a door to a new mystery that had not even presented itself yet.

Anderson felt pulled in two directions. Mostly, that was because he was. The Bureau felt he was the most capable man to investigate what was going on in Belfast, and at the same time the chief entrusted him to find the President's kidnapped son. To say that this was an honor and a curse was to put it mildly.

On top of it all, Anderson had become haunted by dreams of the murders and the victims. Not a night passed when he did not see one or more of them. They attempted to speak to him in the dreams, but he could not hear them. It was if he were deaf or watching a silent movie. Their lips moved indistinctly, and he could not read them. Yet he sensed quite clearly that they were trying to tell him that the Federal Bureau of Investigation and the Central Intelligence Agency, arms of the American government for which he worked, were somehow involved in the crime—that he was there for a purpose beyond merely helping to solve the murders. He was there as a representative of some sort, someone who would carry back a message to his superiors that would lead to . . . what?

One night he bolted upright after such a dream, fully awake and sweating profusely. He had been given an insight but only for a fleeting moment, and he had not been able to hold on to it, to grasp it in his mind. What was it? What was the message that he—and only he—was supposed to receive? What was the *key* to these brutal acts?

Then he had another dream. Or was it a vision? It was something that had not yet happened, but he could not conceive of how it could happen, or when—or why.

He was standing on a stage of some kind. It was almost like an ancient Greek amphitheater with seats that rose up all around the stage, surrounding him. All the seats were filled, and the people in them were cheering loudly, unceasingly. Anderson was no longer alone, and as he looked around, he saw familiar faces elsewhere on the stage. One face in particular—a young man with whom he was very familiar, was Marcus Jackson, the son of the late President of the United States. In the dream Marcus smiled at Bobby Anderson. It was as if they shared some secret knowledge—but again, the FBI agent had no clue what that knowledge was. Somehow he knew, though, that the boy held the key. How could that be? What in God's name had the son of the President to do with these murders in Belfast, Ireland?

A small, still voice within seemed to be attempting to communicate with Bobby, to guide him onto the correct path. What was it? Who was it? Was it anything besides his cop's instinct, which had never failed him, from his first NYPD case till now? He listened . . . listened hard. But he sensed only the faintest "sound" as a tickling of his consciousness.

Overloaded. Oversensitive. Undersleeping. He could not shut off. His mind was constantly racing with symbolism, and now the facts of both investigations were bleeding together. And he was losing objectivity since he felt connected to the family . . . more than most.

During the last presidential campaign, Bobby Anderson had been detached from the FBI for the duration to provide security for Candidate Jackson and his family. It was an interesting assignment, providing him with a close-up look at democracy in action. There was the time the bus broke down outside Ozark, Alabama, and a farmer and his wife fed the thirty-four people who had suddenly become their guests. Before the meal was over, another forty neighbors arrived and Candidate Jackson held an impromptu rally right there.

Bobby remembered one of the guests who stayed in the background. The man had a sour expression on his face and Bobby was sure his ire was racially motivated. It was, but as it turned out his animosity was less toward Candidate Jackson than for his wife.

"I read she was a Vietnamese. She's one of them illegals who come over here on a boat. We ought to put her on a boat and send her ass back to where she come from," the man whispered to his neighbor, who hushed him.

Bobby overheard and kept an eye on him. He was relieved when he saw him climb into an old red pickup truck and drive away.

He also recalled a memorable flight. The chartered 757 that Senator Jackson had used as his campaign plane was named *Chien Thang*. Win had chosen the name, which was Vietnamese for "Victory." On this night, the plane was flying through a storm, and as lightning flashed outside, the plane pitched and yawed as the pilot tried, unsuccessfully, to find some smoother air.

A lot of the passengers on board were visibly frightened, and Bobby recalled that young Marcus had gone out of his way to calm the fears of a female journalist from CNN.

"You don't have to be afraid," Marcus had told her. "Captain Kirby has more than ten thousand hours. Why, he flies through weather like this all the time. And this airplane? It is a Boeing 757, and it is as strong as a tank."

"You seem to know a lot about airplanes," the woman said.

"I've read all about them," Marcus said.

Bobby watched from three rows back, smiling in admiration as the boy continued to ease the young woman's fears until she was actually laughing.

A few minutes later, Marcus walked back to the lounge and put a pack of popcorn into the microwave. When it started popping, Bobby walked back to join him.

"That's smelling awfully good," he said.

"You can share it with me," Marcus said.

"I saw the way you handled that lady reporter. Your mom and dad would be very proud of you."

"I remember what it was like when I was a little kid and would sometimes get scared," Marcus said.

Bobby chuckled.

"I know why you are laughing. You're still thinking of me as kid now. I'm not."

"No, I guess you're not."

The bell rang and Marcus took out the popcorn. "If we both sit there, we can eat it out of the bag and won't have to mess anything else up," he suggested.

"Good idea."

"Mr. Anderson, you investigated those serial murders in New York, didn't you?"

"How did you know about that?"

"I read about them. Do you believe that there is evil in the world?"

"Of course. The person who killed all those people was evil."

"No, I don't mean evil as in an evil person. I mean evil, just all by it-self."

"I don't know. I guess I've never really thought about it that way. Why would you ask a question like that?"

"I don't know. I've been thinking a lot about evil and reading about it. One of my favorite authors is Dawson Rask, and I really like what he writes about. I mean, I don't *like* that stuff, but I wanted to talk to some grown-up about it, but I know that Mom wouldn't want to think about such a thing, Dad doesn't have time to think about it, and none of my friends that are my age would understand it. But you have actually come up against it."

"I know Dawson Rask personally; he is a good friend of mine, as a matter of fact," Anderson said. "I think he is incredibly smart and knows so much about ancient wisdom teachings and the depiction of good and evil in the world."

"That is so cool. Can you introduce me to him some time?"

"Sure. How old are you, Marcus?"

"I'm going on fifteen." He always liked to stretch his age a bit by claiming he was older than he really was.

"You're lying. You are a thirty-four-year-old man in a fifteen-year-old kid's body."

Bobby got to know the Jackson family very well during that campaign, and he had grown especially close to young Marcus. Bobby had never been married, because he would have felt guilty subjecting his wife to the life he lived. But if he had gotten married, and had a boy, he would have wanted him to be exactly like Marcus. Marcus was intelligent, had a very good sense of humor, and beyond that, had an unerring sense of right and wrong.

Considering all that, it was not that unusual that the person who did show up in his dream, the person who was trying to help him deal with the concepts of good and evil, was Marcus Jackson Jr. But he cautioned himself to remain logical and professional. Stick to the data. Stick to the facts.

CHAPTER
72

As he awoke to the new reality, the President had one clear thought: He wanted to see his son. How long had it been? Was Marcus okay? In his gut—well, what had been his gut—POTUS knew the boy was alive, but he desired above all things to see him, to communicate with him somehow, and to bring him back to family and safety in the best way possible.

Likewise, he felt the need to see his own father, who had always remained a presence in his life, long after his death, when POTUS had been much younger . . . a time he had nearly forgotten, which now seemed as if it had been just a moment earlier, like every other event in his life. He existed now in a historical continuum and could access any time period of his earthly existence by mere thought, a sort of mental snapping of fingers to put him exactly where and when he wanted to be. Yet it was not all smashed together; each memory, each moment remained distinct and whole, though connected irrevocably to every other moment.

A light beam enveloped POTUS as he stood in the still-strange new plane of his existence. He did not and could not yet know it was Caleb, his would-be guardian and guide who caused the phenomenon. He felt it as a cool warmth, a light that blinded and illuminated simultaneously, completely cleared his mental vision and the channel that his soul had become.

"Dad!" His father was there, his face and figure before him as if he had always been there and would always be . . . Dad. Every conversation they had ever had ran through the President's memory, every word and gesture of the man who had brought him into the world and held his hand when he was a little boy and shaped his decisions as a youngster, providing guidance by example. "Dad!" POTUS repeated, breathless.

"Son," the man said, speaking the single syllable with a world of emotion.

The two embraced, though neither now existed in a corporeal dimension, in a very hard and very human hug.

"Have you seen young Marcus?" the newcomer asked his father. "I was informed by the Council that he was kidnapped. I need to know more. Is he still alive? Where is he?"

"He is alive. Still alive on Earth."

POTUS had known it in his heart, but this confirmation from the one he trusted above all others gave him a great feeling of relief and comfort. *He may be in danger but he is still alive.* There could be no better news he would ever hear than that.

"I will find him and speak to him, somehow," he vowed.

His father said, in the same voice POTUS so clearly remembered, "What you will do, now that you have crossed over to the side of the light, is what you are meant to do. What you were born for. Yes, you are called to guide Marcus in his time of difficulty and lead him to his own right choices, just as I have tried to do with you."

"You were always saying that to me, Dad. I remember so clearly. When I was little, you always shared the best of yourself with me, teaching and guiding me. And I felt your influence even when you were gone."

The entity who stood before him now, tall and strong, emanated nothing but pure love, unalloyed and without reservation or qualification.

Why did I never fully understand how Dad felt about me when I was young? Even as I matured and could look back and see all that he did for me . . . I never truly appreciated what it all meant and how he shaped me in every way imaginable. Did I make the right choices that he was always talking about— even now? Well, I tried my damnedest to live up to those standards he set for me, mostly by his example.

"Son," his father said, clearly reading the unspoken thoughts, "you were elected President of the United States, for goodness sake. You saved lives when you were in the service. You fell in love and married and had a family of your own. It is not possible to count the number of lives you affected for the good. Nor is it possible for me to express the great respect I have for you and all you've accomplished. But here's the good news: We have all of eternity to have the conversation, and I can try to convey to you how much I love you every minute of those hours and eons. Time is now irrelevant to anything we do—or even who we are. We exist outside the bounds of time and physical space."

Marcus is still alive. My father is here with me to help teach and guide me. I have entered a new place and a new, unending phase of existence . . . As much as I want to know what it all means—right now—*I guess I'll have to just absorb what I can, when I can. It's, well, it's very different than what I imagined it would be. Not that I spent a lot of time thinking about this stuff during my so-called lifetime.*

"So true, son," his father said. "None of us truly understood fully the implications of our actions and the energy we projected during our time on Earth. More will be revealed to you—and to me. More will be revealed."

Suddenly, with the same swiftness with which it had arrived, the brilliant, otherworldly light vanished and a chill enveloped POTUS. He stood alone. Though he knew he was not alone and never would be again, he noted the absence of his father, a source of positive, life-giving energy. He looked around and saw the outline of his new environment retaking definition and shape and dimension. And he saw IRA, standing beside him with an odd smile on his otherwise bland visage.

An insight into the true nature of the guide nearly came to him, but POTUS could not hold on to the thought that flitted across his mind then exited. *There's too much going on right now*, he said to himself.

"You're darn right," IRA stated as if in answer to a spoken statement.

CHAPTER
73

Marcus could only estimate the time that had passed since he had last awakened from a drug-induced sleep. About an hour ago, he had been given some water and dried-out food by an unseen person who had opened the door and silently placed the plate and bottle on the floor, then relocked the door. The room had remained in total darkness, but Marcus could tell by the sound about where the food and water were located. He also discovered, by touch, that there was a plastic container beside the bed, which he guessed was to serve as a kind of toilet facility like they used to have in olden times. What did they call it back then? . . . Oh, a chamber pot. He remembered reading about that once.

He drank a little water and ate a few bites of what tasted like a granola bar. He did not feel hunger, though he knew his body needed nourishment and water. He stood by the side of the bed and walked in place for a half hour or so. He guessed he had been conscious for about three hours at this point.

He had the strong feeling that he was being held—how long, he had no idea—for reasons other than ransom or political leverage. It did not feel like a terrorist kidnapping, either, though he was not sure how he could reach that conclusion without any evidence one way or another. He was just going on his gut at this point. And he tried to think of a way he might be able to escape . . . though that seemed highly unlikely to impossible.

Whoever had done this knew what he was doing. Isolate the prisoner and keep him in total darkness, completely cut off from the world and from any sensory input. Perfect for their purposes, perhaps.

But little would they realize they were creating the perfect environment for him to "see" the Other Side when it needed to connect with him. Then it happened. He again heard his father's voice, but this time it was more distinct and seemed much closer than before. He still had trouble making out the words, so he listened hard. With every bit of energy he could muster, he listened.

"My son, my son . . ." Now the words were audible.

"Dad! Dad!" Marcus said aloud.

"Do not speak, but listen to me, and answer me with your thoughts. Can you do this?"

Marcus bit his lips together so he would not say aloud what he was thinking: "Yes, I think I can, Dad. Is it really you, or am I feeling the effects of whatever drugs they gave me?"

"I'm no longer on Earth, but my journey, my work, is continuing. I've encountered my own father here on this side, and he has given me a better, deeper understanding of what role I am expected to play—and the energy, somehow, has also been given to me. I want you to know that you and your mother have been constantly in my thoughts since what happened to me. I can see you from where I am, and I want you to know that I am fine. This is but another stage of life, another way of being that is tied to my previous life on Earth with you, but there is much peace here. I want you to know that help is on the way."

"I hear you, Dad. I want to believe you. I *do* believe that it is you." In fact, Marcus had been trained, taken through drills by the Secret Service during his father's election campaign, in the event of just such a contingency. He had called it "kidnapping school," and he'd kind of enjoyed it—then. He hadn't taken it all that seriously.

"Don't be afraid to doubt all you want, my son. That is part of being human, part of being the son and grandson of a Jackson. But be assured that I am going to look after you. I have a job to do, and you are going to help me do it."

"What do you mean?" Marcus felt his head spinning, and he felt thirsty.

"Son, I am not completely certain of how this all works just yet, but I know we are connected—and you are in trouble. Just as the rest of the world is in trouble. And I need your help, just as you need mine. Drink some water," POTUS advised him.

Marcus drank the water and it reminded him of a hike he had taken one summer when he came across a windmill that was pumping water from a deep well. The water was cold and sweet, and he had never tasted any drink that was better, not any soft drink, or juice, or lemonade. The water quenched his thirst as no other drink ever had, until now, and this water, which his mind told him was tepid and stale, had the same flavor and coldness as that delicious well water.

"Oh, the water is very good," Marcus said.

"Yes," POTUS said. "It was like the water you drank from the well one summer."

"How did you know about that?"

"You and I are one now, Marcus. We can communicate and share thoughts with one another across time, if we both wish to do so."

"I have been thinking about you, Dad. I can't put you out of my mind, did you know that?"

"Yes, I am aware of such things. Any time you think of me, I am there with you. I know you as well as I know myself, how you think and feel. I am with you now."

"Where am I? Why was I abducted?"

"The simple answer is, you are where you are supposed to be, and all is as it should be. You will not experience pain. I will see to that. I will sacrifice myself for your safety if I must."

"I don't understand."

A thousand thoughts raced through his brain as Marcus tried to hear and understand the words his father spoke to him. None of it made sense, yet he knew it was happening and that he was a part of something larger than himself.

"As above, so below, my son."

"I think my brain is going to explode, Dad. Are you saying you were *supposed* to be killed so that you could communicate this to me?"

"That is exactly what I'm saying, son. But I will also tell you this: I am having trouble accepting that myself. It doesn't make sense to me. I am learning many things since I left the earthly plane, many answers to questions I had been asking my entire life. Here, even though I am safe from any further physical harm, I can see what potential harm you and others are facing—and I am in a position to act upon that knowledge, to help you and others survive the evil that threatens you. Does that help?"

"A little bit." Marcus sat down on the edge of the bed, his legs unsteady. He was trying to absorb all this, realizing there was no time to waver or ask too many questions. There was too much at stake here. "I will do what you tell me to do, Dad," he said in his thoughts.

"I know you will," POTUS answered. "And you will have help on Earth as well as from this side. The forces of good, what we were always taught in Sunday school, are with us."

"You mean, like angels?"

"Yes, that's exactly what I mean. There are angels—and other created beings and many souls of the departed all living in harmony in a beautiful place. I can't begin to describe it to you, Marcus. There are no words to describe the beauty of this place, and there certainly isn't any time."

"Have you been trying to communicate with me when I was passed out?"

"Yes. I have been calling out to you, wanting to speak to you. I had to wait until you were ready and fully conscious to receive my words. As soon as you crossed that threshold, we were able to have a conversation as we are doing now. You will understand when the time is right. So, be prepared. I am going to download information to you."

Young Marcus smiled, despite his pain and confusion. "That sounds good. A data dump, huh?"

"You've got it, son."

· Melbourne, Australia ·

The day dragged on, and Dawson sat completely immobilized as he watched the nonstop coverage of the presidential assassination, watching it over one of the American satellite news networks. He had completed all his media appearances for the book and felt depleted, depressed as he sat in his hotel room watching the terrible news coming from the United States.

"Shortly before driving to the Henry B. Gonzalez Center in San Antonio, President Jackson announced that he had invited Charlene St. John to the White House, where he intended to present her with the Presidential Medal of Freedom, the highest award that can be bestowed upon a civilian. Here, we see President—"

Suddenly and unexpectedly, the pictures became black and white, and the words changed in midsentence.

"—Kennedy as his motorcade drives past the Texas Book Depository in Dallas. But the mood of the crowd alongside the motorcade changed suddenly from one of excitement and joy to one of horror and sorrow as the shots rang out. Mrs. Kennedy, who is resplendently dressed in a bright pink suit, reached first for her husband, then crawled out onto the back of the car, as a Secret Service agent jumped on. The car accelerated quickly, and the president was taken to Parkland Hospital. We are waiting for further word."

Now, on-screen, sitting at a desk in a newsroom, Walter Cronkite stared into the camera.

"From Dallas, Texas, the flash—apparently official—President Kennedy died at one P.M. Central standard time." Cronkite removed his glasses and looked up at the clock. *"Two o'clock Eastern standard time, some thirty-eight minutes ago."* He put his glasses back on, and paused for a long moment

before continuing. His voice broke, slightly, as he went on. *"Vice President Lyndon Johnson has left the hospital in Dallas but we do not know to where he has proceeded."* Cronkite removed his glasses yet again. *"Presumably, he will be taking the oath of office shortly, to become the thirty-sixth President of the United States."*

Dawson was immobilized for a moment as he watched the screen. This wasn't archival footage! He was watching the telecast of the Kennedy assassination as it was originally broadcast on November 22, 1963!

What was happening to him? He hadn't even been born yet when JFK was killed. This entire day had been a series of bizarre events. Had President Jackson been killed? Or was it Kennedy? Was there some sort of warp in the space-time continuum? Was he in the present, or in 1963? He looked at the room receipt and saw that it was dated in the present. Perhaps he was in both time periods simultaneously.

He felt an overwhelming feeling of dizziness and went over to the bed to lie down.

Within a moment, words and pictures flashed by him, and he could feel air rushing by, as if he were riding in a car with his head sticking out the window. Was he asleep?

He felt himself falling, and involuntarily grabbed on to the bed with both hands. He forced himself to open his eyes.

He saw a man standing in front of him. He was pleasant-looking, with relatively chubby cheeks, bald except for a crown of hair that passed around his head just above his ears. He was wearing glasses and clothes from the 1960s.

"Who are you? What are you doing in my room?" Dawson asked, startled by the appearance of the intruder.

The man smiled pleasantly, nodded respectfully, then said one word: "Perelandra."

"What? What does that mean? Why do I keep hearing that word?" Dawson asked.

The man disappeared before his eyes, though like the Cheshire cat, his smile remained for a second longer.

Dawson was breathing hard, and he could feel his heart beating in his chest. He looked over at the TV, which he had left on. When he lay down, the TV was broadcasting images and reactions to the JFK assassination. Now the talking heads were reacting to the assassination of President Jackson. He was back in his own time, but who—or what—was that apparition that had greeted him when he awoke a moment ago?

"*. . . leaves behind his wife, Win, and a son, Marcus Jr.*"

It was one o'clock in the afternoon in Melbourne. The hotel had a convenient time chart in each room and, consulting it, he saw that it would be eight o'clock in Decatur, Illinois, where his parents lived. When he called home, his mother answered the phone.

"It's awful," his mother said. "It is so terribly sad." She began to cry over the phone, and a moment later his father's voice came on.

"She's been crying all day," Alex Rask said.

"It is a sad day," Dawson concurred.

"I remember when Martin Luther King and Bobby Kennedy were killed," Alex said. "I remember the sense of anger I felt, that all of us felt. I mean here we were, fighting a war overseas, while our best and brightest were being killed back home."

"Pop, do you remember when President Kennedy was killed?" Dawson asked.

"Yes, of course I remember," his father said. "Everyone who was alive then remembers it, vividly. I was a student, and I had just gone to the cafeteria for lunch."

"Are you still there, Dawson?" his mother asked after an awkward few seconds of silence.

"I'm still here."

"You need to come home. I'm worried about you being alone, so far away."

"Mom, I've got more stops to make on my book tour."

"That's just the point," his mother said. "I read something about you in a magazine the other day. It said that you are one of the country's most eligible bachelors. That shouldn't be. You shouldn't be alone. You should have a wife."

"No thank you."

"It's been a long time since Mary Beth was—uh, since Mary Beth died. You know she would want you to be married and happy."

"With two kids, living in Middle America in a bungalow with a white picket fence?" Dawson asked.

"I worry about you, Dawson, that's all," his mother said.

"Don't worry about me being alone, I'm doing fine. I just wanted to make sure you and Pop were doing okay. I'll call again when I get back to the States."

Two seconds after he ended the call, his cell rang again, and without reading the caller ID he answered, "What? You forgot to tell me that you love me. I love you, too!"

"Well, I appreciate the sentiment, buddy . . . but let's start with dinner before we get to the 'I love you' stage." Dawson recognized Bobby Anderson's voice. The FBI agent was a friend whom Dawson hadn't spoken to in some time. "Can you talk, Dawson? I need your expertise—and an autographed copy of your new book, so I can personally hand it to Marcus Jackson when he is found."

Anderson and Dawson Rask had met years earlier, before Anderson joined the FBI. Bobby had been a member of New York's Finest then, working on a serial killer murder case and thought that Dawson might be able to help him. Dawson had not yet become a widely known celebrity writer, mentioned on all the TV tabloid shows, and appearing often on Page Six of the *New York Post*. He was, however, writing articles for various publications and had developed a justifiable reputation for his expertise on symbolism. Dawson's unique perspective on the information Anderson brought him helped to solve the case and save a potential victim. And the horror of 9/11 bound them in a tight emotional bond. They were as close as brothers (to tell the truth, Anderson was more like a brother than Dawson's own biological sibling could ever be), and nobody was prouder of Dawson's literary success than Bobby Anderson.

By now, Special Agent Anderson was a veteran of more than 200 homicide investigations, most of them multiple killings, some outright mass murders, others serial crimes, all of them horribly violent and shocking to "normal" sensibilities and emotions.

Even today, as an agent with the Federal Bureau of Investigation, if

Anderson was working on a case that showed certain patterns were beyond the normal police perspective, he would call Dawson. The calls were
always on the QT, out of respect for both of their careers.

"What can I do for you, Bobby? I'm in Australia, so it had better
be important." He was feeling raw from his publicity tour and the strange
visions that still made no sense, and the death of his President was all too
much for one day.

"We're not doing too well on this end of the planet either, pally," Anderson said. The two shared their memories about the President, and there
was a moment where both men were silent.

Dawson sighed. "Sorry, Bobby. This day has been a bear. So go ahead,
tell me how I can help."

"As your specialty is ancient wisdom teachings and the symbols used
by the ancients in their religious rituals, I have some material that has
baffled me but may be child's play for you. I would like to consult with
you on a case that has gotten progressively worse over the past months. It
seems to be pointing to something else, another event independent of the
actual murders, as if predicting a much greater and more horrific event or
mass killings on a genocidal or possibly global scale."

"Is that all? Well, maybe I could add my two pence to your investigation."

Anderson was taken aback at the flippancy of Dawson Rask's remark,
given the gravity of the situation. He, Anderson, had been brought in on
the murder investigation after four of the killings—and there had been
seven subsequent deaths, all following the same bizarre and gruesome
pattern, clearly the work of the same monster, yet each with a distinctive
creative flair (if such acts could be called "creative") and unique symbolism
attached. Early on, he and the local investigators had identified the symbols as possibly related to some larger cosmic pattern but what it was they
were at a loss to identify.

At first glance this looked like a string of run-of-the-mill occult or
Satanic murders, the kind that common criminal minds used to cover
up more simple murders. In his gut, however, the FBI man felt strongly
that there was an evil force behind these killings, something that had
far-ranging consequences.

Anderson said to Dawson, "I must add this: I was *told* to call you. Or,
perhaps I should say, I had no choice but to call you."

Dawson said, "That's weird, Bobby—okay, so where are these murders
taking place?"

"Belfast, Ireland," Anderson said matter-of-factly, as if it were Any-where, Anywhere.

Inexplicably, Dawson felt as if he had been sledgehammered in the chest. Was this another reference to C. S. Lewis? Something was nag-ging at his mind and welling up in his soul. But he was at a loss as to its origin. For several seconds he could not breathe. He thought he might be having a heart attack.

Dawson? Dawson? Are you still there? Are we still connected?" Bobby asked.

The American agent held his BlackBerry away from his ear and looked at it. He did not believe in ESP or in anything that he could not see or touch, yet through this case he had come to believe that he had actually seen and touched—and even smelled and tasted—evil. Now, he sensed strongly that Dawson had experienced the same kind of blow he had when first brought into the investigation, when he had first visited the killing field and seen the beginnings.

Dawson Rask, celebrity author, had been bitten by the same evil in-sect that Bobby Anderson had. Bobby knew it. The silence on the other end of the wireless conversation was loud—and eloquent—testimony.

Dawson finally said, "Northern Ireland. The ancients considered Ireland a mystical, sacred island. I'm sure you know that. The Romans never con-quered Ireland, as they did Britain, not because it was worthless, as they claimed, but because they were afraid. They would never admit that, the macho sods that they were.

"Cromwell finally did the job, but that was very late in the game. And it was at a horrific price that still hasn't been repaid. Such a bloody history, yet the mystical voices and phenomena still echo down through the centuries to our time. I should say down the millennia. Long be-fore there was a Rome, there were priests and seers wandering about Ireland, north and south, east and west. They created signs and sym-bols that represented the stars and planets that fit seamlessly into the belief systems developed elsewhere, until it all became one—a language of the spirit. Spoken by men with good hearts and men of evil inten-tions."

"So, you think the fact that the killings are in Ireland is significant?"

"In a word, yes. That's about as brief a statement as I can give, given that this call is on your cell phone plan."

"But here is the thing. These murders signify something that is happening all over the world."

"Why do you say that?"

"It's a hunch, born of a long time investigating this kind of thing. But it's more than just that."

"All right, what do you have?"

"First, satellite imagery that reveals a chart, with the last two to be found in the field in Belfast at ten and eleven o'clock. The spokes from the circular chart point to all the other places where bodies have been found—in direct lines.

"Further, there is nothing overtly to relate any of these victims to any other, yet every one of them had one thing in common. Carved on their backs, as intricately as any tattoo, is a kind of mystical writing, astrological glyphs and numbers, like latitudes and longitudes. That's one reason I think it is international in scope. Then, how they are arranged for some kind of display or statement to the world.

"And, just inside the left thigh, the words 'Viva Domingo,' are carved on every one of them."

"Viva Domingo? You mean as in Viva Castro, or Viva Perón? Who is Domingo?"

"I don't think that's it. *Viva* means 'live,' and *Domingo* means 'Sunday.'"

"Live Sunday?"

"Yeah."

"What does that mean?"

Anderson chuckled. "Well, Dawson, that's why I called you," he said. "I was hoping you could tell me what it means."

"I don't have any idea."

"Now comes the real freaky part."

"Whoa, wait a minute. Are you telling me it hasn't been freaky until now?"

"Yeah," Bobby Anderson said. "The real freaky part is that the heart has been surgically removed from every one of them."

"Why in heaven's name would someone do something like that?"

"I assure you, my friend, whoever did this, did not do it in heaven's name. In fact, if you listen to Dave Hampton, they did it in Satan's name."

"Dave Hampton? That kook? Who listens to him?"

"Quite a lot of people listen to him."

"What does he have to do with this?"

"You don't listen to him at all, do you?" Bobby asked Dawson. "Otherwise, you wouldn't have asked that question."

"I don't listen to him, and I did ask."

"For the last month, Dave Hampton has been on this kick of good versus evil. This, he says, is a manifestation of evil."

"Well, duh, that's not hard to figure out, is it? I mean that killing someone, mutilating their body, and carving out their heart is evil."

"I think the scope of his shows go beyond that. I think he's talking good and evil without material form or substance."

"Wait a minute, *Viva Domingo*—," Dawson said, interrupting. "Let me check something."

Dawson walked over to the desk, where lay a copy of the complimentary paper. On the front page, above the fold, was a picture of Charlene St. John kissing the cheek of one of the men who had tried to abduct her. On the door behind her were the words VIVA DOMINGO.

"Yes," Dawson said, returning to the call. "Have you seen the picture of Charlene St. John kissing the cheek of one of her would-be captors?"

"I have," Anderson answered. "Written on the door behind her is, *Viva Domingo*."

"That's funny," Dawson said. "I didn't see this the first time I looked at the photo."

"How could you not notice it? The words go all across the door," Anderson said.

"No, I'm not talking about the words. I'm talking about the picture. There is a picture on the door behind the words."

"What picture?"

"Don't you see it? It's of a woman wearing long flowing robes and— huh, if I didn't know better, I would say—it is! It's a drawing of the Virgin Mary. Are you telling me you didn't see that?"

"I'm looking at the photo right now," Anderson said. "There is no picture behind those words."

"Maybe the newspaper airbrushed the picture out."

"I'm not looking at a newspaper," Anderson said. "We've got prints of the original photo. And I'm telling you, there is no picture of a woman behind the words."

"And I'm telling you that . . . ," Dawson said; then he drifted off in midsentence. "That's strange, I don't see it now. It must have been the way the light was hitting the photo or something. 'Live Sunday,' huh?"

"That's what the words *Viva Domingo* means," Anderson said. "But what it means in a greater context, I have no idea. I was hoping you might know."

"I'll have to give it some thought."

"Well, I appreciate it," Anderson said. "Do it fast, though. I have a strong feeling that brief is better—that we are quickly running out of time on this investigation."

"Seems like it to me, as well."

"Thank you, Dawson. May I call again if I have more questions for you?"

"Of course, you have my word I'll pick up the phone, even if I know it's you."

As he broke the mobile connection, Anderson laughed—for the first time in several weeks it seemed. He sat by himself in his hotel room with no lights on as the day ended and the sun fell below the horizon visible from his window. Never before in his life had he felt as lonely or as powerless in the face of evil as he felt at this moment. He wanted to get Dawson's take on the murders but didn't feel comfortable talking to his old friend about his other case, particularly over open lines.

Bobby Anderson had learned very early on in his career as a homicide investigator that it was vitally important never to stop when two plus two equaled four. There was more—there was always more—to the problem than simple arithmetic.

The placement of the bodies and the messages contained within were too close in time and too significant not to be, somehow, related to the global phenomenon signified by the sudden and frequent appearance of *Viva Domingo*. Everywhere it appeared, it was associated with mayhem and violent death. But how was it significant beyond the obvious warning and taunting? Who could orchestrate such a worldwide series of events with a consistent message?

He asked the same question regarding the killing field in Belfast where the bodies had been secretly and carefully arranged after having been marked so brutally. By the same hand? That was virtually impossible, physically and geographically. By the same organization? But *who?*

There was an art to this demonstration of evil intentions. True art, in turn, depends on an underlying unity—a unity of message to the soul, even if the visible result appears to the unschooled eye as abstract or chaotic or violent. Indeed, in the Belfast killings the uniformity was the very essence of the crime—with the promise of more to come, up to the expected total of twelve dead bodies, twelve clearly articulated messages of doom.

Counterintuitively, the "art" of *Viva Domingo,* in its seemingly random manifestations reported by witnesses and investigators in locales that had no unity whatever, spoke to Anderson with a loud, even eloquent voice.

No question in Bobby Anderson's mind, and in his investigator's well-trained nose, that forces were moving in a single, unified direction. That they were aligning in a powerful way that was intended to be visible to everyone in the world—and that everyone in the world, good, bad or neutral—

Bobby had just stepped over the line that separated him from being on the outside looking in to standing on the inside looking out. It would take a while for his vision to clarify, but he had made a significant leap forward in his thinking.

Whatever doubts and questions remained, he felt he had to be on the right path now.

CHAPTER
76

·London·

Omar, must it be Shakir? If this thing is to be done, tell me again, why can it not be me?"

"Remember Abraham, how he built an altar and laid the wood in order, then bound Isaac his son and laid him on the altar upon the wood. And Abraham stretched forth his hand, and took the knife to slay his son."

"But Allah stayed his hand and Isaac was spared."

"That is not the point. The point is, Abraham was willing to show his love for Allah by sacrificing his son. Do you love Allah any less?"

"No."

"Then you will do this thing."

Muti locked himself in a back room so he could think of what he must do. How could he convince Shakir that martyrdom would be a good thing? *Was* it a good thing? He did not want to lose his son, but he felt that he had no choice.

"You do have a choice," someone said.

Startled by the unexpected voice, Muti whirled around to see a man standing before him. The man was wearing richly adorned raiment with a huge turban that featured a large emerald. He had a long gray beard, and there seemed to be a shimmering light about him.

"Who are you? How did you get into this room? And what do you mean I have a choice?"

"You ask many questions, Muti Faradoon."

"And you have answered none."

"I am Suleiman. If it is not too immodest of me to say so, I have been called Suleiman the Magnificent."

"That is impossible. Suleiman the Magnificent died over four hundred years ago."

"Has it been that long? No matter, there is no time where I am now, although, if the forces of evil have their way, time will run out."

"Who are the forces of evil?"

"You do remember, do you not, a visitor to your restaurant not too long ago. I believe you and your brother referred to him as 'the One.'"

"Yes, I remember him. He was a strange man indeed."

"He is from the Dark Forces of Evil. I am from the Light Forces of Good."

"Forces of evil, forces of good, what are you talking about?"

"I am talking about the great battle that will establish forever whether Allah is to rule—or Satan. There are many who serve Satan and are working for his rule. The One is such a person. So is your brother Omar."

"Omar? No, that cannot be true," Muti said. "Omar is a good man who strives always to serve Allah."

"Omar is a man who is driven by hate and revenge for the injustices he believes the infidels have put upon his people. Hate and revenge are not the tools of Allah. If you would serve Allah, you will follow the precepts of tolerance and appreciation."

"But we are in a jihad," Muti said. "Every Muslim must be prepared to die for his belief."

"To die for your belief is a matter of free will. It is not something that should be forced upon you. You have free will. Shakir has free will. Do not send him to die for the evil ones."

"I am very confused. Omar is my older brother, I now must listen to him, do as he says." Muti bent his head and ran his hands through his hair nervously. "But you tell me that I—" When Muti looked up, his visitor was gone. When he checked the door, it was still locked from the inside. How had his visitor gotten in? How had he left? Was his visitor really Suleiman the Magnificent?

What was I doing? I was about to sacrifice my own son. Abraham! As Allah stayed Abraham's hand to prevent him from killing his son, so, too, has Allah, by this visitor, stayed my hand. I will not send him to die!

Omar was in the supply room checking on the inventory when he heard his name called. Turning, he saw the same man who had visited the restaurant earlier, the one he and Muti had called "the One."

"You must hurry," the One said.

"I must hurry to do what?"

"There are forces at work, someone who is trying to prevent Shakir from fulfilling his glorious destiny."

"Who?"

"It is not important. You must go to Shakir now, reach him before his father does, and tell him that it is his destiny to honor his father and his family, that by divine providence has he been chosen."

"Yes," Omar said, his eyes gleaming now in resolute fanaticism.

Where is Father?" Shakir asked.

"Muti does not have your strength and your courage," Omar replied. "He knows that you must do this, that you honor all of Islam by your sacrifice. And he is proud that his son will be remembered forever on earth as a martyr, and will be received into glory by his action. But he is a weak man who does not have the strength to ask you to do what must be done."

"I—I don't want to do this," Shakir said.

"But you must."

"Please, Uncle, I cannot do this."

"Would you rather spend the rest of your days spit upon and scorned because when Allah called you, you were too frightened to answer His call?"

"What must I do?"

"I will give you a backpack to wear," Omar said. "The backpack is a bomb with nails and nuts and bolts sewn into it. I will take you to Piccadilly Circus. There you will get out of the truck and walk to the center, where most of the people will be. When you get there, all you will have to do is open the zipper on your backpack."

"What will happen then?"

"You will feel nothing. One second you will be walking across Piccadilly Circus, here on earth, and the next second you will be welcomed in Paradise. There, you will be treated as a hero and a martyr forever."

"I am frightened."

"You need not be frightened, Shakir. I will be in the truck, watching you. You will know, with your last moment on earth, that you were not alone."

"What about my mother and father?"

"You do this thing, and your mother and father will live in your glory until the end of their days. You will be in Paradise before them, to welcome them. You do want to honor them, don't you?"

"Yes."

"You do want to serve Allah, don't you?"

"Yes."

"Then this is what you must do."

Asima was sitting at her computer, the letters on the monitor flying across the screen in keeping with the rapid motion of her fingers.

> In the days of Aisha Bint Abu Bakr, one of the most famous women in all of Islam, there were no universities such as we have today, and had there been, she would not have been allowed to attend. Despite that, her words are studied in faculties of literature, her legal pronouncements are read in law colleges, and her life and works are researched by students and teachers of Muslim history today, as they have been for over a thousand years.
>
> Are there no such women in the Islamic world today? I think there are many such women, but the unenlightened leaders of our religion and our culture are squandering a great resource by keeping these women down.

Asima had been working at the computer for two hours without a break, and she felt the need to get up, stretch, and walk around. This would be her third book. She had written two previous books, and had printed them out, then bound them . . . for what? She knew that, as a Muslim woman, she felt it was dishonorable to get the books published without her husband's permission, and that would never happen. Once perhaps, but not in his current frame of mind. Still, it fulfilled something in her psyche to write them. Maybe someday, long after she was gone, someone would find her books, read them, and be uplifted by them.

Asima walked downstairs from their apartment that was over the restaurant. The restaurant was busy, there were many diners present, and the kitchen and waitstaff were occupied, but she didn't see Muti or Omar anywhere.

"Margaret, have you seen Muti or Omar?" she asked the hostess.

"I have not seen Mr. Muti Faradoon, but Mr. Omar Faradoon is in the supply room."

"Thank you."

Asima walked to the back of the kitchen, then up a long narrow corridor to the supply room, where extra cooking utensils, chairs, and even some folding tables were kept.

"Mr. Faradoon?" she called. "Mr. Faradoon, are you in here?"

Even though she and Muti had been married for fifteen years, she still called Omar Mr. Faradoon because she sensed that was exactly the way he wanted her to address him.

Omar did not answer her, and a quick perusal of the supply room let her know that he wasn't here. She was about to leave when she saw a piece of paper on the floor. She picked it up. It was an iTelegram, which was used in some places in the world since Western Union no longer sent telegrams. Asima marveled at the fact that there were still telegrams of any kind in existence . . . and that she was holding one in her hands.

When she read it she was horrified.

PICCADILLY CIRCUS 1045 SHAKIR BEGINS HIS VOYAGE TO PARADISE.

Asima's blood ran cold. She knew exactly what that meant. Somehow Shakir had been talked into becoming a suicide bomber.

"No!" she shouted, her voice one long, agonizing wail.

Wadding the note up in her hand, she started back up the corridor. She had to get there in time. She had to.

In the black chambers of the Tribunal, the final murder was being planned. The twelfth victim was to be put into position, which would ignite the renewed media hysteria about the serial killings in Ireland. International headlines would scream from every newspaper, TV broadcast, and Internet outlet that the Belfast serial killer or killers represented a new and unstoppable force in the world. Their minions on Earth, who had already been activated, would understand this call to action for the final confrontation with the remaining, weakened forces of good—their neighbors and, in many cases, their own family members.

Further, when the extracted heart of the twelfth victim was placed into position, the aerial views of the macabre circle would show an astrological chart of attack. The specific date and time displayed would set off the sleeper cells of spiritual terrorists, "alarm clocks," and point them to waves of destruction and fearmongering, from outright terrorist attacks to domestic violence and attacks on the human soul.

There were no boundaries to the Tribunal's active intervention in the world, no religious targets—except all religions and all people. They would use members of all faiths and no faith at all as their agents in the imminent battle for the hearts and minds of humanity. Just as they had harnessed the physical universe, they would harness the psychic and psychological powers of humankind to their ends.

The plan was brilliant in its simplicity, as it would play out against chaos and the clash of energies from every direction and every source. The Tribunal had worked within religions from the beginning, to great effect, destroying some—and their adherents in the process—and weakening others, until today the power of religion, of all religions, was at its lowest ebb in human history.

The One had been appearing to individuals and groups of people all over the world, in all walks of life, to those of all religions, and even those who had no particular faith. The One would, in fact, be one of the chief tools of the forces of darkness poised to be unleashed by the Tribunal. The message: Viva Domingo. The actions: mayhem and destruction in their own lives and neighborhoods, in cities and random locations throughout the world.

This meticulously planned attack of the Dark Forces, utilizing their ability to plug into the hearts, souls, and minds of persons everywhere, would activate the fears of individuals who would "follow the herd" or else suffer waves of fear and self-loathing that would separate them from their fellow human beings . . . It was a vicious circle of energy that entrapped the victim in actions that, whatever choices might be made, would result only in negative results and the release of even more negative energy.

For many years—centuries, in fact—the Tribunal's efforts had infected human existence and development, combating the very idea of individuality that religions and philosophies had promoted. Now it had taken on a viral quality: speed and omnipresence throughout cultures across the entire globe. The decline of individuality and personal responsibility meant that people would seek a leader to lift them from their malaise. The leaders who would rise to the task had already been groomed. Years of ego and entitlement hunger were fed, as were the feelings that they had been personally wronged—whether as a culture or an individual—by family, boss, or society.

Small, localized uprisings had begun in recent years all over the planet. This friction against governments and minorities had sparked larger fires of embattled consciousness that were now ready to be fanned into a major conflagration. The Dark Masters were emboldened and empowered in ways they had not been for centuries on end. Now they held the whip hand.

The Dark Energies would simply plug into this eternal battery of energy, and the earthly plane would plummet into a dark night of the soul as only artists and prophets had ever imagined might actually occur in humanity's lifetime.

The Tribunal had been created by active, restless spirits, the Dark Masters whose eternal reach and depth of malevolence could not be measured. The members of the Tribunal had been plucked from their earthly incarnations and soul-washed into believing they had no choice or ability to evolve from their last earthly life. Many of them believed that they were working off karma and were blindly being led by energies, many of them tricksters like IRA. These energies would be lost in a battle of the Heavens as the Dark Forces of the Tribunal mocked the light energies of the Council of Elders and the angelic hierarchies for not attempting to overthrow their Reign of Enlightenment—as their propaganda and rhetoric implied.

This type of rhetoric was absorbed very easily into the newfound consciousness that awaked in beings on the Other Side from the earthly transition. All the souls who did not seek out any belief, or abandoned their faith on Earth, who did not believe that there was something beyond their egos, who had sadness, loneliness, and despair in their hearts as they lived out their earthly lives were pulled to the negative side of the universe. The thing that IRA and the other tricksters wanted these souls not to realize is that all a soul ever needed to do was use their free will and choose to be in the *light* when they transitioned.

So in the moments of their awakening on the Other Side, as with POTUS, the campaign would begin, and the IRAs of that plane would begin to program them into feeling what they needed to feel in order for the Dark Forces to fuel on the remnants of their terrestrial energy. And the Forces of Light let them do this, for to interfere with a soul's evolution was forbidden to them.

Energy was the answer. Energy was the weapon. Energy was the result. Energy was the Alpha and the Omega, the beginning and the end.

But would the energy of the individual and the masses be bent to the purposes of good or of evil? This was the battle line that had been drawn down through the ages.

The Tribunal, then, motivated their network of soldiers by broadcasting this energetic message of accomplishment: *We are winning. We possess more and more new souls each day. We are the masters of the energies of the world.*

The legions of souls who embraced their messages were seeking community and love, like all people, and would settle for attention and earthly energy and power as a plugged-in resource. Again, it was exactly like the pools of passion that POTUS had experienced. Similar to the way that cigarette makers hook their users, the rush can become a way of life, of habit and ultimate, undeniable need for that cigarette—that experience that answers the cravings of body and soul. The dependency of so many on the *earthly* energy was the structure on which the Tribunal's Army of Souls built its campaign to fuel and manipulate the currency of uncertainty, fear, and control.

This was their means to achieve total domination.

Through their minds, bent as one to destructive purpose, the mantra of chaos coursed like life's blood. The leader of the Tribunal constantly addressed them, wherever they were, whatever time of no-day and no-night, whatever epoch or season—for all melded into the same black eternity of the now:

"The earthly clock is ticking down as the celestial bodies in what men call the skies align in our favor. Just as we have moved the stars and planets with energies and forces stolen from the pitiful humankind, so we have generated even more resources to allow us to grow and evolve, to realize our true power and purpose. Soon we will be able to see our families, who have crossed into the Light and have been kept from *us*! Soon we shall have the order that was promised to us and never delivered in the face of the Source and the promise of love and energy."

The words, uttered in every language ever known on Planet Earth, shouted from the tower that was a corrupted Babel, thoroughly penetrated the network of souls with a message of hate and triumph. A beautiful message: the most welcome vision of a new age of darkness that they could imagine. They—the armies of Angel Emphatic and his co-generals and minions—had been formed and soul-washed over time immemorial to receive the encouragement of the Dark Masters and revel in it. The time was nigh.

Clouds formed in the skies that enveloped the planet, and the hearts and souls of a few humans were beginning to recognize their calling was possibly to save not only Earth, but maybe Heaven as well . . . But how could this be accomplished—how would the final battle be staged?

The few who knew the answers held back from revealing all to their followers. It would be clear enough soon. Scientists were now dangerously close to understanding the significance of the dark matter, evidence that the cloud was expanding more rapidly now. Based on the data, they, too, would know the truth soon. Very soon indeed!

CHAPTER
78

His Holiness has viewed the shows you sent," Cardinal Luigi Morricone said.

"And what did he think?" Dave Hampton asked.

"He was particularly moved that both he and a pastor from Dallas, Texas, delivered the same New Year's Day message at exactly the same hour."

"Will His Holiness speak to me?"

"He will speak with you," Cardinal Morricone said. "But he asks that there be no television cameras or microphones."

"Agreed."

"Wait here," Morricone said.

Dave was Presbyterian, not Catholic, and many of the rituals and rites of the Church were foreign to him, but he felt a profound sense of reverence for where he was and what he had seen since arriving at the Vatican. He didn't know what this room was, but it felt like sanctified ground, with the crucifix on one wall, a painting of the Blessed Mother and Christ child on another, votive candles around, and a softly lit picture of Pope John Paul II on yet another.

As he stood looking at the picture of Pope John Paul II, Genaro came walking briskly into the room. At first, Dave wasn't sure it was the pope. He had never seen him in person, only in photographs in which he was always wearing the chasuble and the double-peaked bishop's cap known as a miter. But now he was wearing a white mozzetta, a gold pectoral cross, red shoes, and a white zucchetto, or skullcap. Dave wasn't sure how to greet him. Should he bow? Dip to one knee? He was sure he wasn't supposed to shake hands.

"Please, Mr. Hampton, have a seat," the pope invited, speaking in easily understandable but Italian-accented English.

"Thank you, Your Holiness," Dave said. At least he had that right.

The pope sat as well. "I am told that you want to speak with me about good and evil," the pope said.

"Yes. But not just—"

"Not just the concepts of good and evil," Genaro said, completing the sentence for Dave.

"No, sir, not just the concepts. Holy Father, I'm not sure how to express this. Well, that isn't true, I have been talking about it for weeks, perhaps months on my TV show. But I am sure that you would have more insight into this than anyone else on earth."

"That is where you are wrong, Mr. Hampton. This insight is not limited to me. I have spoken of it with men of different faiths, who have also been touched by a higher power. The pastor in Texas that you spoke of so eloquently in your television broadcast. I am sure that he, too, has been touched by that same power." Genaro paused for a moment. "As have you."

Dave laughed nervously, then held out his hand. "No, wait a minute, you've got me misplaced there. I'm not a man of the cloth. I'll be honest with you, I'm not even that regular about attending church."

"And yet, God has spoken to you."

"I . . . I don't know," Dave said. "He didn't speak to me from a burning bush, I've never heard voices or anything like that."

"Why have you undertaken this crusade to warn others of the Dark Forces of evil?"

"It isn't just religious. There is a real cloud of dark matter approaching earth—"

"From a galaxy known as Pandora's Cluster," Pope Genaro said.

"Yes."

"But even before you learned of this from the scientists, you were speaking of a—I believe you called it 'sinister shadow.'"

"Yes."

"And where did you learn of this sinister shadow?"

"I don't know, it was just something that I felt. From watching the news and reporting it day in and day out, I formed an opinion—one that I thought would be a shocker for the ratings—but then began to really believe it."

"As I said, you were touched by the hand of God. Mr. Hampton, let me tell you what I think this is.

"I believe that there exists in the world beyond our own two very powerful kingdoms. And it's pretty black-and-white. I would define it as the Kingdom of God and the Kingdom of Satan. Both God and Satan have an uncountable number of messengers, or perhaps, in the case of Satan, minions who are set to carry out their orders.

"These angels are made up of souls who have never incarnated, as well as the billions of souls that have. God's family are good, and contain in their number such notables as"—he pointed toward the picture of a previous pope—"John Paul the Second, Mother Teresa, Saint Peter, your grandfather, my mother—in other words, all who have lived and died with a good soul.

"Now, this battle has been going on from the beginning of time. And even if we are successful, it will continue. But what makes this point so critical is the fact that, for the first time in human history, the powers of darkness feel that the world has moved so far away from God that they can call upon the living manifestations of evil to help them in their battle."

"Like the serial killer in Belfast," Dave said.

"Yes. And those who have taken upon themselves, with unbridled fanaticism, the secular fight to eliminate all vestiges of worship. We have seen so many events recently that test the beliefs of the faithful: terrible earthquakes, planes crashing mysteriously, eruptions of violence in various parts of the world. All evidence of negativity and, yes, evil that only feeds people's perceptions of a world without the presence of a loving, positive force. We in the religious realms call it by many names, but in my heart they all come from the same source. But we have our own source, a well of positive energy to combat this evil. We look there for answers, for light in the darkness. The secular, anti-religious use the negative forces for their purposes."

"I know what you mean," Dave said. "However, I think that there are many people in the world who are atheists and who are good, decent people. Forgive me, Your Holiness, but I truly believe that you don't necessarily have to be a person of faith to have a good heart. But then there are those who have wrapped themselves in the cloak of atheism and are actively trying not to advocate a discussion of reason but to destroy the faith of others. Theirs is a world of hate and fear. The question is, what are we to do about it?"

"You have made a beginning, my son. Your television program reaches millions, and those millions tell millions more. As Christians, we must take up the cross of Jesus, but this battle transcends Christianity. It is the classic battle of good against evil, and in order to win, we will require the combined efforts of not just those of faith but all men of goodwill, whether they agree with my conception of the Creator or not."

"You seem to be more open to the validity of other religions than your predecessors were. May I ask you—?"

"Holy Father," Cardinal Morricone said, stepping into the room at that moment. "You have a full schedule today."

"Please forgive me if I've taken too much of your time," Dave said.

"Any time we are doing God's work is time well spent," Pope Genaro said. He smiled at the interviewer, indicating without words that he had heard Dave Hampton's question.

·South Junction, Jamaica·

On her first visit, a decade earlier, Willi Steenberg had been a tourist looking for a fun, relaxing time at a Jamaican resort in the coastal parish of Saint Elizabeth. But after five days of nonstop sun and rum drinks, she asked the hotel concierge for a car and directions to a "real" town where she could meet some "real" people.

The young Dutch woman drove about forty miles inland and a few hundred feet up in elevation to South Junction, which was little more than just that—a meeting of two main roads, with shops and a petrol station, a bank and a bus stop. Within the immediate vicinity were a few hundred homes surrounded on all sides by farmland and woodland, just a mile from a little river that flowed into the Caribbean Sea below.

Willi had been born and raised in the countryside, then attended university in Utrecht, and moved there to live and work for the rest of her adult life. So she was used to city and country life both. She loved the look of the bustling little outpost of civilization and stopped to eat and refuel her rental car.

A gaggle of primary schoolchildren caught her eye. They were on lunch break and came into the café to buy some patties and cola drinks before returning to classes. She asked one of them where they went to school.

"In the town hall basement," the girl with golden brown skin and night-black hair told her.

"Oh? You don't have a schoolhouse?"

"Our school was blown down by the hurricane last year," another youngster said. "No more schoolhouse for us."

Willi asked around town and found out that, indeed, the five-grade school, which had been little more than a tin warehouse in the first place, had blown away. So, when she went back home after that first trip, she thought about what she could do to help the kids. She priced some inexpensive but sturdy buildings that could be built in the area and researched labor costs and local politics. Her conclusion: She could build a new school with her own savings, some gifts and loans from friends, and credit card equity. It really didn't cost all that much, all things considered.

Now, ten years later, she had returned to South Junction. The schoolhouse she had financed had been in use for three full school years. All the kids she had originally met in the café had long since graduated and moved on, but when she returned to the little eatery for a bite before visiting the building, a dozen or so students came in at midday, just like the first time, and ordered their patties and soft drinks for a quick lunch.

Willi Steenberg walked from the café to the South Junction primary school in the early afternoon with tears in her eyes.

·Melbourne, Australia·

As Dawson sat with his cell phone on the edge of his bed talking to his friend, Bobby Anderson, again, he saw President John F. Kennedy.

Kennedy reached up to brush a fall of hair back from his forehead, and he smiled at Dawson. "That's all right, finish your call," Kennedy said to him. "We'll talk later."

Dawson wondered how he could be seeing a long-dead president—and hearing him. Kennedy folded his arms across his chest and leaned back against the desk. Then the image morphed into that of an animal—a majestic, fearsome king of animals. Dawson saw before him the same lion he had seen when he was in the car on the way to the radio station this morning. As before, the lion was animated, with human characteristics.

"Do you see that lion?" Dawson asked President Kennedy.

In fact, he hadn't actually spoken, as he was still engaged in conversation with Bob Anderson. In some weird way, he was able to think of these words and images and not lose his focus on the conversation with Bob. He realized that he was multi-thinking and reacting.

"Of course I see the lion," Kennedy answered. Now the two images—lion and human—were separate. The handsome president pointed to it. "It's right there in front of us. How could I not see it?"

The balding, chubby-cheeked man who had appeared at the foot of his bed half an hour earlier now appeared alongside Kennedy. He picked up the newspaper that Dawson had been looking at earlier, and turned it so that Dawson could see the front page. Though he was too far away and the type too small for Dawson to be able to read the individual articles, he saw again, as he had seen in the car, disconnected words that grew in font size and became boldfaced, and then floated off the page to hang in the air in front of him.

JOY . . . CANCER . . . BELFAST . . . MERE . . . CHRISTIANITY . . . NOVEMBER

"Perelandra," the balding visitor said. Kennedy nodded as if he understood completely what it meant.

Dawson's fingers started tingling and shaking. His dizziness came and went, and he began getting a weird clarity about his thoughts.

"Dawson, are you still there, buddy?" Anderson asked.

"I'm here."

"Good. I thought for a moment I had a dropped call."

"Bob, what is Perry Landra?"

"What?" Anderson's response was sharp, almost annoyed that Dawson had suddenly changed the direction of the call with such an unrelated, and totally meaningless question.

"What is Perry Landra, or maybe it is Perry Landers. It might be one word, like pere landra, or perrylandra? Does that mean anything to you? I keep hearing in my head."

"I don't know what the hell you're talking about? Dude . . . that has nothing to do with what I am saying to you. Are you listening? Have you heard anything I have said to you?"

"Yes, I've heard everything," Dawson said. "All the bodies that have been found in Belfast have one thing in common, markings and cuts on the body that were done postmortem. And they aren't just slashes and disfigurements. They are numbers or letters, sometimes both, always in the same place. And just inside the left thigh are the words *Viva Domingo* carved on every one of them."

"So you have been listening."

"Yes, I've been listening. Bob, I have to go now, I have to do an interview. I'll call you back, and if you need any more help from me, call me.

"Any more help? Yeah, I'll do that, if I need—any more—help." Anderson set the phrase "any more" apart from the rest of the sentence to emphasize the fact that he didn't feel as if he had gotten much help in the first place.

Dawson caught the inference. "I'm sorry, I guess I wasn't that much help, was I? Let me think about it. If I come up with any ideas, I'll call you back, I promise."

"That's all right," Anderson said. "And thanks, Dawson. I didn't mean to sound ungrateful."

The room phone rang almost as soon as he punched off the cell phone call.

"Mr. Rask, this is Jack."

"Who?"

"Jack, your driver, sir. You have another interview in one hour. I'm downstairs."

"Oh. Thank you, I'll be right down."

Dawson hung up the phone and looked around the room: President Kennedy, the same little man, and the lion had all gone away. Dawson idly wondered if he was going insane. He also wondered about continuing his tour given the events happening back home, but it wasn't as if he could do anything about it.

CHAPTER
80

Dawson was at another radio interview, and as his publicist explained, this one would air during drive time and reach the entire country, so it would be good for sales.

He was met by Tony Gordon, a smiling man with white hair and beard, wearing glasses that reflected so much that most of the time his eyes were hidden.

"I heard about your show with Jim Mayer," Gordon said. He laughed. "The entire country has heard about it."

"Yes, I'm sorry. I don't know what got into me this morning."

"Oh, please don't apologize," Gordon said. "As far as I'm concerned, that pompous ass got just what he deserved. I promise you, our interview will be on the friendliest possible terms."

"Thank you."

The host escorted Dawson into the broadcast booth. There was a newscast on at the moment, which gave Dawson time to settle into his chair and wait for the interview to begin.

"My guest today is the well-known and most accomplished American author Dawson Rask. Mr. Rask, welcome to the *Gordon Hour.*"

"Thank you."

"Has anyone ever compared your work to that of C. S. Lewis?" Gordon asked.

"C. S. Lewis? No, I don't believe so. Though to be honest with you, I'm not that familiar with the works of C. S. Lewis, other than *The Lion, the Witch, and the Wardrobe.* And I must confess that I have never even read that." Startled by the reference to his visions, he wondered where this was going. . . .

"Well, I say that because in your book *The Moses Mosaic*, there is battle between good and evil, your protagonist fights what one could call demons as he travels toward the ultimate goal. Some of these demons are only in his head, in that he is following false leads, and some are real, but it is up to the reader to discern which are real and which are in his imagination. And in the final denouement, we learn that there is an unseen order, and we must adjust ourselves harmoniously with that order. Would you say that is a fairly accurate interpretation of your book?"

As Dawson listened to Gordon's question, which was more of a dissertation than a question, he saw a handsome young man with strong jawlines and a squared chin. He was wearing the uniform of a World War I soldier, complete with the pie-pan helmet worn then. He was smiling at Dawson and nodding in agreement with everything Gordon was saying.

"I must confess that no one has ever made that comparison to me," Dawson said. "And I had never looked at it in quite that way. But now that you tell me your take on it, I can see why the comparison would be valid. And, I hasten to add, I am extremely flattered to have my work compared to that of C. S. Lewis—or even to be mentioned in the same breath, as far as that goes."

"Of course, when you consider that Screwtape is a devil, and not just any devil, but head of one of the chambers of hell, you get a much better perspective. He is someone who understands human weakness very well," Gordon said.

"What? I'm sorry, what did you say?" Dawson touched his headset as if to indicate that it had cut out on him.

"I said that when you consider all the obstacles your character must surmount, that he goes through a veritable hell, you have a better understanding of his human strengths and weaknesses," Gordon repeated.

"Uh, yes, that's true," Dawson fumbled, then tried to refocus.

As the interview continued, the World War I soldier disappeared. Neither his appearance nor disappearance shocked Dawson, nor did the disjointed words Dawson was now hearing—words such as *cancer, Belfast, Bernagh,* and *Warney.*

"How long will you *Belfast* be with us here in Australia?"

"I'll be heading back to the States tomorrow," Dawson replied.

"I do *Bernagh* hope you have enjoyed your stay with us. Of course, the unpleasant episode with Jim Mayer being the *Warney.*"

"It has been most productive and pleasant—for the most part," Dawson said with a grin.

The interview continued for the entire hour, during which time they spoke of writing, and of his experiences and how they helped his writing.

"I feel that experiences are to a writer what automobiles are to a car dealer. A car dealer who has no automobiles on his lot cannot stay in business. A writer who does not have a backlog of experiences cannot write."

"Interesting concept," Gordon said. "My guest today has been Dawson Rask. Mr. Rask, it has been a rare privilege," he said. "Please, if you are in Australia again, stop by and do the show with me again."

"Thank you. I appreciate your insight and this opportunity," Dawson replied with the slightest bit of distraction between what he heard and what he thought he heard.

Dawson was escorted back to the lobby where Jack, his driver, was waiting for him.

"Did you hear the interview?" he asked.

"Yes, they had it on the speaker," Jack answered.

Dawson wanted to ask if Jack thought his performance was a bit off and if he thought it odd that Gordon did not make even one mention of the assassination of the President of the United States.

Returning to his hotel room, Dawson opened his laptop, thankful for wi-fi, and checked into his gmail account. His box had ninety-three emails. At first, the emails pertained to his book and PR tour.

> To: DARbook
> From: Willoughby
> Caught you on the radio. Loved the way you told Mayer what he could do with himself. I served with Americans in Vietnam. Like I've told all my friends, you Yanks do have a way with words, even if you do have a strange accent.

After about thirty emails talking about his book, or the promotion tour, or asking him to read something they had written, so he would recommend them to his publisher, he began reading emails pertaining to the assassination.

> To: DARbook
> From: RKurt
> I don't mean to sound too crass and commercial here, but as your agent I feel obligated to always look out for your best interest. Given your relationship to the president's son, I wonder if you might consider writing a nonfiction book talking about Marcus and how he is coping with the death of the president. Let me know what you think.
> Richard

"I can't believe you," Dawson said aloud. He drummed his fingers on the desk for a moment, trying to decide whether or not to call him. Finally he decided to send an email.

To: RKurt
From: DARbook
No. No. And just in case you don't understand, DEFINITELY NO. To you
and to the rest of America, he was the president. To Marcus, HE WAS
A FATHER. I have no intention of capitalizing on this in any way, shape,
or form.
Dawson

The email had angered Dawson, but the feeling faded just as quickly. Richard was, after all, the quintessential agent, interested only in his next deal. And the truth was, he was a very good agent, and exceptionally honest, a trait that Dawson appreciated. He would send a follow-up email later on, ameliorating somewhat his harsh reply to Richard's suggestion.

But Richard had given him an idea. Dawson had become friends with Marcus—and indeed with the whole First Family—as a result of a fan letter Marcus had sent him. He had been quite surprised to get a letter from the White House, and even more surprised to discover that it was written not by the President, but by Marcus Jackson Jr.

> . . . I think your books are great. All Presidents write books
> when they leave office. When my dad leaves office I know he will
> write a book as well. I will have to tell him how much I like his
> book, but I know it won't be as good as your book.

Dawson had visited the White House shortly after that, having been invited by POTUS. Marcus greeted him enthusiastically, holding up a copy of one of Dawson's books that he wanted autographed.

"Please don't tell my dad what I said about I won't like his book as much as I like yours," Marcus had whispered when he had a chance to speak to him without being overheard by his parents.

Dawson put his finger over his lips. "Your secret is safe with me," he said. Marcus smiled broadly, delighted that he and his favorite author had entered into a conspiracy of sorts.

Thinking about that, Dawson very much wanted to call the White House and see if his little buddy was okay. He knew, though, that he would not be able to get through to him. He looked at the clock, then at the time chart. It was eight o'clock here, so that meant it would be four in the morning in Washington. It wouldn't be appropriate to try calling anyway.

He did, however, feel compelled to write Marcus a quick letter. Even if he was not able to speak to him for a while, he wanted to get his thoughts and emotions on paper. He called up a new Word document on his laptop.

> *Marcus,*
> *I know this is a very difficult time for you. And I know that telling you the entire world is sharing your sorrow doesn't make it any easier. But I just wanted to take this opportunity to . . .*

"To what?" he asked aloud.

He looked through the window of his room and down onto the parking lot below. He saw a family unloading luggage from their car and he watched them for a moment, almost envious of them, of their shared love, contentment, and completeness within their family unit. He thought of Mary Beth. No doubt they would have had a family now.

He looked back at the screen to reread what he'd written, so he could continue with the letter.

Nothing he had written was on the screen. Instead, he saw the words:

DAWSON WILL YOU ASSIST US

WESTON HAS RETURNED

THE LION MUST ROAR

WORMWOOD HAS BEEN WAITING

PERELANDRA IN PERMANENT DANGER

Dawson stared at the words on the screen for what seemed like no more than a few seconds. Where had the words come from? What did they mean?

When the phone rang, it startled him. He looked at the time on his cell phone and gasped. It was now nine o'clock! One entire hour had passed since he wrote the first words of his letter to Marcus. That didn't seem possible.

The caller ID showed that it was Bob Anderson calling.

"Bob, it's four A.M. there, isn't it?" Dawson asked. "What are you doing up so late?"

"Is it that late? I haven't been paying attention. Those disjointed words you blurted out before?"

"Yeah, like I said, I'm sorry about that."

"No, don't be sorry. I ran your info and it's interesting."

"Interesting in what way?"

"Does the name Jack Lewis ring any bells for you?"

"No . . . I don't know any Jack Lewis."

"What if I tell you what his real name is, and not what his friends call him? His real name was Clive Staple Lewis."

Dawson knew exactly in that moment who Bob was speaking about. C. S. Lewis, the writer. And, oddly—or maybe not so oddly the way things were going—the very writer that the interviewer Gordon had compared him to.

When there was a long, pregnant pause before Dawson replied, Anderson chuckled.

"Tell me, Dawzy . . . did I pass your literary test? I'll just bet you thought I had never heard of C. S. Lewis, didn't you?"

"I've no room to talk," Dawson said. "Truth is, though I've heard of him, I've never actually read him."

"That word you gave me? *Perelandra*? That's the name of one of his books," Anderson said. "That's what led me to C. S. Lewis."

Dawson felt as if he were in a carnival hall of mirrors. "All right, well, I'll be here if you need me," Dawson said.

"When did you say you're coming back?"

"I'll be on the plane tomorrow. As a matter of fact, I am flying through L.A. And as you had said you were in the town for a little bit, maybe we could get together during my layover."

"That sounds great. And yeah, I made that flight once," Anderson said. "It's almost twenty hours. I don't envy you."

"I'll be in touch when I get back," Dawson said.

Dawson punched off the telephone call and continued to stare at the monitor. The words had not left the screen. Was he finally losing it? Could it be exhaustion? The traveling? The time zone? What? "Maybe I'm finally losing it," Dawson said out loud to anyone who could possibly be listening.

Where was JFK ? Or C. S. Lewis, for that matter, if indeed that's who the strange little man was? And just what was the deal with the lion? The unreality of the situation, of these visions or hallucinations, had him confused. And why should he even care whether they ever showed up again? Dawson suddenly felt a wave of sadness come over him and he found himself near tears. He hadn't really cried since Mary Beth died. Was he having a breakdown, due to all the stress he had been under, all those unresolved feelings of love and despair that he had shoved deep down inside? Dawson rubbed his eyes and decided to take a short nap. He needed some relief—some break from all of it . . .

·*On the Honduras–Nicaragua border*·

The village was not even big enough to have a name. The people lived poorly, removed from "civilization," which meant that they stayed far from the frequent dangers of civil war that could erupt on either side of the border. They spoke a combination of Spanish and a native tongue that was almost extinct. They prayed to no God or gods and subsisted off the land.

In the middle of the day, a cloud descended like a theater curtain of black and red velvet over the huts and makeshift shelters of the village.

Forty or so people—men, women, and children, including an illiterate elderly couple who had survived decades of wars and massacres—all came outside and looked up into the sky. What they saw was unfamiliar to them. The infants and very young children began to cry. The curtain—or whatever it was—moved closer, falling from heaven.

When they were finally enveloped in the miasma, there was no escape for any of them.

A noxious odor overcame many of them, who fainted. The others, of strong jungle stock, who had experienced very little or no contact with city life or any of the accoutrements of the modern world, stood as long as they could, before the bacteria-laden darkness fell completely to the ground. The babies died first, then the oldest among them. It took about an hour before the last of the villagers succumbed to the mysterious killer disease.

The dead and dying could not hear the cackle of laughter on the other side of the curtain that separated their world from denizens of another, malevolent dimension who had released the dark energies that contained every evil known to mankind and many other kinds that had not yet entered human consciousness.

The experiment had worked. Now others around the world would be surprised by the same random plague designed to incite fear and panic among survivors who would hear of its power and finality.

The sunless chamber that had no visible ceiling housed the Tribunal, as the souls of darkness, who had once been soaring spirits, huddled to speak with one another and to observe what was happening on Earth as they stood around the mirror-like pools of consciousness that dotted the "floor" of the assembly hall.

Their beings vibrated with anticipation of the work of centuries that was timed to culminate in a crescendo of energies that would truly rock the foundation of the world from which they had emerged in previous ages. The choices they had made, both in their terrestrial existence and after, placed them in positions of great jeopardy and great promise. It was exhilarating, this time of waiting and watching.

The humans, it seemed, were all too eager to take the easy way out when presented with moral dilemmas in the course of everyday life. What a delight! How easily malleable they were! There were some exceptions, of course, and the heavenly realm was full of those who, even tentatively or reluctantly, had made a decision at some point in their lives to live rightly or had opted for the good over self-serving evil.

That was a shame, of course. Why couldn't they *all* get with the program?

But then there would be no challenge and no confrontation such as that which awaited the world. What a conflagration of emotions lay in store for the unsuspecting humans when Viva Domingo would become a reality and not just a mysterious slogan and rallying cry for those in the know.

The hourglass had been turned one last time, and the end of time approached . . .

W e call to *dis*order this convention of the Tribunal," the once and future Angel of Darkness, the most senior statesman of the assembly, declared.

A hideous laugh erupted among those gathered with a purpose. To the human eye, the evil senate was only dimly visible, as multiple cloaks of darkness—more accurately, of the absence of light—shrouded the figures, who knew each other well by the sounds of their voices and the distinct odors of translated beings. Most, but not all, had once been human and had retained, even on this side, certain senses and connections to earthly conditions of being.

Angel Emphatic, as he liked to call himself, pretending that he had no care for rank or title, though he clung to both tenaciously and purged any who threatened his preeminence in the governance of the Tribunal, spoke in a booming, mellifluous voice that demanded the attention of all within its range. Silence fell like another cloak over them.

"The time is near at hand for us to broadcast the energetic message of our accomplishments. Legions of souls have already embraced our past messages, even if they do not fully understand why and how this is so." The dictator of the Tribunal paused and peered out at the indistinct mass of those in attendance. If they could see him, they saw his broad, mirthless smile, an evil gash that split his face—if it could be called a face—nearly in half.

"Our agents and avatars on Earth have reported successes at every level, on every continent, especially in North America where they have found the soil of discontent to be richer than it has ever been for many generations of mankind. It is laughable that the African continent is riven with wars and famines, because it has been the case for so long. And the peoples of Asia, who multiply faster than we can calculate, are shouldering the burden of our cause quite reliably.

"For centuries we have discounted the little nations and little people that call themselves Europe, because they do so well at destroying themselves and denying the divine. That leaves us with only the barest toehold among peoples in South America and throughout the Pacific Ocean—both of which are vastly outweighed by our strength elsewhere."

A rumble of approval grew into an unearthly roar from the numberless assembly of beings.

"The earthly clock ticks down as the celestial signs align in our favor, as in distant ages past. But very soon we shall have the resources at our disposal to evolve to the next and final stage of our destiny. Soon we will be able to see ever more clearly the families who have crossed into the Light and have been kept from us. Then we can pose to their souls a choice once again. Soon we shall have that which was promised to us and never delivered: the promise of eternal love and energy—the order of *dis*order.

"That covenant, which was broken by the Supreme Spirit—not by us!—will be fully restored, and I shall be—that is, *we* shall be masters not only in name but in a new reality." Emphatic's demonic voice achieved an unbearably high pitch that, on Earth, would have shattered glass and cracked stone. Human ears would be pierced and bleed at such an ungodly shrieking sound.

The pools of consciousness on the other side of the veil, in what men and women called Heaven, similarly served the Council of Elders and the hierarchy of angelic spirits as a view of earthly activities and helped them know when—or whether—to intervene and attempt to guide humans as they stumbled toward destiny.

In contrast to the Enemy, the Council of Elders and the forces of light and good upheld the concept of salvation. They represented hope for all of humanity, yet theirs was a more difficult "sell" in the turmoil and tribulation of the times. Often the members of the Council and the chief elders themselves felt frustration and even despair at the paltry results of their attempts to guide people to the right choices. The flaw in the human makeup that some theologians called "original sin" and others termed "ego" was so powerful that it sometimes presented a chasm between the subject and the right or moral decision that faced him.

What could be done to illuminate the human mind beyond engineering miracles and phenomena to demonstrate the power of the light versus the destructive might of the dark energies? The Council of Elders did not try to manipulate the celestial mechanics in the way the Tribunal had for centuries and to taint man's search for answers in the heavens with evil and occult meaning.

"Have we been weak or misguided?" Caleb once asked during a difficult assembly of the Council when wars and uprisings seemed to spring up daily upon the earth and the people seemed to be drifting farther from their influence. The Dark Forces were exerting an almost magnetic attraction over the often hapless and gullible human species. "Is it our own fault?"

There was no satisfactory answer to such a question. Caleb and the other Masters of Light—a legion of soldiers who practiced the art of spiritual warfare in the cause of the good—must simply apply their energies more effectively and tap into the energies of the Earth in ways that would block the power of the Tribunal. But how? When? Where? The eternal battle was waged over such questions and with similar desperation . . . and thus it always had been.

The question of free will lay before Caleb and all of mankind. It was clear that each human being in the earthly realm possessed the ability to choose good or evil, light or darkness. That the balance of energy within a person and in the physical world could be manipulated from either direction—inside or outside. Subtle distinctions and choices could, ultimately, tip that balance all to the side of evil or darkness, almost without the person involved knowing what was happening. Education—for good or ill—played such a critical role in human moral development, whether the source was religion or the positive influence of a strong family, in any and every part of the world, be it a teeming city of millions or a small village just one step above tribal existence.

The energies that had been unleashed on the Earth by the Tribunal were aimed at tipping the balance all toward the Forces of Darkness. Was it too late to reach even one human being who wished to make the choice for good versus evil? Had it become too difficult, with such forces arrayed against the light, even to hope for one good soul, let alone enough to restore any hope for the balance of energies that had existed, however tenuously, through the ages?

CHAPTER
83

Anderson felt a little disheartened by his conversation with Dawson and with no new leads on the abduction case he decided that if a thing needed to be done, he would just have to do it himself. He settled down in front of his computer and called up the few scraps of evidence left at the crime scene. Perhaps there was something that would tip him off as to why this island was such a magnet for this series of murders. Poking about on the Internet caused him to look at some of the myths in the Book of Invasions, and deeply embedded in Irish lore, he had to admit it was all fascinating stuff.

Legends had it that the Fomorians were a divine race of demons, who had inhabited Ireland for countless generations. They resisted invaders and all newcomers to their territories. Their leader was Balor of the Baleful Eye, the gaze of whose single great eye caused instant death; he could not be killed by any weapon known to man, nor by any warrior. Balor dwelt on Tory Island in constant dread of the fulfillment of a prophecy, namely his eventual destruction by an unborn grandson. Despite his attempts to forestall this end by keeping his daughter Eithne away from men, she became pregnant and gave birth to triplets. Balor cast them into the sea. But one survived: Lugh, who grew up to lead the Tuatha Dé against the Fomorians and who himself killed Balor with a slingshot through his eye.

The Tuatha Dé Danann also claimed divine origin as keepers of the Light Forces, led by Lugh, revered as a god of light, whose summer festival was Lughnasad—still celebrated in Ireland. The Celtic word *lugos*, Anderson learned, could mean "raven," and there was a link in many of the legends between Lugh and those birds.

Lugh was a warrior-hero, a sorcerer and master of crafts, whom Julius

Caesar called "the inventor of all the arts," In battle, Lugh used his magic powers and an enchanted sword. His surname, Lámfhada, meaning "he of the long arm," possibly reflected his skill with the throwing spear or the sling with which he killed his own grandfather, the evil Balor.

So, if Lugh represented the forces of light and good . . . then why would the serial killer claim, if that is what he was doing, the name of a god of light instead of a figure of darkness? How could so many brutal deaths be done in the name of good?

One other thing kept coming back to him as he kept reading. Unlike our concept of good and evil, these gods and legendary men from the distant past were very ambiguous. To call one good and the other evil simply meant that the victorious side claimed to be "good" and named the other, losing side "evil." Lugh could just as easily have stood for a symbol of darkness instead of light. And maybe Balor wasn't evil—but who was to say?

None of this made much sense to Anderson and whether this would help him or not he didn't have a clue. But he knew that time was running out . . . and that somehow the killings in Belfast had something to do with the President's son being kidnapped. And if he didn't solve one or both of these cases shortly there would be consequences beyond anything he could conceive of.

CHAPTER
84

In the Tribunal, Angel Emphatic called upon his ancient ally, Balor of the One Eye, to speak about the impending firestorm of terror to be unleashed upon an unsuspecting Earth. "All of you no doubt know of the power of the baleful One Eye and how we have all benefited from the generosity of its employment over many millennia of earthly time. Now we shall all see a new world broken through the single evil eye of the Dark Master, Balor."

"My dear Lord Angel and venerable comrades in the cause of righteous darkness. For this moment each of us was created and chosen from the beginning of time by the Source of All and the Giver and Taker of Life. Long ago, many of us transitioned to this side and evolved—through much hard work, I must say—toward perfection." Balor manifested in this setting as a gnarled old man with a wispy white beard and a bald head. His skin was nut brown and wrinkled, his hands large and his legs rather stubby. He leaned on a bent stick as if he required it for support.

He went on, "There is much value in the ancient magics that gods and men wielded for century upon century in places far-flung across the Earth. I came into being in the place that is called Ireland today. It was, during past ages, the Earth's very center of spirits and magical doings, misted in cloud and separated from other lands by harsh seas. There, in the navel of the world, I grew to maturity and ruled over a realm not large in size compared to some but unmatched in power. Gods and men were jealous. Although some, like the mighty Romans, were afraid to invade, others were bolder—and infinitely more foolish.

"Though I was defeated by my own grandson in one battle, by a fluke, I died with honor and left a curse upon the very earth that had been my mother. For she abandoned me and stole my magic for a single moment that made me vulnerable to a slingshot—a stone in my eye." Balor pointed to the seemingly bloodshot orb that he displayed on occasions such as this as a badge of divine honor.

"Because of my eternal curse, the land of Ireland has been plagued with diseases and hungers, with many turmoils and troubles over time. Even the Christians, our mortal enemies—along with all religions—who sought to bring peace and light to the cursed isle, fell afoul of the evil I had wrought and fought among themselves, shedding more blood that I had any right to expect—even at my most optimistic!"

The demonic assembly roared again with approving laughter.

Balor said: "The day of blood is upon us. My trusted minions on Earth have devised an ingenious exhibition that will serve more than one purpose. For the men and women of the terrestrial plane are fascinated with murder and mutilation. They say always that they are repulsed, horrified, shocked at such crimes. But all of them are, more truly, fascinated and attracted to grotesque and violent killings. Well, we have presented them with one of the most delectable serial murders in their history. And upon its completion, ever new horrors and devastations shall be released from the bowels of hell to overrun their land and the entire planet. We are opening a vortex and portal to pass through with ease."

Angel Emphatic grinned like a death's-head and applauded his old friend as the Tribunal erupted with cheers and shrieks that shook the outer realm to its very foundation.

The gods of the underworld, ancient and eternal, were well used to the wars between the Armies of Light and the Forces of Darkness. For millennia the battles had raged—on the subcontinent of India, on the plains of Troy, in dense jungles throughout Africa and Southeast Asia. The gods' agents among mankind, whether they believed in the reality of the divine energies or assumed the struggles were merely between human forces, all too often seemed eager to carry the banners of darkness and light into endless, bloody wars.

To what end? Often they did not know themselves. But our planet was the playground and battlefield of many manifestations of spiritual powers throughout the ages—powers that men called Kali or Zeus or the Sun god or any of a thousand different names, with a thousand different faces. In the end, it mattered not what they were called, only that the energies they sponsored were put to good—or terrible—uses among men, women, and children of Earth.

CHAPTER
85

How can somebody evil make the signs from the heavens hurt people? I thought you always said it was supposed to be used only for good." Ruby was sincerely confused.

Mama G smiled. "People always have a choice to use knowledge for good or for evil, child. People have done that many times, as a matter of fact. Remember in your Bible stories how King Herod wanted the wise men to find Jesus and report back to him where the little baby was?"

Ruby nodded, her eyes wide with wonder and horror. As always, she was learning more from her gramma than she had bargained for, and she loved every minute of teaching, which was better than being in a classroom. Then again, nothing was better than being with Gramma.

"The Star of Bethlehem was a sign from God. For thousands of years, God knew he was going to send the star to lead those good men to the place where Baby Jesus lay in the manger. But King Herod had an evil heart, and he had his own wise men who told him the same thing the strangers from the East were proving: that a new king of Israel had been born who would one day take Herod's place on the throne. They were astrologers just like your Mama G. They studied the stars and the movement of the planets, and this gave them special knowledge about what was happening—and what was going to happen—in the world.

"Well, Herod wanted to use this information for his own purposes and to do harm to the little child. In fact, he killed a whole bunch of young boys so that he could eliminate the threat to his kingship. That didn't work, as we all know now. Do you remember why it didn't work, child?"

"Yes! An angel told Joseph to flee to Egypt with Mary and the baby," Ruby announced.

"How right you are. An angel. Another sign from God Almighty to a man on Earth. See, God doesn't do just one thing or just another thing. He works in many ways—many of them mysterious—to communicate with us, to teach us good things and warn us about bad things."

"Why did Joseph believe the angel? A lot of people today don't believe in angels."

"Child, where do you get your wisdom from? I suppose your mother passed it down to you. She always was a wise little thing. Well, anyway, people don't believe in angels anymore because they've been taught wrong—or they haven't been taught properly how to believe in God. He is mighty and mysterious. He has many powers. After all, He created the Heavens and the Earth and all the creatures of the earth. That means you and me, too. And he could—if he wanted to—make all of us do just what he wanted us to do. But instead, he gave us free will. That means we can do pretty much whatever we want to. Even if we want to go against his ways and team up with the devil to do bad things. Well, now, I'm getting off track. . . ."

Ruby did not want to dissuade her grandmother, Mama Greenidge, from going down any track she chose to travel. It was all fascinating for the child. She hung on every word.

"What my point is, is that every bit of knowledge, every God-given science for understanding his beautiful universe, can be put to good purposes—to help people and to make their lives and their families' lives better. That's what I've tried to do for these past fifty years or so, and maybe I succeeded a little bit at it.

"But by the same token, anyone can turn all that good into bad in a pure second. All the knowledge about the sun signs and the moon signs and all the planets—that can be turned to wrong purposes and make something that is good into something that is evil."

"I understand what you are saying, Gramma, but I don't know why anybody would want to do that."

"Why did Adam and Eve partake of the forbidden fruit of the Tree of Knowledge?"

The little girl shrugged, realizing that the question was rhetorical. She did not want her to stop. Gramma was on a roll.

"Because they wanted to *know* more and to *be* more. They wanted to be like God, or like little gods. That is the root of all evil—not accepting

Jehovah's role as our father and friend. They thought they knew better, just as we do today. It's the same story repeating itself, over and over again. We human beings don't seem to learn very much from our past—or to pay attention to the signs God sends to us. We're too busy trying to figure things out on our own. Now, don't let me discourage you, child, from seeking knowledge and asking questions and trying to figure things out. That's not what I mean. I just want you to know that God is standing by your side with all the answers you could ever want—to questions you will never live long enough to ask. If only you will seek to know what His will is for you as you go along your way, on your journey."

"One of my teachers said that science proves there is no God."

"Lord, Lord, child . . ." Mama Greenidge had little time to refute false teachings, but she wanted her own granddaughter to be clear on this, at least: "Every particle in our little world and throughout the universe, every little breath you take or cell in your body is proof of God. If science has achieved anything over the past thousand years—or a lot longer—it is purely proof that there is something far greater than you or I could ever imagine. Who holds up the stars that men first thought of as signs of the zodiac? Those old Greeks saw something in the sky that they called the 'circle of animals.' The zodiac. Who put those stars there? Who made the animals that crawl upon the earth so that somebody could see them in the sky? Who gave man the intelligence to conceive of names for animals—in hundreds of languages around the world?

"Did you ever think about how a little girl in America could see a frog or a skunk or even an elephant and another little girl in China could see the same thing, yet they have a different way of saying the name of that animal? Or why would they have different names? What makes one human being see the same thing on the Earth or in the sky and call it something completely different—yet they are seeing or experiencing exactly the right thing?

"That's because God gave us the brains and the power of thought to respond to His creation in unique ways as individuals."

"I never thought of any of that, Gramma."

"Of course, you didn't, child. I'm running on with my mouth, and I know you couldn't care less about half of what I say." Mama G took a tissue and patted her temples and her upper lip where she perspired when she got especially excited. "You asked about evil and how man can turn something good, like astrology, to the purposes of evil. I imagine you've heard about the terrible murders in Ireland." She shook her head gravely.

"These evil ones are taking a spiritual tool for teaching and guidance and turning it into a weapon of negativity. Do you understand me, child? They want to make astrology a symbol of evil for those who won't take the time to understand what it is really for. It makes me sick that such a thing could happen. And even more so that little children would hear about it, as you have."

"It doesn't make me scared," Ruby said bravely.

Mama Greenidge took the child in her arms, as she had so many times before, and hugged her tightly. "Well, it scares me, dear. I'm not ashamed to admit it. Maybe you can comfort me and help me not to be afraid. I can be more like you and your mama. You're the brave ones. Your Gramma is an old scaredy-cat, is what I am."

"Oh, Gramma. Stop saying that. You aren't afraid of anything."

The elderly lady who had seen so much in her life—through the astrological charts she had done for thousands of people and her visions of other worlds and the skill in reading people's auras when they sat or stood before her seeking her insights into their lives—all that was as nothing when put up against this rising of a new evil, a powerful new negative force that, in ways large and small, was threatening the entire Earth.

The serial murders in Ireland were, in her estimation, merely the tip of the iceberg. A distraction. As horrific as the crimes were, she saw them as symptoms of the greater disease that had taken root across the planet and threatened to consume all of human life. For many years now she had read the signs of this impending tragedy. Having entered the Age of Aquarius at the turn of the millennium, with so much potential for good to triumph over darkness in all human affairs, she had constantly felt the pushback of the Dark Forces and the presence of a newly powerful evil in certain people, too many people.

How had they—really, how had *we* allowed this to happen?

And what can I do now? she asked.

·Southern Britain·

His parents were not pleased with Ian Renshaw. He was not toeing the family line, like his sisters were. He was right in the middle of two older and two younger sisters. The family lived in a middling section of Hastings, a historic town in southern England, where William the Conquer had conquered nearly a thousand years ago.

The idea came to him when he was watching the telly—when he should have been doing his homework lessons. Ian was a smart kid, but his marks in school did not track with his intelligence level. He would rather be out playing football, whatever the weather or time of year, instead of reading his schoolbooks. Or playing games on his laptop computer or exploring Facebook or texting chums about football scores and plans to play football and surfing the Internet to find out about football and football players.

His misery was compounded by having a broken left ankle that would prevent him from much activity for days—and weeks—to come. It was so unfair. . . .

But rather than utilize the opportunity to hit the books, Ian Renshaw used his time to watch matches of his favorite teams and research their scores and statistics online and scheme about how to get to local games. No question, he wanted to be where the action was, right in the middle of the action, as a matter of fact. Nothing would please him more.

His father had a talk with him, then his mother pleaded with him, and his sixth-form teacher reprimanded him, all to no avail. Ian was no scholar. Not that he wasn't interested in learning. He had a good head about him and was learning all the time—absorbing data and ideas from every source imaginable except his school textbooks.

He fantasized about the roar of the crowd greeting him when he walked onto the field for a crucial tournament game with a professional team. That was after he had excelled in the secondary school leagues and maybe even been the star on his university team. But the way he was going, university might be out of the question. Perhaps a trade school team. Those boys were tougher anyway than the scholarly blokes up at university.

Finally, his dad agreed to take him to a big match in Cornwall, coming up in a few weeks, *if* he would buckle down and get some studying done and pass one or two of his upcoming midterm exams in mathematics and English grammar. He hadn't ever enjoyed either of these subjects, but the prospect of getting out of the house and seeing two pro teams was enough to get him serious about his schoolwork. He passed both tests with flying colors.

Just to prove he could do it.

Before he knew it, Ian and his father were sitting in the stadium amid the roaring football fans from the two competing clubs. They were maniacs, each with a reputation for violence in the stands and around the stadium, though nothing terrible had erupted at this point. Ian's dad had warned him that at the first sign of anything untoward, he was going to take the boy, still on crutches, out of the stadium and head home.

Young Ian felt he was plugged into the crowd and could sense the mood. The two warring clubs were evenly matched, and neither had scored a goal nearing the halfway point of the match. Strangely, Ian felt at home and in his own world there in the stadium. And even more strangely, he suddenly felt the urge to stand up and move. The first period of forty-five minutes was almost over; then there would be the halftime break of fifteen minutes before play resumed. The crowd was restless. It was beginning to feel ugly, not only to the boy but to those around him as well.

He wasn't sure exactly why, but Ian had to do something. He didn't tell his dad, but just as the timer ticked to the end of the half he sneaked out of his seat, using his crutches to move quickly down the stairs from the upper tier of the stands toward the field. His father was distracted in conversation with a man in a neighboring seat.

Ian moved faster than he thought he could, helped by the fact that he was moving down with gravity. The buzzer for halftime sounded just as he reached the gate at the bottom of the rows of seats. No one was looking, and Ian flipped the latch on the gate and slipped to the other side—the field side—and then hobbled directly onto the field and headed toward the home team's bench.

Just then a rumble erupted in some of the upper stands directly opposite where Ian stood. The boy turned to look at the source of the noise and immediately sensed what was happening. The crowd, which had been tense all along, was starting to erupt. No one knew exactly what prompted it, but the hooligans who were looking for trouble had found it.

Ian spotted a microphone that had been set up in the middle of the field at the halfway line for some announcements and some entertainment. He moved as swiftly as he could toward it. When he got there, he stood on his tiptoes and angled the microphone down toward his mouth.

"Oi, lads!" he shouted. His voice carried to the farthest corners of the stadium. "Listen up. We're all here for the match and it's been a great one so far. For once let's have all the rough stuff on the field. *No trouble! No trouble! No trouble!*"

At first there was dead silence throughout the park. Then a few people shouted and picked up a chant, *"No trouble! No trouble! No trouble!"* Then more and more people joined in.

Ian Renshaw's dad, realizing the boy wasn't in his seat but down on the field at the microphone, bolted down the stairs onto the field and snatched up his son, who hung on to his crutches.

"No trouble! No trouble! No trouble!" reverberated through the football

stadium and greeted the players who came back onto the field early to see what was going on. The players stood there with their mouths open, looked at one another, some of them even hugging, and joined into the chant. *"No trouble! No trouble! No trouble!"*

His father deposited Ian back in his seat, with a stern look on his face. "Whatever possessed you, son?" he asked.

"I don't know, Dad. Something made me do it. I thought it was the right thing."

The boy's mother read about the incident in the newspaper the next morning and nearly fainted.

Clive Staple Lewis, who preferred to be called Jack, was born in Belfast, Ireland, on the 29th of November 1898. His father, Albert Lewis, was a lawyer. He had a brother, Warren, called Warnie, who was three years older.

Lewis had a happy early childhood, living in a large, gabled house with dark, narrow passages and an overgrown garden, where he and Warnie played and explored. Albert Lewis kept a well-stocked library where Jack developed his love for books, his favorite being *Treasure Island*.

His happy boyhood came to an end when Jack's mother became ill and died of cancer when he was only ten.

In 1916 Lewis entered the University at Oxford. But World War I was under way, and whether inspired by patriotism, a thirst for excitement, or just curiosity, Jack left school and joined the army where he wound up fighting in the muddy trenches of northern France.

Dawson looked from his research then, recalling the soldier he had seen in the World War I uniform while he was doing his radio interview on *The Gordon Hour* the night before. He knew that he had to get on a plane but wanted to do just a little more reading on the man–ghost—that was appearing to him.

After the war ended Lewis returned to Oxford, where he studied Greek and Latin literature, Philosophy, ancient history, and English literature, graduating with honors. He taught at Oxford, remaining for 29 years, then he became a professor of medieval and renaissance literature at Magdalene College, Cambridge, in 1955.

Even as he was teaching at the university, Lewis began to publish books. His first major work, *The Pilgrim's Regress,* was published in 1933. He published several books that not only won him acclaim as a writer of books on religious subjects, but also as a writer of academic works and popular novels.

Following the publication of *The Lion, the Witch and the Wardrobe* in 1950, Lewis quickly wrote 6 more Narnia books, publishing the final one, *The Last Battle,* in 1956.

After his wife, Joy Gresham, died of cancer in 1960, Lewis's own health deteriorated, and in the summer of 1963 he resigned his post at Cambridge. He died at his brother's home in Oxford at seven p.m. on November 22, 1963.

Dawson examined what he had written, noticing, immediately, the connection between C. S. Lewis and President Kennedy. He made a note of it. Then he looked up pictures of C. S. Lewis. He found a picture of Lewis taken during the First World War. He was not surprised to see that this was the same person he had seen in the WWI uniform when he was doing the interview on *The Gordon Hour.*

And the other picture of C. S. Lewis was the same man he had seen appear in his bedroom, twice, once alone, and once standing alongside President Kennedy.

Dawson looked over the notes he had made:

CLIVE STAPLE LEWIS . . . did not like his name, so he called himself Jack. (President Kennedy was John Fitzgerald Kennedy, but he was called Jack.) C. S. Lewis died at the home of his brother Warren in Oxford, England, at 7 P.M. on November 22, 1963. By some cosmic coincidence, that was the exact moment that President Kennedy was pronounced dead.

As an aside, Dawson also noticed that Aldous Huxley died on the same day, though not at the same time.

He continued to make notes from his research. He made the notes just as they occurred to him, without regard to whether or not they had any specific meaning.

Lewis's wife was named Joy.

The lion that Dawson saw represented Aslan, the iconic symbol of Spirituality and God or Christianity in *The Chronicles of Narnia.*

Weston represented Professor Weston, an evil incarnate individual who wants to corrupt and do evil in *The Space Trilogy*.

Wormwood is a character from *The Screwtape Letters* that also has to do with unleashing Evil against the Enemy: God and Spirituality.

The suite's bell rang. It was housekeeping, and Dawson opened the door to the maid, who was bringing in a tray of fruit, cookies, and bottled water. Her name tag read PENNY. Penny, Dawson had learned in his research this morning, was one of the two main characters in C. S. Lewis's *The Magician's Nephew*.

Was there no end to all this symbolism? Coincidence?

If Dawson had all this figured out, C. S. Lewis, who was now dead, wanted Dawson's help. Help with what?

This was all too ridiculous. Maybe it was nothing but his overactive brain coming up with the next storyline for Matt Matthews. Are writers sometimes forced to live in the very worlds they create?

Who needs his help? A dead writer? Why him? Why now? He wanted to howl, to cry out to the literary gods who had zapped him with some peculiar sort of insanity or inspiration—he wasn't sure which. He stood erect. He knew on some weird level that he was about to walk through his own wardrobe.

CHAPTER
87

Mama G, having consulted her charts all evening, was posting her nightly blog. After noting scores of specifics about alignments, risings and fallings, about the gatherings of stars and shadows and dark matter still closing in, she shared these words:

> From each one, many.
> As above, so below.
> No one sign, no one spirit, no one moves alone.
> No one.
> All one.
> As above, so below.

Mama G had been seeing signs and hearing voices with accelerating intensity, with a greater positive vibration. Sometimes the brilliances of light and energy would wash over her with so much light and power, she would get light-headed, breathless.

But Mama G was feeling her bouts of hopelessness and uselessness and utter sadness beginning to ease. A clearing of sorts. Signs of clearing. Her recent sense of doom now dissipating, even just a bit. More and more, with each post on her blog, she was energized, renewed.

Each answer she gave to a fellow soul who was logged on to her site sustained her feeling of momentum. Like she was going places, every time she pressed SEND.

She knew deep in her heart that she had been receiving floods of good energy, showers of light of hope and love and usefulness, all coming to her from the Council of Elders. She saw the Governor's approving face. All this warm feeling being sustained every time she shared this energy with others.

And they were coming together to do what needed to be done.

She heard, *All. Together. All*

Your choice. Your acts.

Below, as above.

One.

Mama G sat typing at her computer but as she did so, the words that she thought she was putting on the screen didn't appear. Instead she got words like *Hollywood Joe, Hello L.A., Big Warehouse Sale—All Must Be Freed.*

And suddenly Mama G had a vision of a young boy in a lightless place. . . .

Sometimes it was that simple: In this vision she was shown how she could help find the President's son—in Los Angeles. She laughed as she wrote down the information, and then picked up the phone to call Dave Hampton. Surely he knew how to get this info to the FBI. She knew it wasn't much, but merely knowing for sure that the boy was in the city would surely help.

She'd also call Dawson Rask, a truly good man who had come to Grenada years ago to do research for one of his novels and along the way become a trusted friend. Someone had to find that boy, and fast. And she had a sense if Hampton didn't have the resources, then Dawson knew how to reach the FBI even more quickly than she could.

Then she discovered an email from Dawson that she hadn't seen before. . . . When had it come in? She checked: Just within the past hour. As she read the email, she thought, *Whoa, Lord, my instincts are right. You are deep in this thing already, man, and I am glad you are on our side.*

And suddenly Mama G knew in her bones that this was but the start of her journey. That she was not just a messenger in this upcoming battle but a player. It was time for her to pack a bag and leave her beloved island. She would brave her nemesis—her fear of flying—and go to the City of Angels herself.

News brief from *The New York Times:*

Teen's Confession Thrown Out
In Buddhist Temple Massacre

The U.S. Court of Appeals for the Ninth Circuit in Arizona ruled that a teenager's confession to nine killings at a Buddhist temple was involuntary because he was not properly read his rights.

Daniel David Johnssen was 17 at the time of the killings of six priests, a nun and two others during a robbery at the Wat Promkunaram temple west of Phoenix in 2002. He was sentenced to serve 301 years after he was convicted of murder, armed robbery and other charges and has spent more than 10 years in prison, most of that time in solitary confinement.

The Arizona attorney general's office is considering whether to file a petition asking the Supreme Court to review the case or seek to retry Johnssen, who pled guilty to all charges and later claimed he was "ordered" to perform the killings by the Antichrist.

CHAPTER
88

Angel Emphatic, also known as the One, felt self-satisfied at the turn of events. In human form—passing as a Los Angeles white-collar criminal—he had burrowed into the community for several months to establish roots there in anticipation of the critical moves his masters had tasked him to perform. He was a general in command of a vast army that was scattered across the Earth, warriors who had trained and prepared for the battle that would seal the fate of mankind for all eternity. The general was eager to deploy his forces.

Marcus Jackson, the son of the assassinated president, lay in the secure room next to Domingo's office in a warehouse district of L.A.

The plan was simple—and critical. Marcus must be contained until after the revelation by Angel Emphatic of the ascendancy of the Dark Forces. If Marcus were to escape, it could ruin all his plans. The young man had the potential to mobilize Light forces all over the Earth and turn the Dark Matter away. He didn't know his potential, of course, or he would be trying harder to escape.

No, Angel Emphatic was confident of his eventual and total triumph.

The date, time, and place of the announcement of victory was set—and it was now only days away. In that epochal moment, Los Angeles—glamorous Hollywood and all that it stood for—would be at the epicenter of the world. It always brought a smile to his human lips to think of the irony and the absolute rightness of the plan.

Angel Emphatic transported himself across the planes in the blink of an eye to the realm of darkness. There he sought out his lieutenant, known as IRA, to glean the latest intelligence the trickster had gathered from the Council of Elders in the enemy camp.

The two adherents of the Dark Energies met and merged their consciousness in familiar conversation. They had spoken often over many centuries and knew each other's thoughts intimately.

"Greetings, brother," Angel Emphatic said warmly.

"My most esteemed brother and friend," IRA greeted in return.

"So, Clever One, tell me of your progress with the arrogant American leader who is in your capable hands and under your guiding influence."

"He is everything we expected—including naïve. He is dying to do good. Pardon the pun!" IRA was proud of his facility with languages. His "specialty" was rhetoric—influencing others through his clever words and planting tortuous rhetorical thoughts in the minds of earthly men and women to muddy moral issues and debates among them.

"The Council of Elders seems desperate to enlist him in their dying cause, but I have detected a hesitance within him. He is still very new on the Other Side and not yet comfortable there. He is obsessed by what is going on in the human realm and has not yet let go. I would characterize him as stubborn."

"That is excellent—for our purposes. If we can manipulate him, we can move him to delay action by the Elders against us. Do you agree?"

"I agree wholeheartedly, my lord. But I would add this note of optimism. I believe I can turn him to our side, enlist him as an ally to the Tribunal."

"That would be an unparalleled accomplishment, dear friend. The Council might collapse and surrender at word of such a loss. Nonetheless, we hold the winning hand in our game with this so-called President: his son."

Angel Emphatic leered majestically, proud of himself and his comrade, confident as never before in the likelihood that they would achieve ultimate mastery of the created world. If he had been made of flesh, his blood would be running high and hot.

"The son is secure and isolated by our human allies, who were influenced by a powerful flux of energy to do our bidding, to capture him. Our methods, which may seem crude to those of you skilled in the finer arts of manipulation and influence, worked supremely well. No doubt, the President will try to contact him, unless you can dissuade him from that course, IRA. Can you do this?"

"Indeed, I think I can. He is too eager to compromise, I suppose from his long political training. And he pretends to be concerned for what happens to others—especially his family. I cannot believe he will do anything that he feels might harm his only child."

"Yes, that is a weakness of so many human beings and one of our great advantages. It is so simple to put them in situations in which they must choose our way or death and destruction. They are afraid of what others think of them and can thus be paralyzed by simple acts of terror."

"It's what we do," IRA concurred with a laugh.

"Our earthly allies have gotten better and better at it over time," Angel Emphatic reflected with pleasure. "The only downside is there has come to be less need for good old-fashioned mass bloodshed. It would be a beautiful thing in this electronic age of the Earth if there were new massacres and violence to broadcast every day."

"Wouldn't that get boring, too?" IRA always played the provocateur.

"You are incorrigible, my friend. In our realm—and soon in all of creation—there is no limit to the benefit to us of mayhem in every aspect of life, across time and every dimension."

Anak Krakatau, or "Child of Krakatoa," first appeared in 1930 and had grown consistently at a rate of five inches a week or twenty feet per year since then, with periodic activity throughout that time. NASA and world-wide geological institutes kept the island under constant surveillance over the years. For decades, volcanologists expected the site to erupt at any time, but when it finally did, its violence surpassed even the worst predictions and its suddenness took the world by surprise.

The dome of the island exploded with a ferocity not seen since 1883, when Krakatoa had shaken the world. Almost simultaneously, Mauna Loa in Hawaii, the largest volcano in the world, erupted, spewing fiery lava and columns of ash more than a mile into the air.

Within twenty-four hours of these two Pacific Ocean mega-volcano events—the sea level in the world's largest ocean rose several inches, and a tsunami originating from each volcanic site rolled outward into open waters. Geologists and oceanographers calculated that Australia, the Philippines, and eventually Japan would be the largest population centers to be hardest hit, with many of the smaller islands that lay in the paths of the giant tidal waves being obliterated in their wake.

CHAPTER
89

Bobby Anderson went through the case materials again and again, and he came to the same conclusion each time—that there was a definite connection between the Belfast killings and the abduction of Marcus Jackson. There simply had to be one. And as Anderson kept thinking about it, the key seemed to boil down to the phrase *Viva Domingo*. A series of events was unfolding according to plan, keyed to the science of the stars and planets and the impending Age of Aquarius. But what real evidence did he have to support this theory? It didn't help that the only clue that they had on the abduction was that Marcus Jr. was in Los Angeles, and that was from a lone source. Anderson was debating whether he should stay in the city . . . that is, until he was given vital information by Dawson, who had been contacted by noted seer Mama G, giving them a lead, telling him that the boy was *definitely* in Los Angeles. Anderson had always been a little leery of the psychic community, but after what he had experienced in the last few months he was willing to take any help he could, even if it meant relying on magic and on his well-trained gut to lead him forward with the investigation. But he was still hesitant to go forward until he had thought this through a bit more.

He could not clearly prioritize one over the other, Belfast over Marcus Jackson, or vice versa. They both occupied his mind and every waking minute of thought and energy. In fact, there was no "nonwaking" hour for Agent Bobby Anderson, as he had forgotten all about sleep and did not expect to become reacquainted with the concept before both cases were resolved.

Viva Domingo. If you were to take it literally, that would mean "live Sunday." What the hell did that mean? What was so special about a live Sunday? Did it mean any Sunday . . . or this coming Sunday? Anderson knew that events were racing ahead and that they had little time left. He looked up the date in history: March 2. Astrologically, the date fell under the sign of Pisces, the planet Neptune, and the Earth's moon. No obvious significance there. Geography? In the Americas, Asia, Europe, Africa? . . . Northern hemisphere or southern? Bobby laid out his notes and hypotheses and stared at them until he was blue in the face.

He took a break, turned on the TV to catch the news, fearing he would hear something awful that he didn't want to hear, as he almost always did these days. . . . Nonetheless he flipped from channel to channel for several seconds each. He clicked onto a commercial in progress: "This Sunday, the biggest entertainment moment of the year, the Academy Awards, broadcast live from the Hollywood Grand Theatre in Los Angeles. . . ."

That was it! The Academy Awards.

He immediately got on the phone and tried calling Dawson. The call went straight to voice mail, and he left a message to call him as soon as he could—he wanted him to stay in L.A., and not make his connecting flight. He needed his help. And he knew somehow that the tip from Mama G might just be the thing he had been looking for.

On the most popular cable news network in the United States, all news broadcasts led with the disastrous news that in some way affected nearly everyone on the planet:

"In economic news tonight, a strange, unexpected downturn in world markets has put more countries around the world closer to fiscal meltdown than ever before. The economies of Greece and Italy have finally, fully collapsed, and France is facing default on eighty percent of its debt. Ireland is hanging on only because Great Britain and France are supporting that country by a thread. Central and South American nations are holding their collective breath, watching to see what will happen in the United States when our markets open tomorrow. Every indicator up until just last week had been positive, from gross domestic product numbers across Europe and stocks and bonds in Asian markets to the New York Stock Exchange and NASDAQ, both of which had rebounded phenomenally in recent months."

The noon news anchor looked rather ashen and shell-shocked, as she read the bulletin.

"Experts are at a loss to explain exactly why this negative trend is so sharp, indeed, why it has occurred in the first place. Virtually all economic indicators over the past few months have heralded the long-awaited recovery from global recession and near-depression for many nations. Panic has erupted in trading rooms all around the world and huge sell-offs are occurring twenty-four hours a day, even after local markets have closed, with investors seeking to bail out of the markets, taking with them pension funds and small investors, as well as the biggest global players."

Video clips from the past seventy-two hours showed riots in Amsterdam, Hong Kong, Cairo, Athens, Santiago, and Mexico City, with surging crowds protesting the economic woes of those countries, as the rest of the world watched, stunned at this turn of events. And those were just some of the locations that had exploded in violence, including North American cities of all sizes with crowds ranging from a few hundred to a few thousand of every race and economic status.

"Finance and treasury ministers from governments on every continent have been summoned by the secretary general of the United Nations to an emergency meeting in Davos, Switzerland, to address the crisis, but organizers are wondering whether, even if the meeting is held within a few days, it may be too late to avert a global meltdown of currencies, investments, and national systems."

Within the Tribunal, the commanders of the Forces of Darkness expressed their delight that the dark energies had successfully penetrated the lives of nearly every man and woman on the planet with such apparent ease and completeness. This would offer a huge advantage in the coming confrontation.

CHAPTER
90

Mama G boarded the plane and found her seat on the flight to Los Angeles. She hated plane travel, but her thoughts were on the messages all around her, and her heart was full of both fear and joy. She knew that this was a moment for which she had been born, and no matter what the outcome, she knew that she had to do everything in her power to make things right. For herself. For her little granddaughter.

For the world. *It isn't a matter of courage,* she thought, *it's just something that a righteous body has to do.* She settled into the seat and began to do the only thing that gave her comfort, which was to pray.

The Governor sat alone in the chamber. No Council of Elders meeting was slated for this morning. He thought about the good work Mama G was performing. How her circle of "doers" was gathering, and gathering steam. Music filled the Council chamber. It was shimmering colored light, light that sounded butter yellow. *As above, so below,* he thought.

And as the Governor thought, he thought of Mama G, that calm yellow turned to orange, then lavender, indigo, all strands of light, pulsing, circling strands, turnings of a wheel, color-wheel turnings, gatherings of circles, threading into harmony.

Who were the Fallen Masters? POTUS had never heard of the concept. Of course, he had been busy as a soldier and public servant, a husband and father, a doer rather than a thinker. All his life he had devoured books and consumed ideas and theories, but he stubbornly lived in the "real" world of flesh and blood—of life and death—not in the ether of spiritual notions.

He was not one to compromise or consider what might exist "in between" this real world and the next—or any alternative to what he could see, hear, taste, or touch with his own human senses. But his experience in the realm of Light on the Other Side had taught him a radical new curriculum: the spiritual and nonsensory. His entire soul was now open to learning lessons and concepts that had never been a part of his life before.

Through the pools of consciousness he *saw* life on Earth as he had never been capable of seeing when he existed in that realm himself.

As part of the need to communicate the message of hope from the Council of Elders, he now understood that persons like himself had particular roles to play. Guides or angels had served as messengers in past ages. The Bible, world religious texts, history books, hieroglyphics, and even primitive art such as cave paintings all testified to these messengers from beyond the earthly sphere. Now, POTUS clearly understood that he and other historical personages were being called upon in a critical moment in human history to carry down to people words of hope and instruction—and to intervene directly in some cases—to elevate human consciousness and increase awareness of the threat to the earth by the expanding dark matter.

More than that, the Fallen Masters—as chosen messengers—were empowered by the Council to inspire humans to choose the path that would ensure their survival and defeat the powerful forces of darkness.

The Council of Elders had chosen some of the most influential and powerful men and women in history to serve as Fallen Masters. Philosophers, artists, and saints were probably the most powerful of all, and rulers and political leaders, if they had made the right choices during their lifetimes, could also be incredibly effective. The Governor took a very particular interest in who was recruited as a Master, as he had when POTUS had first come to the realm of light from his sojourn on Earth. Not that his arrival had been unexpected; indeed, the leadership of the Council were gifted with sight that was not restricted by boundaries of time or space that included the ability to foresee the arrival of souls such as POTUS. He fit their criteria perfectly.

In this final battle, family members would be dispatched to give aid and comfort to other family members. The cycle of history would turn full circle to counter the energies exerted by the forces of darkness through natural and unnatural means. Falling to Earth, or returning to the plane where they had once known existence themselves, these Masters would break through the invisible barrier that traditionally separated them from men and women. Reentering the dimension they had once departed, the Fallen Masters could communicate with their human counterparts without sound or physical contact—rather by telepathic means, by pure thought waves. The Masters, for their part, experienced the same kind of dislocation that they had when they had died and passed over to the Other Side, in reverse. It taxed their energy and was no simple task.

POTUS was aware that he was being prepared, through his own son, to take on the responsibility of being a Fallen Master and stepping through the portal of time on this mission that would, like those of the other Masters, help equip mankind in its battle against the army of darkness that was powerfully arrayed against it.

It seemed an almost impossible task, yet if even one Fallen Master succeeded, it would make an incredible difference for one human being who could influence countless others. POTUS hoped that he was up to the task, and while he wondered at some of IRA's training methods, he felt that his strength would sustain him and he would be able to be one of the true Fallen Masters. He felt proud to be an instrument of such good.

· *Atlanta* ·

D r. Tyler Michaels had seen it with his own eyes and confirmed it with his companion and sometimes nemesis Rae Loona on the telephone: The invitations from Charlene St. John to be her guest at the Academy Awards ceremony were actually in their hands. As a Best Original Song nominee, Charlene could invite several people to be with her in the audience and backstage—and at the numerous parties to which the A-list types were invited. Yet, though he had seen it with his own eyes, Tyler was having trouble believing it. And he wasn't sure he wanted to accept. Something was holding him back. . . .

"What, are you crazy, Mikey?" Rae chided him. "You and me with Charlene, who is one of my all-time faves, though not even in the same ballpark as you-know-who? This is the opportunity of a lifetime!"

"Maybe you should go, then, without me," he said. A heavy curtain of depression had fallen between him and the rest of the world, and he was almost incapable of action, of making any kind of choice that would be positive for him. He felt the presence of forces "out there" that were pushing him back and down and down and down. From where or to where, he could not tell. He just *felt* a malevolent presence that was holding him back. He wondered whether he should self-prescribe some kind of medication to whack himself back to reality.

"Creation is a thing of beauty. Look around you: See the good in all things. Understand that the people who are in your life—and those no longer in your life—are there for a purpose that is ultimately positive. The motive of the Creator is the source of all positive energy and all light. It is everywhere, if you will just open your eyes to it."

The voice came to him even as he was still on the telephone with Rae.

"Hello, hello, Mikey. . . . Are you still with me? Earth to Mikey! Earth to Mikey!" Rae's insistent tone pulled him back into the conversation they had been having.

"It was him," Tyler said.

"Who?"

"My Swedish friend. I heard him. His voice. Inside my head. I can't seem to get away from him."

"Well, that's not a bad thing, is it?" Rae Loona said. "From what you have told me, he has some pretty interesting things to say."

"Oh, I can't deny that. But it's kind of spooky. I've never been what you'd call a religious guy."

"Don't I know it," Rae said, then thought better of chiding her friend beyond that. She was getting the picture that Tyler was somehow changing, that he was being called to a different level of understanding, and she didn't want to stand in the way or discourage him. He was on his own journey now, *Go-ing Pla-ces.*

Tyler hung up the phone. The philosophical presence was still with him but remained silent for a long time. He sat patiently, something that was different for him; he was always moving, doing something, going from one place to another. Since Karen's passing, he found himself less and less inclined to be always on the go. He was still impatient and wanted things to happen in *his* time, but perhaps he was getting better on that front, learning patience in his "old age," as he liked to put it.

"I want to help you, to guide you. I have been sent for that purpose. It is up to you, however, to want my help, to seek the deeper understanding."

There, it was back.

Tyler said aloud: "All I want is to see my wife, Karen, to tell her I truly love her. To see my son, Jeremy, and to let him know that I am his father and that I love him." Tears blurred his vision. "I know I was so wrong in what I did, that I missed the opportunity to have a family. God knows, I am so sorry for my own arrogance and stupidity."

"That is the key to understanding and to helping others learn and grow. I know that you are confused and uncertain by my presence, by what you 'hear' in my voice. But that is so unimportant. Who I am is the least concern. Karen knew me. Your friend Rae will know me. I am a philosopher, but my philosophy doesn't matter in the least. The message from the ultimate Source, the Creator of all that is good in the universe, is so very simple, for you and for every man and woman: Come unto me. Trust in me and you will find everything you seek."

"So you are the Swedish philosopher that Karen was all hot about. She tried to tell me. I didn't listen. Swedenborg. Funny name. But I can accept it now. I am willing to listen. God knows I have blown it up till now."

"On the contrary. Think of the lives you have saved. You are one point in a vast universe, so insignificant as to be nearly nonexistent, yet so important that many others depend upon you. It is the way of creation. Each of us has a message and a role to play in the lives of those around us—and those we do not yet know exist."

Tyler now was silent himself. Not since medical school had he been called upon to absorb so much information. . . . He hoped he could do it. It was beginning to dawn on him how much was at stake and what he was being asked to do.

"No, you are not crazy. And, yes, you should share with your friend Rae Loona this experience," the man said. *"And you are right, I am the scientist and theosophist your wife Karen told you about, Emanuel Swedenborg. My life among men has ended, but I was sent back to be your guide and to help you accomplish what you need to reclaim those you love and have lost.*

"Your task will be to assist the Forces of Light in the best way you can—by turning your knowledge and the goodness of your heart to the ends of good. Will you choose to accept such a mission in a time when you and those closest to you need you the most?"

"But I—" Again, Tyler felt himself tongue-tied, absolutely out of his depth. What could he do—what had he ever done—to advance the cause of right in the world? It was so big, too big for a person like him. . . . All he had ever done was screw up lives and relationships through his pride and unconcern about others. It wasn't until he lost Karen and his son that he had realized there was something more to this life than career achievements and material wealth.

"I am afraid it is too late," he said aloud. But no one heard him.

At the same time, Tyler was now quickly warming up to the idea of paying attention to the Swede-voice, but to some extent, he was still confused. He was getting more than a tad tired of Rae Loona's endless prodding, and flat-out sick of her relentless John Travolta lovefest. OK, OK, maybe he could see that they were *GO-ING PLA-CES*, but how was this all fitting together?

OK. He was unwilling to give up entirely feeling blue. He was stuck in it, so what? After all he'd been through . . .

He kept listening to Charlene St. John's newest CD and found it consoling.

In his car, heading to meet Rae, he flipped on his iPod, which he'd plugged into his car's auxiliary outlet.

· Atlanta ·

Late at night, after reading Mama G's latest posting on *Putting It Together*—"Now Is the Time to Take Action"—Rae Loona, a long-time subscriber to the seer-astrologer's e-newsletter and podcast, sent an email to the WIN AN INSTANT READING offer on the website homepage. In her entry she asked Mama G, "What action should I take? Please clue me in."

Within a few minutes, Rae had received notification that she had won the prize! "Talk about bizarre," the nurse murmured aloud, staring at her laptop screen. "This is spooky."

Early the next morning, Mama G replied to Rae: "You will search, and you will find. You are on a quest to find the Key. You are not alone. You know you are go-ing pla-ces!"

Before Rae could reply, the astrologer sent another one-liner in addition: "You're going to L.A., aren't you?"

How the heck did Mama G know about Los Angeles? Rae reflected for a moment—breathed in, breathed out—and thoughts about Tyler and fate filled her mind. Feelings of hope filled her heart.

"Yes," she typed.

"There you will be led to take action. You are at the center of it all. I am going to Los Angeles, too. For the first time in my life!"

"So all this is not a coincidence?" Rae emailed back.

"Is your friend's contact with the Swedish philosopher a coincidence?"

She decided not to answer Mama G.

But Mama G came back to her, big time: "You are needed in L.A., child. You have a unique destiny awaiting you there. Save the boy. *Save the boy.*" Rae had no idea what boy was meant by this, but she knew in her heart that if Mama G said a thing, then it must be the truth. She just had to figure it out somehow.

At the airport, less than twenty-four hours later, Rae met Tyler. She had managed to pack her best dress and surprisingly few other items in a single carry-on—to avoid the extra-baggage charge and because she had so little time. The two held their electronic tickets as they joined the line to board the aircraft.

"She said we have a destiny in Los Angeles."

"Who?

"Mama G. The seer."

You know Mama G?" Tyler had long since realized he should never be surprised by Rae's revelations to him, but he'd truly had no idea about this. Even he knew about the world's most famous astrologer, and he had once or twice visited her website himself. A long time ago.

"Sure. I'm a regular. I love all that woo-woo stuff. And Mama is the real thing. I can testify to that."

"I won't ask . . . ," he said simply. Then he turned to her and was completely serious. "My friend Swedenborg came to me again."

"I didn't know he was ever not with you, Mikey."

"Listen, this is important. He didn't give me any specific instructions about L.A. and what we are supposed to do there. But I have a strong thought—knowledge, really—that the President's son is there, and somehow, we are supposed to be involved in finding him and saving him."

"That's it!" Rae exclaimed. "We're going there to be a part of it. That's what Mama G meant when she said, 'Save the boy.'"

The two compared notes as they sat together in their business class seats. Then they were quiet. Rae closed her eyes to get some rest. Tyler flipped on his iPod and settled in to listen to Charlene St. John's newest CD. His eyes remained wide open for the entire flight.

So, they were go-ing pla-ces . . . maybe. But it occurred to the doctor that they were going to one place where they were supposed to be. Perhaps there he would learn how this was all fitting together. It didn't matter anymore what he wanted, or what he thought he wanted. He was being led by his spirit guide, the amazing Swedenborg, and he finally decided not to fight it anymore. To go, to do what he was asked to do, to be who he was supposed to be.

·En route to Los Angeles·

Also en route to L.A., but on a different airliner, Patricia Rose Greenidge was beginning to *see* what lay ahead. Often she had visions, sometimes scattered and unconnected, but of late she was seeing things that were all of a piece: from her encounter with the Council of Elders, which still blew her mind when she thought about it, to her contacts with Rae Loona and Dave Hampton. She had even sent and received messages to Dawson Rask and that FBI agent who was searching for the President's son—and who had the deepest and most accurate insight of anyone else on the planet as to what was happening globally.

Putting it all together . . . now she knew exactly what was happening and why this particular group of people was converging on L.A.

This was the time when the Army of Light, the forces of the Council itself, would reveal itself in a battle against the darkness. It was all coming down to this. And she would be in the middle of it, or present to see it unfold. She was called, just like the others, to be present on the battlefield for the confrontation.

Mama G, along with the whole world, would be there to see it happen.

Mama G saw the Governor sitting across from her, as clearly as if he were also a passenger on the flight. But, instead, she was back in the Council chambers. Her ears were filled with music, her heart with love, and her mind with foreboding. It was like nothing she had ever heard, and yet at the same time the most natural sound in the world. Could it be nothing less than the music of the spheres? Harmonies that set the planets in motion?

Now, with so much gratitude and a loss of fear, she heard the music—whole, eternal, suspended in air. She heard the harmonies that would never be lost as long as she was open to being this in tune with everything around her.

"The signs in the heavens are all converging," she said to the Governor. "That is why I am traveling to the States."

"The time is now. All God's children have their tasks," he said. He really wasn't talking. It was as if his eyes, glinting in the light, were telling Mama G to keep on keeping on. A powerful message.

She responded with a smile. Mere words were of lesser value at this moment.

Mama G had her theme for tonight's website post, which would be done remotely—from L.A. She was grateful to the Council for revealing the truth to her. She felt privileged and in awe of the power of Light in a world threatened by darkness. She had her marching orders. For sure.

Mama G closed her eyes and started to pray. And suddenly, as if words were now becoming pictures, Mama G saw the number *1* slide across her closed eyes, followed by *512*. She sat very still, hoping, for once, her vision was clear as crystal. She heard the word "Jesse" being said as if over a loud-speaker in an airport. Suddenly, Mama G saw herself in an airport terminal, in front of a departures board showing flights. Brightly lit was flight 1512 from L.A. to Marcus via Jesse Airlines.

Mama G was skilled at sorting out symbols, and these were child's play: 1512 had to be an address, and Jesse probably meant the street. She knew that time was of the essence and for once she was happy that she lived in a time of technology. She pulled out her cell phone and accepted the disastrous charges to make some phone calls. She prayed that she would be in time. . . .

This was all too ridiculous. Maybe it was nothing but his overactive brain coming up with the next storyline for Matt Matthews. Are writers sometimes forced to live in the very worlds they create?

Who needs his help? A dead writer? Why him? Why now?

"Because we have come to now," C. S. Lewis said.

Dawson looked up from the notes he was taking, not at all shocked to see C. S. Lewis standing right there in the hotel room with him. No longer in a World War I uniform, Lewis was wearing a tweed jacket and a dark blue tie that was somewhat askew. He had a high forehead and dark, very penetrating eyes.

"Well, so you finally decided to talk to me," Dawson said.

"Oh, but I've been talking to you all along, dear boy. You don't think you were suddenly blessed with the power of precognition, do you?"

Dawson had never seen a film clip of Lewis, and he had no idea what Lewis sounded like, but the accent seemed just right—exactly like that of Ian McKellen. In fact, he wondered if it was McKellen's voice he was hearing. Perhaps it was. Perhaps his subconscious was merely supplying that voice for this occasion.

"Why are you doing this? What is going on? Why am I getting all these visions?"

"Because we need you," Lewis replied.

"Who is we? And why do you need me?"

"We are us, the souls of planet Earth."

"But you are no longer of this planet. You are dead."

"Do I look dead?"

"You look like you just stepped off the set of *The Lord of the Rings*. You know, it was made into a movie long after you were gone."

C. S. Lewis laughed. *"Tolkein and his confounded elves. Never quite my cup of tea."*

"What?"

"I'm teasing you, dear boy."

"You are avoiding the question. What do you mean when you say 'we need you.' Who is we, and why do you need me?"

"I did answer the question. My soul is still of this Earth, as are the souls of all who have gone before. Your Mary Beth's soul, my sweet Joy's soul. The soul of your late President. There are Dark Forces gathering, and the world is in trouble. But you can have a positive influence on stopping the Dark Forces."

"Why me? What can I do?"

"You are a writer, Dawson. Like me. That's why I have come to you. You can change the future and plant seeds of hope with your writing."

"Clearly you haven't read any of my books—my bubblegum fiction, I believe one man called it."

Lewis chuckled. *"I will tell you that you are going to develop a series of books and create a world similar to what I did in Narnia. You will inspire millions of people about the world we live in, and you will influence the choices they make. Choices that will stop the Dark Forces of evil."*

"You really have that much confidence in me, do you?"

"We all do. But, it isn't just your writing. You are going to play a very active role in the events to come."

"How?"

"Via your friend, Bobby Anderson, for one. His role in all this is pivotal. He needs your help, and you are going to supply it."

"You're talking about those cult murders he is dealing with?"

"I am indeed, but they are more than mere cult murders. They are all hooked in to these same, evil Dark Forces."

"So let me get this straight. I'm to help Bobby solve these cult—"

"Not cult."

"These, ritualistic murders, and I'm also to write a series of books that will help turn back the Dark Forces."

"Right you are. And a few other things."

"What other things?"

"When they happen, you'll know."

"Thank you for not saying; 'If they bring a knife, you bring a gun.'"

C. S. Lewis laughed again. *"You're a riot, Dawson. Don't be late."*

"Late?"

"For your flight to LAX."

"LAX? That's a term you're familiar with?"

"I've not the slightest idea what it means. You're the one that put the words in my mouth," Lewis said as he slowly faded from view.

Dawson stood at the large plate glass window in Terminal Two, looking out at the many aircraft waiting to be boarded at Melbourne airport. Because Terminal Two was the international terminal, he heard a collage of languages behind him: Chinese, Japanese, Korean, German, as well as English in dialects from American to English to Australian to Indian.

"Fahrgaste nach Frankfurt sollten jetzt laden. Passengers to Frankfurt should be loading now."

His cell phone rang—another call from Bobby Anderson. He smiled as he punched up the call.

"Tell me, Bobby, are all these calls on your call plan? Or are we poor beleaguered taxpayers having to pay for them?"

"Of course you are paying for them," Bobby answered. "This is, after all, official business. And this is really important—I left you a message which you may not have listened to. I'm just glad I got you before you boarded. I know that we had plans to meet in L.A. during your layover, but I would like you to change your plans and stay in L.A. I need your help."

"What kind of help?"

"Do you remember when I spoke to you about the ritualistic killings?"

"Bobby, that's not the kind of thing that will just slip through your memory. Of course I do."

"Well, I—I almost hate to even bring this up on the phone. You'll think I've gone crazy, but I believe there is much more to these killings than meets the eye."

"Dawson, ask the lad if he thinks there is a connection between these killings and the assassination of the President?"

"Oh great, Ian McKellen is back," Dawson said.

"What?"

"It's not really Ian McKellen, it's actually C. S. Lewis. He just sounds like Ian McKellen."

"Holy crap, I'm coming to you for help and you have gone mad on me."

"Do you think there is a connection between these killings and the assassination of the President?"

Bobby was quiet for a long moment.

"Bobby, are you still there?"

"Yes, I do," Bobby said, the words spoken quietly as if he didn't want anyone else to hear. "I am convinced that there is. Not only that, I believe that these killings are not only not random, but are part of some great plot. I think they are an intricate key of some sort that will, when completed—"

"Loose some cataclysmic, dark—," Dawson interjected.

"Energy shift bigger than anything anyone has ever seen before— almost like a shift in the energy—," Bobby continued.

"Right before a huge storm hits and wreaks havoc," Dawson concluded.

"I knew it," Bobby said. "I knew you would have a handle on this." Then he remembered something Dawson had said, something that Mama G told Dawson. "It's just like Mama G told you. The Key. The *key* to everything will be revealed in L.A."

"Oh, yeah. I've known Mama G for a long time, and I've known her to be dead on the money most of the time."

"Then, you know I'm on to something, too?"

"Bobby, my friend, I don't want to burst your bubble, but right now I don't have an idea in hell what I'm talking about."

Bobby chuckled. "Good, good. That means that we are, at least, reading off the same piece of music. What time does your flight get to Los Angeles, and more to the point, will you stay and help?"

"Twelve noon, your time—and yes."

"I'll meet you at the airport. On your tip, I contacted Mama G, and it appears that the old lady is flying here herself. She should be arriving soon, and I'll check to see when she is supposed to get in."

"So, she's not coming by astral projection?" Dawson quipped.

"Very funny. She probably has a better grasp of reality than all the rest of us put together, friend. Save your jokes for after."

CHAPTER
92

In the precincts of the Tribunal, rumbles of satisfied laughter, at the expense of the hapless victims of Earth, could be heard by any who had ears (physical or spiritual) to hear.

The leaders who would rise to the appointed task at the end of human time had already been carefully groomed. Years of ego and entitlement hunger, feelings that they had been personally wronged, as a culture, or individual against a family member or boss. At the signal from the minions of the Tribunal, small uprisings would be sparked all over the globe, and this friction would spark larger fires of battled consciousness . . . of person against person, son against mother, friend against friend. Pure chaos and negative energy! The masters of this evil agenda then could just plug into this eternal battery of energy and the Earth plane would plummet into a dark night of the soul that had only been seen in movies or read about in books—until now.

What a glorious plan, created in the depths of soul-consciousness and brought to life with malevolent intent! What chaos and misery would result!

In the moments of their awakening on the other side, the campaigning would begin, and the IRAs of that world—twisted guides well-schooled in the arts of persuasion—would begin to program them into feeling what they needed to feel in order for the Dark Forces to fuel on the remnants of their earthly energy. The jolt of negative energy from a familiar source would become a way of life, of habit and ultimate need. That dependency on Earth-sourced energy that falsely lulled and comforted, would motivate the chosen unit of souls to help design, fuel, and manipulate the currency of the earthly world. Through fear, and control. A means to an end . . .

That was their key to success: Harnessing the power of negative energies, on the Earth and in the universe. Dark matter would mingle with dark soul-energy to create an irresistible force to shackle the Earth in its iron cold grip—forever.

The Tribunal motivated their network of soldiers by broadcasting this energetic message of accomplishment. The legions of souls that embraced their messages were, in truth, seeking community and love, but they settled for attention and earthly energy as a plugged-in resource. They were, after all, only human.

Gathered before the pools of passion in their dark realm, the members of the Tribunal presented a motley but unified assembly. "The earthly clock is ticking down as the celestial skies align in our favor. Soon we will have the resources to allow us to grow and evolve. Soon we will be able to see our families who have crossed into the light and have been kept from us. Soon we will have the order that was promised to us and never delivered in the face of the Source and promise of eternal love and energy," the leader of the Tribunal of Darkness proclaimed.

As the network of souls were infused with this message, clouds formed in the earthly skies, visible to the eye and felt in the depths of the soul.

E xcuse me, sir. Are you Dawson Rask?" The questioner was a young
woman. The operative phrase, Dawson thought, was "young." She
couldn't have been much over twenty years old.

"Yes," he answered.

"Oh, I just love your books. I've read every one of them."

"Thank you," Dawson said.

"I wish I had one of my books with me. I would have you autograph it."

"I have some bookplates, I could—," Dawson said, then he stopped.
"No, I'm sorry, I don't. They are in checked luggage."

"Oh, I know!" she said. "I'll bet one of your books is in the terminal
bookstore. I'll go look."

The young woman hurried away toward the bookstore, and as Dawson
watched her, he saw an older couple that he assumed were her parents.

She came back with three books. "I can't go into a bookstore and buy
just one book," she said with a broad smile. "For me, it's like trying to eat
one peanut."

"Speaking as a writer, and someone who has been in the business for a
while, that is a trait I much admire," Dawson said.

The young woman handed a book to him. "Make it out to Susan," she
said. Susan was one of the characters in *The Lion, the Witch, and the Wardrobe*. By now, Dawson was no longer surprised by the coincidences.

The book was *Perelandra*, by C. S. Lewis.

This is just too weird, Dawson thought. He opened the book to the
frontispiece and held his pen poised over the page.

"I'll be happy to autograph this book for you," he said. "But it wouldn't
do you much good to have a C. S. Lewis book signed by Dawson Rask,
would it?"

"Go ahead, laddie, sign it. We're good friends now, aren't we?"

"Oh, heavens," the young woman said. "I handed you the wrong book. My bad," she quipped with a little laugh. She took *Perelandra* back and handed him a copy of the *Moses Mosaic*. "This is yours," she said.

He signed the book, then handed it back to her.

"Thank you," she said.

In the corner of the gate area, a large-screen TV was playing. On-screen now was the replay of the fateful moments when the President of the United States was shot. He had just stepped out of the car in front of the Gonzalez Center in San Antonio. Standing nearby was a color guard, with the U.S. flag, as well as flags of the army, navy, and air force. Standing to either side of the flag bearers were the honor guards, uniformed men holding a highly polished rifle at present arms.

One of the honor guards suddenly brought his rifle down and fired. The President grabbed his chest, fell back against the car, then collapsed to the sidewalk.

After that there were so many people who rushed to the scene that it was difficult to see what happened next. The screen then changed to a picture of the shooter, a man in his early thirties. He reminded Dawson somewhat of Timothy McVeigh, though unlike McVeigh, this man, who was identified as Justin Studdock, had scars and bruises on his face.

"Viva Domingo," Studdock said as he stared sullenly into the camera.

"Studdock," the young woman said. "That's odd."

"Do you know him?" Dawson asked, surprised to hear her reaction.

"No, I don't know him. But Studdock is the name of a character in one of C. S. Lewis's books."

Forty-five minutes later, the Qantas A380 Airbus had reached cruising altitude, and the pilot turned off the seat belt signs. Dawson was settled into his first-class seat, and he looked out the window over what appeared to be piles of whipped cream. He thought of all the unusual events and coincidences that were swirling around him.

Well, they certainly were unusual. The question was, were they mere coincidences? Was there some higher power at work here?

There must be, for there could be no other explanation for it. But why had he been chosen?

Dawson knew that if he continued to dwell on that, it would drive him crazy. So he put on his headset to try and just not think. When he turned on the in-flight entertainment system, there was a tribute to the works of

C. S. Lewis on one of the channels. Dawson laughed. . . . He flipped the channel and found *The Lion, the Witch, and the Wardrobe*.

"Are you kidding me?" he said aloud. Shaking his head and laughing, he flipped gain. *The Devil Wears Prada*. Flipping again, he came upon the miniseries of Sidney Sheldon's book, *Master of the Game*. Next came the '80s children's cartoon *Masters of the Universe*. Then Keanu Reeves was chasing a white rabbit in the *Matrix* movie. Marlon Brando was on the next channel explaining to Christopher Reeve that they can't alter mankind's history, but Superman does it anyway, flying backward so rapidly as to reverse time and save Lois from a landslide.

On the next flip he was watching the opening credits to *Lost in Translation*.

Dawson laughed once more.

Ding!

"Flight attendants, prepare the cabin for landing."

The captain's voice awakened Dawson—who couldn't remember the last time he had slept—and he returned his seat to the upright position, as the flight attendants, two men and two women, moved up and down the aisle checking for seats, trays, and so forth.

"How long before we land?" Dawson asked a young male attendant as he passed by.

"About fifteen minutes, I would expect," the attendant replied.

"Thank you."

Dawson checked his watch, was momentarily surprised by the time, then realized he had not reset it since leaving Melbourne. He looked through the window and saw several boats, some with colorful sails, some without.

He heard the whirr, and felt the thump as the landing gear went down. The airplane banked, rather steeply Dawson thought, to the left, his side, and he was able to look almost straight down as the pilot turned on final. The flaps went down and Dawson felt pressure from his seat belt as the plane slowed precipitously and the nose lowered. They passed over Vista Del Mar and he could see the traffic congestion, then, as they flattened out and he saw another road, a fence, an inner road, then the diagonal white markings at the end of the runway. The plane touched down, and he felt the weight as it compressed wheel struts. A moment later he heard the roar of reverse thrust and was pushed hard against the seat belt.

Dawson was tired, and felt groggy after the sixteen-hour flight from

Melbourne. For a moment he resented the time it took; then he thought of how long it must have taken in the days of ocean liners.

"That's true, but traveling by ship was much more civilized," C. S. Lewis said. *"Dining with the captain, dancing in the ballroom with Joy, strolling along the promenade deck."*

"I thought you were gone," Dawson said. He had not realized he had projected his thoughts to his new literary-agent-in-spirit. It was still a novel idea for him . . .

"Heavens no. I told you, we need you. You have a job to do, and I will be here for you."

"Yeah, well, I don't know if that is good or bad."

"Why do you say that?"

"What if you and I start a conversation in front of Bobby? He will think I've gone nuts."

"Don't you know? No one can hear me, and you don't have to talk aloud for me to hear you."

"That's good to know."

Dawson stayed in his seat for a moment after the plane pulled into the Qantas gate. He waited until the aisle was somewhat clear of the rush; then he stood, took his laptop down from the overhead bin, and walked to the front exit where all the attendants were standing by, smiling and greeting the disembarking passengers.

How do they do it? The flight was as long for them as it was for him, but all of them looked as if they had just stepped out of the shower, and all of them were smiling as brightly as they had been when he got on. And they had to do this all the time.

Agent Bobby Anderson had been at the airport for well over an hour. He had hoped to encounter Mama G but even with some checking couldn't find out exactly what flight she was on. He had bought a paperback novel when he arrived, a western because he wanted to get his mind as far away from the ritual murders, the assassinated President, and his missing son as he much as he could. But even a story of rustlers and steely eyed gunfighters couldn't hold his attention, so he put the book down in the seat beside him then got up and walked around to drain off some of his nervous energy. He checked the arrival board, all it said was: QF93 . . . Melbourne . . . Arrival 1200 . . . On Time.

Bobby missed the days when passengers could be met right at the gate as soon as they stepped off the plane. But those days were long gone. Now he had to wait in the faraway lobby area, and watch as hundreds, no, thousands of passengers came from the security area.

He stepped into a snack area and bought a cup of coffee. When he finished he went back to the arrival board.

QF 93 . . . MELBOURNE . . . AT GATE

Bobby walked over to the nearest information desk and stood there watching the crowd of people, searching for Dawson. His cell phone rang.

"Yeah."

"I'm here, are you at the airport?"

Looking up, Bobby saw Dawson, standing with his back to him. He smiled.

"Turn around."

"What?"

"Turn around and smile. I'll take your picture."

Dawson turned around with a confused look on his face, then when he saw Bobby he smiled and started toward him with his hand extended.

"Welcome back."

"It's good to be back."

"You've got luggage?"

"Oh, yeah."

"Let's get it. I've got a car outside."

"Let me guess. It's about a mile away, right?"

Bobby chuckled. "You know the best thing about being an FBI agent? I have a little shield on my car that lets me park any damn place I want. Right now it's in the taxi queue."

"Ha! You don't have to have all those perks if you have a friend who does."

A few minutes later, as waiting taxi drivers glared at them, Dawson threw his luggage in the trunk of Bobby's white Ford car rental.

Bobby's phone was ringing just as he pulled away from the curb in front of baggage claim, and the Bluetooth picked it up.

"Anderson."

"This is your Mama G," came the unmistakable lilting voice. "I'm on my way. But that's not important now. You need to be at 1512 Jesse Street."

"What?"

"I'll say it one more time: 1512 Jesse Street. I would bet my life—and yours—that that poor boy is there. Don't you worry about Mama. I will meet up with you soon. I can't stay on the line right now because you have to *go!*"

"Hello?" There was no answer. "You still there?" Bobby asked. There was no further response. She had hung up. He was anxious to see her.

"That was strange," Bobby said as he punched off the call. "It was Mama G. She gave me an address."

"Do you know that area?" Dawson asked.

"Yeah, it's all warehouses."

"Well, if you don't think it is anything real, I need to get to the hotel and take a shower. I am positively rank."

Bobby said, "Yeah, you are. But we have to move. Mama G made it sound as if this is as real as it gets, and if she is right, we have a shot at getting the boy."

"Next time you are cooped up for sixteen hours on an airplane, see how good you smell. What was the address Mama G told you, 1512 Jesse Street?"

"Yes. Put it in the GPS while I'm driving."

Dawson did, and the GPS displayed the route immediately.

Bobby pointed to the glove compartment. "There's a rotating red and blue light in there. Get it out, plug it into the cigarette lighter, then set it up on the dash as close to the windshield as you can get it."

Dawson got the light out, but even before he had it plugged in, Bobby was doing ninety miles per hour on the 105 Freeway.

Mama G held the phone in her hand. She had set one pair of hands to do the Lord's work but she realized that her job was not yet done. Suddenly a scene popped into her head and she punched up her database and located Rae Loona's cell phone number. . . .

Rae and Tyler, having been given their own instructions from Mama G, arrived at a warehouse at 1512 Jesse Street.

"Look there, Mikey," Rae said, pointing to a group of men who were just on the other side of the barbed wire–enclosed compound. "They're wearin' army suits."

"Uniforms," Tyler said. "They are called uniforms."

"Yeah, well, whatever they are, what are they doing there? They are American soldiers, aren't they?"

"Yes. You think the President's kid is really there?"

"That's what Mama G said. And she hasn't been wrong yet. She also told me . . ."

"What? What else did she say?"

"That someone will die. She has this idea that there is a whole army behind the abduction and—well, everything else. Anyhow, something is there, that's for sure. I can't see any other reason to have a bunch of soldiers walking around carrying machine guns right in the middle of the Los Angeles Warehouse District."

They sat there for several minutes as one Humvee arrived; a moment later, that same Humvee left. As each vehicle entered or left, the guard pushed a button that rolled the gate open, then shut.

"What is in there?" Tyler asked.

"I think it's the President's kid," Rae said.

"I wonder if there is another way in."

"We aren't supposed to do anything yet, remember? We have to wait until all the keys fall into place," Rae said. "Mama G told me we were to wait until we see a wolf. Then after the wolf, we'll hear three gunshots."

Rae saw the look on his face. "I know how it sounds to you, but that's what she told me."

"Yeah, that's what makes me think this whole thing is just some crazy idea," Tyler said. "I mean, how likely are we to see a wolf? We're in downtown Los Angeles, for crying out loud."

"Downtown Los Angeles? It sure doesn't look all that glamorous, does it? All I see is a bunch of warehouses and factories."

"That's because we are in the Warehouse District."

The two sat in the SUV with the windows rolled down for several more minutes. A large eighteen-wheeler rumbled by on Imperial Street, and a train sounded its horn on the nearby railroad tracks.

Inside the warehouse, Marcus lay on his cot with his hands laced behind his head.

First Lieutenant Jeff Kirby came into the cell and looked down at him. "Are you afraid?" Kirby asked.

"No," Marcus answered.

"How is it that you aren't afraid? Don't you know that you may be killed, sacrificed to a greater order?"

"Yes."

"How do you know this?"

"I know this because my father told me."

"What do you mean, your father told you?"

"I spoke to him." Marcus was having difficulty shifting from one reality to another—from being a prisoner to being free. And from being the victim to being the messenger. When he could breathe and think, he could see a bit more clearly. . . . He had, after all, been to "kidnapping camp" and he had been in touch with POTUS, and there were forces at work that not everyone knew about—yet—who were at war with one another. Even the "bad guys" in this incident thought they were doing good, having been influenced by the negative energy that so effectively corrupted people.

Marcus continued: "From the Other Side. He comes to me. He speaks to me. I am the Key."

"The key to what?"

"The Key that will unlock the forces of good to overcome the forces of evil."

"Who are the forces of evil?"

"I don't know. I haven't been told. But I know that there are Dark

Forces on this side and the other side that are evil, energies who want to destroy our world."

Kirby stroked his chin. "Do you think I'm evil?"

"He is not evil, but he is serving the forces of evil," POTUS said.

Marcus repeated his father's words: "You are not evil, but you are serving the forces of evil."

"No, I'm not. We have to hold you here to protect you, don't you see. We aren't your kidnappers, we are your protectors."

"Ask him if he really believes that."

"Do you really believe you are my protector and not my jailer?"

"I—I just looked in to see if I could do anything for you."

"Yes, you can. You can take me back home."

"No. I'm sorry. I can't do that."

Lieutenant Kirby stepped out of the boy's cell, locked the door behind him, then walked down to the little room that had been established as the orderly room.

Marcus had called him a jailer. Though he had dismissed the idea in that moment, it now came back to him as he saw what was happening here through new eyes. Marcus had kept his cool—remarkably for such a young person—and acted like he was being "protected" by an unseen hand. Whose hand? A small but powerful voice inside him was speaking more loudly now. *Release the boy. This is* wrong. *It is up to you.*

He would have to override all his training and upbringing to do what he knew was right. He would have to make a choice . . . the most difficult choice of his life.

Colonel Boyle was sitting at a desk, reading a magazine and listening to a CD of Charlene St. John.

"How's the kid doing?" Colonel Boyle asked.

"Colonel, are we his protectors? Or are we his kidnappers?"

"What difference does it make?" Colonel Boyle asked.

"It makes all the difference in the world. I was told that after the President was killed, there was a plot to kill the child as well."

"What would be the purpose of killing him? He's worthless to us dead."

"Worthless to us? I don't even know what that means. Worthless to us."

"Think about it, Lieutenant. You can't be all that dumb or you never would have gotten your commission. As long as we have the kid, we can exert pressure."

"Pressure on who, to do what?"

"Pressure on the powers that be to do anything we want." Colonel Boyle smiled at Lieutenant Kirby, but it was a grim smile, completely without humor or mirth.

"No," Kirby said, holding out his hand, palm forward. He started backing away from the colonel. "No, I don't want any part of this!"

"It's too late, Lieutenant. You are a part of this now. Whatever happens, you own it."

"No!" Kirby said. "I'm not going to let you get away with this. I'm not going to be involved in the killing of the President's son."

"What are you talking about? We're not going to kill him. I told you, he is much more valuable to us alive than he is dead."

"I'm not going to let you use him, either. This has to stop here and now. I have reason not to trust our orders, Colonel." He had removed his service pistol from its holster and held it at his side.

"Son, it doesn't matter who gives the orders. We're just here to obey them, soldier!"

"I'm doing what needs to be done." He did not intend to use the gun—unless he had to—but he would go down fighting if he had to in order to stop this.

"You are insane! Put that gun away! Guard!" Boyle shouted. He held out his left hand in a defensive mode but shifted and used his right hand to pull his own gun up at the same time.

In the SUV parked outside the warehouse, Rae looked through the windshield and saw a gray canine run across Mateo Street, then up Jesse Street. "Mikey, look! That's a wolf!"

"It's a coyote, but that's close enough," Tyler said. "If we hear three shots, I'm going to . . ."

Even before Tyler finished his sentence, they heard two shots.

Kirby shot Colonel Boyle in the leg—not to kill—then, when the guard came running in, in response to Boyle's shout, Kirby shot him as well, also to wound rather than to kill.

———

That's only two shots," Tyler said.

"Who's counting, for crying out loud?" Rae said. "We've seen a wolf, and we heard two shots."

Inside the compound, inside the warehouse, Lieutenant Kirby looked at the two men he had just shot and knew that he had reached the point of no return. He put the barrel of the pistol to his temple, held it there for a moment, then moved it down to his chest and pulled the trigger.

You wanted three shots, you've got three shots," Rae said.

"Damn!" Tyler said.

"That's it! We've got to get in there!" Rae said as she opened the door and jumped out of the SUV.

"Rae, wait!" Tyler called, but she paid no attention to him and moved quickly toward the gate.

"Open that gate and let me in!" she called to the guard.

"No, ma'am! This is a restricted area!" a young man in a private's uniform replied. "No civilians are allowed inside."

"Someone was just shot in there," Rae said. "Didn't you hear the shooting?"

"Yes, ma'am."

"I'm a nurse."

"That don't matter whether you are a nurse or not. I can't let you in."

"Look here, sonny," Rae said with as much authority as she could master. "Do you see that black Escalade sitting over there? There is a cameraman in there right now, and he is taping this. Now you've got two choices: You can either let us in to tend to the wounded, or you can watch this whole episode on the six o'clock local news tonight. Local my foot. I know you've got the President's son in there. This will be on every national and international news service in the world, and your butt will be toast in a couple of hours if you don't let us in."

The young guard looked at the angry expression on Rae's face; then he glanced over at the black Escalade. That was when he made his decision. He pushed a button in the guardhouse, and the gate began to draw open.

Rae ran back to the SUV. "Come on, Mikey! We've got to get in there!"

Tyler looked at Rae in astonishment. "Damn, Rae, I've seen you do some difficult things before. But this wasn't difficult, this was impossible. How on earth did you do that? What did you say to the guard?"

"I can't be giving you all my secrets now, can I, Mikey? I have my ways. Come on, let's go in before that kid at the gate changes his mind."

As Tyler got out of the car to join Rae, a white Ford raced through the open door, then skidded to a stop. Bobby and Dawson got out of the car and came under fire as soon as they did so. Bobby returned fire, killed one of the guards, and wounded the other.

"Where's the kid?" Bobby shouted to the gate guard, who had thrown his weapon down and put his hands up.

"Who are you?" the young gate guard asks.

"FBI."

"What are you doing here? We're protecting him."

Lieutenant Kirby came staggering out of the warehouse then, holding his hand over a bleeding wound in his chest.

"The boy is inside," Kirby said. "At the back of the building, last door on the left. Here is the key."

Bobby took the key from him.

"Lieutenant, what's going on? Why are you giving up the boy?" the guard asked.

"Don't you know? We weren't protecting him. We were holding him prisoner."

Kirby leaned back against the wall, then slid down as blood spilled through his fingers.

Tyler rushed over to him. The first thing he did was make certain the tongue was out of the way so Kirby could still breathe. Then he applied pressure to the wound to stop the bleeding.

"Call 911," Tyler said.

"Who are you people?" Bobby asked. "What are you doing here?"

"I'm Dr. Tyler Michaels, and this is Nurse Rae Loona. We came here to find the President's son, to save him if we could," Rae said.

Bobby looked surprised. "What do you mean, save him? How did you know he was here?"

"Mama G told us," Rae said.

"Okay, so the old lady is sending in all the troops, it seems," Bobby said.

"But it appears that the President's son is here, and unlikely as that may seem, we are here, too."

"Yes it does. It is all beginning to fit together now," Dawson said. "Don't worry about Dr. Michaels and Rae. I have a feeling in my gut that they are good guys."

Sirens could be heard now as police cars and ambulances were speeding toward the scene.

"Doc, have you got him stabilized enough to leave him for the EMT people?" Bobby asked.

"Yes, I think so."

Bobby handed the key to Tyler. "To tell you the truth, I don't know who to trust anymore. But, for some reason, I trust you. Get the kid, and get him out of here."

Tyler and Rae hurried into the warehouse, then back to the last door on the right. When they unlocked it, they saw Marcus sitting on the bunk bed. They expected to see him very frightened, but he was smiling at them.

Hello," Marcus said.

"Hello, Marcus. Don't be frightened," Tyler said.

"I'm not frightened. Dad told me you would be coming for me."

"Your dad?" Rae asked.

"Yes. He's here with me now. You can't see him, and you can't hear him, either. That's right, isn't it, Dad? They can't hear you or see you?"

"That's right," POTUS said.

"We want you to come with us."

"You can trust them," POTUS said.

"I know I can, Dad."

"Mikey, I believe this kid really is talking to his dad. Mr. President, I'm sorry you were shot. I want you to know how proud I was to have you as President of the United States," Rae said.

"Tell Rae Loona I appreciate that," POTUS said.

"Dad said, tell Rae Loona that he appreciates that."

"How did you know her name?" Tyler asked.

"Dad told me."

"I told you, Mikey, Marcus really is talking to his dad. But, Marcus, we have to get you out of here now, while there is still time."

"Tell them to take you to the Hollywood Grand Theatre."

"Dad says take me to the Hollywood Grand Theatre."

Tyler, Rae, and Marcus hurried out of the compound and toward the Escalade. They met up with Anderson and Dawson and told them what—supposedly—a dead President had told them to do.

And Anderson was left with one of the most important decisions of his life.

Bobby Anderson made one of the most critical decisions of his law enforcement career. Against all protocol, but going with his strong instinct in this moment, he allowed Dr. Tyler Michaels and Nurse Rae Loona to accompany Marcus Jackson Jr. to the Hollywood Grand Theatre. He had never felt a "hunch"—a term he hated violently—as strongly as he felt this one. It was a voice in his head that kept telling him to do it. *Rae and Tyler have a role to play and a reason to be here, just as Dawson and Charlene do—just as Bobby Anderson, big-shot FBI investigator does. . . .* It was the same voice that had guided his thinking to the truth about the Belfast killings: that they were a part of this conspiracy of forces beyond his understanding. And then there was Mama G. She told him to trust these people, and while it may be going against everything he had ever been taught about security, Anderson knew in his heart that it was the right thing to do. He nodded and sent Rae, Tyler, and the boy into their car.

"Come on, Dawson, let's get out of here, too," Bobby said. "I don't want to be around when everyone gets here. I don't want to answer any questions, and I honestly don't know who to trust."

Bobby and Dawson were two blocks away when they saw the first of many emergency vehicles speeding to the scene.

At almost that same moment, Intercontinental Airlines Flight 1331 from Miami to Los Angeles crashed in the western Nevada desert, killing all passengers and crew. It had been a normal flight up to that point, and weather had been clear, with a strong tailwind that promised to deliver everyone on board early to LAX. Later it would be determined that a very small superheated meteorite had pierced the right wing of the aircraft, a freak accident—a one-in-ten-million occurrence.

Within the precincts of the Tribunal, a shout of triumph arose. Another manifestation of the awesome power of the dark energies as they massed in strategic locations around the Earth to create just such havoc and instill fear in people everywhere.

CHAPTER
95

After Bobby dropped him off at the hotel, Dawson had only one thing on his mind, and that was to get up to his room and take a shower. He stood in front of the elevator, suitcase on the floor beside him, watching the numbers count down, hoping it didn't stop anywhere on the way down. It reached the lobby and the doors swooshed open. The elevator was empty, and Dawson was glad. He stepped in, then turned to punch his floor on the number panel.

"Hold that elevator!" a female voice called, and Dawson felt a moment of frustration. He didn't want to share the elevator with anyone, not as grubby as he was. He wanted to push the close button to hurry up the process, but he thought better of it, and pushed hold.

"Thank you. It seems like these elevators take forever," the woman said as she stepped into the elevator.

Dawson's breath was taken away by the beauty of the woman. Her skin was a smooth, mocha latte color. Her eyes were large and expressive, her hair jet black. Then, even as he admired her beauty, he realized who she was. This was Charlene St. John, the famous singer.

"You're Dawson Rask, aren't you?" Charlene said.

Hearing his name come from her lips was like a blow to the solar plexus. He was amazed—and if he admitted to himself, flattered to no end—that she had recognized him.

"I am a big fan of yours," Charlene continued. "And I've seen you doing interviews on television."

"You are a fan of mine?" Dawson said. "I—I don't know what to say. I mean, you are, arguably one of the most famous people in the entire world. I just got back from Australia, and they love you down there. Oh," he added quickly, "I just got off the plane a short time ago. Excuse my grubbiness."

Charlene laughed, and to Dawson, her laughter sounded like the tinkling of perfectly harmonized wind chimes.

"You call it grubby, I call it masculine," she said.

"Oh, I assure you, Miss St. John—"

"Can't you call me Charlene? I mean, as one 'famous' person to another, don't we have that right?" She emphasized the word *famous* to indicate that it was tongue in cheek.

"I would hardly put myself in your league. I am famous only to the person who happens to be reading my book, and notices my name."

A moment earlier, Dawson had wanted the elevator to race up to the fifteenth floor. Now he wished it would creep up. He was enjoying this time with Charlene St. John. No, *enjoying* wasn't quite the word, enjoying didn't cover it. He was intrigued by her, and for the first time since Mary Beth had died, he felt a connection, a real connection to another person. That she was drop-dead gorgeous hadn't escaped his attention either.

Charlene, in turn, was shocked by her reaction to this man. Not since Ryan died had she even so much as thought of any kind of a relationship with another man, and yet there was a definite spark between them.

The elevator stopped on the fifteenth floor and the doors slid open. There was nobody waiting. In a move that was so uncharacteristic, nobody who knew Charlene could believe it of her, she punched the hold button. She felt as if another hand was moving hers, and she suddenly felt a familiar presence standing next to her. Could it be—?

"I wonder who pushed the button on fifteen?" she asked.

"No clue," he volunteered.

"A ghost?" Each of them said exactly the same thing at exactly the same time. They laughed.

"I don't believe in ghosts—" Again, they spoke simultaneously, the words tumbling out without thinking. He chuckled, and Charlene rolled her eyes in amusement.

After a somewhat awkward pause, he asked, "Do you think two famous people could have dinner together in this town without causing a problem?"

She looked at Dawson directly in his eyes. "Better yet, want to go to the Academy Awards with me?" She had just blurted it out, but it felt prompted, somehow. Then it dawned on her with a certainty born of her entire life's experience: It was Ryan. He had brought them together somehow and was prompting her to keep the conversation going.

She pulled her business card from her purse and held it out to him.

Meanwhile, Dawson Rask was speaking: "Like this. Me all grubby and all? And no car." Dawson smiled. He felt touched by her seeming awkwardness. Beneath it all, he could sense her sincerity and genuineness. He *liked* her. World famous, though she was.

Yes," she said. Inside, she could not believe she had just done this. But she had felt moved to ask, and she felt drawn to him, suddenly and powerfully.

Dawson took the card. It was a business card with no name, just a telephone number. "All right," he said simply. "Thank you."

When Dawson reached his room, he set his suitcase down, then started toward the bathroom, stripping out of his clothes along the way. When he stepped into the shower he just stood there for a long moment, letting the needles of spray massage his jet-lagged body.

He began singing in the shower, but not just any song. He was singing the song Charlene was best known for: *Someone, Somewhere.*

> *I've a life to live*
> *Open up my heart and give*
> *To someone, somewhere*
> *I know that we will be together*
> *Heart touching heart forever*
> *Someone, somewhere*

CHAPTER
96

When Charlene reached her room, she saw a beautifully wrapped gift basket on her bed. The card read:

To Ms. Charlene St. John—
   We are so pleased you chose our hotel. Please accept this gift basket, as a symbol of our appreciation. From the manager and staff of the Ritz-Carlton, Los Angeles.

"Well, that's very nice of you," Charlene said aloud. "But I didn't choose you, Paul Maxwell did." She smiled. "But I am the one who will get to enjoy it."

Taking off the gold foil wrap, saw a bottle of Cabernet Sauvignon Napa Valley, vintage 2007. There were also a few bars of Swiss dark chocolate, two blueberry muffins, and several packets of gourmet coffee. There was also, she noticed, a corkscrew. She uncorked the wine, poured it into a wineglass that was on the bar in the room, and let it sit there to breathe as she took her own shower.

She had just returned to her suite after a rehearsal of the Academy Awards ceremony at the Hollywood Grand Theatre. As she was showering, she thought of Dawson Rask, the man she had met in the elevator. Dawson Rask was best known for his Matthews character, in his thriller novels. But Charlene liked one of his earliest books, *Moon Song*, a story about a Midwestern man trying to adapt to New York, and a hip New York girl that he met on the subway. They have nothing in common but love, and share everything but time. One week before their wedding, she is killed by a mugger. It was that, the sudden and unexpected death of one so dearly loved, that drew Charlene to the story. It was more endearing to know that he, too, had lost his wife and had plugged into that type of loss and was writing about it from his own experience.

When she finished her shower, she put on her dressing gown, then looked at her cell phone to see if anyone had called while she was in the bathroom. No one had.

It was three o'clock, four more hours until the Academy Awards ceremony. Charlene sat in the lounge chair, picked up the remote, and turned on the TV. She had thought there would be nothing but endless coverage of the upcoming Oscar night, but instead there was a picture of a warehouse and several police cars.

"We don't know exactly what happened here today," a male reporter said, standing in front of all the activity and speaking into a handheld microphone. "The police were summoned by a 911 call and arrived to find four men out of commission, and one seriously wounded man—the wound, apparently, self-inflicted. There was one uninjured survivor, Private Matthew Dagan, and this is the intriguing part, Diane. Private Dagan says that they were a special military guard unit to protect young Marcus Johnson, the son of the late President.

"Everyone has believed, up until this time, that the President's son had been kidnapped. Now, what makes this even more intriguing, is that the officials at Fort Ord, as well as officials at the Pentagon, deny that there was any such military operation taking place here. And now, to add to that mystery is the fact that if the President's son was here, he is here no longer. According to Private Dagan, he left with a man and woman, who had identified themselves to Dagan as a doctor and a nurse."

"Phil, did they take the boy by force, or did he go willingly?" Diane's voice-over asked.

"Apparently he went willingly," the on-site reporter replied. "There were two others here, who also left, one of whom had identified himself to Dagan as an FBI agent. Again, according to Dagan, Marcus seemed to know both of them."

"What about the self-inflicted wound?" Diane asked.

"Yes, well, we have no further information on that—his wound was quite serious, and he was taken to the hospital immediately."

"And Private Dagan?"

"As you can tell from the report I've been giving you, Dagan was a good source of information. However CID agents from the army have since taken Private Dagan into custody, and I haven't been able to follow through for any more information."

"But the bottom line is, the late President's son is safe?" Diane asked.

"Well, we can't say that for sure. We know that by all accounts he was alive two hours ago, and we know that he was apparently comfortable with whoever it was that took him. But for now, we have no idea where he is."

After that report, the news did turn to the Academy Awards ceremony that was to be held tonight, and they discussed the pictures that had been nominated for Oscars. *Glory in the Ruins* seemed to be the odds-on favorite for best movie. Ryan Frederick seemed to be a lock for best male actor, while Damaris Royce had the nod for best female.

Charlene herself had a song nominated for the Best Original Song award, which she would be singing during the ceremony. They also discussed Charlene's role in the ceremonies tonight, and had a clip from her performance in Mexico City.

Charlene turned the TV off, looked again at her cell phone. Dawson hadn't called her. Maybe he didn't think she was serious when she'd invited him to call. Ha! Why wait on the invitation? This was the twenty-first century, after all. Why not call him?

Charlene picked up the phone and dialed the hotel operator.

"Yes, Miss St. John?"

"Would you ring Dawson Rask's room for me, please?"

"Yes, of course."

Charlene heard the ring and for just a moment, almost hung up. Her mind raced along the now-bright path of time and opportunity that lay ahead. Now that she had been given a clean bill of health and had experienced more than one real miracle in her life, she felt a renewed zest for living. She couldn't help but think Ryan had something to do with it. He had always been a positive force radiating creative, loving energy. She felt she was being guided by him in this moment—perhaps she had been for some time and never realized it.

She decided not to hang up the phone.

Dawson had been watching the same news program as Charlene, and when they finished the report on the happenings at the warehouse at 1512 Jesse, he turned it off. Lying on the table beside him was the card Charlene had given him. He picked it up and looked at it for a long moment.

Had she been serious? Did she really want him to call? Or was this simply a "we must do lunch sometime," with no specific date stated. He turned the card over a few times in his hand as he thought about it. Why not call? Why not call now? He didn't know that, just as he was deciding to call her, she was dialing his room number . . .

Just as he reached for the phone it rang—the ringing startling him. This had to be Bobby. He picked it up.

"Okay, Bobby, what can Jack Lewis and I do for you now?"

"Uh, Mr. Rask?" It was a woman's voice.

"Oh, I'm sorry," Dawson said quickly. He chuckled. "There's no caller ID on these phones, and I thought you were someone else."

"This is Charlene."

"Charlene?" It couldn't be, could it?

Charlene laughed, and again, there was the sound of perfectly harmonized wind chimes. "We met in the elevator, remember? One famous person to another?"

"Yes, yes, of course I remember! How could I not remember? It's just that, I didn't expect, I mean . . ." Then he blurted: "You won't believe this, but I was just reaching for the phone to call you."

"I choose to believe it. That way I don't feel like I'm intruding."

"No, no, not at all!"

"Good. Dawson, you do know that the Academy Awards are tonight, don't you?"

"Yes, I know. Oh, and I even know that you will be singing at the awards."

"That's true. And I have a ticket for an escort. I really was serious in the elevator—I wonder if you would be my escort?"

Dawson wasn't sure he had heard what he thought he heard, and he sat in stunned silence for a moment.

"Dawson, are you still there?"

"Yes, yes, I'm here."

"What about it?"

Dawson looked up and saw a smiling C. S. Lewis. *By all means, my boy, do accept. You will have a splendid time.*

"Yes, I would love to escort you. I wasn't sure if you really meant it when you made that generous offer, but I can't think of anything in the world I would rather do."

"I am in room 1912. Call for me at five thirty, that will give me time to nibble on a cracker and have a glass of wine or something to calm my nerves before we go to the Hollywood Grand Theatre."

"I will be there, bright-eyed and bushy-tailed," Dawson said.

"Oh, like Mr. Fitzpatrick."

"What?"

"My pet squirrel."

"You have a pet squirrel?"

"Never mind. I'll see you at five thirty."

Dawson hung up the phone. "Yes!" he shouted. He saw C. S. Lewis and raised his hand. "High five!" he said.

"*I beg your pardon?*"

"Never mind, you couldn't do it anyway. Damn, my tux, it will be a mess!"

Ordinarily, Dawson wouldn't even have a tux with him, but he had taken it to Australia because there was supposed to be a black tie event in his honor, sponsored by his Australian publisher. The event was canceled after the President was shot, and Dawson's trip cut short.

He took the tux from the suitcase and groaned. It looked as if it had been slept in for a month. He took it in the bathroom, hung it on the towel rack, then turned the shower on as hot as it would go.

An hour later he fought his way through the steam in the bathroom, turned off the shower, then brought his tux out into the room, where he hung it up to let it dry. He was pleased to see that his impromptu pressing was successful. The formal attire was wrinkle free.

When Charlene heard the knock on her door, she looked over at the digital clock. It was exactly five thirty and she smiled, wondering if Dawson had waited in the hall until the exact time. She opened the door.

"Oh, you are in a tux!" she said.

"Shouldn't I be?"

"Yes, you look wonderful in it. It's just that I asked you on such short notice, I wasn't sure you could come up with one in time."

"I always keep it with me, just in case."

"In case what?"

"In case a beautiful woman asks me to escort her to the Academy Awards."

All the time Dawson was talking, he was holding one hand behind his back, and she leaned around to look. "What do you have?"

Dawson brought around a single daisy. "I brought you a flower. You should put it in water right away."

Charlene laughed. "Put it in water? It's silk. In fact, it looks suspiciously like the ones in front of the elevator down in the lobby."

"It is," Dawson said. "But you aren't supposed to call attention to that."

Charlene took it. "It's beautiful. I'll get it in water at once." She put water in a drinking glass, dropped in the plastic daisy, then scooped up her bag and wrap. "Shall we go?"

"Yes, we should get a move on. But . . . I kind of want to tell you something, though, before we go." It was as much a question as a statement from him.

"Sure. What is it?"

"I want you to know where I was earlier. I mean—what I was doing. We rescued the President's son from his kidnappers. The FBI did, actually. A good friend of mine, Agent Bobby Anderson." He related the whole story, including the bizarre coincidences of Mama G's metaphysical involvement and Rae Loona and Tyler Michaels's presence on the scene.

Charlene took it all in without batting an eye, though her pulse was racing quite a bit faster than usual. "You don't say," she offered when Dawson had finished his account of the adventure. He looked a bit shell-shocked. "You don't say . . ."

A thought was forming in her mind as she fiddled with her wrap and let him help her put it around her shoulders. Then she calmly added, "I will tell you about my conversation with the President when we are in the car. It all fits in."

Thinking to herself, she also realized she could top even that event with her vision of the Blessed Lady who had, she believed, cured her cancer. That, too, fit into this plan that was unfolding before her very eyes. Tonight would represent a major step forward for her—well beyond the Oscar nomination for her song. No, something more, something bigger, something *much* bigger than she had ever experienced lay ahead.

Omar drove the truck all the way around Piccadilly Circus, showing Shakir where five major streets joined. "As you can see, some moments there are more people than other moments. In order to have the maximum effect, we need to detonate the bomb in the middle of the largest crowd."

"All those people will be killed," Shakir said.

"Yes, that is the point."

"What if I can't do it?"

"What do you mean, what if you can't do it? How hard is it to drop a backpack? That is all you have to do."

"Yes."

"There, look," Omar said, pointing to two buses that were loaded with Japanese vacationers. They began spilling out into the plaza.

"Allah has provided for us," he said. "Go, now. Get in the middle of them. If you are lucky, you can get over one hundred of them."

Omar reached across in front of Shakir and opened the door. "Go now," he said. "Go quickly. Fill your mind only with the thought of paradise, for that is where you will be, one minute from now."

Omar did not notice that tears were streaking down Shakir's face. And even if he had seen them, he would have misread them. He would have thought that Shakir was frightened because he was about lose his own life. Shakir was frightened, and saddened that his action could take as many as one hundred innocent lives, and no doubt grievously wound many others.

As Asima hurried to Piccadilly Circus, she checked her watch. If Omar was on schedule, and she had learned that he was very much a man of structure, she had only three minutes remaining in which to stop it.

Then, unbidden, a memory of her days in college flashed back to her. She was in the market when an older woman approached her. At first she thought the woman was going to ask her for money, and she felt embarrassed because she had no money to give.

Do *not be afraid of me, Asima," the woman said.*

"Who are you? How did you know my name?"

"I am Patricia Rose Greenidge, but many call me Mama G. May I touch you?"

Asima was startled by the strange request, but there was something in the old woman's eyes that calmed her, and she knew that the woman offered no danger. The old woman touched Asima . . . putting her hands on Asima's cheeks.

Asima felt a strange surge, almost like a wave of electricity emanating from Mama G's hands.

"You are a very special woman, Asima," Mama G said. "One day you will make the greatest sacrifice and it will help so many"

Up until this moment, Asima had always thought that the sacrifice was giving up her own hopes and dreams to help Muti raise their family. But now she was looking at it with a whole new perspective . . . a perspective of sacrificing her son.

She saw him getting out of Omar's truck. He was carrying a backpack.

"Shakir! No!" she shouted. "No, please, don't do it!"

"Mama!" Shakir called back.

"Lay down the backpack! Come to me!"

"Mama, I can't. I have to do this!"

"No, you don't!" Muti shouted, and looking around, Asima saw her husband coming up behind her.

Shakir looked at his parents, then back toward Omar, who was still waiting in the truck. He hesitated for just a second, and then laid the backpack on the ground.

"Good!" Muti shouted. "That is good! Now, come to us!"

Shakir started toward them, and Asima was overwhelmed with a feeling of relief and gratitude until she saw something that made her blood run cold. Omar had come out of the truck, and now he was punching numbers into a cell phone.

Asima knew exactly what that meant. He had no intention of letting Shakir make up his own mind. There was a cell phone embedded in the backpack, and the moment the cell phone rang, it would send a charge that would detonate the backpack. Dozens, perhaps hundreds would be killed, and everyone would report that the last person they saw with the backpack was Shakir.

Asima started running toward the pack, dashing by Shakir without so much as a greeting.

Asima!" Muti called, "What are you—?"

Then Muti saw Omar dialing the phone and he knew exactly what Asima was doing.

"Asima! No!" he shouted.

Witnesses would later report that they saw a beautiful woman come running from nowhere to grab the backpack. They watched her strange action and were confused by it. Some thought perhaps she was stealing it, but in instead of trying to run away, she jumped over the concrete wall of a trash-collecting bunker.

There was a loud explosion. Smoke, flame, and pieces of body flew into the air—Asima's body and the concrete walls absorbed both the blast concussion and the shrapnel. Asima's was the only life lost.

Mama G envisioned this scene as if she were there in London, watching, moving with the crowds.

She felt the impact of the bomb, like a fierce burst of hot air against her face, pushing her body back. She caught her breath and wiped tears that were running from her eyes.

Watching what the signs of the skies had foretold—the darkness spreading, now below as above—overwhelmed her with sadness. Asima . . . the young woman had never been far from Mama G's mind, and the seer now felt even closer to her than ever. How many years ago had it been since they met face-to-face? Even then, the older woman felt there was something special—a spiritual strength and deep inner compassion—that marked

Asima and set her apart from others. She had hoped the young student would have a long and productive life, but she knew in her heart that a shadow lay across Asima, and the stars were not aligned in her favor.

Still, she also felt that her relationship with the intelligent young Muslim woman would continue for a long time—a very strong feeling, which Mama G now knew to be true.

Yes, Asima was gone, but so many other lives had been saved. The yin and yang of existence continued. Yet the forces of darkness still seemed to be getting the upper hand.

And the final battle for the hearts and souls of all people everywhere was beginning in earnest.

Bobby Anderson was in his office grabbing some last-minute things before heading out to the Hollywood Grand Theatre. He was grateful that the President's son was found safe but knew that things weren't over yet, and the pressure to solve his other case suddenly felt overwhelming. He knew that there was some missing piece, some vital sign that he had overlooked. From the insights he had gained over the past forty-eight hours, and especially the last twelve, he knew that the whole thing was tied in—that is, random acts everywhere and heinous crimes that had made headlines around the world, were all of a purpose, and all were leading to one final criminal manifestation that would put even these unspeakable acts to shame.

He checked his watch. It was Sunday in Belfast. But it wouldn't be Sunday for much longer, as he was several time zones away. And suddenly he knew. That was the key—Sunday! Not only for whatever was going to happen at the awards ceremony but for the damned murders as well.

This was the day. *Viva Domingo.* The lives of many would be changed—or ended—on this day, if he didn't move.

He called the chief investigator on the scene in Belfast.

"It's going down today. The final murder that is going to trigger everything," he blurted. "Seal off the field in every direction, and station at least a hundred officers around the perimeter. We need air cover, as well. I'm sure the U.S. Air Force can support your own forces. Nothing can move in or out of that area for twenty-four hours. The murderers intend to signal the end of one phase and the beginning of the endgame. If they cannot gain access today, they cannot send their message in time."

"How do you know all this, Agent Anderson?"

"Don't ask. The short answer is, I don't know how I know. But it all fits. I've been thinking about this ever since I left. The fact that I was called away was a part of the plan, too. Don't ask any more questions—just do as I say. Please. For God's sake."

His colleagues in Belfast had quickly come to the conclusion that Bobby knew exactly what he was doing, and his expertise made everyone around him look good. They responded without further delay. Word went out, and within the hour the killing field was swarming with Irish cops and national security agents. Police and army helicopters swarmed like bees over the crime scene.

In the city itself, on an obscure street, the man who had been stalking a woman who had been drugged by another man and pushed out of doors closed in on his prey. His intention—on orders from higher ups in his gang—was to take her to a nearby cellar where she was to be executed. The money was good for this job. The anonymous man followed the anonymous woman into an alley between a pub and a factory. This was where he would seize her. The chamber that awaited her was just two blocks away.

A street cop, whose shift was almost over, sighted the woman entering the alley, stumbling, apparently drugged or drunk. He then saw the man follow her, walking into the shadow of the tall factory building. He moved across the street and entered the alley himself. . . .

In the reaches of the Tribunal, among the hordes of howling and hungry soldiers of darkness, the leaders could not believe what was happening. They had been ready to execute the twelfth victim and plant the body in plain sight for their purposes ordained from the beginning of time. Their plan, so perfectly constructed and flawlessly executed, had nonetheless encountered resistance from unexpected quarters. In fact, it was falling apart.

There was no time to repair the damage to their plan. *This* was the ordained day. Sunday.

Who was this Bobby Anderson, and who was giving him this information? Somebody would pay dearly for their interference.

Part

·FOUR·

CHAPTER
98

· Los Angeles ·

The Academy Awards ceremony was scheduled for Sunday, March 2. The annual broadcast of this glittering Hollywood tradition was expected to be viewed by at least 3 billion people around the world, the most ever to watch any televised event in human history. Given the international scope of the film industry and the many nominees for awards from outside Hollywood, USA, segments of the awards show would originate in Mumbai and London for the first time, which promised to draw an even larger audience than usual.

The aborted London bombing had made headlines around the world on the eve of the awards telecast, darkening the otherwise almost giddy, festive atmosphere surrounding the event. Although Londoners were used to threats and bombings by now, the U.K. studio was especially somber as the broadcast hour approached and a smaller than anticipated crowd gathered outside the studio that night. The crashed Intercontinental flight was also leading the news, with word that there were no survivors of that Miami-to-L.A. airliner that had been downed, apparently, by a meteorite . . . and somber pictures of the crash site in the desert haunted viewers as they learned of the unusual accident that had claimed so many lives.

An army of technicians had occupied the Hollywood Grand Theatre in Los Angeles for a month before the date of the broadcast, wiring every inch of the house, building sets on an enlarged stage, even reupholstering every single chair to color code the live audience of celebrities, award nominees, Hollywood power brokers, and spectators lucky enough to snag tickets through whatever connections they could call on to get through the doors.

Seats in the front row center were reserved for the crème de la crème, including Charlene St. John McAvoy and the family of the late President of the United States. But questions arose as to whether the former First Lady would actually attend, in light of her son's abduction. The outcome of that crime remained a public mystery as the Oscars approached, further dampening the mood anticipating the event.

· *Vatican City* ·

The pope reconvened the Council of Faith on Ash Wednesday, the beginning of the Christian holy season of Lent. For other faith leaders, the impending change of seasons and the approaching spring equinox (in the northern hemisphere) were significant, as well. The Jews would anticipate the celebration of Passover and Muslims the pilgrimage of countless men and women to Mecca, known as the hajj. For the Chinese, in their native land and around the world, it was a new year.

"My brothers," the Holy Father said, "we have made precious little headway in reaching people of faith across our globe, in sincerely penetrating their souls with the urgent message of impending disaster and tragedy. We have redoubled our prayers here in Rome and in churches everywhere. Some of our people have responded and taken measures to prepare for their families and themselves—and to help others. Every day I pray for guidance and for the Lord God's mercy to shower the Earth and cleanse us all of sin and error.

"Yet, I cannot testify that the Creator has heard my prayers or those of the faithful."

The Dalai Lama spoke from his heart in response: "Dear brother, you have lived up to your responsibility very nobly and with much love in your heart. Suffering is a part of the human condition, sometimes by individual choice, most often by the circumstances of life. We cannot interfere with the divine plan, even if we wished to do so. But we may walk with one another through such times of difficulty and help our neighbors to understand and grow stronger."

Murmurs of agreement rose from those who sat around the table, a now-familiar gathering place for these religious leaders who, in normal circumstances, would likely not even acknowledge one another's existence, let alone speak with such respect and even affection for each other.

"God is great," the imam stated with conviction. "May He sow the seeds of peace in the souls of all humankind. If we continue to pray without ceasing, as Your Holiness has done, no evil can befall us. Paradise awaits the righteous."

The chief rabbi smiled sardonically. He kept his gray beard trimmed neatly and wore a black yarmulke. "Yahweh be praised. He will protect His people as He has throughout all ages."

The pontiff sat back in his chair as others joined the dialogue. He was utterly pleased that these men had answered his call in good faith and were willing to lend their prestige to this cause that he now—privately—considered hopeless. For in his heart he understood that forces outside his control, or the influence of any in this magnificently adorned chapel, had already set in motion the tribulations that lay ahead.

No prayers, acts of charity, or pure intentions could stop the impending days of reckoning. He prayed silently: *God help the people of this Earth to choose the right path—the way of survival and the way of light. . . .*

· Houston ·

Dr. Jason Chang drove to his office at NASA headquarters on this day, just like any other. He didn't know what else to do. For a scientist or any rational person of any professional discipline, routine could be a welcome refuge in times of uncertainty. And *uncertain* was a huge understatement of the situation in this case.

He had marshaled the very best minds and resources he could muster in creating a world-class study team to identify the source and nature of the threat. In fact, it was one of the greatest scientific discoveries of all time to have uncovered the existence of the dark energies that threatened the planet. But what had it gained him—or anyone else? Having turned the world's strongest brains to the task, what solution had they come up with? None. Zero. Zilch. Nada.

If he were susceptible to emotion, right now would be the perfect time for Chang to weep rivers of tears. Instead, he was bone dry—incapable of feeling anything but black despair.

Once he arrived at his office, he sat at his desk and picked up the telephone. He called his opposite number in the Russian space program. But Dmitri Kolnikov, one of the most adept administrators and accomplished physicists he had ever known, was also at a loss. The two spoke for twenty minutes but came up with nothing new, no breakthrough to hope.

Dr. Chang then called his chief researcher to meet with him and review the latest meteorological data from around the world. He held this update daily, usually early in the morning, but today everything was pushed back an hour or so because he could not wrap his mind around what was happening—and what he could not do about it.

Jason Chang was living in a state of total exhaustion. Over just a few weeks, the data his team and other organizations around the planet had gathered pointed to only one conclusion: the fast-increasing presence of a new and distinctly dangerous form of energy—dark matter. Heavier and denser than anything known on Earth. Yet not a substance. A presence that could be described as a black hole—or a series of such holes.

What is it? Where is it? When and how was it generated? Where is it going? And why and what can *it do?* Far more questions than answers.

Ever since the discovery, he had not slept for more than one hour at a stretch. For at least twelve hours a day, Chang sat before a high-def computer monitor searching obscure websites for clues outside the scientific mainstream. The other half of his day was spent consulting colleagues and connecting disparate bits of data among them, planning the next convocation of brains—if there was to be another. If there was enough time.

Now, David Gyles, one of the most respected weather and climate guys in the world, brought the latest satellite and Earth station readings to his boss.

"Here's something interesting, sir. There is a fissure or a fault in the weather over California. That is to say, there is an *interruption* by your mysterious matter—or antimatter, as the case may be—in the regular meteorological patterns in two places on Earth. I would almost classify these interruptions as sunspots, or 'anti-sunspots.'"

"You're not making a whole lot of sense."

"I know. Sorry."

"And where are these sunspot fissures?" Chang asked.

"Very clearly Los Angeles, California, and Belfast, Northern Ireland."

Chang and Wolcott immediately logged on to Google Earth and searched the two cities. There, as clearly as could possibly be seen, the strange gap in the weather patterns was visible.

"Is there such a thing as finality, as objective truth? My entire training and orientation in life cry out against such absolutes or final ending points." He sat back in his chair, perplexed.

Gyles was baffled by Chang's philosophical outburst. He could see that his boss was deeply troubled and confused by the masses of evidence of strange phenomena that overturned his scientific understanding of the world. And he wasn't the only one. Craig Wolcott himself had infinite doubts and questions about what was happening and what it all meant.

"None of us have been trained for this, Dr. Chang," he said. "There is no history of such astronomical phenomena affecting the entire Earth. I don't know how we could have predicted it."

It was true: There was no current theory into which these strange phenomena could be fitted. The idea of so-called dark energy was not new, but the activity that had so rapidly unfolded before their eyes was totally unexpected.

"But we are responsible for finding the answer," Chang replied.

"What if we don't?"

"Well, we may not be around to know what the consequences of our failure will be. Nor anyone else."

Our philosophies have proved inadequate to the task of understanding the threat we face—and our scriptures seem but fairy tales in the face of such evil," the rabbi stated.

"Or are *we* inadequate?" the pope reflected aloud. "I mean, it is possible that we have not read deeply enough or reflected seriously according to our religious traditions. That is why we must help each other now. Never before has universal healing and understanding been so important."

The Shinto priest, Hira, spoke up, which he seldom did, preferring more often to offer up prayers to the ancestors of the world to guide these imperfect men—including himself and everyone else—to understanding and acting correctly to the benefit of the whole of mankind.

He said, "Holy gentlemen, it has become clear, if nothing else, that societies are in jeopardy without exception—everywhere. It is my belief that the most sophisticated cultures are the most vulnerable to this evil threat. We represent the vast majority of those cultures and the way they approach the divine nature. Yet we are stymied in our efforts to lead them to the truth. I feel it is both the foundation of our faith and our practice of faith that have betrayed us. In my sincere opinion, we have utterly failed to protect the souls who have been entrusted to our care."

The silence among the Council of Faith and their secretaries and acolytes was deafening.

CHAPTER
99

The sky was slate gray with thin clouds sweeping across the expanse in every direction. So far, there had been no rain, but it looked as if the whole world was wrapped in a soft, gray-blue blanket that prevented the sun from shining down on the Earth. A sense of foreboding overlay the otherwise festive bustle that surrounded the biggest international awards ceremony in the history of mankind.

Los Angeles had seen eruptions of street crime and political unrest in recent weeks, so the police presence had been more than doubled, and the police chief himself stood close to the red carpet at the main theater entrance, where the attention of the world was focused. From about 4 P.M. Pacific Standard Time on this Sunday evening, a steady stream of limousines pulled up in front of the Hollywood Grand Theatre to let out their famous—and some infamous—passengers, who then strode in their finery along the carpet under the glare of lights, cameras, reporters, and thousands of screaming movie fans.

Also present—omnipresent, as it were—was one who glistened with centuries-ripe anticipation of what was to come within just a few hours of this auspicious, cloud-laden moment. Known by many names, including Emphatic and Angel of Darkness, he was a perfectionist in the practice of the arts of darkness and the expenditure of energies in the service of his masters on the Tribunal. *He* was the actor behind the Viva Domingo call to the world. Nothing pleased him more than a gathering of the proud and amoral for the purpose of puffing themselves up and preening and strutting across the stage in view of the entire world.

Ah, the glory of their downfall is mine! he crooned silently.

He breathed in the physicality of the Dark Matter that now loomed so closely to the Earth that he could smell it. The millennial threat that so thrilled his spirit being was palpable now as it had never been for him— nor for all but a very few souls in existence at this moment in history. He looked up at the steely canopy of clouds that moved imperceptibly across the unseen sky, marking the impending sunset.

The physical world was about to be destroyed by the Dark Energies he represented. He laughed silently at the efforts of esteemed scientists, in- cluding recent winners of the Nobel Prize for physics, who seemed so proud of themselves for "discovering" what Angel Emphatic and the Tri- bunal had known for millennia existed, and upon which they had put their own energies to bend to their will.

These Earth creatures who were so weak and fickle would soon know the awesome power of the Dark Matter and the masters who could—and would—turn it to their own purposes.

Moments later, Angel Emphatic moved stealthily behind the stage, whispering in producers' and technicians' minds. In this way, he had in- fluenced the seating arrangement throughout the theater so that his min- ions would be omnipresent and their presence amplified by strategic placement among the audience members. Many of them were well-known people in the Hollywood community, some less well known but up and coming stars, all of whom had, at one point in their lives, decided to ac- cept the promises of the Dark Forces to advance themselves and to live for the destructive purposes that their master, Angel Emphatic, or the One, directed.

The dark master smiled inwardly, knowing that in mere Earth hours a synchronized level of evil would ignite fear in every sector and heart on the planet. This, he knew, would be the culmination of not only the past few decades of concentrated effort by the Tribunal, not only the past few months of warning humanity of the great coming of the end of the age— but of more than two thousand years of preparation and warfare on the Forces of Light that had often come close but never fully yielded the final victory. If he had possessed feelings it would have felt good—no, exqui- site. As it was, the being that Angel Emphatic, one of the lords of dark- ness and masters of evil, had become deeply appreciated the moment and the glory it presaged.

IRA appeared at his side. The wall between worlds had been breached, and tonight it would open wide as a floodgate of sorts, revealing both sides to each other in new and profound ways. As above, so below. IRA and Angel Emphatic, ancient rivals for the favor of the Tribunal and servant-allies in their constant work of sowing seeds of dissatisfaction among men, greeted each other like brothers.

"My dear one, Emphatic," IRA said in affectionate shorthand talk.

"And my oldest friend, Salazzarm," Angel Emphatic answered, using one of IRA's many past identities—of which there were too many to enumerate. He saw, in once glance, all the various guises IRA had ever taken, including his most recent as spirit guide for the dead President of the United States on the Other Side.

For countless centuries they had moved between worlds but spent most of their time on Earth fomenting crises of choice and battling for the bodies, minds, and souls of mankind. They had devised a system that often worked to perfection: Each would choose a side in a potential human conflict and inflate the egos and motivations of the opposites, ensuring that one or the other would inevitably strike and spark open warfare. The longer such battles lasted the better for the Dark Forces, of course. They had become experts at prolonging wars, sometimes for decades or even centuries, keeping alive the flames of hatred and mistrust that caused entire nations to risk their existence over false conflicts and perceived self-interests.

What indescribable pleasure it gave these creatures of black mist and mystery!

Of course, each longed for primacy over the other, for control of the Tribunal. Such were the egos of these dark spirits. For now, the One was leading. But IRA hoped his mastery of POTUS would so impress the Tribunal that he would triumph over Angel Emphatic at last. POTUS was the key to victory, for only he could aid or hinder his son, who was the key for the hated Forces of Light.

They could regale each other for endless hours and days at a time with tales of their glorious achievements for the Tribunal. But all that seemed to pale beside the event unfolding on this day of days before the largest human audience they had ever mustered for one of their extravaganzas of evil.

"I have guided POTUS to be present tonight at this Academy Awards show," the guide said with undisguised glee in his otherworldly voice. One of many voices he possessed. "And he is completely unaware of the purposes of his being here. He thinks it is because of his son."

"Yes," the One answered, struggling not to shout, which would in fact shake the foundations of the Hollywood Grand Theatre with the ineffable power of his words and his intent. "And the other players on this

stage"—he pointed to the floor on which he stood in corporeal form—
"nor do they have the faintest clue. For they think this evening is about
them!" He wanted to howl and shriek with ungodly laughter, but restrained
himself yet again.

The stagehands and camera crew, as well as some actors, the production
staff of the awards ceremony, and the network executives scuttled unaware
past the two demonic entities, engrossed in their tasks. The One and IRA
reveled in the scene, which only confirmed how their power was in large
part based on their ability to be anonymous, even invisible, to human beings. They were so good at what they did that they scared themselves sometimes.

CHAPTER
100

Outside the Hollywood Grand Theatre, in a trailer that was used as a production center for the television network, Marcus Jackson waited in a tiny makeshift room, sitting on a folding chair. Agent Bobby Anderson stood over the young man, half protector and half disciple—unsure which role he would be called to play tonight in the drama that was about to unfold in Los Angeles. Anderson had arranged for the use of the trailer in order to provide as much security as he could without alerting their enemies. He had a brief conversation with Nurse Rae and Dr. Tyler a few moments earlier, and he thanked them for all their efforts, both in their help in rescuing the boy and bringing him here to this locked-down location. He told them that he would take over and they could go to their hotel to get dressed for the big night and to meet him back at the site as soon as they were ready. Anderson tried to keep his tone light, but he distinctly sensed the same hovering presence of darkness that he had felt in the killing field in Belfast throughout his investigation at that unspeakably horrible crime scene.

"I still don't know exactly how I got here," Marcus said. "And *why* I am here. This is one of the weirdest things I've ever been through. Even weirder than being kidnapped, if that's possible."

"Well, I don't have all the answers for you, other than you and I both are supposed to be here. I'm not sure what that means, exactly, but we have both felt the presence of your dad and the idea that he has a message for the world that only you can receive and interpret." He shook his head, baffled and ever alert to any sign of threat to his charge that could arise at any second.

"Okay, I'm willing to do what is asked of me. You know that. I have had the strongest feeling all along, even when I was a prisoner, that my father was looking out for me, praying for me, along with Mom and the rest of the family. And a lot of other people."

"That is true," Anderson said. "You probably had millions of good people praying for you."

"But what does that prove? That there are millions of good people, or that prayer—even by one good person—really is answered when it is sincere and well intentioned?"

"Maybe all of the above," the FBI man ventured. "I am no expert on religion. All I can tell you is that I got down on my knees each and every day in Belfast and asked for answers." Anderson prayed silently again that the police in Belfast would be able to stop the last murder.

"Did you get the answers you were seeking?"

"The honest answer is no—but I got other answers, better and more important ones."

"What do you mean by that?"

"We've known each other for a long time, though it's been a while since we've seen each other."

"Yeah." Both Bobby and Marcus fondly remembered the campaign days, the energy that experience had generated, the feeling of mission and purpose each of them had felt—and the lifelong friendship that had grown out of that time. Marcus had been a boy then, but thanks to all he had been through, he was quickly growing into a man now, in Bobby's eyes and soon in the eyes of the entire world.

"It's like we're having a reunion or something. Or—well, I don't want to get all misty-eyed." But he felt that way.

Bobby acknowledged the crack with a half smile. He said, "So, you know how I work. I was focused completely on solving the crime that was in front of me. That was all I could handle, frankly. It is what I do, what I was trained for many years to do. And that's as far as I could see. What came to me, however, was different."

Special Agent Bobby Anderson wanted to smoke a cigarette right now. He had not had that urge since he had quit several years ago, when the Bureau had gotten on his case about it. It came on him all of a sudden with a power that almost sent him reeling. Then he knew: It was yet another sign of the presence of darkness—his enemy who wanted him dead—here and now, in this place and time, just as it had been omnipresent in the murders in Ireland. It wanted to taunt and tempt him with things that were bad for him—forcing him to make a choice, pressing him to make the wrong choice.

"It was," he continued, "on the level of a revelation—I think that's how I would describe it. Someone a lot more religious than me could probably understand it better, but I'm telling you what I thought and felt. I saw things with new eyes. I read the evidence in new ways. I saw little glimpses of the future, including tonight.

"It has become clear to me that the role of the individual in all this—you, me, people we know, people we will never know—is most important. The choices we make affect the good of everyone on the planet. I was given more *information* than I could process at the time, to be honest with you. But all of it was a gift of some sort. And I always thought of your father during that investigation. Those days weren't so long ago, just weeks, but it kind of seems I was given a whole year's worth of insight and experience. Now I'm finally learning how to handle the gift. I have been prepared—for something. You might know better what it is than I." Anderson thought again about that sudden flash of insight earlier in the day and wondered—was it just his "gut instinct" or had there been something more?

Marcus laughed—the first time he had seen any humor in his life in a long time, through all that had happened to him and to his family of late. "I guess I do. But at the same time, I cannot articulate it all that well myself. I know exactly what you are describing. The same thing happened to me when I was being held all alone and in darkness. My mind opened up and I saw a blinding light, something I couldn't avoid, couldn't close my eyes to. Everything was clear in the moment, and I haven't forgotten any of it. Yet I wasn't given the full understanding of what I was seeing at the same time I was seeing it. Does that make sense?"

"Perfectly." Then Anderson paused and felt prompted to ask a question. "What do you see now, Marcus?"

"A lot is coming clearer to me. Like, why I am here rather than at the FBI office. You must have a clue, too. That's your job, after all!"

Bobby was impressed with Marcus's insight. He had matured a lot in a very short time. "This is as safe a place as I can get you to," he said. "We expect your mother to be here any minute. I know you'll want to see her as soon as you can."

"My mom is coming here?" Marcus was overcome with the thought that he would soon see and be able to hold his beloved mommy long before he expected to. "You're a good man, Agent Anderson," he said in his all-grown-up voice.

"I could say the same about you, Mr. Jackson."

P leasure and excitement welled up within Angel Emphatic's being. It
was an exquisite feeling that motivated him to exert his every energy
to fulfill the mandate of the Tribunal—and his own desires for power and
control over the minds of human beings. It was a thrill unlike any other,
better than any sensual pleasures known to these hapless, self-centered
creatures.

Laughter rose within the sly dark lord as well, but he did not—could
not—let it out to be heard by others. If his true thoughts and feelings were
known by these people, they would be repulsed by the dank ugliness such
thoughts represented. He knew from long experience that he must hide
his true nature when among impressionable humans, for whom he had no
respect whatever. His laughter could split a person's skull or bend steel if
unleashed in full fury.

Angel Emphatic said to his companion: "The Tribunal has been pleased
with us thus far and expect a glorious cataclysm for the ages. We have a
grave responsibility to carry out their directives as their ambassadors on
the Earth. I intend that we shall win a great victory here."

IRA, for his part, had spent enough time with the assassinated POTUS
and among the grim and self-satisfied Council of Elders to feel super-
confident in his own abilities and the ultimate strength of the Dark Forces
in this new battle for the ages. He felt almost disappointed that it would be
so very easy to subdue the enemy this day, as he assumed would happen.

How the histories would be written and the psalms sung when the
Dark Energies took their rightful place as universal rulers of all realms,
visible and invisible!

Looking around at the bustle backstage, IRA replied to the one to
whom he looked as to his commander in the field, "We stand here at the

436 · JOHN EDWARD

tip of the spear. It is ready to pierce the flesh of these poor beings—for their own good, as well as ours. How can they not know what is going to happen to them?"

He was pleased at his sly reference to an old triumph—the crucifixion of Jesus two thousand years ago. This, however, would be even more thrilling for the evil being.

"Some do," Emphatic said, almost absently. His thoughts, too, had already turned to the aftermath of victory and the celebrations that would shake the heavens. "But they cannot convince enough of their brother beings to make a difference in the outcome."

IRA's unnatural teeth flashed. He was dressed in a tuxedo in order to blend in with the award-ceremony attendees. His earthly form was unremarkable, except for his eyes, which bored into whatever he looked at with singular intensity. His face shimmered in the shadows cast by the intense stage lighting, to which he turned his back. He did not love light; it upset his sensibilities. "They are weak in both thought and action."

"That is, in part, how they have survived for so long," the other said. "They can bend with the prevailing winds and thus survive the most intense storms. Their lack of strength has been an effective evolutionary trait for a long time. But now we are going to press them down as never before—until they break."

The red carpet scene outside the Hollywood Grand Theatre was a mob scene: flashing paparazzi cameras, iPhone video cams, shouting and screaming by fans, press milling everywhere looking for that "exclusive" interview, and show business celebrities and Oscar nominees arriving in limousines every few seconds. It was late afternoon, Pacific standard time, and the rich and famous squinted or wore sunglasses against the natural glare that was amplified by tens of thousands of watts of electric lighting.

Charlene St. John and her entourage arrived early, because she would be singing her new song live early in the broadcast. Her special guests, Rae Loona and Tyler Michaels, were already at a backstage cocktail reception.

During the previous week, she had rehearsed it endlessly—not only the singing but also the choreography—to get the timing down to a science. She had a long-established reputation as a perfectionist who rehearsed relentlessly and drove herself and others. Now, on the evening of the performance, she was relaxed and ready to give it her all.

As she stepped out of the limousine, with Dawson Rask as her escort, along with her publicist and secretary, Charlene looked around at the familiar scene. How many times had she been here before? Hundreds of concerts and dozens of award shows over nearly two decades came back to her in a flash of memory that nearly overwhelmed her. She paused to catch her breath. In her heart she carried her song, *the* song of her life. She touched Dawson's arm to steady herself.

He looked at her and saw that her face was bathed with dying sunlight, seeming to radiate back even more powerfully than the klieg lights and strobes. Never had she looked more beautiful or healthy, or more in command of her awesome talents.

He felt her grip tighten on his arm.

Charlene propelled herself forward, head held high, past doubts and pains and memories. In her own heart, she held the image of the Lady who had given her back her life and purpose. She needed nothing else to sustain her, and she cared nothing for what might happen to her beyond the present moment.

As was the case at her concert in Mexico, she felt a sudden sense of purpose, of knowing what to do, of understanding why she was here on this Earth. It felt good, though it frightened her, and she hoped and prayed she could do what had been asked of her, that she could perform tonight as on no other night in her life.

Dawson looked over at Charlene, who was in her element among her fans, in front of the cameras and microphones. For a second she stopped on the red carpet. She was glued to this spot, anticipating . . . something.

How the heck did I get here? he asked himself for the thousandth time. He added the question: *How the heck did we get here?*

The whirlwind events of the past few hours were something of a blur to him, but one thing stood out: Between Charlene and himself there was no awkwardness or any discomfort whatsoever, just palpable chemistry rippling out to form an aura of peace and newfound affection around them both. That woman was beautiful not only on the outside but she also radiated the goodness of a pure spirit within. It was a source of intrinsic beauty that bowled Dawson over, and for the first time in years, he could envision a life that wasn't filled with sorrow. He almost wept at the thought.

As they moved closer to the theater entrance, they were relentlessly pinned down by microphone-wielding questioners and handheld video cams and lights.

Charlene spoke to a reporter who had a microphone to her face. "I am grateful to God for everything in my life that he has touched—and for the good in this world. I know that a lot of bad things have happened to me, some very publicly, and some are happening right now, but faith is the answer to all that."

"Yes," the reporter said condescendingly, "but what about your song?

It has been nominated as Best Original Song. Do you think you'll win the Oscar?"

"No, I don't," she said simply.

"How can you say that? You are the odds-on favorite to win."

"I've already won," Charlene St. John said with a bright, familiar lilt in her famous voice. "I don't need a statuette to tell me that."

She felt Dawson Rask's hand on her arm. It gave her a warm jolt of positive energy to know that he stood beside her now, in a moment that meant the world to her. If anyone could see into her heart, they would see her pure joy. And there was one who could see and know all. The Lady of Guadalupe, who seemed to appear everywhere she looked.

Early on the red carpet trail, Charlene had been sure she'd seen Our Lady, but on second glance, it was Salma Hayek!

Even here, amid the glitter and glamour of the photographers and screaming fans, with the eyes of the entire world focused on the spectacle of the Academy Awards, with the reporters scrambling to obtain screen time with the pop icon and the roar all around her, Charlene's mind and soul were focused on the Lady, her spirit guide and master on this journey. She constantly saw imagery of her on the way there, including a bumper sticker and a tattoo on a cameraman's arm.

As she moved along the red carpet with Dawson at her side and shouts from everywhere, she noticed a figure that seemed to be moving with her in parallel off to one side and slightly ahead: a woman with a blue veil whose face was partly obscured by the angle at which she walked. There she was! Charlene was elated as the noise about her abated. Smiling serenely, Charlene gave her fans and the television audience a radiant image of the singer at the peak of her powers and in the flower of health and well-being.

Still, even with the comforting presence of the Lady guiding her, even with her heart full of prayer and goodwill, a sense of foreboding suddenly descended upon Charlene. She looked down at the bright red carpet and, for just an instant, saw a river of blood flowing beneath her feet—and instead of the screams of her fans, she heard the cries of the damned and the wailing and gnashing of teeth of her fellow human beings, thousands, even millions of them. One instantaneous, terrifying moment. At first, no one else saw what she had visioned. In anguish, she turned to Our Lady, who seemed to pause and hold out her hands.

In her mind, Charlene heard these words: *"My child, the sins of mankind are many, but the love of God is greater still for all that. Do not be afraid as you enter the temple of the evildoers, for they are as nothing before the power of your loving Father whose angels once vanquished the forces of evil and will do so again. I promise you. . . . Pray with me."*

Then the woman in the Basilica, the woman whose image on the poor Aztec peasant's cloak had touched millions of lives, was visible to those close to Charlene.

For just another brief moment, Our Lady of Guadalupe could be seen by the fans and media, causing a hush. Charlene squeezed Dawson's hand. "Do you see her? Do you see her?" she whispered urgently.

"Yes. And I can't believe it." He stood with her, enveloped in a strange light, experiencing the same feeling he had known when visited by his guide, C. S. Lewis—but somewhat more powerful, definitely more *feminine,* and infinitely more peaceful.

As they resumed walking the red carpet, the vision quickly faded, but the presence remained for Charlene and Dawson. It was clear to Charlene that the image of the Lady was no longer visible to the people and the paparazzi, but the voice—a strong yet gentle voice that sounded otherworldly—came clearly to her: *"Use your voice. It is your gift to bring all who hear you closer to the Source of all goodness. Use your voice."*

CHAPTER
103

A bove the clicking and flashing cameras and in the realm beyond human sight, the Dark Forces swirled and roiled in a frenzy as they realized they were losing ground.

It had been a hot day in L.A., getting hotter not cooler as the celebs strutted down the red carpet in the late afternoon for the pre-awards telecasts, even with the overcast sky.

The Dark Forces had long-planned chaos on their side, and they saw an opportunity to touch the minds of some of those present at the scene and set in motion a series of events during the short span of two minutes. Just ten yards from where Dawson and Charlene were standing, a scaffold holding cameramen for a South American TV company collapsed into a sea of journalists, some fans, and even some of the arriving stars: Jennifer Aniston's leg was broken, and Barbara Walters would be taken to Cedar Sinai Hospital for a concussion—and giving Joan Rivers and Kathy Griffin more fodder for comedy than a team of writers could write in a lifetime.

A sea of black town cars stretched for over two miles, waiting to drop off the who's who of the Hollywood world, the very epitome of ego, entitlement, fashion, beauty, and immeasurable wealth, fame, and talent. The wreckage of the scaffolding and the injured were cleared out within several minutes, reopening the flow on the red carpet.

By this time, Charlene and Dawson had been whisked safely into the theater by a skilled security team. The air crackled with chaos and anticipation of—something. . . .

This was a "red pool" moment, recalling for IRA and POTUS the time the latter was led into such a pool to experience the almost blindingly orgasmic experience of dark energies and misdirected emotions that lay at the foundation of the Tribunal's scheme for domination of malleable and imperfect human beings to their purposes. People on Earth, many of them, saw celebrity and fame as an elixir of life, as the *answer* to so many problems and desires, when the reality was it could only be a distraction at best and an obsession at worst. The Dark Side sought to feed into the voyeuristic ego of people, forcing them to focus only on the ego or the self and thus shut themselves off from the promise and energy of the light. At least for the next few hours, they were in for a treat: a veritable orgy of ego and glitter in the form of an entertainment extravaganza like no other in the world.

For several long seconds, a strange and powerful layer of light surrounded the Earth, causing power to flicker and fade, communications blackouts to roll across entire continents in response to the surge of dark energy that had been harnessed by the Tribunal from solar flares and black holes that swirled and shot through space toward the planet.

Although they lasted less than a minute in total, the interruptions in electrical power across every grid in every city on Earth caused telephonic and wireless communications to cease. Only the broadcast from Los Angeles was relatively unscathed, protected from the malevolent forces because of the huge surge of positive energies and lightness of spirit that had gathered—or been summoned—there.

Mama G's spirit reached out to cover those present with Marcus in the secure waiting room and the members of the Academy Awards audience who were in tune with Forces of Light. Everyone she touched felt her gentle breath and the scent of a breeze from the Caribbean.

The Academy Awards broadcast was already under way. A few power issues and celestial displays would not be enough to stop this world-wide event, which was so important to so many powerful figures in media and entertainment. Already, it was estimated that more than three billion people would see the ceremony this night.

Bobby Anderson met up with a band of agents he personally knew were on the right side . . . He had called to make the First Lady aware directly, via a secure line, that Marcus Jackson, Jr. was alive, and she was in the air on a private jet on the way to collect her son. Probably she was 30,000 feet over Nevada right now.

The FBI agent arranged to get all his security people inside through the stage entrance of the theater. He had two guards posted outside the door and outside the utility trailer where he had deposited Marcus in the care of Tyler Michaels and Rae Loona, who were escorted backstage from the A-list cocktail party.

Much to her surprise, Charlene's work had been nominated for Best Original Song for one of the most popular movies of the year, *Rainfall*, and tonight, with the whole world watching and listening, she would sing it live. Just as she was getting ready to leave her seat to perform, a seat stand-in was sent down the aisle to make sure that no seat was left empty in the shots of the show that are broadcast. Charlene asked Dawson if he would mind walking with her backstage. Barely able to keep his eyes open—the time change from Australia, the ordeal in rescuing Marcus, and the energy drain happening all around him—he accepted, even though he had always wanted a front row seat at a Charlene St. John McAvoy concert. Little did he know that this would turn into a "front row seat" for a life with this woman with whom he was rapidly falling in love.

As they made their way backstage amid heavy security, Dawson noticed Bobby and waved to him. The two friends came together and embraced. They had become even closer, forging a bond of a lifetime over the past few weeks—especially the past twenty-four hours.

"Bobby, this is—"

"Charlene St. John," Bobby Anderson finished, taking the performer's small hand in his. "You are my biggest fan," he said with a grin, purposely mangling the line like many a starstruck fan. "Seriously, I love your music and wish you the best of luck with your nomination tonight."

"Thank you, Agent Anderson. I have heard a lot about you in a very short time from Dawson."

"Always the man of well-chosen words," Anderson acknowledged. "Look, I have some serious work to do here, as you probably know. I hope we can meet again sometime soon."

"Oh, we will meet again," Charlene said, looking between Bobby and Dawson.

"We were able to bring the President's son here, as we had hoped," Bobby said to Dawson. Charlene could not help but overhear. The FBI man said to her. "Marcus Jr.'s backstage, you know."

Charlene had a lightning-bolt moment of clear understanding and vision. She said, "During my song, while all the attention is supposed to be on me—I want you to bring Marcus out onto the stage. I will cut my song short, use the time I've been allotted to bring out a special guest. The whole world will be watching. Dawson?" She looked to the man that she had just met but somehow she knew in her heart that she was falling in love with, seeking his approval for her bold idea.

Dawson, in turn, looked at Bobby Anderson. "What do you think, partner?"

"I must be nuts, but I think it was meant to be," Bobby replied.

And Dawson heard the sonorous Ian McKellen voice of his guide, C. S. Lewis, intone: *"It is exactly suited to the purpose of our being here. Deus volte. God wills it."*

"That's pretty heavy," Dawson blurted, forgetting that the others couldn't hear the voice of his Fallen Master—yet.

Charlene thought he was responding to Anderson. She said, "Darn straight, it is." Her smile dazzled the men around her, and each found himself more than a little in love with her. *She* saw her Fallen Master, the Lady, again in the two-piece white business suit, standing close by and nodding with approval.

Of course, the masters of the dark energies needed to stop this. They triggered a rolling blackout throughout L.A. The theater lost power for several seconds. No power, no show . . . Backup generators kicked in with somewhat weaker power, but it was power nonetheless. The show would go on.

Rae had been mothering Marcus in the trailer just off the employee entrance of the theater. "Don't be nervous, boy," she found herself saying to the son of the late President of the United States. Her smile was infectious, and her maternal concern had its intended effect.

Tyler and Rae were trying to help Marcus, who was still a bit shaky after his ordeal. He was saying that he needed to get inside. But they were uncertain what he was to do once there. They agreed it was just to show the world he was alive—a happy ending to a sad story.

Marcus assured her that he was not nervous. "I'm okay, ma'am," he said simply. "I kind of know what I have to do—what I have to say. My father has given me the words."

Tyler said, "I know what that's like. I've had someone putting words in my mouth and thoughts in my head for some time now."

Rae knew he was thinking of his Fallen Master, Emanuel Swedenborg, but she couldn't resist: "Oh, Mikey, *I've* never put words in your mouth."

"Nor have you ever let me get a word in edgewise," he said, unable to resist.

Rae turned to Marcus and put a warm nurse's hand on his shoulder.

He possessed a quiet cool about himself. He missed his dad more than anything. The only thing that kept him going was the promise that he would be able to see POTUS again. When he had learned that his dad had been killed and wouldn't be there for him anymore, it almost destroyed his will to live. And when he had been kidnapped, he had to struggle to regain his survival instinct to fight the utter despair he felt.

When POTUS had come to meet him during his abduction, however, and he received the charge to take on his father's destiny, a change came over him. This brought about a calmness within him and all around him. Then he had been rescued by the FBI . . . in his mind it all fitted into a pattern of events unfolding in the world. He was not aware of all the events—for good and ill—that had transpired over the past several days leading up to the Academy Awards evening, but he didn't have to be tuned

into the latest breaking news. He was "on schedule" for his part. He would
do what he had been led to do and trust that the results would follow with
the intended effect.

What could he do now but trust? After all, he had been brought to
this place safe and sound—for a purpose.

Suddenly there was a knock on the door. Tyler opened it. Bobby Anderson
stood there, one of the network producers behind him. "Time to move," he
said simply to his young charge and the nurse and doctor.

As Marcus Jackson was being escorted into the Hollywood Grand Theatre
by a security detail supervised by Special Agent Bobby Anderson, IRA
turned to POTUS with a look of contempt and utter betrayal. The boy had
been abducted and held for future use by the Tribunal—but now he was
free!

Then another figure appeared, and IRA recoiled. It was Caleb, who
had finally replaced him as POTUS's evanescent spirit guide and now was
making himself visible. Caleb appeared as an aqua blue aura within whose
enveloping presence IRA's former target stood taller and loomed larger
than he had previously. Caleb and POTUS together emanated hugely
positive energy all around them.

POTUS said simply, "Your masters' plan is about to fail, my friend. The
world will *not* be bent to their dark purposes. This I can now see so very
clearly, and this I promise you through no power of my own, but with the
goodness in every man or woman to throw against you."

The trickster guide loosed a scream from the core of his being: "HOW
COULD YOU DO THIS TO MEEEEEEE . . . ?"

This visceral attack of energy that reverberated throughout Heaven was
the precursor of the intentional attack IRA was directing at the being
with whom he had been working and programming for destructive intent.

The time had come. POTUS had, from the first moment he had
crossed over to the Other Side, been absorbing impressions and data like a
computer hard drive, and processing everything that was thrown at him.
It was not unlike when he was in school and college, or in the army when
he had learned to observe and act with as much precision as humanly possible. Now he was in a realm that called upon all the resources his mind
and soul could tap into. Now he would confront evil face-to-face. *Mano a*

mano. Yet there was something unfathomably poignant about the figure before him. A trickster and false friend who had, the President presumed, once been good—or could have chosen the good over the darkness that consumed him. IRA's skills were formidable, his message compelling, but POTUS did not fall victim to all his energies and wiles, instead becoming a worthy adversary. To no avail.

POTUS instinctively realized that, in himself, he was no match for the energies being unleashed upon him. He was not yet mature enough in his new state of being, nor did he know how to combat the force of the evil targeting him. So, he simply surrendered to it and allowed his soul to be offered up now for what he recognized was a second time to save his family back on the earthly plane.

But what happened next, nobody expected . . .

The loudest *crack!* and *crash!* imaginable were heard throughout the worlds of humans and spirits. On Earth, it was described as if two planes had collided, yet there was nothing visible in telescopes. The world took a deep breath and watched for something akin to a miracle—or the ultimate doom to occur. A heavenly telecast was about to be delivered. . . .

All communications ceased, as a huge solar flare erupted and reached the Earth, creating a layer of light around the planet, knocking out cell phones and electronic communications everywhere for a few seconds. The Earth, in effect, blinked as it recoiled from the intensity of the flare, behind which the dark matter that threatened all was stopped, at least temporarily, in its path.

Dr. Jason Chang felt the reverberation and immediately ordered a check of all instrumentation at NASA.

Pope Genaro I was on his knees in prayer in his Vatican chamber, and his entire body shook when the cosmic boom echoed across the heavens.

"O Creator," he prayed, "open our eyes and ears to Your voice—before it is too late."

Rae Loona was standing behind Marcus Jackson Jr. when she heard it: a familiar and comforting sound. Music to her soul. It was a voice, *the* voice she had longed to hear in person. As she turned in slow motion to look, the bluest eyes she ever saw were staring back at her: John Travolta.

Marcus felt a shift in Rae's energy. He immediately turned to crane his neck to see who it was. At first, he didn't recognize him; he was too young. He asked his friend in a stage whisper, "Who is that?"

Rae was speechless, unable to blink or breathe. John Travolta *smiled at her*, as if he knew what she was thinking. . . .

Rae began to babble like a crazy woman all about the events that led them to that very moment, randomly pulling out pieces of the storyline, hitting Travolta in the arm and telling him how shocked she was that he was standing next to her.

Tyler was standing in the wings, laughing his butt off. He regained his composure after a moment and said to Rae, "You're going to give Mr. Travolta a black-and-blue, Nurse Loona."

That's when John Travolta kissed Rae on the cheek and thanked her for her heroism. "Rae Loona," he said, "stands for *real nurse*." He flashed his billion-dollar box office smile at her.

At that, Rae passed out. Travolta was there to catch her, and Tyler found a chair backstage on which to deposit her temporarily. But the star couldn't linger to tend to his Number 1 fan. He walked out onstage to introduce the next act: Ms. Charlene St. John.

Charlene walked partway onstage as the orchestra struck up the over-ture to her popular Oscar-nominated song. Then she waved at the conductor as she hesitated just beyond the curtain. The orchestra stopped, with the conductor somewhat confused about what was happening. This had not been rehearsed. The spotlight remained on Charlene. She was warmly lit and had never looked more lovely or winning, even at that his-toric Super Bowl not so many years before. . . . Tears filled her eyes as she announced to the world that President Jackson's son, Marcus, had been rescued.

"He is alive and well," she stated in her clear, sonorous voice. It almost sounded like a song. "And he is *here*."

While the whole world watched and sat back, stunned, Marcus walked quietly and confidently onto the stage to a standing ovation. The Holly-wood Grand Theatre went wild. Charlene opened her arms, and the young man hugged her as she greeted him.

The broadcast control room erupted into a panic. The director screamed, "Time! Time! We're supposed to go to commercial in sixty seconds! Somebody help me here!" Ten cameras captured the President's son as the director lost it. The executive producer looked at him as if he had gone crazy: After all, history was being made here, and they were producing it for the whole planet to see.

The television cameras panned the audience of A-list celebrities. Tears fell down everyone's cheeks. These moguls and entertainers were no longer celebrities—just people having a very real moment. They were witnesses to a miracle and a true Hollywood happy ending. This night would be writ-ten about in the history of the awards as the most memorable in the first century of the Oscar ceremony.

The director of the show now embraced the meaning of this historical broadcast. He immediately projected an image of the late President of the United States onto the enormous screen behind young Marcus. Seeing the larger-than-life image of his dad, he could not help being overcome with emotion. Knowing he would never feel him again, never get to hug him one last time, only fueled the deep feelings stirring inside him.

After several minutes of the standing ovation, Marcus took the microphone from one of the technicians who had been quickly dispatched to mic him up. There was a pause in the pandemonium as the oxygen in the theater became rarified and everyone held his or her breath.

Onstage and in the theater there was absolute, dead silence as Marcus Jackson stood center stage, his hands folded in front of him, wearing a black suit, white shirt, and no tie.

H*e looks like he belongs there, in front of the world,* Rae Loona thought. She, like everyone else in the audience, was totally absorbed in the scene, focused on the young man who looked eerily like his father, the slain President of the United States.

Some members of the audience later said they could also see the late President himself standing there behind his son, smiling and encouraging him as he spoke.

What Marcus and Rae and all the others could not know was that across the globe, billions of people were also silent, as if a curtain had descended over the Earth and absorbed every wave of sound and blanketed the planet in utter silence.

Dawson Rask, Bobby Anderson, Tyler Michaels, and John Travolta— who stood arm-in-arm with Rae, wrapping her arm through his—watched from backstage. Anderson scoped out the crowd with a practiced eye, looking for signs of threat. He felt, oddly, that the danger had passed.

Charlene glanced back to blow a kiss to Dawson. Was this really happening? What in heaven's name did it mean? Everyone present knew that something bordering on the supernatural had occurred—was occurring. But *what*?

M ama G stepped toward the small group backstage. She thought she heard the voice of the Governor of the Council of Elders whispering in her ear. "Do you see now what your purpose has been? You have been a part of bringing all these people together. You and the Fallen Masters who have guided them. Just as I have guided you."

There stood Asima, visible only to Patricia Rose Greenidge—just as Mama G was visible only to those in this immediate circle of living human beings and Fallen Masters.

She silently thanked the Governor. The visions she had been privileged to see all came flooding back to her, jolting her with the force of a positive, powerful electricity, then gave way to a glimpse of the future . . . almost too bright to behold. Would it come true?

The words of the Governor now filled her consciousness: "Behold, as the stars and the planets align in their courses and the people of Earth choose the Light over the Darkness, this shall come to pass. The shadow *will* be lifted, if the people heed the words they will hear this night."

Dear Lord, Mama G prayed, *thank You for Your gifts to me. Please help me be worthy and to be grateful for all You have done. And let me know what else is left for me to do for You, as long as I am on this Earth.*

"Come, dear Mama," Asima said. "Your time on this plane has ended. I am here to escort you to the Other Side. You are one of us now—one with us in the realm of the spirit."

"But how—why?" She was confused, but she did not resist the gentle voice and the unworldly "touch" of the spirit guide, the lovely young woman who had given her life to save her boy's life—to give him life a second time, at the cost of her own.

"Come. You shall see. All shall be revealed to you, as it is written."

"In the stars?"

Asima smiled. "Yes, in the stars that represent the souls of all who have come before us."

What is happening? This thought was the one thing that all those in the Hollywood Grand Theatre and billions around the globe were wondering. The moment unfolded before their eyes as if in a dream.

Marcus finally spoke.

"Ladies and gentlemen, I am sorry to interrupt tonight's broadcast. As you can see, I survived and am grateful to those who found me and rescued me today. People who were entrusted with my well-being kidnapped me and caused a great deal of suffering to my family. Although I am looking forward to going home and being with my mom and family, I won't be reunited with my dad—my best friend and the best dad in the world—who was taken from this world . . . our world—" He paused, swallowing hard. "—*my* world. Tonight I stand before you and ask you in his honor to make a choice. He inspired me to look for the goodness or *God*ness in every person. When 9/11 happened over ten years ago, he told me even then, that those men were good at their core but just chose evil instead.

"My father is alive, though he is not with us in body," Marcus said. The hush became even deeper, as if everyone had stopped breathing.

"My father is dead. You all know that, and you know that I was kidnapped. I still don't know why this has all happened, just that it has. And it is over now. But my father is still with us. He has spoken to me, and he wants me to share what he said with everyone who can hear me—with everyone who will listen.

"There are bad people and bad spirits threatening us. Just like those who kidnapped me. I guess they thought they could make some kind of big deal about having the son of the President in their power. I don't know. But I do know that my dad was able to break through the wall that separates us from souls who are dead. If he has the power to do that, then he has the power to fight evil.

"He told me that I have the ability to make the right choice—that all of us have the same power, to choose right over wrong, love over evil, light over darkness. I believe him.

"The words I am speaking are not my own. As you can see, I'm just a kid, really, with a pretty good education—at least my parents have sent me to good schools, even if I haven't studied all that hard all the time. But I did not know anything about the world and the truth of the world, until I was taken from my family, until I lost my father and my best friend. What do any of us really know about life until we experience pain and loss and disappointment? What can we know about happiness unless we have known about sadness and experienced it in ourselves? Like I said, I didn't *know* anything, and I can't claim to even now—but I am here to share with all of you what has been shared with me.

"The message is this: Together we can turn back the forces that want to destroy our world. We have seen this with my kidnappers and the one who shot my dad. There is evil all around us. Look at your own lives. You will see it. To resist such evil is simple but not easy. And we can do it right now—together."

As one, the Hollywood Grand Theatre audience took in a deep, gasping breath.

"I have been given the Key of Understanding by my father. My message is, *Do not give up your freedom. Make a different choice—the right choice.* As hard as it is at a time like this when so much seems to be going wrong and the Earth itself is threatened by physical and spiritual forces beyond our understanding . . ." The young man paused and unfolded his hands, raising them to shoulder level and looking directly into the primary television camera.

"My message is not really my message at all, but comes from a Source of all that is good, a creative, loving Source that wants all human beings to be happy and fulfilled in their lives. Whatever your religious faith, or whether you do not have any faith in your heart—that is not the point."

Rae Loona and Tyler Michaels were transfixed. Neither said a word, but they looked at each other for a second in total understanding. Never had Tyler felt moved in this way, and he could feel the presence of Karen and his unborn child. He also felt another unseen presence, one that had been "dispatched" by Karen and had watched over him for a long time, ever since her death.

Charlene had walked backstage and now stood next to Dawson. Neither said a word but drew closer together.

Marcus was speaking, teaching this unbelievably enormous audience, leading them to a new understanding of their shared purpose—of what was possible through individual choice to do good and to be good.

"Religion and God are like a pyramid: What you see depends upon what angle and what time of day you look at it. From my perspective I see it as red, with deep green shadows. From your view, it may appear bright gold with no distinct edges against a bright sky. If you don't get up out of your chair and look at the pyramid from many angles, get up and walk around the pyramid and really look at it, you will never know the many colors of God.

"You will never see what you are supposed to see—which is everything and every color and every aspect of creation. It is all visible to us, if we will just open our eyes and look at what is before us."

He paused for several seconds and looked around him.

"I have said that these words are not my own, yet I am saying them. If you think that is weird, how do you think I feel?"

The people in the theater, most of them hard-bitten, no-nonsense show business professionals, released some of their tension with a ripple of laughter. Elsewhere around the world, when Marcus's words were translated, the same effect was felt, and people of every imaginable color and culture smiled.

Marcus spoke slowly and deliberately. Instinctively, he knew that his words were being translated into various languages and that he was being dubbed, or subtitles were being streamed across TV screens in many places.

He looked over at Tyler, remembering what Tyler had said about his boy—wishing Jeremy could have grown up to be like him, to be *with* him—and remembering the story of the butterflies. Marcus continued, enunciating each word carefully, "In honor of my dad, I just want to say a proper good-bye. He loved blue butterflies. Can you find a blue butterfly on your iPhones or BlackBerries or whatever phone you use—and hold it up to show that we are choosing goodness or *God*ness over darkness? Every person who hears my voice in this broadcast: Take your cell phones, wherever you are. Place a call to someone you love or just turn on the phone and hold it up to the sky so that the light can be seen from above."

Some people at the back of the theater and in the upper tiers moved toward the exits to make their calls and hold up their phones to the sky. The majority of the crowd on the orchestra level stayed in place, awaiting what Marcus Jackson would say next with rapt attention.

As Marcus delivered his appeal for peace and love, the Council of Elders and the Tribunal both looked down at the Earth and were able to see blue lights blinking across the planet. An inspirational message of love and hope from Heaven was delivered, and the response from the people of Earth came shining back to the Other Side.

It was visible to all who had the ability to see, whatever side they had chosen.

The members of the Council of Elders and souls on the Other Side who had chosen rightly—whether in their earthly existence or after—rejoiced.

Amid these shifts of planetary and celestial consciousness toward the light and away from the darkness, IRA realized there would be casualties for his side—new arrivals whom he would be meeting to recruit, to claim as he had tried to claim POTUS, to feed on the energy of the world they were leaving. The Tribunal would need many victories, even minor victories, in the face of losing this battle for power.

Have we lost? IRA asked himself in desperation, fighting to hang onto the denial that fed his own sense of power and worth in the face of disaster and destruction. It was unthinkable. Yet neither he nor his brother spirits of the Tribunal could deny what was happening before their eyes.

IRA rejoined the Tribunal, who had gathered around the pools of passion, now clouded with warring energies, no longer showing a clear path to victory for them. It was dawning on the leaders that their campaign of manipulation, playing off the powerful fears and uncertainties of human beings, was disintegrating before their eyes. Just as they had enlisted more and more new souls, seemingly every day, they were now losing control of those same souls in the blink of an eye—in the flutter of a butterfly's wings. . . .

Legions of souls who had embraced their message would be betrayed, lost to them forever. The choice of Darkness over Light, of mayhem over peace, had seemed so simple and attractive to so many within the sway of the Tribunal's forces, but what now? Panic spread rapidly through those gathered in the realm of the dark energies like a cancer. Black holes bloomed in the space that surrounded their stronghold.

Shrieking and gnashing of teeth erupted among them. It was horrible to hear.

This was the beginning of the end for their drive for total domination.

"We shall fight on! O Masters of the dark design and hellfire, we shall rise once more to battle the puny powers that have thwarted us this day!" The hapless guttural oration of the chief general, standing over a bloodred pool of consciousness and desire, filled the mind of every soldier, spy, and ambassador of evil within his range. A black miasma seeped from the dark matter moving through the universe, which had been diverted, by pure energy, from its destructive path.

IRA joined the others in issuing an ugly, bowel-wrenching scream that shook the foundations of the universe.

· *Vatican City* ·

The pope had walked across the beautiful Vatican gardens after night-fall to spend some time with his science team at the space observatory located within the tiny city-state. The structure had been built in the time of Galileo to study and chart the movement of the stars and planets. The popes then had felt they needed to get a handle on the cosmos and not leave it completely to the secular scientists who were busy upending the traditional understanding of the Earth and the solar system in the post-Renaissance era.

The Vatican science team reported to him twice daily, but the rapidity of developments caused him to call them more often than that—and to come out tonight to see for himself what data they were monitoring.

As he stepped into the room where several priest-scientists were working, one of them immediately said, "Holy Father, you have to look at this!"

· *Houston* ·

At the same time, Jason Chang, on twenty-four-hour duty at NASA in Houston, suddenly sat up straight at his monitor. As he did so, his arm caught the cup of cold coffee that sat next to his keyboard and spilled the cream-laden liquid across his desk.

Cursing, he jumped to his feet. Two assistants came running with paper towels and sopped up the coffee, which miraculously had not spilled onto the keyboard or any other electronic component. Then he sat down again and stared at the data that moved across the screen in front of him.

He couldn't believe what he saw!

Dr. Chang picked up the phone and called a colleague in Greenwich,

England, with whom he generally spoke three or four times a day since the discovery of the creeping dark matter.

"Are you seeing what I'm seeing?" he asked.

"Sure thing," confirmed Alan Sanders, one of the most competent astronomers on the planet. "Pandora's Cluster has shifted, and there is a sudden and substantial change in the composition and location of the dark matter."

"What do you make of it?"

"Take a look at your satellite imaging."

Within seconds, pictures from United States and international satellites flashed across Jason's monitor. He punched a few keys and sent the images to the larger screens in the data room outside his office. The technicians there all looked up at the images that were now appearing on high-def monitors all around them. He could hear a collective gasp from the room.

Clusters of light emanated upward from every city on Earth, and smaller twinkles—still quite visible—from less populated, more rural areas. Nearly the entire expanse of the United States was lit up, and the same with China and India, which meant that vast numbers of people in those countries were signaling the heavens.

"What the heck—?"

"It's the Academy Awards, boss," one of the senior techs called out to him. At her station, the woman had been streaming the ceremony and the speech by the President's son. "You should watch it."

No longer surprised by such a bizarre suggestion, Jason Chang returned to his own computer and clicked onto the broadcast feed of the Oscars to see what the heck she was talking about. . . .

As events unfolded on Earth, both the Tribunal and the Council of Elders gathered around the many pools of consciousness on the other side of the veil to take in and reflect on the cosmic shift that was transpiring before them.

The Fallen Masters had already been dispatched and were directing other Earth guides in action.

POTUS, whose astral eyes had been opened to IRA's manipulation and the Governor's genuine goodness, stood with the others of the Council by the pools, remembering his ugly experience there of the destructive energies that the forces of the Tribunal had hoped to marshal to their ends . . . No, it wasn't going to happen that way.

With a swiftness that surprised him, POTUS was able to receive from the Governor his portfolio of power and his mission and moved like lightning from the heavenly realm to the earthly plane. He felt as if he were being sucked into the engine of a huge jet aircraft, the kind that had transported troops during his days in the army. But there was no thought of combat or conquest—only justice.

The loudest *crash* and *crack* imaginable—even beyond imagination—was then heard, as if two planets had collided and released the energy of tens of thousands of nuclear weapons in the explosion.

The vibration and crash felt on the Earth plane were, for the people in the Hollywood Grand Theatre, not unlike earthquakes they had experienced before, but with a difference: The physical jolt was less than the emotional and spiritual impact on each person present.

One by one, the people who had been led there that evening by their Fallen Masters—whether they knew it or not—saw their guides materialize on the stage behind Marcus Jackson.

Marcus himself turned and saw his father smiling at him, his arms outstretched, and standing behind his father were other relatives who had passed to the Other Side when Marcus was much smaller. They were silent at this moment, but manifestly present not only in the space POTUS occupied but in the boy's heart and mind as well.

Charlene knew that the Blessed Virgin of Guadalupe, who had entered her consciousness in Mexico, had even before Mexico been very much alive and walking closely with her on her journey. Now, in Charlene's eyes, the entire theater was bathed in the light of the Virgin.

From the audience, Tyler now distinctly saw the figure that had been only a shadow to him and whose purpose had been only dimly perceived—even though it had brought him here to this particular place at this specific time: Emanuel Swedenborg, the philosopher and scientist who had glimpsed the purpose of God in his lifetime. He had never seen a portrait of the man, but he knew without a doubt who it was. Tyler's mind was illuminated, and he smiled genuinely and without irony for the very first time since Karen's death. And, there she stood, as well, holding up the baby's hand in a wave that only he could see.

Dawson felt a tap on his shoulder, a firm, physical sensation that caused him to turn and let go of Charlene's hand. *I didn't know I had been holding her hand,* he thought, partly embarrassed and partly elated.

The words did not come from C. S. Lewis's mouth but were as clear in Dawson's mind as the tap of a hammer upon a nail: *"You see, this is the church of the world. You do not have to travel far to be in the presence of God, nor do you have to be a believer. He believes in you. He will find you. He will seek you out and protect you from those who would see you in Hell."*

POTUS, having crossed over definitively and feeling his feet on the stage behind his son, scanned the faces in the audience and the production crew behind the stage. There—he knew it!—was IRA, watching the scene unfold and standing with a figure that appeared to POTUS as a distinguished statuesque person of undetermined sex. As he watched, the figure assumed various aspects, and he realized it was a kind of angelic being, albeit one with evil intent.

In return, Angel Emphatic, who was boiling with anger, met the gaze of the President. IRA looked from one to the other, fear and disgust scoring his face, an ageless face of deceit, a blank slate upon which darkness could write with a cold hand. IRA disappeared from the scene, transporting himself back to the Other Side, where he released yet another wrathful scream from the core of his being, a visceral attack of energy that expressed the betrayal he felt at POTUS's turn. The One greeted him there, then wordlessly banished him to a lower level of existence as punishment for his failure. No further sound came from IRA, nor would it for all eternity.

Blue butterflies—by the thousands and tens of thousands—filled the stage, then the entire theater within a matter of seconds. Television viewers around the world saw their screens filled with wings of many hues and heard an unearthly sound caused by the beating of so many wings. It was musical, but not quite music as most people understood it, an eerie yet soothing chorus that flowed and flickered, keeping time with the myriad wings and the movement of the beautiful creatures in every direction before their eyes.

Marcus Jackson stood center stage, his arms uplifted and his face full of wonder. Having fulfilled his mission, the young man felt the immense relief of someone who had just completed a difficult race and crossed the finish line sapped of every ounce of energy he possessed. He breathed in the fragrance of the butterflies as they moved through the air in the theater and captured the attention of everyone present.

Apart from the strange sound generated by the butterflies, there was dead silence.

During their lives on the temporal, earthly plane, the Fallen Masters who stood now by their earthly subjects—Marcus, Charlene, Dawson, and Tyler—had not known or interacted with one another, but in this time and place they were together in common cause, just as those they had guided stood to witness and participate in this world-altering event.

Dawson, in particular, saw the significance of the spirit guides assembled near the President's son, alongside Charlene and the others—seemingly unrelated and chosen at random by unseen forces—who had been drawn, or transported here for a purpose.

Why me? he wondered, not for the first time.

Perhaps there was no answer to the *why* question . . . Maybe there was only the *this is* answer to any and all questions tonight. It would certainly be something for Dawson Rask to write about—and for Charlene St. John to sing about for many months and years to come, In fact, the words and music of a new song had already begun to form in her mind and on her lips.

Just as Dawson was looking at her with deep love in his eyes, Charlene turned to look at him, though his image was blurred by the tears that welled up there—tears of great joy and understanding. She then walked out onto the stage and cued the music to resume for her interrupted song. Standing next to Marcus, her arm entwined with his, she sang like she had never sung before in her life.

Rae Loona looked up at Dawson and could sense the wheels turning in the writer's brain. She now realized that she had been gifted for her entire life with a special sensitivity to others' thoughts and needs. It was part of her genetic makeup. The two were natural healers and bridge-builders in a world that so desperately needed such skills, and now more than ever after the cosmic rift they had just experienced.

Her Mikey would never be the same after this. She knew that much. And for that matter, neither would she . . . Something had been revealed to Rae—something deep and mysterious and entirely magical—and she was super-excited to find out how it would unfold in her life. She said a silent prayer of thanks.

Bob Anderson felt the weight of the world lift from his shoulders. *It's over,* he thought, and then: *No, this is just a beginning. The world has been preserved—that is, the* good *in the world has been saved, at least for now. And it is up to the rest of us to make the choices that will keep hope and light and good alive.*

· New York ·

D ave Hampton watched the unfolding events on a studio monitor in New York, just as billions of people around the world watched on TV screens, on their handhelds, and on computers and tablets—everywhere on Earth. Only the most impossibly remote tribesmen or purposefully tuned-out human beings were unaware of the message that had been so powerfully delivered and the victory that had been achieved.

Patricia Rose Greenidge, known throughout the world as Mama G, was dead. She had been killed, along with seventy others, in the strange crash of Intercontinental Airways flight 1331 in Nevada. She had flown from Grenada to Miami, and from there was on her way to Los Angeles.

Mama G had once told Dave that she was terrified of flying. It must have taken every ounce of courage she had for her to get on that plane— two planes, really—to fly out to Los Angeles. He could guess (and he would investigate in coming days to confirm his hunch) that she had played a part in the Marcus Jackson Jr. scenario, somehow influenced what had happened there on the Academy Awards stage that sparked a new consciousness in the world and somehow—no one yet knew exactly how or to what extent—averted a cosmic disaster for everyone on Earth.

This was potentially the biggest story he had ever covered, and now he was obsessed with it.

The famous broadcaster wrote out a few notes but did not feel like speaking at this moment. The images from the stage of the Hollywood Grand Theatre spoke for themselves and needed no embellishment or explanation from his silver tongue—or anyone else's. There would be time enough for that.

Why do I feel so satisfied and happy? Dave wondered. It was as if he had just partaken in a particularly fine meal with his very best friends, and he was savoring every bite. Yet it was more—so much more—infinitely more—than that.

It was beyond the realm of the senses.

Then Angel Emphatic, the defeated eternal avatar of the dark energies, rose as a shadow to enshroud the stage of the Hollywood Grand Theatre and everyone on it. Marcus and the others felt a stabbing chill as the shadow fell upon them. Angel Emphatic gathered power from every source he had ever tapped throughout the ages to express his rage in a dark manifestation and with a soundless scream that tore through the idyllic vision of the shining blue butterflies. But then he was gone. Though most people were unaware of his presence or even who he was, at least for now. . . .

CHAPTER
107

Charlene drank in the applause after she finished her song. She wasn't going to but the receding negative vibes that washed over them all were so strong that she felt that all needed something to bring them back to the feeling that they had but moments ago. The audience in the theater gave her a standing ovation. They all knew something extraordinary had just happened, but they wouldn't know the extent of the drama on a cosmic level until much later. The last thing on her mind now was the actual awards ceremony or whether her song would win in its category. She was humbled—and exhausted.

After her performance, Marcus was escorted by the security team back to the trailer that had served as his green room. The others in his new "entourage" came along, as well: Charlene, Dawson, Tyler, and Bobby Anderson, who was responsible now for his safety.

The Fallen Masters were present, too, though not yet completely visible. They were veiled in a way that would not overwhelm the intimacy of this moment. Each guide was connected mentally and spiritually with each earthly subject. The bonds had become irrevocable and unbreakable.

Marcus sat alone now, completely depleted and utterly exhausted. He was depressed, mournful over his dad's death, and missing his mom. His dad would never return.

Charlene sat closely next to Dawson, almost in his lap, on a large chair across from Marcus. They were *together,* that's for sure.

Dr. Tyler Michaels was reviewing what had just transpired, his mind racing back and forth in time, gently shaking his head, and thinking, *If Karen could only see me now.*

Bobby Anderson had his hands full dealing with the security issues of who wanted to gain access to Marcus Jackson—for interviews, for business arrangements, and who knew what else. Bobby still needed to protect the youth, since those who kidnapped him were still at large. Arrests were pending as suspects had been identified, and the investigation continued at a rapid pace.

He had established a ten-yard safety zone around the location. His hand-held phone was pressed against one ear and an audio bud was in the other. He was receiving information in both ears even as he observed what was going on outside the production trailer with both eyes.

Suddenly, the unmistakable voice of Rae Loona (who had been separated from the group), threatening one of the security men if he wouldn't let her pass, could be heard above the general din.

Agent Anderson walked to the door and signaled to the guard that the nurse should be allowed through his security checkpoint. He quickly stepped aside.

Once inside, the scene struck Rae as something out of a Broadway play. A scary play, at that, populated with all kinds of characters and ghosts.

She assessed everyone in the room, and her maternal instincts immediately kicked in as she saw Marcus sitting alone on the couch, staring at the floor. It seemed he did not quite understand the magnitude of what he had just accomplished. She also guessed that he was reliving the loss of his father all over again.

And Rae sensed that he was missing his mom, terribly. She went and sat next to him and put her arms around him. "It's okay to cry, you know," she said softly. For once in her life, she wasn't sure what else to say.

But that was just what he needed to hear. Marcus took a deep breath and let the tears come, releasing a torrent of emotion suppressed for so long. The cry was so visceral and so intense, it created an energy whirlpool effect that touched everyone nearby. Then another L.A. rolling brownout hit them—crazy, considering that the Oscars were happening, but that's L.A.—the lights flickered a few times before going out.

The people in the trailer stood and sat in the dark, waiting and waiting for the generators to kick in, the only light from the red EXIT sign above the door. There was silence, except for Marcus's heartrending sobs, as all were frozen in the red-tinted dark. In that moment, the EXIT sign began to glow much brighter, then brighter still.

All who were present heard a voice: *"Son?"*

No one could mistake that voice. Marcus wiped his tears and looked up. Rae's arms stayed around him for support—she hadn't let go since he had started to cry.

CHAPTER
108

M arcus saw his dad, the President of the United States, almost in full corporeal form. POTUS radiated pure positive energy and light, and he smiled that familiar smile that had made tens of millions of Americans vote him into the presidency.

"Come, give your father a proper hug and hello!"

Marcus ran into his father's arms—that is, his dad, not the President of the United States—and refused to release, absorbing every energy-infused second. He was not sure how this could be happening, but he did not question it in the least: His dad was with him now!

"I only wish Mommy was here for this. . . ."

Everyone in the makeshift green room heard a brief commotion out-side before the door of the trailer opened. After having successfully run the security gauntlet, the former First Lady stepped inside just as Marcus was speaking, and she replied, "I am here."

The First Family, dispossessed now of their historic role and torn from one another cruelly by violence, were together again for a brief reunion. "Amazing," Rae breathed, stunned by what she was seeing.

Then, one by one, they stepped into view for all to see . . . the Fallen Masters.

Rae's eyes opened brighter than ever before in her life. Her husband and child, who had passed so many years ago, also stepped into view with the other beings from the Other Side. She shook her head in happy dis-belief, tears dripping down her face.

The spirits were glistening and *alive* with energy. They were *there*, no doubt. Rae reached out and touched them, first one, then the other. *Thank you*, she mouthed in a prayer to God, realizing her faith had allowed this to happen.

How all these beings could fit into such a small space was another amazing phenomenon, but everyone was there and no one felt cramped—and all could see one another in a radiant otherworldly light in the otherwise darkened room.

The energy in the room provided the narrative for those who were there. It seemed like everything was happening telepathically, that they were all able to understand who everyone was, with tacit knowledge of their entire backstories. No one said a word, yet all were talking at the same time.

Another pair of figures stepped forward, a woman who was not known to the others on the earthly plane and a man, also unknown. The whole thing was wonderful in its strangeness. These two were Asima and her guide, Ziryab, the Arabian Fallen Master.

"Even more amazing," Rae Loona said, still breathless.

W hy?" Charlene asked the question that was in all their hearts and minds. "I mean—" She struggled for a moment, looking from Marcus to Dawson to her friends, and then to the Lady of Guadalupe, the President, and the other Fallen Masters. She knew this was a historic moment like none other. But *why* now, and *why* had she and the others been chosen to receive this special kind of revelation that so few human beings ever experienced?

She didn't have to elaborate verbally. All the apparitions heard her loud and clear, and they were used to unspoken words of the heart, as was the source of her simple yet profound question.

"Because it was ordained that when the time came, your souls would be united—for a specific time and with a specific purpose—with others from the realm of Light. We are those others, and we are your guides. Everyone on the earthly plane has a guide, but not everyone is open to knowing or communicating with that guide." No one among the Fallen Masters spoke this response, but all spoke it, or *thought* it simultaneously, and it came through to all who were present.

In the same voice, as one, they reached out to their living counterparts with a simple message: *"You chose to hear us. You chose the path that would lead you, ultimately, to the Light. You had the will and the strength not to answer the dark energies swirling all around you. . . ."*

POTUS remembered in that moment—and relived—his first immersion in the pool of consciousness and understood with even more clarity what that signified—for him and for all mankind.

Then it was communicated to everyone who Asima was and what she represented. Here was a woman who had stood against the forces of evil that threatened to take her son and the lives of many others by means of violence. She had given the ultimate sacrifice—herself—in order to preserve a precious life. She did so because she loved her son and had chosen to give him the opportunity to live, even as she ended her own time on Earth.

Ziryab beamed proudly, eloquently, as everyone acknowledged Asima prayerfully.

Then the room in which they stood opened to the Other Side, as if there were no walls, only light and space and another dimension of experience. . . .

Rae looked over at Tyler and smiled as she walked toward her husband and son—there, standing before her, waiting to greet her. "I told you, Mikey. We are go-ing pla-ces . . . ," she said with tears in her eyes.

For Tyler Michaels, this was the most moving and significant experience of his lifetime. He was happy for everyone. He looked over and saw Charlene talking to someone who seemed to be her late husband—and to her father. Dawson was next to her, reunited with a younger woman who Tyler knew instinctively was his late wife.

He was happy for everyone *else* but was not thinking this could happen for him, even though he had been communicating with a dead Swedish scientist as his Fallen Master. Talk about improbable!

Rae looked over at him as she hugged her husband. He heard her voice, even though she did not move her lips: "Mikey . . . anything is possible . . . as long as you believe."

Tyler tried to believe. He wanted to. But even after having all these amazing experiences, he still found himself trying to analyze and scientifically decipher this mass hysteria of coincidences. Then his own guide, Emanuel Swedenborg, walked over and began communicating with him telepathically.

"For me," he explained, *"I had a passion for scientific inquiry that led me to an understanding of God, of the spiritual side of life, if you will. Then I discovered what was colored in the black-and-white. It came to me in that brief moment. And only then did I realize that I had wanted to believe. I had told myself that I couldn't—but the power I sought had been seeking me and wanted me to believe, to give myself over to something far greater than myself."*

At that moment, a teenage boy walked into the light from somewhere beyond Tyler's vision. He said, *"Hello, Dad. It's Jeremy."*

Tyler caught sight of this perfect blend of himself and Karen—and just started to sob. He grabbed at the boy's face and pulled him into his body to "feel" his essence, breathing him in, letting go of his regret for every wasted moment he had ever spent—or squandered—in the name of his ego and career.

He looked at Jeremy again, and that's when he heard Karen's voice: *"I told you God's got a plan for you, Tyler. He's got a grand plan. Just open your eyes and allow it to happen."* The same words her mother had uttered at her funeral. She walked over calmly and serenely.

"Tyler, you couldn't handle me coming here tonight with a baby version of Jeremy. So, we wanted you to meet your son and know he exists on the Other Side—if not in your world, he exists in mine. You will see him again. We will be together again. But find your purpose." She looked over at a smiling Nurse Rae Loona. *"Hello, Rae,"* she said simply.

By this time, Rae Loona was holding her own son, standing next to her husband, and of course smiling. She winked at Karen. In that moment *she* relived the night in the hospital when Karen, barely clinging to life, had asked Rae to take care of Tyler in case anything happened to her. . . .

"You honored your promise, Rae. I thank you," Karen communicated to Rae, her voice inside the nurse's head.

Our Lady of Guadalupe, the one honored by so many in the world as the mother of us all, moved closer to Charlene St. John with a fluid grace that seemed other than human. The Blessed Lady smiled as she maternally touched her cheek. Charlene knew deep within that she was forever changed from this experience. Changed again. She turned and her late husband, Ryan, was no longer there, though the warmth of his loving presence remained—as it always would remain with her.

"Don't lose your way, Charlene," the Lady told her. *"You are a beacon of Light for so many. Spread your message of hope and love with your music. Tell our story in song. Write the theme song for* his *book, which will then become a movie for millions to see."* She looked over toward Charlene's future husband—yes, that's how it came into Charlene's mind. . . .

In that instant, Charlene saw a flash of her future as Mrs. Dawson Alexander Rask, with three beautiful children, one of them adopted from a children's hospital in Africa that Dr. Tyler Michaels would found in honor of his family—and the teachings of Emanuel Swedenborg.

In that same instant . . . Dawson had his moment with C. S. Lewis, the esteemed English author who had inhabited his dreams and many waking hours of late.

"Your task is to inspire *readers with spiritual and thought-provoking ideas—to inspire and to* teach. *Take them on your own journey of self-discovery. Finding your Narnia and the Shadowlands no longer in peril. Go there. Take others there. Be there. Even as you are* here *with the ones you love."*

Dawson turned to see Charlene. They exchanged a very intimate look of understanding with each other. From that time and forever, they knew what their future held for them—together—and they were excited to embrace it, without fear or guilt any more.

The red light of the EXIT sign flickered and resumed its steady glow. The regular lights in the trailer flashed back on, causing those inside to squint as their eyes got reaccustomed to the bright fluorescent glare. Rae, Dawson, Tyler, Charlene, Marcus, and the First Lady stood there in the no longer crowded space, much smaller now that the walls surrounded them once again. They all knew that the Fallen Masters would always be with them, even if they couldn't touch or see them. Looking from one to the other, they knew they were changed—for the good and for all time. They had been given glimpses of the future, of their hopes and goals.

They would each get there, having taken a huge step forward this day.

Marcus Jackson smiled and hugged his mom.

No one said a word for a long time.

EPILOGUE

Mama G was exhausted, as if she had just taken a long, difficult trip. Of course, that's exactly what she'd done. From her new vantage point on the Other Side, she observed her many friends through a pool of consciousness that Asima had led her to. Despite her bone-tiredness—or whatever spiritual exhaustion could be called—she was anxious about what was happening in the world she had left behind, and the people she loved. Especially Ruby.

The girl would inherit Mama G's legacy—and her fortune. Mama G spent little during her life, but she had banked some impressive sums in later years when she became world-renowned as a seer, adviser, and astrologer.

Indeed, she felt as if she had a lot of work yet to do. It would take a while, Asima told her, before she could relax and enjoy this new dimension of existence. But one thing she felt already, and quite strongly: Her faith had sustained her in both life and death.

Faith had always been the foundation of her life and the source, she believed, of whatever psychic powers or knowledge she might possess. She did not give herself a lick of credit for any of it. In fact, she fully expected that one day she would wake up and have none of the special abilities that she had stewarded over the past several decades. . . . It was all a gift. All of it. Even life itself.

Mama G was not in a position to tell anyone what they should do, now or ever. But she certainly wanted to share her insights into the meanings that she saw clearly in the revelation the late President's young son had shared with the world. She worried a bit about him and promised herself that she would reach out to him and his mother. They were in her prayers, to say the least, and she looked forward to the possibility of meeting them.

Still, she wanted to help . . . Dave Hampton, for example. Maybe she could guide him along his path. She had been working on his chart before she died, and she had seen something remarkable. She was grateful she had been able to speak to him before she left for her flight to LAX, her final flight on Earth.

On that fateful day, she phoned Dave Hampton in New York. He picked up immediately.

She said to him, simply, "You will run for political office. I see it so clearly, it scares even me."

"Will I win?" Hampton asked.

"You know I cannot answer that. But if you ask me, I would say, yes, you must win—and after you win, you must make the right choices. If not, we haven't learned anything from what has just happened. Good-bye, young man. Be well."

· Vatican City ·

The week after the amazing events at the Academy Awards ceremony, Dave Hampton traveled to Rome to interview the pope again. It was always a long shot, if not an impossibility, to get the Holy Father on camera, but he had been lucky before with such an "impossible" interview, so he chartered a flight for producers and crew and flew out of JFK. He had a few shows in the can for the first part of the week, and he would broadcast live from a studio facility in Italy, so his bases were covered.

Against all odds, within twenty-four hours of touching down at Leonardo da Vinci Airport in Fiumicino, outside Rome, he had been personally invited by the pope to an audience in the Vatican, so the lights and cameras were set up in the papal garden with a spectacular profile of the dome of St. Peter's in the background of the interview—and, fortunately, excellent spring-like temperatures and sunshine.

At the appointed hour, Pope Genaro I, accompanied only by his communications man, a youngish priest who had been in the job less than a year, appeared and took his seat so that he could be miked up and a bit of pancake applied to the face and high forehead. He tolerated all the fussing and made small talk in English with Hampton and the crew. It all went amazingly well and put Dave off guard a bit; he had been expecting a more aloof or taciturn subject for the interview, but the pontiff seemed very much at ease and in control without showing any symptoms of entitlement or discomfort.

Not knowing how long he would have with the pontiff, Dave plunged right into his questions for the religious leader.

"Thank you for agreeing to speak to us, Your Holiness. Why don't you tell our viewers exactly what the so-called Council of Faith was all about."

Genaro spoke in concise, clipped sentences in perfect English. He explained that he had been inspired to call together the leaders of the world's religions at a time that boded ill for all people of Earth, to rally the forces of peace from a spiritual perspective.

"After all, one could argue that all of our problems as human beings are of a spiritual nature. It is when we wish to disconnect ourselves with our Creator that we experience the deepest pain and frustration. For so many people in our world, the choices they make without proper guidance or prayer are wrong, destructive choices."

"Was that the cause of the threatened upheaval in your opinion?"

"The cause was evil, the absence of good, the absence of grace. Evil will fill the moral vacuum wherever it exists. That is the purpose of evil, to turn men and women away from the light for a destructive purpose."

"So, do you think religion is the answer?"

The pope smiled. He seemed very tired, his thin frame even more wraithlike than it always had been. His spokesman shifted in his seat off camera, but the pontiff waved at him to sit still. Despite his apparent exhaustion, there was a palpable sense of power and authority in the man. His answer surprised Dave Hampton.

"No. Although I am by vocation a priest and I live a religiously oriented life, I do not think religion is the answer to everything. I know this may shock you, Mr. Hampton—and your many viewers. But I will say that people everywhere may find answers in the religion of their choice. The questions we face each day as human beings—the choices we must make—almost always boil down to choices between right and wrong, good and evil. In small matters and large."

Pope Genaro I took a sip from the water bottle the priest had handed to him.

"You made such a choice yourself. When the forces of darkness were reaching into men's lives and causing many to lose their faith and opt for the negative, you could have fueled the dark side in your broadcasts. After all, it was a sensational situation, an apocalyptic scenario that would have made for some incredible television shows. Your ratings likely would have gone through the roof, as you might say."

Hampton couldn't help smiling at the man's turn of phrase, and he was intrigued by his point. He kept his mouth shut and let the pope continue to speak his mind.

"Instead, you chose to emphasize the good, to seek out people who represented the positive outcome for humanity. In that way you played a part in the ultimate outcome of the crisis. You helped tip the scales of history for good, not evil."

"I'm going to play that clip for my many critics, Your Holiness."

"As well you should. I do not mean to give you credit beyond what is due. After all, you are but one man, as am I. But when we come together for the common good, as I did with the representatives of faith traditions with whom I often disagree, it can never be wrong. And the result is almost guaranteed to be positive. Do you agree?"

"All I know is that I felt guided in some way—I don't know by what or whom—to seek out the positive energies that seemed to be in danger at the time. Maybe it was instinct. Maybe it was faith. It definitely was something that I still don't understand."

"But you will understand one day. I can guarantee you that," Genaro said. "If you keep asking questions, keep pursuing the truth. More will be revealed to you and more questions answered than you can even conceive to ask."

When the interview was over, Dave was still pumped—and would be for days to come. Then his producer panicked, came running over to the anchor. "There's a problem with the playback. There's no audio—and no video!"

The pope chuckled and reached out to touch Dave's arm and calm him. "Perhaps this was a part of God's plan all along," Pope Genaro said.

"But I can get the message out to millions and millions of people!" Hampton protested.

The pope smiled and said, "Faith is not something that can be demonstrated in an interview. It comes from within and is demonstrated in our experience. All the preaching and all the TV broadcasts in the world mean nothing if the human heart is not touched."

Dave Hampton heard the words, but he was still devastated by the loss of the interview.

"Every true teaching is meant to inspire and increase human understanding, not to tell people what they must believe," the pope said. "The word of God is clear in every language and in every heart. That alone is our guiding light . . ."

Then Dave remembered Mama G's words to him. He knew that his on-camera career was over. He also knew in that moment that his political career was about to begin. He would say nothing about it, but something inside him had changed fundamentally.

·*Los Angeles*·

Rae Loona offered her electronic airline ticket to the gate attendant. "Honey, if this flimsy thing will get me on a plane, I'm gonna fly far away!" She flashed her trademark smile and entered the jetway along with her fellow passengers in the first class section.

Tyler had insisted that she fly first class on the return to Atlanta. She had not wanted to leave on her own. Tyler wanted to stay behind for a few days for what he called a "retreat" farther up the California coast. He was insistent. She didn't yet trust that the good doctor had fully recovered his senses and his spiritual balance. But she knew she had to trust him, and she knew that the events of the Academy Awards night had made a deep imprint on his soul—as well as on hers and on people around the world. Something was different, even in the quality of the air she breathed.

Her seat was in the third row by the window, and when she stepped onto the aircraft she saw that someone was occupying the aisle seat already. She brought on only one small bag, a colorful *Grease*-themed carryall that held her makeup, billfold, and various sundries that she rarely used or even noticed. So she clutched the bag to her and said, in her sweetest Nurse Loona voice, "Excuse me, sir, I—"

The man raised his head from the magazine he was reading and smiled brightly, then quickly stood to allow her to scoot into her assigned seat.

Rae's jaw dropped nearly to the floor of the jet as she saw who was standing there, big as life, gesturing for her to take her place by the window in the luxury seat. She stuttered, "You're—you're—you're—"

"Yes, ma'am, I'm John," the tall man said. He had a full head of dark hair and an unmistakable face with a million-dollar smile and warm eyes. "Please take your seat. You don't want to hold up these other nice folks."

There was no question that Rae's pulse rate had increased, just as before, from the moment she realized that she was right next to her all-time idol and the true love of her life—again. Having met him face-to-face at the Academy Awards, she had thought then that her life was over . . . or that nothing could ever top that moment. Now she felt the blood rushing to her face in embarrassment, and she looked down at her hands—the hands that had touched her all-time idol and true love.

"Yes, yes, I'm fine," she managed to say. "I guess I was just shocked to see you sitting there. And me right next to you. I thought . . . I mean, I didn't think . . . Oh, I don't know what I mean. Do you know what I mean?"

"Yes, I think I do," Travolta said. "It happens to me all the time. In my business I get to meet a lot of people who I've never seen before except on TV or in the movies, and they don't even seem real when I finally do meet them. My wife and I talk about it all the time. But then, after a while, I realize they're just plain people, like me and my family."

"I suppose you're right. Well, I *know* you're right." A calmness passed over Rae Loona at that moment, and she felt at home. Despite the stream of passengers onto the aircraft, it was as if there was no one else there and they were sitting in her living room. She laughed, though a bit more discreetly than her normal loud cackle.

"So, I guess it wasn't a coincidence that we met the other night," he suggested with a rakish grin.

"I—I guess not . . ." Rae managed. Barely.

The flight attendant brought water for John and hot tea for Rae as the final group trickled onto the plane. Soon the door was closed and the large jet was preparing to taxi over to the runway for takeoff.

"I thought you flew your own planes everywhere," she said,

"I usually do," he said, "but this was an unexpected trip, and I had to leave the family behind, so I thought I'd just hop on one of these commercial flights and try to remember what it was like in the old days, flying with the hoi polloi." He said it with a wink, so she knew he was teasing her.

She felt a strong sense of his humility as a person and genuine warmth and interest in her. He didn't seem bothered by her staring at him and questioning him.

"If I were you," Rae said, "I would tell me to shut up and mind my own business."

"That's the difference between us," Travolta countered. "I'm just a regular guy who wants to be liked, and you're a celebrity totally wrapped up in yourself and your own ego-world."

Now she let loose with a huge cackling laugh that caused several passengers to turn to the source of the disturbance and the attendant also to glance her way. "Oh, John, you're such a hoot," she said. "I could take you home and have you for supper!"

"I hope you're really hungry," he said out of the side of his mouth.

"Ladies and gentlemen," the voice over the plane's PA system announced, "we are third in line for take-off, so we'll be airborne shortly."

John leaned over to Rae and half-whispered, "Does that apply to those of us who are not ladies, nor gentlemen, either?"

"Oh, *John*," Rae Loona said. In her mind, she was thinking: *Lord, I have died and gone to Heaven! Please don't let me wake up from this dream . . . ever.* Then she thought, *I wish Dr. Tyler Michaels were here to see me now. He wouldn't believe it.*

Silently, she said a prayer for her friend who had lost his wife and child so tragically, and who had regained life and purpose after all that. She felt her stomach drop as the jet aircraft lifted off from the tarmac into the sky.

In that same moment, she felt John's hand touch hers, but she could not tell whether he was just comforting her or feeling the moment of uncertainty between heaven and earth as a passenger on a flight over which he had no control instead of in the pilot's seat as he was used to.

"I'm not a control freak," Rae Loona said, her eyes closed tightly and teeth clenched during the takeoff. "I just like things to go the way I want them to."

"I'm sure that's true, Nurse Loona," John Travolta said. "And I'm sure you usually get your way in the end."

"Yes," she replied with a bit of a hiss through her teeth. "I usually do."

·*Fast forward*·

Rae Loona stood beside Dr. Tyler Michaels, and both admired the sign that he had just hung up over this small building, which would be an inspiration for education as well as healing. In a remote area of South Africa, Dr. Michaels would begin his new life, inspiring "his" adopted kids in the worlds of both science and faith. He would teach and heal them. He had come to understand his calling in a new way.

Rae told him he needed to add a new wing to the building. "I think the 'Rae Loona Pavilion' has a nice ring to it, don't you?"

He pretended to ignore her. "When are you going back to the hospital?" he asked.

"I'm going to follow in my sister's footsteps—at least for a while—

working with one family, taking care of all their needs. It means I'll be on call 24/7," she noted.

"It means they will be very well off, if they can afford you," he chided her.

Both laughed, and they hugged.

"Will you see me off, Mikey?"

"Don't call me that! How many times . . . ?"

She pulled him closer to her once again. "I'll call you that every damn time I see you. You'll always be my Mikey, you big white ape man."

They walked outside, arm in arm, in the sweltering African heat. In the distance on a makeshift runway, Rae's new boss awaited her, standing beside his private plane. He called out to her: "You ready, Nurse Loona?"

Tyler laughed and waved as Rae sauntered up the steps to a shiny new private jet . . . with Academy Award-winning actor and producer Mr. John Travolta himself in the cockpit. Rae turned and yelled back to Dr. Tyler Michaels, "I told ya, Mikey. We are going places. *Go-ing pla-ces!*"

Tyler climbed into his jeep as the jet took off. He had to run into "town"—a village just a few kilometers down the road—for some supplies. As he drove, he passed a new hand-painted sign that read: St. Jeremy's Hospital, South Africa.

Charlene St. John McAvoy Rask and Dawson became accustomed to working together every day in her company's studio to record the theme song for the movie version of Dawson's record-breaking *New York Times* bestseller, titled *Fallen Masters*. It was an inspirational novel based on the incredible story of how the two had fallen in love during the tumultuous events that challenged the entire world, now only a memory—though a vivid, life-changing one for them.

Charlene was expecting their second child. Their first, a boy born less than a year ago, had been christened Clive Stapleton Rask. He was a healthy, beautiful child, asleep now in a nearby room outfitted for him, while his parents worked.

Dawson rose from his worktable and went to her as she stood by the watercooler and looked out of a tall sun-splashed window. He put his hand on her full, burgeoning belly.

"Do you ever think what it would be like if we had never met?" he asked.

"I never think about things that are impossible," she replied. "Or that which never was. I can now see clearly that every moment in our lives up until we first saw each other put us on the path to be together. And our adventure together—" Charlene and Dawson called their time in L.A. their "adventure." She paused and turned to face him fully. "The Lady brought me to you, and your master brought you to me. Both brought us to the place where we could help Marcus share his message with the world. Now *that* was impossible!"

She smiled her billion-dollar smile that would one day grace another Super Bowl show. He pulled her to him gently and kissed her on the forehead—and then on those lips he loved so much.

Charlene thought briefly of the other loves in their lives–those here and those gone on. She thought especially of Ryan, and Dawson's late wife Mary Beth . . . and she knew in her heart that the happiness they had with their lost loves would never truly go away and that somewhere they understood this new joy and were happy for both Charlene and Dawson. And as love finds love and all the paths of light seek each other out, they would all someday join in each other in joy. . . .

Marcus Ellis Jackson delivered the valedictory address upon his graduation from William and Mary College, where he graduated at the top of his class—two years early. Bobby Anderson sat in the audience at commencement ceremonies next to Marcus's mother.

To no one's surprise, he used the occasion to announce his intention to run for political office sooner rather than later . . . maybe even against the ever-popular ex-TV news anchor Dave Hampton, now a second-term Congressman from Virginia.

"All of us graduates have a lot of people to thank for helping us get through our college education. My mom, Win Jackson, has never been far from my side—even when I didn't really want her there, so close—every step of the way. And my dad, though he was taken away from all of us, has always been there, too. Always.

"I want to say a special word to my dad, because I know he is here, and he is listening. I can feel his presence and almost see him.

"Dad, you and Mom not only gave me life, but you saved my life when I was most in trouble. And you not only saved me, but, in a very real way, you saved the whole world. We are all in your debt."

Tears filled the eyes of everyone in the audience.

Bobby Anderson, who had known Marcus Jr. from when he was a boy, felt his heart fill with emotion—and pride. He felt Win's hand enfold his, and both squeezed hard. This was a family truly worthy of being called America's First Family.

Marcus Jackson waved to his mother from the podium and gave Agent Anderson a big thumbs-up and a smile.

"That young man is going places," Anderson said, half-aloud. But Win could not hear him amid the cheers and applause.